'TIS THE SEASON TO DIE

As connoisseurs of the season and of trees, Penelope and Mycroft knew that, with patience they could find the perfect tree. They would suddenly approach, perhaps turning into a new row, and there it would be, waiting for them. Sometimes Penelope would find it first. In other years, like last year, Mycroft would find it (of course, Mycroft hadn't bothered to announce his find and went to sleep in the tree, just waiting for Penelope to come along and pay for it. He still couldn't understand what the big deal was).

It seemed to be Mycroft's turn again this year. He saw it at the very back of the lot. There it was. The perfect tree. Not too big, not too small, not too anything, except . . .

There was a body beneath it.

"Mycroft," Penelope called, "don't go too far."

Big Mike stopped and looked back at her. Hurry up! He turned and raced toward the tree. He wasn't fat at all. He *was* big—and fast.

Penelope followed hurriedly. Then she saw it too.

Penelope warily circled the tree while Big Mike took the more direct route of burrowing beneath the thick branches, disappearing from sight. Good God! It was Santa Claus—reeking of cheap whiskey, wearing a red cap, white beard and little else.

Santa was curled beneath the tree—a most unwelcome present, since he appeared to be either dead drunk, or simply dead. Penelope knelt for a closer inspection, putting her fingers to Santa's neck to feel for a pulse.

The flesh was cold . . . colder than Mycroft's nose.

—from *CHRISTMAS CAT* by Garrison Allen

MURDER MOST MERRY

GARRISON ALLEN • BARBARA BLOCK
TONI L.P. KELNER • J. DAYNE LAMB
JAMES R. McCAHERY • J.F. TRAINOR

Zebra Books
Kensington Publishing Corp.
http://www.zebrabooks.com

ZEBRA BOOKS are published by

Kensington Publishing Corp.
850 Third Avenue
New York, NY 10022

First Printing: November, 1994
10 9 8 7 6 5 4 3 2

Printed in the United States of America

Table of Contents

Christmas Cat
by Garrison Allen

I

It wasn't every day—or every holiday season for that matter, thank God—that a Christmas tree was tagged as evidence in a murder case, especially one that Penelope Warren and Big Mike had chosen to grace their living room. It certainly made for a memorable Christmas.

Big Mike, AKA Mycroft, the Abyssinian alley cat from Abyssinia, enjoyed Christmas. He liked the egg nog (with a dollop of brandy but no nutmeg) that Penelope, his friend and mentor, always served her parade of guests. He loved the tree and the presents under it with the yards and yards of brightly-colored ribbons emanating in all directions. Mycroft also liked the carols and Christmas songs that Penelope played throughout the festive season. "Rudolph, the Red-Nosed Reindeer" was among his favorites, although Mycroft was a dedicated Parrot Head and carols could not truly replace Jimmy Buffet, his favorite singer. As Penelope always said, "Of course, he's going to like anyone named after a cat food."

For Penelope, the holiday season was a two-month love affair, always beginning on November tenth when she celebrated the Marine Corps birthday, drinking a toast, or two or three to the Corps. It continued through Thanksgiving and Christmas and finally ended with the last football game on New Year's Day. One might assume, and correctly so, that Penelope was a holiday freak. Football freak, too.

But for Mycroft, the holidays did not truly begin until he and Penelope went to pick out the Christmas tree. It was his very, very, very favorite part of the joyous season and on that fateful day he waited impatiently while Penelope fussed with the last preparations. The couch had been moved away from the picture window, leaving a huge open space for the tree. The stand was in place on a snowy-white covering. Cartons of decorations were ready. Penelope stood, biting her lip in concentration, visualizing the tree's beauty.

Mycroft rubbed against her leg. Although he loved Penelope dearly, and never regretted falling out of the Ethiopian bougainvillea practically into her gin and tonic, she could be *so* slow. Not at all quick and decisive, like a cat.

Penelope looked down and smiled. "Okay, Mikey. Let's do it. We have to be ready when Stormy gets here."

Finally. Hot damn!

Driving through her adopted home town of Empty Creek, Arizona, Penelope admired the new holiday decorations strung across the main street for the thousandth time. The city council had finally appropriated the money for their purchase after Penelope had appeared at a council meeting the previous summer and pointed out—for the thousandth time—that the old decorations were quite threadbare, even ratty. "You're going to drive all our business to Scottsdale!" Penelope concluded indignantly. That did it, of course. The city fathers and mothers hated Scottsdale, as did just about everyone else in the eccentric and free-spirited community of Empty Creek. Empty Creek was . . . it was . . . well, whatever it was, it sure as hell wasn't Scottsdale, that trendy haven of golf courses and snow birds and art galleries.

This was Empty By God Creek, Arizona, as Red the Rat was fond of declaring to any stranger who mistakenly wandered into the Double B Western Saloon and Steakhouse, which establishment Penelope and Mycroft were passing at the moment.

Since Mycroft & Company, the small mystery bookstore Penelope had founded and named for Big Mike, was directly across the street from the Double B, they passed it simultaneously as well. Penelope noted (with some degree of horror) that Timothy Scott, carrying a thick sheaf of manuscript, was entering the bookstore. Young Scott, who might be a poet of some accomplishment one day, waved the manuscript at her cheerfully. Kathy Allan, the subject of young Scott's adoration, worked full time in the bookstore during the holiday season, thus freeing Penelope for the serious preparations necessary for the festive season.

"Good grief, Mikey, he's written an epic this time." Penelope shook her head and drove on, passing Alyce Smith's little astrology parlor with the sign in the window offering Christmas enlightenment through gift certificates.

A little farther on, Penelope saw her very own beloved, Harrison Anderson III, sitting on the balcony outside the second floor offices that housed the Empty Creek *News Journal,* the biweekly newspaper he edited. She honked. He leaped up, startled from his reverie (one in which Penelope played a starring and enthusiastic role) then waved as she pulled to the curb.

Beaming, Andy loped down the stairs, doing his Ichabod Crane imitation, although he didn't know that's what he was doing. It was Penelope who thought he resembled the fictional character, or at least what she envisioned Ichabod to look like—tall, skinny, gangling. It didn't matter. She loved him anyway.

"Slow news day?" Penelope queried lightly, a question she might not have asked had she stopped at Alyce's for just a moment or two and inquired about the position of her planets.

Andy didn't answer. First things first. Who cared about the news in the presence of Empty Creek's sexiest bookstore owner? He leaned into the Jeep and kissed Penelope.

His lips tasted like candy cane. Penelope detested candy canes, one of the few things about the season she could not abide, but she rather liked Andy's lips and decided on seconds. And thirds. Then she said, "Mmm, hold that thought for tonight, Marine." Andy had not been in the Marine Corps, but who cared when he could kiss like that?

"Christmas tree day?" Andy said.

"Yep," Penelope drawled. "Stormy's arriving this afternoon. You know how she likes to decorate the tree."

"Are you sure you don't want me to come along? Remember what happened last year."

"Mycroft's promised not to do that again. Haven't you, Mikey?" Penelope said, tweaking his ear.

Boy, talk about holding a grudge. All he had done was find a good place to take a quiet little nap.

Without telling anyone, of course.

Frantic, Penelope had quickly organized a search party of sales staff and families who wandered into the madness thinking they were going to purchase their tree and go right home. Ha! Instead, they wandered through the Christmas tree lot for the better part of an hour calling, "Mycroft, Mycroft."

The little boy who finally discovered Mycroft sleeping in a very thick Christmas tree said, "He's fat."

"He likes lima beans," Penelope explained before rattling the tree and crying, "Mycroft, you get out of there right now!"

Ah, Christmas memories. Only in Empty Creek.

"We'll be fine," Penelope now said. "See you tonight, but stop slurping on those damned candy canes."

"I like candy canes," Andy protested.

"Yuk," Penelope said, slipping the Jeep into reverse. "Lips that touch candy canes will never touch mine."

"Oh, well, in that case . . ."

* * *

There appeared to be no hard feelings among the sales staff at the huge tree lot. Indeed, the proprietor, a rotund little man chomping on a fat unlit cigar, greeted Penelope and Mycroft rather effusively, in keeping with the season, going so far as to produce a handful of lima beans for Mycroft who sniffed the offering disdainfully.

"I thought you said he liked lima beans."

"Cooked," Penelope said. "The kind that come in cans."

"Ah, cooked."

A little boy said, "He's still fat."

Talk about *déjà vu*. It was the same boy.

"He's not fat," Penelope said defensively, hoping there would not be a repeat of last year's performance. "He's big."

That was indeed true. Mycroft was not fat. He was big, all twenty-five pounds of him, but the little brat was having none of it.

"Fat."

Penelope, with Big Mike at her side, bypassed the smaller trees at the front of the lot. They ignored the trees that had been painted silver. Both woman and cat were traditionalists. No silver tree for them.

Instead, they wandered deeper into the forest, leaving the sounds of whining children, frazzled parents, and traffic behind. It was peaceful amidst the trees and the sweet fragrance of the pine needles.

Together, Penelope and Mycroft rejected one tree after another. Too small. Too big. Too skinny. Too fat. (Damned little brat anyway.) Too lopsided. Too short. Too tall. Too crooked.

As connoisseurs of the season and trees, Penelope and Mycroft knew that with patience, they would find the perfect tree. They would suddenly approach, perhaps turning into a new row, and there it would be, waiting for them. Sometimes Penelope would find it first. In other years, like last year, Mycroft would find it (of course, Mycroft hadn't bothered to announce his find and went to sleep in the tree, just waiting for Penelope to come along and pay for it. He still couldn't understand what the big deal had been).

It seemed to be Mycroft's turn again this year. He saw it at the very back of the lot. There it was. The perfect tree. Not too big, not too small, not too anything, except . . .

There was a body beneath it.

"Mycroft," Penelope called, "don't go too far."

Big Mike stopped and looked back at her. *Hurry up.* He turned and raced toward the tree. He wasn't fat at all. He *was* big—and fast.

Penelope followed hurriedly. Then she saw it too.

The perfect tree.

Oh oh!

Mycroft was sniffing at the big toe of a very bare foot, protruding from underneath the perfect tree.

Now, December nights in Arizona can be cold enough to cause even witches to wear furry underwear, and that carries over to the days, giving the air a crisp tang. In short, it was not a day to be going around barefoot and sleeping on the ground, so Penelope approached cautiously, hoping that it was no more than another of Empty Creek's eccentric citizenry inspecting the tree for some imperfection from the bottom up.

Along with his other attributes, Big Mike was possessed of a cold nose, but in this case it provoked no reaction from the owner of the foot. He looked up at Penelope. *See what I found?* Mycroft, no doubt, thought it was better than the lizards or the occasional bunny rabbit he usually gave as presents.

"Hello," Penelope said hopefully. Perhaps it was a homeless person and she could perform a good deed in the spirit of the season.

There was no reply from the foot, nor any other part of the person's anatomy. Penelope warily circled the tree while Big Mike took the more direct route of burrowing beneath the thick branches, disappearing from sight.

Good God!

It was Santa Claus!

Santa Claus, reeking of cheap whiskey, wearing a red cap, white beard, and little else.

Santa was curled beneath the tree, a most unwelcome present since he appeared to be either dead drunk, or simply dead. Penelope knelt for a closer inspection, putting her fingers to Santa's neck to feel for a pulse. The flesh was cold, colder than Mycroft's nose.

Santa was dead. Penelope carefully raised a branch to find Mycroft inspecting what appeared to be a small caliber bullet hole. Santa was stark naked, white save for the dark trickle of dried blood originating from the wound in his chest. From the whiskey bottle clutched in his hand, Penelope suspected that Santa was probably dead drunk at the moment of his death.

She let the branch drop and, very shaken, went to call the authorities.

Big Mike clambered into the tree to stand guard over it—and Santa Claus.

"I knew him," Larry Burke said.

"So did I," Willie Stoner said.

"Everyone knew him," Penelope pointed out, feeling a little like Hamlet with Yorick's skull. Empty Creek's crack homicide detectives could be so, so . . . Well, they were sometimes known as Tweedledee and Tweedledum, nicknames Penelope had thoughtfully provided during a more tempestuous time in her relationship with the two cops.

Santa Claus, whose real name was Wilfred Maxwell, was a retired engineer who had lived in Empty Creek for many years, a respected and much-loved member of the community, especially at the Senior Citizen Center and among the children at the elementary school where he worked as a crossing guard when he was not pursuing his hobby and looking for lost treasures. And, of course, the former Wilfred Maxwell was Empty Creek's very own Santa Claus, a jolly ho, ho, hoer who delighted the children because he always promised everything on their lists, much to the dismay of their parents, who had to explain why Santa had failed to put the AK 47 beneath the tree.

Larry Burke stooped and peered beneath the tree. "Hmm," he said.

He was joined by his partner who said, "Mmm."

Not to be outdone, Penelope knelt beside them. After all, she was an honorary member of the Empty Creek Police Department, a distinction she shared with Mycroft. "Aha!" she said.

"Aha what?" Tweedledee and Tweedledum chorused.

"Just aha."

"Oh." Another chorus from the detective pair. They were certainly disappointed.

Mycroft watched the proceedings from his perch in the now less than perfect tree. That was just fine with Tweedledee who had once had an unfortunate encounter with Big Mike, receiving a vicious swipe across his cheek during an argument over who was going to drive the police car. The confrontation ended with Big Mike under arrest for obstruction of justice. Penelope, of course, had protested the ridiculous situation only to be arrested herself on the same charge, handcuffed, and tossed unceremoniously, if momentarily, into the local hoosegow.

The editor of the Empty Creek *News Journal* arrived breathlessly, ducking beneath the yellow tape that secured the crime scene from the curious onlookers.

"How come he gets to go in?" the brat whined.

Andy turned and flashed his police press pass on the youngster. "Clark Kent," he said.

"You're too skinny."

"Shh," the brat's father said. "Santa Claus is dead."

"I knew I should have come along with you," Andy said, moving alongside Penelope.

"How was I to know there would be a body beneath *our* Christmas tree?" Penelope protested.

"Death follows Penelope Warren," Andy intoned solemnly.

Penelope and Mycroft *had* developed the disagreeable habit of stumbling across the odd body or two. Penelope was about to deliver another protest when a cry was heard from the dry creek bed that gave the community its name.

"Over here!" Sam Connors shouted.

Everyone creaked to their feet except for Mycroft, who emerged from the tree in a flash.

Aha, indeed.

Sam was standing over Santa's red suit and the pillow that Wilfred Maxwell had used to expand an already ample belly. The pillow was shredded, as was everything else.

Standing atop the bank with the others—even Tweedledee and Tweedledum knew enough not to rush into Empty Creek, obliterating evidence—the scattered pile of feathers from the pillow reminded Penelope of a time in Ethiopia when a smug Big Mike returned from a nighttime foray with scabbed claw marks in his heavy shoulders. She was positive that some night bird of prey had spotted some slight movement on the ground, gone into a headlong dive, expecting to come up with a juicy mouse for dinner only to go beak over teakettle when it found itself attached to a very large, very irritated cat. Penelope could just imagine the ensuing conversation.

Hello, turkey.

Oops!

Penelope had searched all morning for the pile of feathers but never found them.

Which, in turn, reminded Penelope of the Thanksgiving in Ethiopia when the little community of American teachers—mostly befuddled missionaries—had invited Penelope and Mycroft to join their celebration. The only catch was that they had to bring the frozen daiquiris *and* dress up as pilgrims. Now, Penelope didn't mind furnishing strong drink to missionaries (she rather thought it might improve them somewhat), but she just didn't see herself as Penelope Pureheart the Pilgrim, nor could she see Big Mike—who wasn't so big at the time—wearing a cute little pilgrim hat willingly, so she had spent that Thanksgiving drinking *tej*, eating *wat*, and discussing the merits of translating *The Brothers Karamazov* from English into Amharic, with *Ato* Haile Mariam, a young Ethiopian poet and socialist who had enthusiastically embarked on the translation as a lifelong project. Unfortunately, Mycroft—still in the throes of a playful kittenhood—had developed a life-long aversion to Russian novelists when he skidded along Haile Mariam's desk into the thick manuscript, fell off the desk, and was followed by an avalanche of the Brothers K right on his head. With no additional assistance from Mycroft, whatsoever, Haile Mariam had reached the Grand Inquisitor chapter when Penelope's Peace Corps service had drawn to a close. (They never did dress up as pilgrims either.)

But, while these memories were pleasant and amusing (except for the bird with poor eyesight), they weren't solving the murder of Santa Claus, AKA the much-beloved Wilfred Maxwell. So Penelope said, "The killer was searching for something that Wilfred had hidden away."

"What?"

"I don't know," Penelope admitted. "Money, jewels, a treasure map. Wilfred was always searching for lost gold mines."

"Treasure maps are everywhere. Red the Rat's got dozens of them."

That was true. Lost treasures were abundant in Arizona; a testimonial to prospectorial ineptitude or the fierce Indians of yesteryear, sometimes both. Probably everyone in the state of Arizona had a map purporting to show the location of the fabled Lost Dutchman Mine in the Superstition Mountains. That's why it had remained lost.

"Yes," Penelope agreed. "So whom do you suspect?"

"Everyone," Burke replied. "Whom do you suspect?"

"Ebenezer Scrooge," Penelope said. "The Grinch."

That ended that.

Andy dashed off to write his story on the demise of Wilfred Maxwell.

Penelope watched sadly as her Christmas tree was tagged as evidence by one of the crime lab guys. It had been such a perfect tree, too. Oh, well. Although the body had been removed now, Penelope could still see the bare foot protruding from beneath the tree. In fact, she could still see poor Santa's bare everything. "Keep it moist," Penelope told Burke.

"Moist?" Burke said.

"The tree. You know. You have to put the tree in a stand and keep water in it. Otherwise it'll die."

"It's already dead," Burke pointed out. "Just like Santa."

Tweedledee had a point there.

But since Empty Creek's crack homicide detectives, Larry Burke and Willie Stoner, seemed baffled again, Penelope added a note to her mental list of things to do before Christmas Eve—clean house, buy presents, stuff turkey, pick up Muffy and Biff at airport, host engagement party for Stormy (although her sister did not yet know she was about to receive a proposal of marriage), solve murder. While Santa's holiday season may have been spoiled, Penelope saw no reason to have it ruin everyone else's.

Penelope and Mycroft had no sooner arrived back at the remote little ranch they shared with Chardonnay, a sweet-tempered Arabian filly who did not like candy canes, lugged their second choice of tree into the living room (Penelope lugged, Mycroft supervised), and deposited it in the stand when the telephone rang.

It has to be Laney, Penelope thought. Elaine Henders was Penelope's best friend. A ravishing redhead who had her bodice ripped as often as the heroines in the steamy romance novels she wrote, Laney also had a network of informants who gleefully informed Laney of everything that happened or was about to happen in Empty Creek.

"Hello, Laney," Penelope answered. "I see the desert telegraph is hard at work."

"Death follows Penelope Warren," Laney said.

"That's not funny."

"But it's true. We were playing Christmas Tree when I heard the news," Laney said.

Penelope hesitated for a moment, wondering whether or not she wanted to hear the rules of Christmas Tree, then decided she did. Laney had such a fertile mind when it came to devising imaginative games to play with the male of the species. She called it research for her novels.

"And how is Christmas Tree played?"

"Oh, you just decorate your man like a real Christmas tree. You'd be surprised how many places Wally has to hang decorations. Andy too. You should try it."

"Frankly, it doesn't sound like much fun if Wally's just standing around pretending to be a tree. It sounds like something out of a Beckett play."

"Oh, the fun comes when he gets to his present under the tree. That's me, of course. He eventually gets to untie the big red ribbon."

Mmm. It was beginning to show possibilities. She could just see Andy now. Penelope knew exactly how she would decorate him . . . She shook her head to clear her mind of naughty thoughts. She didn't have time for a cold shower just now. Stormy would be arriving any minute.

"I have to go now, Laney."

"Yes, well, you keep me posted on events. You *are* going to solve the murder?"

"Of course," Penelope replied. After hanging up, she added, "Somebody has to."

The tree began to shake like a big bowl of Jell-O.

"Mycroft!" Penelope cried. "Get out of the Christmas tree right now!"

What an old poop she was turning out to be.

II

While Mycroft went off to sulk after being unceremoniously tossed from the tree, Penelope swept up the trail of pine needles that led from the Jeep through the front door and around the couch to the tree itself. She paused momentarily at the door, staring at two copper pennies glued there, constant reminders of two other murders. If not for Big Mike, the killer might have added Penelope to the list of victims.

Penelope had discovered both bodies. Actually, Penelope had found poor Louise Fletcher on her doorstep simultaneously with Andy and Mycroft. And it was Mycroft who discovered Freda Alsberg's body on Crying Woman Mountain, but Penelope had been the first person on the scene, if you did not count Mycroft as a person (which Penelope did when he wasn't off having a hissy fit).

And there *were* those unfortunate deaths at the Empty Creek Almost Authentic Elizabethan Spring Faire when Queen Elizabeth I was assassinated, setting off a string of murders that included what seemed to be half of a Not-So-Merrye Olde England. Penelope had an iron chastity belt (unused, of course) and a scold's bridle (she was tempted to employ it on a few of her more talkative friends) in her study to remind her of that case, another occasion where it had been a damned good thing Mycroft had come along when he did.

Perhaps death *did* follow Penelope Warren. Or Big

Mike. Or both. And now Santa Claus. Good God! What was the world coming to?

Still thinking of poor Wilfred Maxwell, Penelope swept and swept. The damned second choice tree shed more than Big Mike during the blistering Arizona summer.

Mycroft announced Stormy's arrival by rushing to the front door from the kitchen where he had gone to sleep on the window sill, but only after Penelope had promised to buy two trees next year, one for decorating and one for sleeping. No matter how much time passed between Stormy's visits (not much anymore, at least not since she had fallen in love with the Empty Creek police chief), Mycroft always knew when the big white limousine turned on to the old dirt road that led to the ranch. It was one of Big Mike's uncanny skills. He *always* knew who was coming to visit, sometimes before they did.

Cassandra Warren exited the limousine regally, as befitted her status as Empty Creek's very own reigning star of the silver screen, although her film appearances were under the stage name of Storm Williams, the result of her agent drinking a little too much one evening at the Polo Lounge during a long reminiscence about the great burlesque queens of his youth. One Irma the Body had been his favorite, but as he had explained to Cassie the next morning while gulping aspirin and black coffee, "You just don't look like no Irma." Gulp. Swallow. "The name," he added hastily, "not the bod. You got a great bod, kid, major league boobs, almost as good as Irma's. I still got the rose she threw me. It's in a scrapbook somewhere. You wanna see it sometime?"

Cassandra Warren, who was about to become Storm Williams, could have cheerfully throttled Myron Schwartzman on the spot but since he had just obtained her first starring role in a film to be called *Biker Chick*, she refrained, at the same time politely refusing Myron's generous offer to view his faded rose (or anything else for that matter). Besides, she did have a great body and she was positive it was as good or better than Irma's—as all the world would soon discover, much to the dismay of Muffy and Biff, Cassie and Penelope's long-suffering parents.

Storm Williams was now quite popular in Europe, particularly in Germany where she was the idol of a number of Teutonic fan clubs, the result of such epics as *Space Vampire, Amazon Princess and the Sword of Doom, Return of the Amazon Princess,* and the soon-to-be-released, *Pirate Queen* (everyone said Stormy was much better than Michelle Pfeiffer). They were also quite popular rentals in the Empty Creek Video Emporium, which was located next door to Mycroft & Company.

But if the truth were known, Cassie had grown quite fond of Myron's creation. She liked being two people. As Storm Williams, she could play whatever role she wanted in her personal life. As Cassandra Warren, she could be Penelope's younger sister with all the bother *that* entailed.

Mycroft positively galloped to the limousine. He absolutely adored Stormy. *She* wouldn't kick him out of the Christmas tree.

The stately and dignified Storm Williams role didn't last long. "Mikey," Cassie squealed.

Mycroft leaped into her arms, a habit he had picked up from his best friend, Alexander, a diminutive Yorkshire Terrier who lived with Laney and Wally. The force of his enthusiastic leap nearly bowled her over.

By the time Penelope came out into the yard, Mycroft was happily nestled against those major league boobs. *So there,* his expression told Penelope. *See if I ever get in your tree again.*

"Penny," Cassie squealed for a second time, depositing Big Mike on the gleaming white roof of the limo before rushing to embrace Penelope. The two sisters were the best of friends.

"Hello, John," Penelope said, offering her hand to Stormy's perpetual chauffeur. He had also been on Crying Woman Mountain, along with Penelope and Stormy, that fateful day when Mycroft had found Freda Alsberg's body. Despite that grim experience, John was now a fixture in Stormy's visits. "How have you been?"

"Quite well, thank you," he answered.

"Well, let's unload the presents," Cassie said. "John and I are absolutely perishing for one of your delicious egg nogs."

"A virgin for me," John said. "I'm driving."

"Ha!" Stormy cried. She teased John unmercifully about his sexual preference. "Do you mean a virgin, or a *virgin?*"

"Both."

"My God," Penelope exclaimed when John opened the trunk. "What do you have in here?"

"Clothes for a two-week stay and videos of *Pirate Queen* for everyone. Autographed, of course."

"Of course."

In due time everything was unloaded and drinks were poured.

"What a lovely tree," John said.

"It wasn't our first choice," Penelope said. "We found Santa Claus dead under the tree we really wanted. He was shot. And naked. *That* tree is evidence in a murder case now."

In another, more normal, household, this pronouncement would have provoked disbelief. Here, however, Stormy only groaned, "Not again."

"Death follows Penelope Warren," John said a little queasily.

"Et tu, John?" Penelope said.

"Well, I remember what happened the last time." He looked around the living room nervously, as though expecting to find a cadaver or two parked behind the furniture.

"And the time after that," Stormy said. "You weren't here, John, when Penelope was almost burned at the stake."

"Beheaded," Penelope said. "As the Queen, I was to

be beheaded, a privilege of royalty. It was Alyce and Sharon who were going to be burned as witches."

"Whatever, and you had me put in that horrid scold's bridle and—

"Well, you were talking too much."

"There I was wandering around the whole night and no would help me."

"I still have it, you know," Penelope said.

"You wouldn't dare," Cassie laughed.

"Yes, I would. I'm your older sister and you have to do whatever I say."

"Well, it was a good thing Mycroft showed up when he did. He's my hero, aren't you, Mikey? Come to Auntie Cassie." Mikey didn't have far to go since he was sitting in Auntie Cassie's lap. She ignored that simple fact and gave him another big hug anyway.

Myron Schwartzman was right. Major league all the way.

John left, wishing one and all a very merry. Penelope thought he seemed to be a little too eager to get away from the Warren sisters, although she couldn't blame him for being nervous in their presence. They did seem to attract death.

But he was quickly replaced by another John, chief of Empty Creek's finest. John "Dutch" Leonard had fallen in love with Storm Williams on the steps of the police station on the day when Stormy led a demonstration to free the "Empty Creek Three," two of whom consisted of her sister and Big Mike, both arrested for the aforementioned obstruction of justice (that day had not turned out to be one of Tweedledee's best; he should have just let Big Mike drive the damned police car).

Mycroft grudgingly gave up his place on Stormy's lap as she rushed to greet her beloved. Stormy, too, had been deeply smitten that fateful afternoon, especially after he asked for her autograph (take that once more, Jane Fonda!).

Penelope discreetly removed herself and Mycroft to the kitchen, allowing the happy couple a few moments to themselves. Being somewhat of a voyeur, Mycroft wasn't especially pleased at being forcibly removed from the living room. After all, he might learn something he could teach Murphy Brown, that sleek calico who lived down the road a piece. But the sound of the electric can opener distracted him. He whirled around in that graceful dance known only to cats and was rewarded with a generous helping of lima beans. He decided to forgive Penelope on the spot. After all, no one in the entire world could play the electric opener as well as Penelope, not even Stormy, who spoiled him rotten.

When the happy couple finally consummated their reunion with one last lingering kiss, they strolled hand in hand to the kitchen where Dutch presented Penelope with a folder.

"I thought this would save you a trip to the station," he said.

Penelope smiled. There were advantages to having your future brother-in-law double as the head cop. "I appreciate your thoughtfulness, Dutch," Penelope said as she leafed quickly through the police report, statements from employees at the tree lot, and interviews with Maxwell's neighbors at the Burning Cactus Golf and Condominium Club. Tweedledee and Tweedledum had been busy.

"We don't have much yet," Dutch said. "Maxwell was apparently killed with a .22 caliber bullet that ricocheted off a rib right into his heart. Bad luck for Santa Claus. We'll know more after the autopsy."

"I'd rather go back to smooching," Cassie complained. "That's all you guys ever talk about. Murder."

"In a minute, dearest sweetheart of my life."

"Isn't he wonderful?" Cassie said, ending that conversation with another big smooch.

It seemed to Penelope that her sister was becoming as sex-crazed as Laney and everyone else in Empty Creek.

* * *

Andy was the next to bop in. He, too, was rewarded with a copy of the crime report. In exchange, he distributed drafts of his story on Santa's death to Penelope and Dutch.

Reading over Dutch's shoulder, Stormy exclaimed, "What a wonderful lead. It's so visual. You should be a screenwriter."

"Don't put things into his head," Penelope commanded. "He's got a thing about Daryl Hannah."

"She's a liberal, you know," Cassie observed.

"Andy wasn't thinking about her politics," Penelope said. "It is a good lead," she added, reading it aloud. " 'Not a creature was stirring when Santa Claus was murdered beneath a Christmas tree Tuesday night. The nude body of Wilfred Maxwell, Empty Creek's own version of the beloved St. Nicholas, was discovered by prominent local bookseller Penelope Warren.' " Penelope groaned. "Did you have to put that in?"

"Death follows Penelope Warren," the trio recited in unison.

The Ravishing Redhead of Empty Creek soon swooped down upon Casa Penelope with her entourage in tow. Actually, only the laconic Wally, Laney's unemployed cowboy, was in tow. Alexander the Yorkie raced ahead, trumpeting their arrival loudly. He might be tiny, but he had the bark of a German Shepherd—several German Shepherds.

First greetings and then drinks were dispensed all around.

Mycroft took Alex on an inspection of the tree before settling down to await developments.

Stormy and Laney, the two underwear freaks in the gathering, went off to examine Stormy's latest acquisitions in naughty lingerie catalogs—they were both much too modest to shop in person.

Andy, Dutch, and Wally, drinks in hand, gathered before the fireplace to discuss football.

Penelope was tempted to join them—she was the most rabid football fan present, after all—but decided to go off and feed Chardonnay before things got too frantic. So she gathered a few peppermint candies for the filly—Penelope didn't know any normal animals—and walked down the hill to the stables where she was greeted with an enthusiastic whinny or two. Chardonnay munched the peppermints contentedly while Penelope prepared the healthy concoction that would be the Arabian's dinner.

Somehow, the Christmas tree was decorated and dinner was served.

After dinner, everyone gathered in front of the television while Penelope popped *Pirate Queen* into the VCR.

The opening credits rolled over a rebellious Storm Williams in a judicial dock protesting her innocence with heaving bosom to a leering, bewigged, and unsympathetic English magistrate who summarily sentenced Elizabeth Barrett to seven years penal servitude in the colonies.

"What did you do?" Penelope asked, since the screenwriter apparently forgot to put it in.

"Stole a loaf of bread to feed my starving little brother."

"That was nice of you."

Apparently, there were only female criminals in the writer's vision of eighteenth century England, for the screen dissolved to a long line of women in irons trudging up the gangplank of the prison ship about to set sail. And, equally apparent, all of the female criminals of England appeared to be beautiful and buxom. There wasn't a hag to be seen.

Storm Williams, in her screen persona of Elizabeth Barrett, stood at the ship's rail with the other beleaguered women, shaking her manacled wrists at England's dreary shore. The young woman next to Stormy cried as the dock receded. Stormy offered what comfort she could.

It was really quite heart-rending, although Mycroft promptly fell asleep in Stormy's lap. Penelope thought it a mark of his good breeding and intelligence that he always fell asleep during Stormy's films, usually before the main credits drew to a close.

Of course, a leering sailor quickly appeared below decks to rip away at the bodice of Elizabeth's new friend, receiving a good whack from Stormy for his efforts.

Now Stormy was dragged into the captain's cabin.

"My God, it's the judge," Penelope whooped. It was indeed the judge from the earlier scene, sans powdered wig, of course.

"We were on a tight budget," Cassie said.

"I'll say."

Mycroft snored quietly.

Sentenced to thirty lashes, a subdued Elizabeth was brought on deck before the assembled crew and convict women as a cabin boy solemnly beat a tattoo on his drum.

Ropes waited to secure poor Elizabeth to the mast. The first mate stood with coiled whip.

Ta dum, ta dum, ta dum, the drum roll continued.

Bravely, poor Elizabeth went to the mast.

Ta dum, ta dum, ta dum.

The first mate stepped forward. His hand was at the neck of her dress, ready to bare poor Elizabeth's back for the whip.

The screen suddenly switched to a beer commercial.

"Popcorn!" Stormy cried. The remote control was in her hand. "I want popcorn before my big scene."

"Damn," Dutch complained. "She's always doing this to me. Sometimes I think it would be better to watch her movies without her."

"And I was on the edge of the couch," Andy said. "You were being so courageous too."

"I'm always courageous," Stormy said, "but I'm more courageous with popcorn. Buttered popcorn."

Intermission over, the audience supplied with bowls of popcorn, napkins, and replenished wine glasses, Stormy looked around and said, "Everyone ready?"

Ta dum!

The first mate went whoosh as Stormy delivered a vicious elbow to his gut. He whooshed again when she delivered a stunning knee to a place no knee should ever go, unless it involved an evil first mate.

As the first mate lay gasping on the deck, Elizabeth pulled his pistol from his belt and popped the captain right between the eyes. Apparently, poor Elizabeth was a crack shot, if a poor bread thief.

The convicts joined the fight and quicker than you could say Errol Flynn, they subdued the ship's crew and set them adrift in a lifeboat, all except for the cabin boy who blubbered something about being unable to swim and a fear of sharks and begged to stay with Elizabeth. Because he, no doubt, reminded her of her baby brother still starving back in England, Elizabeth granted his request and acquired a devoted servant.

Standing at the rail, brandishing the pistol in one hand and a cutlass in the other, Stormy shouted to the crew, "You tell them back in England that they haven't heard the last of Wild Liz."

"Wild Liz," Penelope chortled.

"You need an eye patch," Laney said. "All good pirate queens should have an eye patch."

Mycroft snored louder.

"It wasn't in the budget," Stormy said.

"Wild Liz," Penelope hooted. "Eye patch."

Dutch shushed her. "This is terrific," he said. He couldn't do anything about Big Mike's snoring, however.

There was a great deal of sailing about, punctuated with booming cannons, swashbuckling, swinging from ropes and masts, even a few tender moments with male pirates suitably awed by Wild Liz's wild bunch. The judge who doubled as the captain appeared twice more, once as Wild Liz's love interest (but she made him walk the plank when he proved treacherous) and again as Lord Nelson, lying gravely wounded on the deck of his flagship.

The film's time frame got a little obscure right about there because Wild Liz and her stalwart crew somehow wound up at the battle of Trafalgar, saving England's bacon to the uproarious cheers of the British Navy, and soliciting a royal pardon and the gratitude of the entire nation.

Wild Liz was finally reunited with her baby brother who, to Penelope's mind, looked as though he hadn't missed a meal in his entire chubby life.

As the closing credits rolled, the swashbuckleress was rewarded with a loud round of applause. She was quite pleased with the audience reaction, although Mycroft continued to snore, awakening only when Dutch's beeper went off.

"Oh, God," Laney exclaimed. "It's probably another murder."

"Or a bank robbery," Andy said hopefully. After all, you could never have enough news.

"I hope it's a barking dog," Dutch said. "I've had enough crime for one day. I'll use the phone in the kitchen so I don't disturb you."

There was little chance of that, since the assembled company trooped to gather around the kitchen door to eavesdrop. They were unrewarded, however, because Dutch's end of the conversation consisted of "Okay . . . uh huh . . . I see . . . all right." He hung up the telephone and turned to find himself the object of intense scrutiny. Even a grumpy Mycroft was waiting impatiently to hear the latest, although he wasn't at his best just after waking. Still, Dutch's beeper hardly ever went off. This could be important to Big Mike's investigation.

"Well," Stormy demanded, "I hope you don't have to go rushing off into the night."

"That was Burke. They found a suicide note on one of Maxwell's computer disks."

"What an odd place to leave a suicide note," Laney said.

"What an odd place to commit suicide," Stormy offered. "Under Penelope's Christmas tree."

"Did he read the note to you?" Andy asked.

"There was no need," Penelope said. "It wasn't suicide."

"You saw the body, Penelope," Dutch said, waiting for her opinion.

"The shot was fired from more than eighteen inches away. There was no gunpowder burns. Just the entrance wound."

Dutch nodded.

"Did Larry dust the keyboard for prints?" Penelope asked.

Again, the chief of police nodded.

"Wiped clean, right?"

"You've got it."

On that somber note, the little party soon broke up. Stormy dragged Dutch off to her lair, no doubt for a late night discussion of cinematic theory. Big Mike was a little miffed when he was not invited to participate, but he had been known to use an occasional male appendage as a scratching post. It could dash a bucket of icy cold water on the most amorous of activities.

Laney gathered a sleepy Alexander into one arm and wrapped her other arm around Wally's waist, standing on tiptoe to whisper something about an eye patch in his ear.

Penelope strained to listen in, but for once Laney was discreet. Penelope suspected that Wally was in for a rousing game of Pirate Queen, imagining that he would soon be walking the plank into the Ravishing Redhead's bed.

Alone at last, Penelope and Andy tidied up the kitchen. Penelope smiled and did a little whispering of her own. "How would you like to play Christmas Tree, Andy?"

"I don't know how."

"I'll teach you," Penelope said, gathering up some red ribbon and leading Andy off to her bedroom.

Big Mike followed eagerly. The evening might not be wasted after all.

"Who invited you, Mycroft?" Penelope asked archly. The door was shut firmly in his face.

Oh, well. There was always the Christmas tree.

III

The Burning Cactus Golf and Condominium Club was a snooty snow bird haven, a gated, security-conscious way station on the railroad track leading to eternal reward. Supposedly open to senior citizens aged 55 and older, Penelope thought that there might be some sort of unofficial restrictive club policy in force if the gentleman at the gate was any indication—he was at least 90, perhaps more.

Penelope flashed her honorary police badge and identification card at the old man.

"What's that?"

"Police," Penelope answered.

"Lemme see." He leaned into the Jeep for a closer look, squinting at the I.D. card, or so she thought—at first.

The old doofer was looking down the front of her blouse!

She snapped the badge case shut. "I'm investigating Wilfred Maxwell's murder."

Foiled, the old man cackled. "Name's Ed. I'm old, but I ain't dead. Remember everything right back to day before yesterday. Wanna go dancing?"

"Not right now."

"Too bad. Show you a good time. Who's that?" He leaned in again to get a closer look at Mycroft. Mycroft stared back, perhaps contemplating taking Ed home as a trophy.

"Well, I'll tell you, Ed, if you'd stop trying to undress me, you'd see it's a cat. His name is Big Mike and he doesn't care for anyone who tries to mess with me. He's a cop too."

"Didn't know they had police cats."

"It's the latest thing in law enforcement. They're smarter than dogs."

"Had a dog once." Ed paused to consider that for a moment. It must have been further back than the day before yesterday, because he said, "Sure you don't wanna go dancing? We could snuggle real close."

Penelope sighed. It had to be something in the water that turned Empty Creek residents into raging hormonal bombs, ticking away ominously while awaiting their next encounter with the opposite sex. "Call me the day after tomorrow. Right now I have to investigate a murder."

"Knew right off you liked older fellas. What's your telephone number?"

Penelope rattled off Laney's number. "Ask for Laney," she said. The Ravishing Redhead could teach the old guy a game or two. Perhaps they could play Elderly Patient and Devoted Nurse.

"That thing you got says your name's Penelope."

"Laney's my nickname. Better than Lopey."

"Okey, dokey. Now, you just head on up to the community center. That's where everybody is this time of day." Ed leaned in again.

Penelope shook her head, suppressing the urge to just get it over with and bare her chest for the old geezer. It wouldn't do to induce cardiac arrest, and besides, she didn't have time to play nurse, although it might be interesting with the right patient.

"Them men up there. You watch out for them. They're all woman crazy. All they think about is sex. Gals, too."

No kidding.

* * *

A gaggle of senior citizens, clenched fists swinging with determination, power walked down the road past the club's very own paramedic station. Since a sign at the entrance to the club proclaimed that residents—like elephants in Africa—had the right of way, Penelope pulled to a stop next to the seventh green of the Burning Cactus golf course, allowing the power walkers to get some distance ahead.

She watched as a golfer wearing bright yellow trousers and an equally bright green shirt flailed away, trying to extricate his pink ball from a sand trap off the seventh green. Sand flew everywhere, but the ball stubbornly refused to move. Finally after seven or eight ferocious swings Yellow Pants leaned down, picked up the recalcitrant ball, and threw it on the green. It went directly into the cup.

Penelope smiled.

"Nice hand wedge, Herb," his companions called out.

"I'll take a bogey on that," Yellow Pants said.

Penelope drove on. That was the way to play golf. Cheat.

She parked the Jeep in a visitor's spot at the community center and looked down at Mycroft. "I don't suppose there's any chance you'd care to wait in the car?"

Nope.

A volunteer manned—actually womanned—an information desk in the lobby. She wore a tag that said her name was Cora.

Mycroft leaped to the desk top.

"Ain't supposed to be no animals in here," Cora said, giving Big Mike a pat on the head. "Except seeing eye dogs. Got some of them here alla time."

"Mycroft is a senior citizen cat."

Big Mike shot a miffed look in the direction of Penelope. He wasn't ready for the American Association of Retired Cats by a long ways, but Cora smiled and said, "Senior citizen cat. That's a good one."

Penelope asked for Elise McMahon Harper Stewart

Halsey, a name cited as Wilfred Maxwell's neighbor in the crime report.

"I know who you are now. You're that detective lady I read about."

Penelope admitted her identity and repeated her request.

Cora sniffed. "You want the Iron Lady," she said. "Just finished leading her aerobics class. Saw Tilly Cramer crawling down the hall, gasping for breath. Killed four husbands already. Gonna kill one of her ladies one o' these days. All that running and jumping around. But it means the Iron Lady's on her break now. She'll be in the snack bar, guzzling that mineral water. You like mineral water?"

"Not much."

"Me neither. Iron Lady don't drink nothing else. Me, I like scotch. Don't trust no one who drinks mineral water."

"How will I recognize her?"

Cora sniffed, again, haughtily this time. "Can't miss her."

Cora was right. Penelope could not have missed the Iron Lady even if she hadn't been the only woman in the snack bar.

A handsome woman in her early sixties perhaps, Elise McMahon Harper Stewart Halsey was an Amazon. Penelope could see how she had sent four husbands to an early death. If they hadn't died in bed, they had surely died trying to keep up with their beloved on the jogging track, the swimming pool, the weight room, bicycling, or racquet ball.

Her short blond hair was lustrous and without even traces of gray. The only indications of age were slight wrinkles around her eyes. Tall and muscular, Elise McMahon Harper Stewart Halsey could have posed for the senior citizen hard body centerfold. Her breasts, firmly encased in an athletic bra, should have been registered as deadly weapons in this fragile male setting, although the man in the room looked as though he might enjoy a game of Russian Roulette with the Iron Lady.

Even Mycroft was impressed, allowing the woman to scratch his ears. He ignored the man, going off to inspect the vending machines, perhaps hoping to find a package of lima beans.

"You're way too young to be hanging around here," the Iron Lady said.

"You look way too young yourself," Penelope said.

The Iron Lady smiled, pleased at the compliment. "I'm sixty-one, but I have to keep showing my ID card. Prove I'm old enough to belong. I'm Elise McMahon Harper Stewart Halsey and this is Leonard Trope."

Leonard tore his admiring glance away from the Iron Lady's body long enough to say, "It's very nice to meet you." Leonard was perhaps a few years older than the Iron Lady and was tanned and fit. He was also drinking a bottle of mineral water.

Perhaps it contains some sort of beneficial preservative, Penelope thought. "I'm Penelope Warren," she said. "I'd like to ask you a few questions about Wilfred Maxwell."

Elise McMahon Harper Stewart Halsey's face stiffened. Suddenly, she looked her age. Older. "Would you excuse us, please, Leonard?"

"I think I should stay. Wilfred was my friend too."

The Iron Lady shook her head. "I'll be all right."

"I'll be right outside if you need me, Elise." Before he left, angry at the interruption, Leonard gave Penelope a dark and malevolent look. It was the first variation of expression Penelope had received from a male member of the Burning Cactus community, but at least he didn't try to look down her blouse. That was a welcome relief.

The Iron Lady went to a vending machine, but before she turned away Penelope saw the tears in her eyes. Another bottle of mineral water thundered down its chute.

"Would you like something?" Elise asked, her back

still turned. "Or the cat? Perhaps a carton of milk." Her voice broke only slightly.

"No, thanks," Penelope said. "We're fine."

"Are you a policewoman?"

"No. I found Wilfred's body. I'd rather like to find out what happened."

Always sensitive to another creature's pain, Mycroft rubbed against the Iron Lady's legs, purring. When Elise turned back, she had regained her composure and her youthful appearance.

"Mrs. Halsey. . . ."

"Please, call me Liz."

"Wild Liz?" Penelope said. "I'm sorry, that just slipped out. My sister's an actress, a very good actress, but her movies . . . well, they're sort of stinko. In her latest, she plays a pirate named Wild Liz."

"Johnny—he was my second husband, Johnny Harper—he used to call me Wild Liz right up until the moment he died. I was, too, but I shouldn't have insisted he make love to me three times that night. Poor Johnny." She turned an appraising eye on Penelope. "I'll bet you have a streak of wildness in you."

"I have my moments," Penelope said, thinking of the red ribbon she had worn last night. Laney had been right. Christmas Tree was a fun game.

"I kept all of my husband's names as a memorial to them. I was extremely lucky with my men. They were kind and thoughtful, but they lacked staying power. They all died loving me. A woman can't ask for more than that, can she?"

"No," Penelope said, "she can't." Thank God staying power wasn't a problem of Andy's.

"Wilfred was like that, too," Liz said. "He was so . . . so . . . loving. We were going to spend our declining years together. And now he's gone." She bit her lip and stroked Mycroft, who had wormed his way into her lap.

"Is there anything you can tell me?"

"He didn't have any enemies," Liz interrupted. "Everyone liked him. I can only believe that he was mugged and it turned violent."

"It wasn't a mugging or a chance robbery, I'm afraid. Someone was searching for something. His clothes were shredded. Do you know what he was doing at the Christmas tree lot? That's an odd place to be at night."

"No. We had spent the evening together and I wanted him to spend the night, but he said he had to be up early and didn't want to disturb me. He was so thoughtful in little ways like that. I should have insisted. He'd be alive now."

Penelope wasn't so sure of that, not with Elise et cetera Halsey's record with husbands who all died of love. Still, it was better than being shot and left wearing nothing but a beard and a red cap beneath a Christmas tree.

"Are you all right, Elise?" Leonard asked, re-entering the snack bar.

"I'm fine. Penelope and I are going home. There's something I want to give her."

"What about our walk? I thought we were going for a walk," Leonard said. "Alone," he added emphatically, rudely.

"Another time, Leonard."

He face turned dark, brooding. Leonard stalked off down the hallway.

"He's not a loving man," Liz said. "He tries, but he's not."

Liz opened the door and ushered Penelope and Mycroft into her home, grabbing a device from a coat rack. As she conducted the tour, Liz pumped the machine, flapping her arms in front of her like some demented bird. "It's good for the breasts," Liz explained. "Keeps them firm. Men like that."

"It certainly seems to work for you," Penelope said, looking around.

Wild Liz's townhouse resembled a gym. There was a speed bag mounted in the living room (Liz set it to dancing with several well-placed jabs) and an exercise cycle in front of the television. Instead of magazines, books, or newspapers, the coffee table sitting before a white couch was laden with small barbells. The kitchen contained a small trampoline (Penelope imagined Liz bouncing to the ceiling in between stirs of the simmering sauce). The second bedroom had been converted into a weight room. The master bedroom contained a king-sized bed and some kind of stair climbing contraption.

"Make yourself comfortable," Liz said. "I'll be right back."

Penelope and Mycroft settled on the couch, the only place empty of athletic equipment.

Liz returned quickly holding a refrigerator magnet in her hand. "I hope you don't like children," she said.

Remembering the little brat at the Christmas tree lot, Penelope said, "Not much."

"Good. They're disgusting and demanding little creatures. Here, this is for you. And Big Mike, of course."

"Let's get rid of all the children," the magnet's message said. "The cats are allergic to them."

"That's wonderful," Penelope cried. "Mycroft would certainly agree with the sentiment."

"Would you like some tea?" Liz inquired.

"That would be nice," Penelope answered, and Liz retreated into the kitchen again.

Things happened quickly then.

Big Mike, as was his custom while investigating crimes, had been exploring enthusiastically. Unable to dislodge the barbells, he had turned his attention elsewhere. Burrowing around between the cushions of the couch, Mycroft emerged, waving his paw furiously trying to dislodge the plasticine covering of a computer disk from his claw.

The doorbell rang.

"Get that would you, please, Penelope?" Liz called from the kitchen.

The disk skidded across the hardwood floor, and Penelope picked it up on the way to the door. Wilfred Maxwell's name was written on the little sticky thing. She dropped it in her jacket pocket and opened the door.

Tweedledee and Tweedledum.

Surprised, Penelope blurted out, "What are you doing here?"

"What are *you* doing here?" Larry Burke asked. He was equally surprised.

"I asked first."

"We've got some more questions to ask the Iron Lady."

"If you're referring to Mrs. Halsey. . . ."

"Detectives," Wild Liz said, "What are you doing here?"

"We've got some more questions to ask," Tweedledee said.

"We'd like you to come down to the station," Tweedledum said.

"Of course, just let me get my wrap." She headed back into the kitchen.

"What's up?" Penelope asked.

"Maxwell left a will on a computer disk."

"Don't tell me . . ."

"That's right. Everything goes to her."

"But Wilfred had children."

"Two daughters, ex-wife. All cut out of the will completely."

The kitchen door slammed.

"Oh, shit," Tweedledee said.

Penelope and the detectives arrived at the kitchen door in time to see Elise McMahon Harper Stewart Halsey jogging determinedly down the street, past an old man pushing his walker.

The detectives raced to their unmarked squad car, clamped the Kojak light to the roof and squealed off in pursuit.

Penelope and Mycroft took up the chase on foot, an endeavor that lasted half a block. With Wild Liz pulling away steadily, Penelope and Mycroft retreated to the Jeep and renewed their pursuit, arriving at the golf course in time to see Liz vault the wooden fence.

The police car screeched to a momentary halt and Tweedledee jumped out. The car roared away again in an apparent attempt to cut Liz off on the far side of the course while Tweedledee gathered his breath for a foot pursuit.

By the time Penelope and Big Mike got there, the unfortunate police officer had been surrounded by power walkers. He fought his way free and attempted to imitate Wild Liz's leap over the fence, succeeding instead in imitating the Keystone Cops, falling flat on his face while leaving a substantial portion of his trousers behind on the fence. Bright red underwear flashed through the tear in Tweedledee's pants.

Penelope giggled, though normally she did not like to find humor in another human being's distress. But *this* was funny. Penelope screeched to a halt, gathered Mycroft in her arms and, ignoring the cries of the power walkers, dashed through a gate in the fence just as a pair of golfers drove up in a golf cart.

"Police business," Penelope cried, depositing Big Mike in the cart. She jumped in, hit the accelerator, and roared off.

"Wait! I need my three iron." The plaintive cry echoed over the golf course.

Wild Liz was two fairways away.

Penelope and Big Mike passed a huffing Tweedledee. Let him commandeer his own cart.

"Fore!" rang out the warning cry.

The golf ball struck Tweedledee a glancing blow, but it was enough to fell him. He wasn't having a very good afternoon. But he was determined and resumed the chase, one hand holding the seat of his trousers together, the other rubbing the bruise on his forehead.

Penelope and Big Mike were gaining on Wild Liz now. My God, that woman could run. She was passing the clubhouse and starting down the first fairway.

Penelope circled the practice green, swept past the foursome on the tee, and followed. Big Mike was hanging on, mewing with excitement. He had never been in a golf cart before and thought it was pretty cool.

Penelope later thought that they might still be chasing Wild Liz if it hadn't been for the creek running in front of the first green. Wild Liz's athletic prowess finally failed her as she attempted to clear the creek in a single leap. She almost made it. She would have made it, except for the duck that waddled right into her landing spot. In mid-air, Wild Liz flailed and backpeddled out of compassion for the duck, who saw the strange apparition looming. The duck quacked and went straight up. Wild Liz managed to abort her running broad jump, but she landed just at the edge of the creek, hit a spot of mud, and fell backwards into the creek.

A very bedraggled Elise McMahon Harper Stewart Halsey crawled from the creek.

"Why did you run?" Penelope cried.

"They always arrest innocent people on 'Murder, She Wrote.' I watch all the reruns," Liz explained.

My God, she wasn't even breathing hard. Penelope handed her the towels hanging on the golf bags.

"Then you should know that Jessica always gets the innocent people off. And, besides, you weren't being arrested. They just wanted to ask you some questions."

"But after asking a *few* questions, they were going to arrest me. Anyone could see that. I loved Wilfred. I didn't kill him."

The whine of a siren announced Tweedledum's arrival. An enraged shout announced Tweedledee's arrival in a course marshall's cart.

"You're under arrest," Tweedledee wheezed. "You have the right to remain silent." Wheeze. Pant. Cough. "You have the right to. . . ." Hack. Puff.

"You can't arrest her for jogging," Penelope cried.

"Assault on a police officer . . ." Wheeze. ". . . for openers. I was almost killed back there."

"He yelled fore. I heard it distinctly."

"Aw, shit," Tweedledee moaned, leaning over to put his hands on his knees. "All we wanted to do was talk."

"So talk. She's right here," Penelope pointed out in what she thought was a rather reasonable manner. Sometimes you just had to do everything yourself.

And how was your day, dear?

Well, first I was propositioned by a horny old security guard at the senior citizen community. Then, I chased a sixty-one year old Amazon across a golf course. Then I had tea with said Amazon and watched as she mended the rip in Tweedledee's pants. And then . . .

Cinderella's wicked stepmother and two wicked stepsisters, shrieked like harridans, and invaded the happy little domestic scene, pushing their way past Penelope, who opened the door, accusing poor Liz of alienation of affection, fraud, theft, harlotry, and a variety of lesser transgressions, all apparently committed in the attempt to cheat the former Mrs. Wilfred Maxwell and her daughters of their rightful inheritance.

"You parked your high heels under the wrong bed this time, you—you—old bimbo!" the former Mrs. Maxwell—who was far more wrinkled than Elise—sputtered.

In her dismay, Liz pricked her finger with the needle, jamming the wounded member into her mouth.

Mycroft screeched when Wicked Stepsister Number One stepped on his tail.

Wicked Stepsister Number One screeched when Big Mike returned the favor, shredding her pantyhose and leaving long red, deep scratches across her calf.

Wicked Stepsister Number Two attempted to avenge her sister by aiming a kick at Big Mike, who dodged the daintily clad foot rather easily.

That was a definite no-no, in Penelope's eyes and Wicked Stepsister Number Two, who was not so agile as Big Mike, was leveled when Penelope kicked her right square in the shin. Since Penelope was wearing pointy cowgirl boots at the time, a howling Number Two joined her still-screeching sister on the floor.

Mycroft grinned placidly at Penelope after the brief encounter—she swore he winked at her. *What a team.*

While attempting to calm the former Mrs. Maxwell, Tweedledee's red underwear only enraged the furious Wicked Stepmother, who then accused the detective of conspiring with Elise to steal her riches.

Tweedledee, who hadn't managed an arrest all day, soon rectified that matter. Still clad only in shirt, jacket, and red underwear, he marched them off to the police car where he stuffed them in the back seat to cool off before questioning them.

Heading for home now, Penelope decided not to answer if Andy, or anyone else, for that matter, should ask about her day.

And we still don't know who killed Wilfred Maxwell, Penelope thought, although she had placed the former Mrs. Maxwell and her daughters at the head of the list, displacing Wild Liz for the moment. There had been definite malice and avarice in the three pairs of beady eyes and anyone who would kick a cat was certainly capable of patricide. Penelope liked Wild Liz but also wondered if she was as accomplished a killer and liar as she was an athlete and seamstress.

Penelope shook her head. All we really got out of the day was a cute refrigerator magnet and a computer disk! Penelope patted her jacket to make sure that magnet and disk were still separated. It wouldn't do to have the magnet wreaking havoc on the disk's files.

IV

Penelope was aching to get to Wilfred Maxwell's computer disk.

But no.

An irate Ravishing Redhead waited on her doorstep. "Penelope Warren," Laney cried, "I'll never forgive you for this."

Even Mycroft (who understood Laney better than most) was confused.

"What have I done now?" Penelope asked wearily.

"What did you do? Write my telephone number on the men's room wall out there? Call Laney for a good time and the last rites?"

"Oh, that."

"Oh, that! I'm getting obscene phone calls from Cackling Ed and all you've got to say is, 'Oh, that.' "

"Well, I didn't want to give him my number."

"So you gave him mine!"

Big Mike retreated to the Jeep. He had seen Laney's Irish temper before. Not only was sitting on the warm hood, pleasant and out of harm's way, it afforded an excellent view of the proceedings.

"I'm trying to solve a murder," Penelope explained. "I don't have time to listen to the ravings of a deranged and oversexed senior citizen. I didn't want to be impolite and I thought you'd like to help." She smiled the very sweetest of her smiles.

"Argh!" Laney said. But the show, such as it was, was

over. Laney dearly enjoyed the machinations of Empty Creek society generally and the puzzles provided by Penelope and Big Mike's investigations specifically. Besides, Cackling Ed did have some interesting suggestions.

A disappointed Mycroft followed them into the house and into Penelope's office. At least, he would be able to help them on the computer (which he believed Penelope had purchased for him as one of the more expensive cat toys in history). He seemed to think that the printer only worked when he helped it along by sleeping on it. He like typing, too, and had once rewritten an entire book order for Mycroft & Company while Penelope went to the kitchen for another cup of coffee.

So as Big Mike hopped on the printer and Laney drew up a chair, Penelope slipped the disk into the B drive and fired the machine up.

At the C:\> prompt, she typed: Dir B:*.*.

Viola!

Wilfred Maxwell's directory appeared on the screen.

CS.WM	1092	12/4	15:37
LIZ1.WM	1483	11/4	09:47
LIZ2.WM	9772	11/17	10:22
LIZ3.WM	8653	12/9	08:45
LIZ4.WM	763	12/11	23:48
LT.WM	4761	10/13	13:45
MC.WM	981	12/11	23:57

"Mmm," Penelope said.

"What?" Laney asked.

"Zzz." Big Mike was taking a nap.

"Two of the files were last used the night before Wilfred died."

Penelope retrieved LIZ4.WM.

My Dearest Liz, it began.

Penelope blushed after the first paragraph.

After writing so many lurid and colorful ravishments in her romance novels, it took Laney two paragraphs before her cheeks matched her hair. But blush the Ravishing Redhead did.

LIZ4.WM was a love letter. Although brief, it described what Wilfred and Liz would do during their next tryst. In detail. In great detail.

Penelope exited the file.

"Wait," Laney cried. "This is great."

"You're a snoop."

"I didn't know old people did it. I mean like—like that. Like young people."

"Liz isn't old." Penelope brought up the second file from December 11th.

The screen filled with letters and numerals.

H7 C12 R14 K10.

Penelope scrolled down.

More letters and numerals.

"Map coordinates," Laney said.

"Of course," Penelope replied. "The file was labeled MC. For map coordinates."

"Well, do you want my help or not?"

"Yes, I do. Tell me what map the coordinates come from. *That* would help."

"Oh, sure. I get all the hard ones. You want the easy stuff. Some detective you are."

Penelope went to a bookcase and brought out a road atlas of the United States and turned to the Arizona map. She put her finger on the line where H intersected with 7.

Sedona.

What the hell did that mean?

C12 put her finger at Four Corners, where Arizona, Utah, Colorado and New Mexico joined.

There was no R14 in Arizona.

K10 was on an Indian reservation.

Penelope flipped through the atlas, choosing another state at random. Kansas. H7 in Kansas was no yellow brick road. It was a plain white spot to the northeast of Garden City. The Pawnee River ran through it. Who in the hell would want to live in H7? In Kansas?

"Go back to LIZ1," Laney said. "I'll bet there's a clue."

Instead, Penelope brought LT.WM to the screen.

"Well, isn't that interesting?" she said.

"What's so interesting about loaning someone $15,000?"

"He loaned it to Leonard Trope. I met him today. Liz introduced me to him."

"I still think we should go back to LIZ1. It's probably chockablock with clues."

"Chockablock?"

"Oodles."

"I know what it means."

The telephone rang. Penelope answered it, listened for a moment, and handed it over to Laney. "It's for you."

Expecting that her Wally was lonely and desperately missed the pleasures of her company, Laney said, "Hello, Sweetie."

"That's better," Cackling Ed said. "How 'bout you and me just drive on up to Crying Woman mountain and park? We can watch the moon come up."

"Argh," Laney said for the second time in the space of an hour. She hung up, waited a moment, and then took the phone off the hook. "There."

An insistent beep told them the phone was off the hook and awakened Mycroft, who looked sleepily at LIZ1, which Penelope had brought up on the screen. He was the only one in the room who didn't blush. His taste in the written word tended more to the complete works of William Shakespeare anyway. He used the thick volume of the Bard's collected poetry and plays as a scratching post.

"You're going too fast," Laney complained.

"We're looking for clues," Penelope said, "not titillation."

"Speak for yourself. This is great stuff. I could get inspiration for my novels."

"You don't need inspiration."

"Even America's greatest living writer of romance novels needs inspiration," Laney said. "On rare occasions."

Penelope slowed down, just a little. It was great stuff. Andy had never written a love letter like these to her.

Wilfred Maxwell had possessed a most inventive mind, devising one method after another for pleasing his lady love in the solitude of their bedroom. The lady love in question had apparently been more than willing to participate in whatever Wilfred came up with, even suggesting a few ideas of her own.

The letters should be sent to the Kinsey Institute archives or Masters and Johnson for preservation.

But they were singularly lacking in clues as the identity of Wilfred Maxwell's killer.

"I'm going home," Laney announced after Penelope had turned the computer off. "I think we're going to play Beautiful Female Private Detective and Client."

Penelope hoped poor Wally had taken his nap. He would need his energy. "I'm going to the Double B and then to the library," she said.

"How dull."

The Double B Western Saloon and Steakhouse was a gathering place for Empty Creek's elite. Penelope parked next to Daisy, Red the Rat's old mule who was tied up to the hitching post outside. The Double B catered not only to the elite and desert rats such as Red, but to the horsey set who liked to ride into town for Sunday brunch.

"Come on, Mikey," Penelope said.

Big Mike needed no special urging. It was his custom after working all day with Penelope at Mycroft & Company to cross the street and belly up to the bar for two ounces of non-alcoholic beer. (He used to drink real beer, but after an unfortunate incident with a tipped over bottle and the living room curtains, Penelope had put him on the wagon.)

Big Mike took his accustomed stool which happened to be next to Red the Rat's customary stool. Big Mike was the only one in town who didn't mind the smell that usually emanated from Red's direction.

"How do, Mike," Red said politely. "How do, Penelope."

"How are you, Red?"

"Getting closer. Almost found it this time out." Red the Rat had been searching for a lost gold vein reputed to be north of Empty Creek for upwards of thirty years now. He sometimes strayed for a few months and went off looking for another vein or mine, but he always returned to *his* search.

Debbie D leaned across the bar and gave Mycroft a scratch under the chin before pouring his libation into a saucer. "Hey, Mikey, how's my favorite cat?"

Mycroft appeared tempted to cross the bar and give Debbie a rub or two in return, but the beer won.

"Hi, Debbie. Where's Pete?" asked Penelope.

"Oh, he's taking a few days off. I'm filling in. I like it. Gives me a break from the cowboys out there." Debbie D nodded at the cocktail tables where she usually worked as the Double B's favorite waitress, a popularity she had gained for two very apparent reasons. She was possessed of a most magnificent chest, often described as "national monuments." Everyone loved Debbie, but her heart belonged to Sam Connors, one of Empty Creek's finest.

"Chardonnay?" Debbie asked of Penelope.

"Please."

"Be right back."

Penelope turned to Red. "Did you know Wilfred Maxwell?"

"Sure. Use ta come in and talk. We'd swap a few lies. Too bad about old Wilfred."

"Yes, it is."

"You going to find the killer, Penelope?" Debbie asked as she returned with the glass of wine. "Sam told me you were working on it."

"I'm going to try."

"You be careful," she said. "You, too, Mikey."

Having finished his beer, Mycroft followed Debbie down the bar. It never hurt to give one of your favorite people a nuzzle or two.

Red the Rat watched him go. "Helluva cat. Helluva woman. You, too, of course, Penelope."

Penelope smiled. "You're right on all counts, Red. Do you know what Wilfred was searching for?"

"Lost Patrol," Red said solemnly.

"Lost Patrol?"

"Yep. I was probably the only one he ever told."

"What's the Lost Patrol?"

"Oh, musta been back about 1881, maybe '82. Cavalry had a patrol out that got ambushed by Apaches. When they sent a relief column, they found 'em all dead, 'cept for one, and the sun had fried his brains. He was just sitting there tossing these gold nuggets up in the air. Each of the dead men had a bag of gold nuggets. The survivor babbled about gold just sticking out of the ground, but nobody ever found it. People been looking for them nuggets ever since."

"And that's what Wilfred was looking for?"

"That's what he said."

"Where was the Lost Patrol when they were killed?"

"Somewhere in the Mazatzal Wilderness."

"I have a computer disk of Wilfred's. One of the files is nothing but what appears to be map coordinates. M3. That sort of thing."

"Sounds like they might come from one of them government maps they do up for the tourists."

"Did you ever ask specifics about where he was searching?"

Red the Rat shook his head. "Ain't polite, Penelope. That kinda thing could get you shot in the old days."

"Apparently, it can get you shot today, too," she said grimly.

* * *

Penelope still whispered in libraries, a trait instilled by Sister Mary Joy of Jesus during Penelope's seventh grade year in Catholic school. Sister Mary Joy of Jesus, despite her religious name, was singularly lacking in joy. Sister's real name was Agnes. She looked and acted like an Agnes.

Leigh Kent, however, was no Agnes.

When Leigh became the Empty Creek Public librarian, a passion for things literary soared among the male population until the library rivaled the Double B Western Saloon and Steakhouse as a gathering place for bachelors (and more than a few of the lecherous husbands in town). Leigh shattered librarian stereotypes, demolishing a multitude of hearts, young and old, in the process. Even Red the Rat renewed his library card, something that had not happened since the Johnson administration, when he had suddenly developed an inexplicable passion for Lady Bird and haunted the library to pore over news magazines searching for photographs of the First Lady.

Leigh was quite simply beautiful, not in the classic sense, but sexy?

Wowee. Oh, double wowee!

Our Leigh (for that is how many referred proudly to the librarian) is a dark-haired, wide-eyed, sultry and exotic, mysterious heartbreaker. In the words of Red the Rat, definitely a fine figger of a woman.

Our Leigh seemed unaware of the effect she had on men. As a consequence, many a young puppy wandered out of the library, arms laden with books, to stagger home dazed with love. Even Andy, dear old Andy who was so hopelessly in love with Penelope, admitted to being smitten by Leigh, confiding that he wanted to reach over and slowly remove Leigh's glasses (the vast majority of Empty Creek's male population wanted to take her glasses off, along with a few other items of apparel) in that ageless movie cliche that transformed the prim and proper librarian (or teacher or businesswoman) into a wanton beauty. It was a good thing for Andy that he had never tried it. Leigh would have slapped him down good, to say nothing of what Penelope would have done.

Penelope, of course, delighted in Leigh's friendship, her only flaw being that Leigh was a dog person and didn't really like cats, although she tolerated Mycroft's presence. In Empty Creek, tolerance was an excellent trait to possess and necessary for coping with the somewhat addled population—male, female, and animal alike.

Mycroft, of course, knew immediately on first being introduced to Leigh that she was not a cat person and set out on a single-pawed mission to rectify the matter. He delighted in rubbing against her legs and settling into her lap, purring loudly all the while to show what a good and forgiving fellow he truly was.

So, Big Mike hopped into Leigh's lap while Penelope whispered, "Where is the map collection?"

There was no need to whisper. The library was, for the moment, empty of Leigh's many admirers, and during Christmas vacation, singularly devoid of young scholars from the high school questing for knowledge.

Leigh answered in a whisper anyway. "You know perfectly well the maps are kept in the Local History Room."

"Yes, but I like to ask questions. It makes librarians feel useful."

"Where is the restroom?"

"You don't know where the restroom is after all this time?"

"That's the most frequently asked question of librarians. Where is the restroom? You should ask sometime. Add to the statistic."

"I know where the restroom is," Penelope said.

"That's not the point."

"Ou est la Tour Eiffel?"

"In Paris."

"I know it's in Paris. You can see the bloody thing for

miles. But I had to learn that question when I took French. It's no wonder my French is abominable."

"I hear you're working on Wilfred Maxwell's murder. That's why you want the map room."

Penelope nodded.

"I hope you find the killer. I liked Wilfred. He was always so polite."

Not at all like his greedy little family, Penelope thought.

Finding the map was easy. Red the Rat had been right. It was a government map published by the Forest Service. Unfolded, however, the map was more than three feet long. There were half-inch squares, each indicating one square mile—hundreds and hundreds of square miles. H7 alone contained eight hundred square miles. According to the legend, none of that eight hundred square miles had been accurately surveyed yet. It was just what the name indicated.

Wilderness.

Whatever coordinates had interested Wilfred Maxwell were buried in a maze.

Big Mike burrowed under the map and went to sleep on the library table. Big help he was.

According to the circulation card—the maps were not on the computer system—Wilfred Maxwell had checked the map out. Of course, he appeared to have checked every map out at one time or another.

So had Leonard Trope.

Shortly after each map had been returned by Wilfred, Trope had taken it out.

"Isn't that interesting, Mikey? And Trope owed Santa Claus $15,000."

The map rustled as Mycroft emerged to look quizzically about the room, and Penelope idly leafed through some of the other folders and their maps.

"Did you find what you need?" Leigh asked from the door of the small room.

"I found it, but it wasn't much help. Are there any maps missing?"

"Probably. Something's always missing."

"Treasure maps?"

"You mean like the Lost Dutchman?"

Penelope nodded.

"We have some copies of old maps like that. They're just facsimiles of some prospector's dream. We had a display last year. The snow birds like to pore over them and wish."

"Where are they?"

"Under T, of course."

"Of course."

"I'll get them for you." Leigh went to a file cabinet and pulled the drawer open. Mycroft followed, leaping from the table to the top of the file cabinet in two fluid bounds.

"That's strange. The file is empty."

"The maps?"

"Gone."

"Did one of the maps show the location of the Lost Patrol Vein?"

"Yes. I remember it distinctly."

Mycroft had lost interest in Leigh and Penelope for the moment. He had found another computer disk on top of the file cabinet. Perhaps remembering the other disk that had caught in his claws, he gave it a stalwart whack, launching it like a technology-laden frisbee.

Penelope and Leigh watched it sail to the table, slide across the map, and fall to the floor.

"Where did that come from?" Leigh picked it up. "It says Wilfred Maxwell on it."

"Now, that *is* strange," Penelope said.

"Well, how was your day?" Cassandra asked merrily. Obviously, she had thoroughly enjoyed her reunion with Dutch.

"Don't ask," Penelope replied. "You don't want to

hear. First, we met the Iron Lady and then we had to chase her across the golf course in a cart and Mikey got a computer disk caught on his claw. . . ."

Cassandra shook her head in disbelief. "You're right. I don't want to hear."

"Where's Dutch?"

"Oh, he wanted to go into the office for a while. He's so dedicated. He'll be by for dinner, naturally. What are we having, and what can I do to help?"

"Hot dogs."

"Super! I'll chop the onions and tomatoes. The guys can barbecue."

"I'll be out in a minute. There's something I want to do on the computer first."

To his credit, Mycroft wavered, trying to decide whether to provide Penelope with his company *and* his valuable assistance or to oversee the dinner preparations of Cassie. Dinner won. It always did. He padded happily after Cassandra into the kitchen to provide instruction in the ever-changing nuances of pleasing your favorite cat.

In the lonely office—Penelope had grown accustomed to Mikey's presence and his ready willingness to help—she turned on the computer and put another of Wilfred Maxwell's disks in. He appeared to have left computer disks all over town.

This one was a disappointment.

No love letters.

No map coordinates.

There was only one file. It was labeled IOU.WM.

Penelope entered the file and read it.

TO WHOM IT MAY CONCERN:

I owe you ten (10) facsimiles of historic maps.

WILFRED MAXWELL

Why didn't he just leave a note? Why didn't he just check the maps out? Why . . . ?

Penelope decided that chopping onions would be more therapeutic than staring at Wilfred's IOU.

Wait.

"I should have done this before," Penelope told the computer.

Dit dit dit dit dit dit, the computer replied, telling Penelope that it was saving the file every three minutes as she had instructed. Please wait, flashed on the screen. It was a very polite and well-mannered computer.

Penelope ignored it as she usually did. It always caught up eventually.

Penelope loved her adopted state of Arizona, and like most good Arizonans, she subscribed to *Arizona Highways,* which published a regular feature entitled, "Legends of the Lost." Since she was neat and tidy with all things printed, if somewhat messy otherwise, her collection of the magazine was neatly bound, complete with yearly indexes. She only had to go four years back to find the Lost Patrol Vein, complete with an illustrated map. The story of the Lost Patrol essentially matched what Red the Rat had told her.

Unfolding the map she had borrowed from the library, she easily matched the government map with the magazine map, pinpointing the location within eight or ten square miles. A paved road ran twenty-five or thirty miles into the wilderness area, then it turned into a dirt track. Then . . . nothing. Penelope sighed. It might easily be a hundred square miles or more. Miles and miles of empty and uncharted desert around Bootleg Springs and Lion Canyon.

It was definitely time for a therapy session with the chopping knife.

Penelope had borrowed Laney's recipe for Nuclear Meltdown Hot Dogs and simply changed the name. Penelope's Boom Boom Hot Dogs were quite simple to prepare. Chop up a mess of onions and tomatoes, stir in a jar of hot dog relish, add Tobasco Sauce to taste—Penelope's taste ran to about half a bottle—char the hot dogs on the barbecue, smear some non-fat cream cheese substitute on the buns, and there you were. Boom

Boom. You had to be a real man, woman, or cat to eat the damned things, though. Fortunately, both Andy and Dutch were real men and no one would ever dare question Penelope or Cassandra's womanhood. Real women? Damned straight! As for Mycroft, he thought he was a lion anyway.

Which might come in handy when they reached Lion Canyon, since Dutch had rather summarily rejected Penelope's solution of Wilfred Maxwell's murder.

"But it's the only thing that makes sense," Penelope had protested.

"You think some person or persons unknown," Dutch summarized, "shot Maxwell, stole his treasure map or maps, and is now out there?" He stabbed the empty trackless desert waste portrayed on the map with a finger. "And whoever we find looking for the Lost Patrol gold mine is the killer."

"It's a vein, not a mine," Penelope said.

"Whatever."

"And my money's on Leonard Trope," Penelope said, "or perhaps the mother, although it could be the daughters. They looked like they would cheerfully steal the pennies from their dead father's eyes. It might even be the Iron Lady, but I don't think so. I hope not, anyway. She gave us the nicest refrigerator magnet."

Dutch groaned. "Do you have any other suspects?"

"Nope, that's it. Mikey and I have solved your murder for you. Again! If you don't want to do anything about it, that's fine with me."

"It would take the National Guard to find anyone out there. It's impossible."

"So what are you going to do?"

"Wait for our person or persons unknown to return with a pot full of gold."

"Ha!" she snirred. "With that kind of attitude, it's no wonder we have so much crime in society today." Some brother-in-law he was going to be.

* * *

It took Andy quite a long time and a rousing game of Let's Make Up, although Andy had done nothing, to restore Penelope's good humor. Sort of.

"Andy?"

"Mmm." He was quite exhausted. Let's Make Up could be rather strenuous.

"Why don't you ever write me love letters?"

Oh Oh. That got his attention. He didn't like the tone in Penelope's voice. The Mysterious Female was emerging from her den. "What did you say?"

"A love letter. A billet doux. An expression of affection."

"But I never go anywhere and I see you almost every day."

"That's no excuse."

"It isn't?" Oh oh. Again.

V

Penelope sat at the kitchen table drinking coffee and making a list of things to do. It was quite simple really. 1. Feed Mycroft. (If the grump ever decided to get up.) 2. Call Laney. 3. Load Jeep. 4. Find killer.

If all went well, they could be back before dinner. And once the killer—or killers—were behind bars, she could return to Christmas preparations. After all, Muffy and Biff would be here in a few days and she wanted everything set for her parents.

But first someone had to find Wilfred Maxwell's killer.

Saddle up! as Marine Corps gunnery sergeants were fond of saying.

Penelope went to the telephone and quickly dialed Laney's number.

"If you call me one more time," Laney shrieked into the phone, "I'm going to come over there and do unspeakable things with rawhide to your horny old body!" The phone was slammed down.

What was that all about, Penelope wondered as she redialed.

"I warned you!" Laney shouted.

Penelope shouted right back. "It's me!"

"Oh. I thought it was Cackling Ed again. He should be locked up as a pervert. Do you know what he said?"

"You can tell me later. Want to go on an adventure?"

"An adventure? Absolutely. Anything that will get me away from Cackling Ed's indecent suggestions."

"It might be dangerous," Penelope warned, knowing that Laney would ignore the warning. Laney was always up for any exploit.

"Danger is my life," said the adventuress. "I'll be right over."

"We're going into the desert and we may have to stay over a night, so bring your sleeping bag and some extra clothes."

"Oh, goody. A desert slumber party. Who's bringing the marshmallows?"

"I hate marshmallows."

"Who cares?"

The first thing Penelope did after hanging up with Laney was load two magazines for the AR-15, the civilian version of the military's M-16 rifle. Penelope's salty old sergeant major called it a mouse gun, but mouse gun or not, what good was all that excellent marksmanship training in the Marine Corps if you didn't take advantage of it when necessary? Besides, Lion Canyon didn't get its name by accident. Neither did Dead Man's Wash. Penelope had no intention of providing a new sobriquet for some desert landmark. Dead Penelope's Mountain. Thank you, no. The mouse gun was going along.

Death follows Penelope Warren. The chant of her friends echoed in her ears.

By the time Laney arrived, the jeep had been loaded with sleeping bag, pup tent, camping outfit with stove, ice chest (soft drinks, beer, and a bottle of chardonnay), rifle, canned foods of various sorts, two jerry cans of extra gasoline and one of water.

Mycroft, finally awakened by the unaccustomed flurry of activity (he was not a morning cat, anymore than Penelope was normally a morning person), demanded to eat, gathering his strength for the impending ordeal, and then went to sit in the jeep, assuring that he would not be left behind. He also made sure that sufficient quantities of cat food had been packed. Someone had to take charge of these expeditions. He eyed Laney suspiciously. He growled softly. *You're not taking my place.*

Laney, looking for all the world like she had stepped from a full page safari ad for Abercrombie and Fitch or the Banana Republic, twirled for Mycroft and Penelope. She seemed to possess a mail order catalog for every occasion. "Do you like it? It's the very latest in bush wear."

Penelope, who wore jeans, a bulky red sweater, and boots, admitted Laney was very fashionable. "You certainly have enough pockets. They may come in handy for toting gold or something."

"Well, thank you, Penelope. I may forgive you for giving that dreadful old coot my telephone number."

"We have to stop by Burning Cactus first."

"Why on earth for? That's where Cackling Ed is."

"The person I think will be in the desert may be at home. I just want to check," Penelope explained.

"Why did we get ready for an adventure if the villain is sitting at home in front of the hearth?"

"He's just the one I *think* I'm looking for. The villain could be someone else entirely."

"Why don't you just call?"

"That's no fun."

"Well, just put a blanket over me. I don't want to see Cackling Ed. More to the point, I don't want him to see me."

"He's harmless."

"Ha!"

"And he may not be on duty."

"Let us pray."

Penelope left a note on the kitchen table. "To whom It May Concern: Back Soon. Penelope and Mikey."

Laney had no intention of hiding her bush ensemble with some old blanket, but prayers went unanswered. Cackling Ed was on duty as the security gate of the Burning Cactus Golf and Condominium Club.

He positively danced, clipboard in hand, to the Jeep. "How do. Knew you'd change your mind."

"Well, actually, I haven't. Perhaps Laney has."

"Oh, Gawd, I'm in love. Never could resist a lass with red hair."

"Well, you better fall right back out of love. I have a gun and I won't hesitate to use it. No court would convict me. Justifiable homicide. I looked it up."

"Gawd, I like a woman with fire."

Laney shook her head helplessly.

"We'd like to go in and see Leonard Trope."

"Ain't here. Gone for the holidays."

"How about Elise Halsey?"

"Iron Lady's gone, too. For the holidays."

Gone where? Surely, the police had asked her to remain until the murder was solved. Surely Tweedledee and Tweedledum had watched enough cop shows on television to know that much.

"How about the former Mrs. Wilfred Maxwell?"

"Gone."

"The daughters?"

"Gone."

Hmm.

"I'm here," Ed added optimistically. "You could come in and see me. Be off duty soon."

"Thank you, no," Penelope replied. "We have to be going."

"Where you headed with all this gear?"

"We're having a slumber party in the desert," Laney said. "And you're not invited."

An hour later, the paved road ended. Thirty seconds after that, the desert had swallowed them whole. The desert was like that. Everything was normal and then the terrible sense of isolation descended, and you might be the last creature on earth. The dirt road, rutted and corrugated from the rains, was the only sign that man had ever traveled into this bleak and harsh landscape.

For a moment, the desert reminded Penelope of a passage from Kafka. "What could have enticed me to this desolate country except the wish to stay here?" It was from *The Castle* and K's utterance had remained with Penelope ever since first reading the novel. Now she hoped they weren't going into the desert to remain there.

Dead Penelope's Mountain.

Penelope was alone in the desert, except for a murderer and the skeletons of the Lost Patrol, grimly guarding their secret. But then she shook her head and glanced to her right. Laney smiled and hummed a snatch of a tune. Mycroft stood in her lap, front paws pressed to the dashboard as he watched the approaching landscape with interest. He seemed to be smiling.

And the desert was beautiful and majestic, if intolerant of man's unthinking transgressions. Penelope would miss it if ever she should leave, as desperately as she now longed for the gracious expanses of Africa. Stately saguaro cactus stood guard on both sides of the dirt track. Silent mountains, born of some ancient volcanic eruption, were outlined against the clear blue sky.

"It's lovely," Penelope said.

"Savage Love," Laney replied, pointing to stark mountains to the north. "I've decided to call my next novel Savage Love, and that's where they're taking poor Jessica. To their mountain stronghold. They're going to do unspeakable things to her with rawhide. That's where I got the idea to dissuade Cackling Ed."

"It didn't seem to work."

"I rather think he liked the idea, the horny old coot."

"Will the dashing Captain Walters arrive in time to rescue poor Jessica?"

"Oh, no. Harry Scott will do that. He's the savage lover. Jessica could never love Captain Walters. He's much too genteel. All that West Point folderol. Jessica loves Harry. He was raised by Indians, you know. Sort of like Paul Newman in *Hombre.*"

Penelope slowed and then stopped completely as they

rounded a bend. The deer stood in the middle of the road, unafraid, staring at them curiously.

"He's beautiful. I'll put him in the novel," Laney declared.

"Don't kill him."

"Of course not. Harry lives at one with his universe. That's why Jessica loves him."

"It's too bad some other people don't adopt that philosophy," Penelope mused as the mule deer ambled off into the desert and disappeared.

"I hate to admit it," Penelope said, "but this was a really dumb idea."

They had left the road hours ago, following the rim of Lion Canyon south to a spot overlooking Bootleg Springs, the landmark reputed to be nearest the location of the Lost Patrol Vein. They were only five miles—Penelope had noted the odometer—from the road, but they might have been on a planet populated only by birds and coyotes. There was nary a killer to be seen anywhere.

"Well, there might be whole civilizations behind the next cactus and we'd never know it," Laney said.

"No, I'm afraid Dutch was right. We'll never find anyone out here. We might as well go home."

"Penelope Warren! It's not like you to give up."

"It seemed like such a good idea at the time, too." Penelope took a last sweep of the desert through the binoculars. Still no sign of life. "Oh well," she said, dropping the binoculars, "we might as well start back."

"I think we should spend the night—take another look in the morning. Then we can head back."

"Well . . ."

"Mikey wants to stay. He's having a grand time."

"Well . . ." she hesitated. Mycroft did seem to be enjoying himself. He had industriously explored and staked out his territory, and at the moment, was busy explaining to a lizard that there was a new sheriff in town.

"We'll have a campfire. Cook out. Have a singalong."

"The only song I know is the Marine's Hymn," Penelope said. "All three verses."

"We'll have to skip the singalong then. I don't know any songs either. I was counting on you. We should have brought Wally along. He knows all the good songs. We'll tell ghost stories instead."

"We will not. Mycroft doesn't like ghost stories."

"Who doesn't like ghost stories?"

Penelope shivered. "Neither of us," she admitted. "My imagination is too vivid. I start believing there really are things out there in the night."

"But, Penelope, there are. Whooo!"

Mycroft looked at Laney when she groaned. He was upset. Maybe he really didn't like ghost stories. Big Mike, who wasn't afraid of anything. "I'm disappointed in you, Mikey," Laney said. "Just wait until I tell Alexander. Whooo!"

"Stop it, or we're leaving right now."

By the time darkness fell, the ladies were sipping wine from plastic cups. The tent had been erected, a canned stew supplemented with Tabasco simmered merrily away on the small stove, and Big Mike slept before the small fire.

The night was cold. The sky was clear and filled with stars. A full moon peeped over distant mountains, rising slowly until it seemed to fill the eastern horizon.

Laney held her cup out for more wine and said, "This is wonderful. We should do it more often."

"What? Go into the desert looking for murderers?"

"No. Get away. Camp out. Next time, I'll bring Alexander."

"He's a city dog. He wouldn't like the bush, not like Mycroft. He grew up with hyenas, jackals, wild dogs."

"Weren't you afraid for him?"

"Not after I learned he thought he was a lion. No one messed with him. He was the toughest critter on the campus."

"Still is," Laney observed.

"That's true."

A real lion had lazed the afternoon away in a mesquite tree watching the inordinate amount of activity in his parish with a considerable degree of interest. The mountain lion had seen man before—although the midget lion was new to his experience—and was not particularly alarmed. The ugly and foul-smelling creatures usually poked and prodded the earth for a day or two and went away. Still, if this kept up, it might be time to move on. But being feline, and of a most inquisitive nature, just like a real cat, he decided to hang around for a while, await developments, maybe even pop over for a quick visit. That midget lion *was* most curious.

The trouble with camping out was that there wasn't really a whole lot to do after singing all the snatches of Christmas carols they could remember—they made it all the way through Silent Night—and running through the Marine's Hymn three or four times. Sit around in the dark—it wasn't even that dark, with the full moon and all—and watch the dwindling fire.

Or go to bed early.

Alone.

In the pup tent, snug in her sleeping bag next to Penelope, Laney said, "Next time we should bring the boys. We could play Intrepid Pioneer Women."

Warm and happy between the two women, Big Mike purred contentedly. He was having a fine time as Pioneer Cat.

"How does that one go?"

"I'm not sure, but I'd think of something."

"Go to sleep. Think of cold showers."

Penelope tried to drift off to sleep, but she kept wondering what Leonard Trope was doing tonight. Probably in a nice warm bed someplace where a rock wasn't digging into *his* back. This was really, really dumb, Penelope told herself. You don't even know he did it. It could be any of the others. Checking out a slew of maps was *not* evidence of murder.

Dumb, dumb, dumb.

Mycroft growled softly.

He was answered by a snort outside the tent.

"Penelope," Laney hissed. "Wake up. There's something out there."

Always a very sound sleeper, Penelope only said, "Mmph?"

Laney shook Penelope's shoulder.

"Mmph?"

Mycroft growled louder.

"Penelope, please."

Enough pussy footing around. Big Mike threw down the gauntlet and squalled like a banshee.

That got Penelope. "Humph!" She sat up just as a mountain lion stuck his snout into the tent to see what the racket was all about.

That was a definite oops.

Big Mike punched him out good, raking sharp claws across his feline cousin's most sensitive nose. It wasn't very neighborly, but it was effective.

The lion hastily withdrew, whining as it loped out of the campsite. That little sucker packed a wallop.

Big Mike punctuated the lion's retreat with another loud squall before sitting back, looking rather pleased with himself, although he might have sprained his paw. That was one big nose.

And that took care of sleep for that night, unfortunate for several reasons.

First, the dawn found two very tired ladies draped in

their sleeping bags, dozing fitfully before a dying fire. Mycroft, on the other hand, had slept quite well, although he wondered what all the fuss was about. It was just some dumb oversized cat. Second, all of the squalling and roaring of the night had attracted attention.

Third, Leonard Trope got the drop on them.

Sort of.

To his credit, Big Mike tried to warn Penelope, but she was never at her best without a solid ten or twelve hours of sleep and Trope, after removing the rifle from Penelope's lap, practically had to shout to get the drop on them.

"Hands up," he bawled finally.

"Wah," Laney said.

"Humph?" Penelope said.

"Well," Penelope said, "at least I was right." She was still embarrassed at being so easily disarmed by Trope.

"A fat lot of good that does. He's going to kill us, you know."

"Probably."

"You don't have to agree with me. Can't you get loose?"

Penelope and Laney sat where Trope had left them, their backs to the saguaro cactus, their wrists encircled with rope and raised above their heads and tied to the arms of the cactus. The ropes were very tight.

"I don't want to disturb Mycroft." Big Mike was asleep in her lap. "How about you?"

"All I've done is make the ropes tighter. What are we going to do?"

"Wait."

"For what? He'll be back soon."

"I don't know. Something."

"Ha! Now I know how poor Jessica feels. At least, Harry is going to rescue *her.*"

"Listen!"

"I don't hear anything."

"There. I heard it again. He *is* coming back."

"He's whistling. Do you think he found the gold?"

"I don't know. Be calm."

"I am calm. I'm always calm just before someone kills me."

"The Marine's Hymn? He's whistling the Marine's Hymn?"

He was, indeed, but he broke off to say, "How do, ladies?"

"What are you doing here?" Penelope and Laney chorused.

"Came to find you," Cackling Ed said. "Looks like a good thing too."

"My hero," Laney said. "Now untie me."

"Gonna give me a kiss if I do?"

"That's blackmail."

"Yep."

"I wouldn't kiss you if you were the last man on earth."

"Gawd, I like a woman with spirit."

"I'll spirit you—"

"Oh, all right." Cackling Ed pulled a giant knife from a scabbard on his belt and cut Laney free and then turned his attention to Penelope. "You wanna tell me who did this?" he asked.

"Leonard Trope," Penelope said, "and we have to get out of here. He's got my rifle."

"Good idea," Laney said, "for a change."

Too late.

"Don't move," said Trope. He stepped into the clearing with Penelope's rifle leveled at the quartet of women, man, and cat.

"Never did trust you," Cackling Ed said.

"Shut up."

"What are you going to do now?" Penelope asked. "As you can see, there are people who know we're out here."

There certainly were.

"Thank God, I've found you!" Elise McMahon Harper Stewart Halsey said, emerging from the trackless waste. "I've been wandering for hours. I heard the greatest racket last night. It sounded like mountain lions fighting."

"Get over here, Elise," ordered Trope.

"Yesterday," Penelope complained, "we couldn't find anyone. Now half of Empty Creek seems to be out here." Some trackless waste this turned out to be.

"Listen," Laney said.

It was the faint but unmistakable *chug-chug-chug* of an approaching helicopter.

"And here comes the other half," Penelope said.

"I said, get over here, Elise. You're coming with me."

"You killed poor Wilfred," Wild Liz said. She didn't look very wild now.

A police helicopter circled the clearing and then swooped low, sending dirt flying everywhere.

Trope grabbed Elise's belt and pulled her close. The rifle barrel touched the back of her head. They backed away as the helicopter hovered low.

Dutch was hanging out of the passenger side, gun drawn. The helicopter inched forward.

Trope and Elise inched backwards.

Gunfight at the OK Corral time.

Penelope started to shout a warning to Trope, but—Oh well. He'd figure it out soon enough.

There is a cactus in Arizona known as the jumping cholla. It gets its name for obvious reasons. Whenever man or beast gets too close, its sharp spines jump into the nearest target. A smart man or beast doesn't get too close to the jumping cholla.

Leonard Trope wasn't too smart. He backed right into it.

This jumping cholla, a particularly vicious specimen, did exactly what it was supposed to do. It jumped. Well, not exactly. The plant didn't move, but the rest of it sure did, filling Leonard Trope's backside with a number of stout and very sharp spines.

His screech almost matched Big Mike's squall of the night before. The rifle flew out of his hands as he clutched his backside. He screamed again as the spines penetrated the palms of his hands. There was a third—and final—scream elicited from Trope as the Iron Lady turned and delivered a most unkind, if effective, kick to the area where he never wanted to be kicked.

Was the Iron Lady into Kung Fu as well, Penelope wondered as she leaped through the swirling dirt kicked up from the helicopter and retrieved her rifle.

The fight was over, to the disappointment of the arriving cavalry. Tweedledee and Tweedledum roared into the clearing in a police four-wheel drive vehicle.

Andy, Wally, and Cassandra followed right behind them in Laney's Bronco.

"Do you know what renting this helicopter has done to my budget, Penelope Warren?" Dutch cried after the helicopter was shut down and everyone could hear again.

"It's not free?" Penelope asked sweetly.

"No," Dutch shouted, "it is not free."

"Penelope, don't ever do this to me again," Andy cried. "I was worried sick."

"Me, too, lambkins," Wally said, taking Laney in his arms.

Lambkins? What kind of way was that for a cowboy to talk?

"And Dutch proposed and gave me a ring and everything and I rushed right home to tell you that I want you to be my maid of honor and you're not there and no one knows where you've gone and what is that 'to whom it may concern' stuff anyway, Penelope?" Cassandra finally had to catch her breath.

"I still think I should get a kiss," Cackling Ed said.

"When I'm seventy and wearing purple," Laney said, at last relenting, "but not a day sooner."

"Hell, I'll only be a hunnert and thirty or so," Ed said. "I'll wait."

Laney groaned. He just might.

"Help."

The chorused cry was faint, but unmistakable. The wicked stepmother and two wicked stepdaughters had been heard from. The party was complete, or would be when the three women were located. Sounds were deceiving in the desert.

"We'll get 'em," Tweedledee said. Burke and Stoner roared off.

Penelope turned to Trope. The Iron Lady was solicitously picking spines from his backside. She seemed to have a remarkable capacity for charitable forgiveness.

"I believe it's time," Penelope said, "for the big confession scene. All the best murder mysteries have them."

Dutch read Trope his rights.

"Go to hell," Trope said, groaning.

The Iron Lady jabbed Trope with a cholla spine.

"Ow, damn it, Elise, that hurt!"

"Talk, buster."

"I know about the loan," Penelope said. "Was that why you killed him?"

"That was only part of it," Trope said. It seemed that he had waived his right to remain silent. "Wilfred had everything. Money, Elise, everybody liked him. It didn't seem fair for him to have the gold too. He didn't need it. Still, I didn't want to kill him, so I made him an offer. We'd find the gold together and split it. That would have taken care of everything, but he just laughed. He shouldn't have laughed at me."

Tweedledee and Tweedledum returned with three very subdued and very bedraggled women. "He buried them up to their necks," Tweedledee announced. "We had to dig them out."

"He kidnapped us. He was going to kill us," the Wicked Stepmother said.

Penelope turned back to Trope. "Why?"

"That was my backup, in case I didn't find the gold. I figured I could marry Elise and get the money anyway, but they were going everywhere saying how they were going to sue for their inheritance. I couldn't take the chance—Owwww!"

The Iron Lady stomped off. So much for charity.

Mycroft batted a small rock toward Penelope. There was a tiny glint in the sunlight. She leaned over and picked it up. There was a definite glint. Penelope rubbed the dirt off.

"What is it, Penelope?" Andy asked.

"It appears to be a gold nugget," she announced.

"Mycroft," they all shouted. "Where did you find it?"

Big Mike refused to tell. That gold had caused enough trouble.

VI

'Twas the night before Christmas, and the house was anything but quiet. Indeed, creatures were stirring everywhere. Empty Creek's very own carolers had just left, bouncing away on the flat bed truck that carried them to the more remote homes, after beautiful renditions of "God Rest Ye Merry Gentlemen" and "Come All Ye Faithful."

Biff—Penelope and Cassandra's father—was holding court in the living room cheerfully dispensing drinks and advice to Andy, Dutch, and Wally, who were swearing over the assembly of some difficult toy to be delivered to the children's ward of the hospital the next morning.

Laney absolutely adored Biff—his real name was Jameson, but no one ever called him that—and agreed with his every word offered to the disgruntled assembly line workers.

Mycroft was under the tree for a change, burrowed among the presents, although he was sorely tempted to offer his own help on the assembly line. Big Mike's faithful canine companion, Alexander, was next to him, black eyes glowing with excitement. His tail thumped furiously against a wrapped box.

Muffy—her name was Mary, but no one ever called her that, either—had taken command of the kitchen as was customary, because both her daughters believed her to be, rightfully so, the greatest cook in the world. The three of them were busily engaged in preparing the

Warrens' traditional Christmas Eve repast of roast beef and Yorkshire pudding, the conversation skipping haphazardly between wedding plans and murder most foul.

"I think a spring wedding," Cassandra said. "Don't you, Muffy, when all the flowers are in bloom?"

"Yes, dear. I'm so glad you want to be married in our back yard. The view will be beautiful." The Warrens—*père* and *mère*—still resided in Southern California, high above the Pacific Ocean on the Palos Verdes Peninsula. Penelope and Cassandra had grown up in that very house. "But I still don't understand how you knew the killer would go prospecting like that, Penelope."

"I didn't really, but I figured that whoever had killed Wilfred Maxwell would be in a hurry to get the gold before anyone else had a chance to get it."

"After the honeymoon, we'll have a reception for our friends in Empty Creek."

"Well, I wish you wouldn't get yourself in such situations. I mean, after the last time . . . It's so dangerous."

"Death follows Penelope Warren," Cassandra said, "but she's going to be my bridesmaid, anyway."

"Well, that's that," Muffy said. "Everything's done for the moment."

"Let's go sit down for a while," Penelope said. "It's time."

"Time for what?" Muffy asked.

"You know," Cassandra said.

"'Twas the night before Christmas . . ."

Muffy said the same thing every year. "Aren't you getting a little old for that?"

"It wouldn't be Christmas without it, Muffy." The tradition had started when they were little girls. Every Christmas Eve, Muffy recited "A Visit from St. Nicholas." After dinner it would be Cassandra's turn to read O. Henry's "The Gift of the Magi." That was a tradition, too.

"Oh, very well."

Muffy took her place on the couch. Everyone gathered around her while Penelope turned out all the lights except for those on the tree.

When Muffy began reciting the old poem—she knew it by heart—Penelope closed her eyes and returned to those magical days of her childhood.

> " ' 'Twas the night before Christmas,
> when all through the house
> Not a creature was stirring—not even
> a mouse;
> The stockings were hung by the chimney
> with care,
> In hopes that St. Nicholas soon would
> be there . . .' "

Penelope listened to Muffy's melodious voice and was a little girl again, sitting beside Cassandra, the both of them trembling with excitement and anticipation. The jolly St. Nicholas, indeed, soon would be there.

" 'Happy Christmas to all, and to all a goodnight!' "

Christmas, Margaritas And Murder

by Barbara Block

Favors for Manuel always had a tendency to spiral out of control. That's why when Tim called me from the store and asked me to do one for him I wasn't exactly pleased.

"Robin, don't worry," Tim assured me over the phone. Our connection was bad and his voice kept fading in and out. "It's nothing major."

"It never is." I lit a cigarette and blew out the match. "That's not the point. What's he doing down in Cancun anyway?"

"He's staying with his aunt and uncle. Apparently it's one of those spend-Christmas-vacation-with-your-relatives deals."

"I bet they were in for a surprise," I murmured.

I could just image how they'd take Manuel's current enormous shorts, knee length Metallica tee shirt, and pierced ears. Of course they wouldn't have taken his side burns and pompadour any better. Like most sixteen-year-olds, Manuel was a stylistic chameleon.

"Probably." Tim coughed. He had a classic midwinter Syracuse cold. "So how's the conference going?"

"The conference is going fine," I replied as I pulled my bathing suit up and started slathering suntan lotion on my legs. They were nice and long. If only they weren't so scarred, I thought regretfully. Skin grafts can only do so much. Two years and I still had trouble looking at them. Not only were they ugly, but they reminded me of the person who'd tried to kill me. But then, that person had tried to kill Manuel too. That's how we'd met. We'd become friends during our physical therapy sessions at the hospital. I sighed and put the bottle of lotion on the nightstand, then I brightened. Bill Coborn didn't seem to care, so maybe I shouldn't either. We were having dinner tonight and after that, who knew? I smiled thinking of his warm eyes and easy laugh. Two years was a long dry spell. And after all, I was on vacation. And it was Christmas. maybe Bill would be my Christmas present to myself.

"You buy anything for the store?" asked Tim, interrupting my fantasy.

I came back to reality. "Five ball pythons and half a dozen Mexican tree frogs from Ray. He's gonna ship 'em up in a couple of days." I studied the view out of my window. The water was turquoise and aqua, the sand a pure creamy white. I could have kissed whoever had decided to hold The International Collectors Herpetology Conference at the Cancun Sheraton in December. "Now you want to tell me what this is about, because I was just heading down to the beach."

"Light, you're a cruel woman," Tim moaned. I laughed. "You know what Manuel's like," he continued. "Well, it seems he lost his money somewhere, and since you're down there too his mother wanted to know . . ."

"If I could loan him some?"

"Just to tide him over."

I said I would. I should have known better, because as I said, nothing with Manuel is ever simple, but in this case I figured: what could go wrong?

What went wrong was this. Manuel and his aunt and uncle were screaming at each other when I walked into their house. When they saw me his aunt and uncle started screaming at me. My Spanish isn't very good, but I did manage to get the gist: something about Manuel sneaking out of the house at two in the morning and that they were fed up with Manuel walking around with his pants falling off, sleeping till noon, and hitting on all the girls on the block.

"We are decent people," the uncle pronounced through clacking teeth. "And already the neighbors are talking. We think you should take him back to the hotel. He will be happier with other Americans."

"Fine with me. I'm outta here," Manuel said and jetted out the door, past the crêche, and into the waiting taxi before I could stop him.

But I thought, okay. We'll go back to the Sheraton, I'll call Manuel's mom, she'll call her sister and everything will get straightened out. Wrong again. The uncle absolutely did not want him back; they'd get a cousin to deliver Manuel's clothes to my room. I was stuck with him till the day after tomorrow, when I could put him on a plane back to Syracuse. Manuel was delighted. I was not, especially since the hotel was booked and we would have to share a room. We spent the rest of the day at the beach. That evening Bill, Manuel, and I ate dinner together at the hotel. It was not what I had planned. Neither was the rest of the evening.

"Mind if I come along?" Manuel asked when I told him Bill and I were going for a walk on the beach. I glared at him. "Of course," he continued, choosing not to take the hint. "If you don't want me . . ."

I didn't, but I couldn't say that—at least not in those words. But while I was thinking of a polite way to tell Manuel to get lost Bill shrugged philosophically and told me he had to get up early the next morning anyway. He suggested it might be better if we met after I put Manuel on the plane. Then he gave me a peck on the cheek and said goodnight. I spent the next twenty minutes sulking. I would have sulked longer but someone was setting fireworks off down by the beach and it's impossible to sulk when Roman candles are lighting up the sky. By the time the display was over I was in a better frame of mind. Manuel and I went back to the room and I phoned Tim to check on the store. Then I settled in with a guide book to Chichen Itza called *The Yucatan.*

I'd booked the tour to the ruins through the conference pre Manuel and had seen no reason to change my plans. Of course, Manuel didn't want to go, but that was too bad. He was coming anyway. I wasn't about to leave him to his own devices for the whole day. Given his prior history with the court system I didn't have much faith in his judgment.

Aside from two snoozing bellboys and six sleepy-eyed people waiting for the van, the lobby was empty when we came down at seven the next morning. I stifled a yawn as I introduced Manuel and myself to the tour group members. Conversation was desultory. No one wanted to talk. It was too early. Cradling my cup of coffee in my hands, I leaned against one of the columns and wondered where the driver was. By my reckoning he was now ten minutes late, ten minutes I could have used to sleep. Five minutes after that he pulled up in a dented maroon-colored van and we all trooped out and got aboard. As soon as we sat down Manuel closed his eyes and went back to sleep. I spent the next two and a half hours alternately dozing, studying the scenery—which mostly consisted of scraggly trees, shacks, children, chickens, and goats—and watching the other passengers, who seemed to be doing the same things I was.

Except for the couple sitting in front of me, that is. They spent the trip down arguing. I couldn't hear what they were fighting about, but it was obvious from the ferocious whispers and glares being exchanged they weren't billing and cooing. They'd introduced themselves to me as Milagros and George Schmick back at the hotel and told me they ran a pet store out in Queens called Pet Paradise. I'd been struck then by what a contrast they were. He was thin, she was fat. He was blond, she was dark-haired. She had a low forehead, he was balding. Maybe it's true that opposites really do attract. That had certainly been the case with Murphy and me,

I thought as I closed my eyes. I was just dozing off when Percy Sorbus tapped me on the shoulder.

"Want a cookie?" he asked after I'd turned around. His voice was high and squeaky. When he'd introduced himself I'd thought he'd sounded like a mouse. Now I realized that he looked like one too.

I thanked him and shook my head. I had a chocolate bar in my pocket I was planning on working on. Then Sorbus asked James Johnson, the man sitting all the way in back, whether he wanted one, but Johnson shook his head too and went back to fiddling with one of the buttons on his white short-sleeved shirt. The tic under his left eye that I'd noticed at the hotel seemed to be getting worse. Despite the air conditioning, his face was shiny with sweat.

"Hey Johnson, what you got in that pack of yours anyway?" The man sitting next to Sorbus asked as he pointed to the black backpack by Johnson's feet. His name was Adam Neyhart. He had a moon-face, close set eyes, and a receding chin.

"I got stuff," Johnson said shortly.

"What kind of stuff?" Neyhart insisted.

"None of your business stuff," Johnson retorted.

Neyhart's face went red. "What's the matter? Why don't you wanna answer? Maybe you got something venomous in there? Maybe we should take a look."

Before Johnson could say anything, the last member of the group, Sam Walker, looked up from the guide book he was reading. He was tall and thin and delicately featured with skin the color of an ebony statue. "If you don't mind," he said to both Johnson and Neyhart. "I'm trying to read."

"Good for you," Johnson replied and proceeded to look out the window.

Neyhart opened his mouth to say something, thought better of it and closed it again. No one spoke for the rest of the trip. I went back to sleep. I was still sleeping when we pulled into the parking lot at Chichen Itza. I woke up just in time to see the driver, Hector Robles, point to the building off to the right and inform us a buffet lunch would be served at the Plaza Hotel from twelve to three. Then he gestured to the visitors center and the gravel path to the main ruins and told us we were free to wander where we wished.

As I got off the van and the sun hit me I couldn't help wondering if I'd been wise to come after all. Sometimes visiting the scene of old loves and happier times isn't a wise thing to do. It opens up too many wounds. Then Manuel asked me where we were going and I put those thoughts aside.

"There," I said pointing to El Castillo, the largest pyramid at the site. I beckoned to Manuel to follow me. Everyone else walked off to the visitors center. I didn't mind. I don't like being part of a group anyway.

"You know, if you gave it half a chance you might actually learn something," I told Manuel as we entered the clearing to the Temple Of The Warriors. He'd been whining ever since I'd decided we were going to visit the old part of the ruins, a twenty minute walk away from the main attractions.

"All I can see is bugs and bushes," he repeated for what must have been the hundredth time. I was about to say something nasty when he made an odd strangled noise. "What's that?" he whispered pointing to the altar in the center of the clearing.

I took a look and felt the bile in my stomach rising.

Ringed by three vultures, James Johnson was splayed out on a stone block in front of the temple. A trickle of blood ran out of his ears and down the granite surface. Someone had stuck thorns through his eyelids and protruding tongue. His chest had been torn open. His heart was missing. The two statues on either side of the altar stared out into the jungle with blind eyes. I followed their glance. No one was there. Except for the sound of Manuel retching the silence was absolute. Not even the insects were whirring in the hot noonday sun.

I closed my eyes and swallowed hard, but Johnson was still there when I opened them. I'd been hoping I was seeing things, but unfortunately I wasn't. Part of me wanted to run, the other part of me wanted a closer look. After having been involved in two homicide cases in as many years corpses didn't scare me anymore, and anyway the truth was I still couldn't quite believe what I was seeing. I half expected some director to jump out from behind the scrub trees and yell, "Cut" and Johnson to get up, dust himself off, and call for some mineral water. Only he didn't. Neither did the vultures. I guess they didn't want to leave a good meal. Most of us don't.

"Get out of here," I yelled waving my hands in the air and stamping my feet.

The three giant birds stopped pecking at Johnson for a second, looked at me, and went back to eating. I picked up a rock and threw it at them. One of them gave me a speculative glance, then it and its two brethren rose into the air. Their wings blocked out the sun as they glided to the top of a nearby dead tree. We can wait, they seemed to say as they preened their feathers. We have all the time in the world. I shivered and averted my eyes. As I did I caught a glint of something grey lying in the scrub grass by my feet. I crouched down to get a better look. It was a glasses case.

I picked it up. It was one of those soft leather jobs, the kind that the opticians give you when you buy expensive frames. I looked inside. No name. I was trying to remember whether or not I'd seen Johnson wearing glasses when I heard a sharp crack behind me. I jumped up and whirled around. But there was nothing there, at least nothing that I could see. Just the jungle and the quiet and the Mayan warriors.

"Let's get out of here," cried Manuel.

"Sounds like a good idea to me," I agreed as we hurriedly backed out of the clearing.

When we hit the trail we started running, and we didn't stop until we reached the lobby of the Plaza Hotel. It wasn't until after I'd told the hotel clerk to call the police that I happened to look down and see that I was still holding the glasses case in my hand.

"Damn," Adam Neyhart said when I told the tour group what had happened. He threw down his napkin and petulantly pushed his plate away. It hit against one of the terra cotta Christmas angels decorating the table. "There goes my meeting with Wagner for tonight. We were supposed to close on three of my big Burmese. Now we'll probably be stuck here," he lamented. "Why couldn't Johnson have gotten himself killed in Brooklyn like everyone else? Why did he have to come out here to do it?"

Sam Walker pursed his thin lips disapprovingly. "Why do you always have to be so callous?"

I gave a guilty start because I'd been thinking about how inconvenient Johnson's death was too. All I wanted to do was get back to Cancun tonight so I could get Manuel on the ten o'clock plane tomorrow and call Bill, and now it looked as if that wasn't going to happen. I mean, of course I was sorry Johnson was dead, but I was sorry in an abstract way. The truth was I hadn't met the man until this morning and the little I'd seen of him I hadn't liked.

"I'm not callous," Neyhart retorted. "I just call them the way I see them—not like some I could name."

Walker leaned forward eagerly. He looked as black and sleek as one of the vultures I'd seen earlier. "Honesty does not excuse one from observing the common decencies."

Neyhart rolled his eyes. "You weren't observing them with Johnson over at Ray Malone's booth."

"That was because he wanted to know if I wanted a Yucatan crocodile." Walker sat back and put his fingertips together.

"And you said no?" George Schmick raised his thatched eyebrows in disbelief. "Milagros, tell the man what those things are worth," he ordered. But instead of answering his wife bit her lip, looked down at her plate, and pleated her napkin.

Walker ignored her. "I know what they're worth," he told Schmick. "But they're also on the endangered list."

George scowled and began spinning a peso he was holding on the table surface. "Well, if you ask me I think that list is bullshit. It's totally political. A lot of the items on it have no business being there."

Walker drummed his fingers on the table. "You would think that. If people like you had their way nothing would be protected. And you know what would happen?" Since it was a rhetorical question he didn't stop for an answer. "Well, I'll tell you. Everything would be extinct in ten years."

Neyhart snorted in derision. Then he leaned forward. "You know some of us make our living selling reptiles. Some of us don't get paid to sit on our asses and compose long, learned monographs about field conditions they know nothing about."

"Are you saying I don't know my subject area?" Walker demanded.

"I'm saying that there's an enormous difference between theoretical and practical knowledge."

Walker's mouth tightened, but he didn't say reply.

"You say Johnson's heart was ripped out?" Percy Sorbus asked me. A retired mail carrier from the Bronx, he was a serious herp collector and had been telling everyone who'd listen that he hadn't been able to resist the combination of Christmas in Cancun and a herpetology conference. "Who would do something like that?" Sorbus demanded, his eyes blinking rapidly.

No one answered.

"Does anyone know what Johnson was doing down here?" I inquired.

Neyhart began bending his straw into a triangle. "Looking to make a buck, I'd say. After all, that's what he did best."

George Schmick ran his hand through his thinning

blond hair then readjusted the collar of his silk shirt. "He probably had orders he was filling."

I looked around the table. "So you're saying he was a dealer?"

"Yes," Milagros whispered. She was still pleating her napkin.

"I understand the Feds were thinking of investigating him." Walker put his hands down on the table and pushed himself away. "Something about Indian pythons."

George continued spinning the peso. "It wouldn't surprise me at all. Not one single bit." He flattened the peso with the palm of his hand and looked at his wife. "Honey, do me a favor and get me a beer."

Milagros bit her lip. Reluctantly she got up and walked over to the bar. I was getting up to join her when our driver Hector Robles tapped me on the shoulder.

"The police want to speak to you and the boy," he said, pointing to Manuel. "Come. I take you." He began chewing on the tip of his mustache. "It is not good to keep Lagartos waiting."

As we passed the Christmas tree with its blinking lights and candy canes and strands of bougainvillea I decided this might not be such a merry Christmas after all.

Detective Hernando Lagartos was not pleased. He wasn't pleased to have his lunch interrupted. He wasn't pleased to have to deal with a corpse. And since Manuel and I were the ones who had found it, he wasn't pleased with us either. At all. A fact his scowl made abundantly clear on the ride back over to the old ruins. When he saw the vultures ripping away at Johnson's body he scowled even harder. Then he took out his gun, a Glock 9mm, aimed, and fired. Pow. Pow. Pow. The birds fell over one after another like cardboard cutouts in a shooting gallery.

"I don't like pests," he announced looking directly at

Manuel and me as he reholstered the gun. "Do you understand?"

"I think we've got the message," I replied throwing a quick glance in Manuel's direction.

He looked as if he were going to throw up all over again. My stomach wasn't feeling so great either. Seeing Johnson again, plus watching Lagartos shoot those vultures, was not a good combination. I swallowed hard. I'd been just about to tell him about the eyeglass case I'd found in the grass by the altar, but not now. No way. I wasn't going to take a chance and do something that would put me in a worse position than I was already in. The eyeglass case could just stay in my pocket. It probably wasn't relevant to Johnson's murder anyway. Lots of people drop stuff like that out of their pockets. I know I sure as hell did. That's why I didn't have a pair of sunglasses right now.

My heart was pounding as I watched Lagartos lift up Johnson's body. I kept wishing I had a drink or a candy bar or a Valium—anything to take the edge off the anxiety I was feeling. A moment later he put him down, straightened up and wiped the blood off his hands with a handkerchief offered by an assistant hovering nearly.

"No es el MSM," Lagartos said to him.

"What did he say?" Manuel whispered to me.

"That's it's not the MSM, the Mayan Separatist Movement," Robles whispered back as he stepped away from the shade of a tree. Little beads of sweat dotted his forehead.

"What's the Mayan Separatist Movement?" I asked.

"A group that wishes everyone who is not Indian out of the Yucatan," Robles replied, raising his voice slightly.

"She does not have to be concerned with this," Lagartos said as he approached us.

Robles melted back into the shadows. Unfortunately Manuel and I couldn't do the same.

"The hotel clerk told me your name is Robin Light," he said. "Is it?"

I nodded.

"And you are from?"

"Syracuse." The jungle seemed to swallow my voice.

"And what is Syracuse?"

"A city in Central New York."

"And what do you do in Syracuse, Robin Light?"

"She runs a pet shop," Manuel replied, jumping in with the answer.

Lagartos half turned and glared. Manuel cringed. "Sorry," he stammered.

Lagartos turned back to me. "Ah. I see." He put his hands together and held them in front of his mouth. "And what do you sell?"

"Everything. Snakes. Lizards. Birds. My store is called Noah's Ark."

"So you are here on business?"

"I'm attending the herp conference at the Cancun Sheraton."

"With him?" He indicated Manuel, his glance taking in Manuel's attire and finding it wanting. "He is your son?"

I started to explain about Manuel and his aunt and uncle, but Lagartos held up his hand. "Is he staying with you now or not? Yes or no?"

"Yes," I replied.

"That's all I wanted to know. And you didn't know this man?" he gestured towards Johnson. His voice was soft and insinuating as the moss on the statues's crevices.

"I've seen him at the hotel but I never spoke to him before this morning."

Lagartos lifted both eyebrows. "I've been told he sells things you might be interested in buying."

"You're mistaken," I replied in as forceful a voice as I could.

"Really?"

"Yes, really."

Manuel gave me a uneasy look. I guess my voice had gotten too loud, but sometimes I do that when I get nervous.

Lagartos stroked his chin. "May I ask why you came to this spot in particular? It is not a popular one with tourists."

"I wanted to show my friend the old ruins, to see the way Chichen Itza looked before it was restored."

"I see." Lagartos frowned and stroked the Glock's handle. It was obvious he didn't believe me. "So our young friend is a lover of *arqueología.*"

Manuel looked at the ground and fidgeted.

Lagartos lifted Manuel's chin up with the tip of one of his fingers. "Well, are you?" he asked.

"Oh, yes. Definitely," Manuel stuttered. "I love all that old shit."

Lagartos's scowl deepened. He looked from Manuel to me and then back again. For a few awful seconds I was afraid he was going to take us in for questioning. My stomach started to churn as I remembered all the horror stories I'd heard about the Mexican police. But instead he ordered us back to the hotel.

"We should have stayed at the beach," Manuel hissed on the ride back. "But, oh no, you had to see the ruins."

"Give it a rest," I snapped as I lit a cigarette. I was in a very bad mood.

We finished the rest of the ten minute ride in silence. Lagartos joined us twenty minutes later, took everyone else's statement and cautioned us against leaving the area. We were not under arrest—yet, he emphasized. We could wander around the ruins, but we were not to go back to Cancun. We would have to remain here at the hotel for the night and possibly even longer. Our tour guide, Señor Robles, would see to the arrangements.

"Do you have any idea how long we'll have to stay?" I asked.

"Until I say you can go," Lagartos replied.

I thought of Bill's hazel eyes and lopsided grin and groaned. He was going home in three days. If Manuel missed his flight tomorrow morning it would be at least a couple of days before I could get him another seat, which left Bill and me no time at all. This was not fair.

"I don't understand why you're keeping us?" Sorbus asked Lagartos in a plaintive voice when the policeman was done talking.

"Obviously because he thinks one of us did it," Neyhart growled. "Isn't that right?" he asked Lagartos.

But the Mexican didn't answer. He just smiled the way a crocodile does when he spots his prey. I ignored him and went off to find a phone.

"Robin." Manuel jiggled my arm just as I was biting into an enchilada. A piece of tomato dropped out of the tortilla and onto the table. "I got to talk to you."

I picked the piece up and put it on the side of my plate. "Go ahead. I'm listening," I said reluctantly. I wasn't in the mood to talk because I was still brooding about Bill.

Manuel licked his lips. "Now you promise you won't get mad."

I most definitely did not like the sound of that. I put the enchilada down and pushed the plate away. My appetite had suddenly disappeared. "What did you do?" I demanded.

"Nothing. I swear." Manuel raised his right hand. "We just gotta go back to that temple."

"The place where Johnson was killed?"

Manuel nodded.

"Forget it," I said thinking of Lagartos. The last thing I wanted was more trouble with that man. Even though I'd seen him and his men leave, I didn't know whether or not he'd posted someone at the crime site. If he had, we'd end up being questioned all over again.

"No, Robin. Really. We gotta go back," Manuel repeated.

I studied his face. He looked very young and very scared. What had this kid done? One thing was sure: whatever it was, it wasn't good.

I crossed my arms over my chest. "You want to tell me what this is about?"

"I dropped something there," Manuel muttered.

"Like what?" My stomach began to churn.

"An envelope." Manuel had dropped his voice so low I had to lean over to hear him.

"And what's in the envelope?"

"A couple of joints," whispered Manuel.

"Jesus," I hissed as I restrained myself from putting both my hands around Manuel's neck and squeezing. I fumbled for a cigarette while I struggled to calm down. "Okay," I said when I felt I could talk sensibly. "How is anybody going to know the envelope is yours? I mean, it doesn't have your name on it, does it?" I enquired anxiously. I was half joking, half not.

"No."

"Good." A wave of relief washed over me.

"It has my aunt's."

I just stared at him in disbelief. How anyone could be such a moron was beyond me.

"So you can see why we got to go back," Manuel pleaded.

For a second I was tempted to tell him to forget it. But I couldn't do that. Possession of a couple of joints in the United states earned you an appearance ticket. Possession of a couple of joints in Mexico could earn you a stay in jail. That was not a fate I would wish on anyone. Not even Manuel.

I pushed my chair away from the table and stood up. "Let's go," I said even though that was the last thing I wanted to do.

Manuel and I walked along the path in silence. I was still too angry to speak and he was too scared. I kept a fast pace for the first ten minutes but then the heat got to me and I slowed down. So did Manuel.

"What happens if Lagartos left a cop behind?" Manuel asked five minutes later finally breaking the silence between us.

By then I had calmed down sufficiently to answer. "I'll just say I dropped my lighter and I came back to look for it," I told Manuel.

"But you don't have a lighter," he protested.

"I know." I half turned towards him. "What is the matter with you, anyway? You can't lace up your sneakers without getting into trouble."

Manuel studied the trees we were passing with an intense amount of interest. "I guess I should think a little more," he finally said. "It's just that I get an idea and go with it."

"What you need is a better class of ideas."

"That's what my probation officer says."

I was just about to tell him I agreed when I heard a strange whirring noise.

"What's that?" Manuel asked as he hiked up his shorts. Even with his belt they were in perpetual danger of falling down to his ankles.

I shook my head. "I'm not sure. But I don't like it."

"Me either," Manuel said and he reached in his pocket and pulled something out. I heard a click and a skinny vicious looking eight-inch blade shot into view. I couldn't believe it.

"Stilettos are legal down here," said Manuel defensively when he saw my expression.

"But not in the States." I wanted to strangle him all over again. "You'd better get rid of that before you get on the plane," I warned.

Manuel didn't answer. He was too busy listening to the whirring, which was getting louder. And closer. He took a couple of steps back. So did I. I couldn't imagine what was making that noise and I didn't think I wanted to find out, either.

I was just turning to run when a wizened old man dressed in a vanilla-colored suit stepped out from behind a red ginger tree. Manuel gasped. I almost clapped my hands with delight and relief.

"It's a beetle man," I cried. I'd heard about people like him from a friend of mine who'd lived down here for a while, but I hadn't believed him.

"A what?" Manuel asked. He was slack-jawed with amazement.

"A beetle man. See." And I pointed to the cloud of blue green dragonflies whirring around the man's head.

They were attached to his wrist by strands of white thread. Large, black beetles dotted the lapels of his white suit. Two waved antennae in my direction. The man gave a little bow. Then before I could say anything he began to talk.

"You want?" he asked us, pointing over his head to the dragonflies. "I give them to you cheap. Forty thousand pesos. Five dollars. Or one for five thousand pesos."

I shook my head.

"For him?" he said indicating Manuel.

"Thanks." Manuel retracted the knife blade and dropped the stiletto in his pocket. "But I think I'll pass."

The old man turned back to me and indicated the beetles. "Then a pretty pin for your niña. For Christmas. Also cheap. I already sell the fancy ones."

"Sorry." I shook my head again. "I don't have a daughter."

The Mexican shrugged fatalistically and trudged on, a fantastical figure followed by a blue-green cloud. As I watched him go I wondered if there wasn't something to be said for Barbie dolls and plastic after all.

"Does anyone ever buy those things?" Manuel asked as the Mexican disappeared around a curve in the trail.

"Someone must," I replied as I lit a cigarette. I tugged on Manuel's sleeve. "Come on, let's get going."

The path was empty. As Lagartos had observed, not many people visited the old part of Chichen Itza. It was off the beaten track, a fast twenty minute walk from the hotel—half an hour if you were taking your time—over a barely traceable path. It was easy to get lost and there wasn't that much to see. Most of the ruins on this side were smaller. Some were piles of rubble. Everyone wanted to see the big pyramids, the ball field, and the table of skulls on the other side of the road.

The real reason I'd wanted to come here, a reason I hadn't shared with Manuel, much less Lagartos, was that I'd been making a sentimental pilgrimage—Murphy and I had visited this place twenty years ago, knocked back a quarter of a bottle of José Cuervo, and made love wedged inside the Temple Of The Warriors. Even though he'd been dead for a little over two years I still couldn't seem to get the man out of my mind—maybe because we'd had such a lousy marriage. Which seems unfair. I mean, why are bad memories so much stronger than good ones? I've asked everyone I can think of and no one seems to have the answer.

I shook my head to clear it and then I started thinking about Johnson. Why had Johnson come, anyway? What had brought him to this spot? A business deal? Was he buying something he shouldn't have? After all, everyone had pretty much indicated he trafficked in restricted items. A desire to get away from the tour group? Had his death been coincidence? Had he been jumped by some crazed person? Lagartos obviously didn't think so, and neither did I.

No, he thought either I or someone in the tour group had killed Johnson. But I knew I hadn't, and while I could picture people in our group killing Johnson, try as I might I couldn't picture them mutilating the body like that. Why had that been done anyway? Rage? Possibly, but I didn't think so. The mutilations had been too deliberate, too ritualistic. Something a group like the MSM might do. After all, the Toltecs had ripped out the hearts of their victims. Maybe this group had just gotten their history a little confused. I was thinking about that when Manuel shook my shoulder.

"We're almost there," he said.

I immediately stopped thinking about Johnson and the MSM and started thinking about how I was going to handle meeting one of Lagartos's men. But except for the two vultures feasting on their dead brethren the clearing was empty. I breathed a sigh of relief. The birds paused for a few seconds when we walked in and then went back to their meal. What they didn't take care of the beetles would, and then the vines would come and cover the bones and there'd be nothing left.

Suddenly Manuel darted ahead of me. "Here it is," he cried triumphantly a moment later as he stopped about five feet from the altar and pointed to a crumpled, dirty envelope.

It was lying in plain view. Probably the only reason one of Lagartos's men hadn't picked it up was because it looked like another piece of trash, of which there was a plentiful amount. Manuel ran over and scooped it up.

I held out my hand. "May I have it, please."

"But the grass is a Christmas present for Rabbit," Manuel cried.

"Then I guess you're going to have to get him someone else," I told him.

Manuel started to say something, stopped himself, and reluctantly handed it over. I opened up the envelope, took out the two joints, and crumpled them underneath a bush. Then I put the envelope in my pocket. Manuel let out a moan. I could sympathize, even though I'd never have said that to him. I wouldn't have minded a smoke myself, but it wasn't worth the risk. I was just about to tell Manuel that we were going when my eyes fastened on the pool of blood on the stone. Something about it wasn't right, but I couldn't figure out what it was. I walked over to the altar and studied it, while Manuel stayed where he was and kicked dust up with the toe of his sneaker. I ignored him, brushed off a fly that had landed on my shoulder and concentrated. Suddenly I knew. It was so simple I wondered why I hadn't seen it sooner.

"There isn't enough blood on the stone," I announced thinking out loud. "There would be more if Johnson was killed here. He was murdered somewhere else."

"Who cares," Manuel muttered sulkily, still obviously brooding about the lost contents of his envelope.

"I care," I shot back, thinking that maybe there was a way to get back to Cancun in time to put Manuel on the plane tomorrow morning after all.

I smiled. From what Lagartos had said to the group before he left it was obvious to me he thought Johnson was killed here. Well, he hadn't been. Maybe Lagartos was wrong about some other things too. Maybe Johnson really had been killed by the MSM. Whoever had murdered him had clearly wanted him found. Otherwise they would have dumped him in the bush. Maybe Johnson was a message from the group. If I came up with some answers I could tell Robles and Robles could tell Lagartos and we could all go home.

I looked up. Had the death occurred inside the temple? I took a deep breath and went inside. A shaft of light streamed through a narrow window high up in the wall. The air smelled vaguely of leaf mold. I looked around at the small room I was standing in. I'd remembered it as being larger. For a few seconds I could smell Murphy's sweat and hear his groans and then the image was gone. Outside of a brown spider running across its web over in the corner there was nothing to see except the gray of the quarried stone walls.

I kicked aside a Coca-Cola can and willed myself to study the earthen floor. For some reason it was less painful than remembering. There was no blood. No signs of a fight, but then the ground really was too hard-packed to show anything. I sighed and went back outside. As I stroked a leaf from one of the bushes around the perimeter, I noticed that some of the vegetation near the temple had been trampled down. But that could as easily have been from Lagartos's men as from anything else. I reached up and wiped the sweat out of my eyes.

If Johnson hadn't been murdered in the temple, where had he been killed?

It couldn't have been that far away.

Johnson was too heavy to drag over a long distance.

It had to be somewhere close. I scanned the ground again. It was another five minutes before I saw what I was looking for.

I don't think I would have noticed the path if I hadn't paused to admire a helmeted iguana sitting on a rotted tree branch. The light green lizard was about five feet long with a crest extending from the middle of his head to his neck. I stopped and he cocked his head and regarded me. Then he stuffed the rest of the dragonfly he'd been eating in his mouth and scurried down the log into the underbrush and vanished. That was when I saw the etching of a path. It was so faint it was barely discernible among the brush, but it was there if you looked carefully. I knelt down to get a better view. The vegetation was trampled—which meant someone had walked on it recently.

I signaled to Manuel. "This way."

He looked at me as if I'd lost my mind. "You want *me* to go in there?"

"I am." And I took a step into the bush. "And you are too. From now on I'm not letting you out of my sight."

"Jesus," Manuel moaned looking around. "How do you know where you're going?"

"See." I showed him the trodden down plants. "Someone has come through here recently."

"Don't they have big cats and stuff like that down here?"

"Mostly," I replied sweetly, "they have leeches."

Manuel let out a strangled yelp.

"Just kidding," I said turning my head slightly so Manuel couldn't see my smile. I still hadn't forgiven him for the envelope.

I kept my eyes glued to the ground and started walking. Manuel followed. We were a couple of feet in and the underbrush was thicker now. Tree roots snaked out of the dirt, but I could still see the trampled vegetation.

Except for the occasional shriek of a parrot it was quiet. The bush would come to life at dusk. A butterfly flitted in front of me and landed on a red flowering vine off to my right. I paused for a minute to admire it. Then it flew away and I continued on.

"Where are we going?" Manuel demanded after we'd walked about five more minutes.

"Wherever this path leads." The truth was, by now I didn't even know what direction we were heading in. Everything was starting to look the same.

"Fucking great," Manuel muttered in my ear. "We're going to die in some fucking jungle and no one is ever going to find us. I should have stayed in Syracuse. Even shoveling out the driveway is better than this."

"Think of the stories you'll have to tell your friends when we get home," I said, trying to cheer him up.

"*If* we get home."

"Look," I said with more assurance than I felt. "All we have to do is follow the path back and we'll be fine." The problem was in the last minute or so I wasn't so sure we were on the path anymore. But I didn't say that to Manuel. He was nervous enough as it was. An emotion I was starting to share.

"And there's something else." He pulled at my sleeve and drew me close. "I get this funny feeling someone is watching us," he whispered as he took out his knife and clicked it open.

I gave a nervous little laugh. "It's just your imagination," I tried to reassure him as much for my sake as for his. "If anyone was here, we'd hear him."

"I don't know," Manuel said dubiously, his eyes scanning the brush. "I just got this bad feeling."

This was not something I wanted to hear. I was spooked enough as it was. I took a deep breath to calm myself and knelt down and studied the ground. All I wanted to do was get the hell out of there. But everywhere I turned all I saw was underbrush and tree roots and tiny black ants scurrying here and there.

"So?" Manuel asked.

I held up my hand. "Give me a minute." My heart was racing as I scoured the ground again. Just concentrate, I told myself as a large black beetle hurried past my foot.

"We're lost. I knew it," Manuel cried.

"You're not helping," I snapped. "Now be quiet and let me look." Manuel mumbled something I didn't hear and I went back to searching the ground. "See over there," I said a moment later and pointed.

Manuel bent over. "What? I don't see anything."

"These." I indicated a couple of crushed plants off to the left. "Come on. We're on the path after all."

A moment later we stepped out into a clearing. It was amazing. One moment we were in the bush, the next we were in a wide open space. I was so thankful I could have kissed the ground. Instead I burst into a gust of hysterical laughter.

"I can't believe it," I said looking at the back of the Plaza Hotel. "And here I was thinking we were in the middle of the jungle when we were probably never more than twenty feet away from the ruins." We'd just taken a short cut.

Manuel muttered something and scratched his arms. They were covered with large red welts. Insect bites. Then I realized my arms and neck were itching too. I'd been too worried to notice when we were in the bush, but I was sure noticing now. I knew I shouldn't scratch, I knew it was the worst thing you could do to a bite, but I couldn't help myself. I did it anyway. The pleasure was so intense I nearly groaned. It wasn't until I saw the dots of blood on my arms that I managed to make myself stop and the way I did that was by jamming my hands in my pockets.

The faint sounds of clinking silverware and scraping chairs drifted over from the hotel dining room. I heard a short burst of Mayan, then a snatch of "I'm Dreaming Of A White Christmas" sung in Spanish. Had Johnson stood here earlier in the day and heard what I was hearing now? I surveyed the scene in front of us more carefully. Unlike the front of the hotel, which was carefully manicured, where even the sand in the ashtrays was colored and swept into patterns, the back of the hotel was a mess. The space between the back of the building and the bush was filled with dead tree trunks, vine-covered rusted-out water heaters, discarded card tables, and beer bottles poking out among the saw grass.

I pushed aside a broken-bottomed chair. A fat brown and green spider scurried away. "Come on, Manuel," I said. "Help me look."

He stopped scratching. "For what?"

"Some sort of evidence that Johnson was here."

He went back to scratching. "Forget it. You wanna waste your time on some wild goose chase just because you wanna get back to whats-his-name . . ."

"Bill," I said through gritted teeth. Manuel knew his name, he just didn't want to say it.

"Whatever."

"Whoever."

"Okay. Whoever. Be my guest, but me—I'm going up to the hotel. I've had it."

I stalked over to where he was standing. A day and a half with Manuel and already I understood why military boarding schools existed.

"Really?" I put my hands on my hips.

"Really."

I was steaming. My foot was beating out a tattoo on the ground. "I just have two things to say to you: one, my private life is no concern of yours. And two, if we hadn't had to go back to the altar to look for the joints you dropped we wouldn't be here now, so don't bitch to me."

"Fine." Manuel glared at me. "I get the message. You don't have to be so pissy."

I opened my mouth to say something and closed it again before something horrible came out. I was not going to let a sixteen-year-old get the better of me.

* * *

Manuel and I split up. I searched the ground near the edge of the bush while Manuel looked nearer to the hotel. A couple of minutes later he found a large, black canvas sack lying besides a pricker bush and picked it up. I ran over to take a look.

"Johnson was holding something like this on the ride coming down here this morning," I exclaimed trying to contain my growing excitement.

Manuel shrugged. "I didn't notice. I was sleeping."

I indicated a white stain near the bottom. "This *is* his. I remember the mark." I opened the flap. The initials J. J. were written inside in white magic marker. "See." I showed them to Manuel. "J. J. short for James Johnson. The bag is definitely his."

Manuel shifted his weight from one leg to another. "Can we please get out of here now?"

"In a minute." I opened the bag and peered inside. It was empty. I cursed. Then I saw a small, flat, whitish fragment of something lodged in the bottom seam. I reached in and drew it out. Bingo. I started grinning.

Manuel watched with curiosity as I held up what I'd taken out to the light. "What is it?" he finally asked.

"Part of a shed."

"A what?"

"A shed from a snake," I explained. "The snake that was in here was shedding," I continued. I tapped the skin. "It left this behind."

Manuel's eyes darted down to the ground around his feet. "So where is it now?"

"I don't know. Maybe it crawled away. Maybe whoever killed Johnson has it."

Manuel took the fragment of snake skin out of my hand and rubbed his fingers over it. "This feels like paper."

"I know."

"How do you know this isn't old?"

"Because it's still soft. It hasn't dried out yet. The snake this belonged to was in this bag fairly recently."

"Maybe Johnson just liked carrying snakes around,"

Manuel suggested. "Maybe it was his pet. Remember when Rabbit was carrying around that Gaboon viper strapped to his waist?"

"Rabbit is crazy," I reminded him.

"Maybe this guy was too."

I ground the Camel out on the wall of the hotel and flicked the butt into the undergrowth. "I'd be more inclined to agree with you if Johnson wasn't a dealer." I scratched my cheek and came away with a mixture of insect repellent and suntan lotion under my nails. Charming. I looked around. "Okay. Just let me think for a minute. Now we know that Johnson was here." I knelt down and began checking the undergrowth. "The question is: was he murdered here too?"

I was betting that he was. It didn't take me long to find out I was right.

A minute later I spotted a rusty stain on the leaf of a large white flower. I rubbed my fingers on the stain and smelled. A faint coppery odor rose. It was blood.

Then I noticed another spot on another plant leaf and another and another. I rubbed my finger off on the back of my jeans and kept going. Soon I saw a patch of rust colored earth half hidden beneath the heavy undergrowth. Manuel came over and stood besides me.

"So he was killed there?" Manuel asked gesturing to the spot where I was kneeling.

"I'd say so." I stood up and dusted off the knees of my jeans. I reached into my jeans pocket for another cigarette but stopped myself before I took one out. Enough was enough. If I couldn't give up smoking at least I could try and cut down a little. I chewed on the inside of my cheek instead. "I think that Johnson met someone here and that that someone stabbed him, took whatever was in his backpack, then dragged his body to the altar, mutilated it, and left it for someone else to find."

"Do you now?" a voice behind us said.

We both jumped as Adam Neyhart came into view.

* * *

Neyhart's face was covered with beads of perspiration. His blue tee shirt was sweat stained around his chest and under his arms. His arms and legs were cross hatched with the same kind of welts Manuel and I had.

"I was trying to catch a baby iguana and I ran into a pricker bush," he explained following my gaze.

"Really?" I replied, thinking that maybe Manuel had been right after all. Maybe there *had* been someone following us through the scrub and that maybe that someone was standing in front of us right now.

"Really." Neyhart pointed a little to the left of where I was now standing. "So this is where the son of a bitch died."

It wasn't really a question, it was a statement of fact. Which got me wondering even harder about where Neyhart had just been.

I nodded. "You don't seem too broken up about it."

"I'm not."

Despite myself I raised an eyebrow.

Neyhart scowled. "If everyone else was honest, if they weren't such hypocrites they'd tell you the same thing." Neyhart pushed his sliding sunglasses back up the bridge of his nose. "Johnson was a rip-off artist. He burned everyone. Ask Walker. Ask him about the green tree boas Johnson sold him."

I folded my arms across my chest. "Why don't I ask you?"

Neyhart was just about to reply when Lagartos and Hector Robles appeared around the corner.

The following hour was not pleasant, especially for me. When Lagartos was done questioning me I had the distinct feeling that I was now in first place on his suspect list, a place I was not anxious to occupy.

Robles patted me on the arm after Lagartos left. "My cousin is just mad that he did not find this first." Robles indicated the bloody patch of ground.

"Your cousin?" I asked in amazement.

"On my mother's side." A blue and yellow butterfly

landed on his arm and began drinking his sweat. He flicked his wrist and it flew away.

"So you're friends with him?" Things might be better than I'd thought.

"Yes," Robles said slowly.

I leaned forward. "Does he talk to you about his cases?"

"A little." Robles looked at me cautiously. "Why do you want to know?"

"I just wondered if you knew why your cousin thought our group killed Johnson instead of the MSM?"

Robles began gnawing on the tips of his mustache again. "He didn't say."

"Tell me who the MSM are again," I asked. I wanted to be sure I got this right.

Robles stopped chewing. "They are a group of *indios*, Indians, who do not want the *gringos* coming down to their temples and making them dirty with their trash."

"Are they killing people?" Neyhart asked in alarm.

"No. No. No." Robles waved his hands in the air. "They only sacrifice animals. So far. It is only a small group. I," and Robles pointed to himself, "am an *indio* and I love all tourists. Without tourists my family and I would not eat."

"Then why doesn't Lagartos want to talk about them?" I asked remembering that he hadn't answered the question I'd asked.

"It is because he does not want rumors to get started. He is really a nice man, *muy simpatico.*"

"You could have fooled me," I replied, thinking of our last meeting together.

"He was angry because his pride was hurt. He is a man with much dignity. But I am glad you told him what you did. Very glad." He beamed and rubbed his hands together gleefully. "Even though he does not want to admit it, maybe what you found will help my cousin. Maybe we will get to go home."

"I hope so," I said fervently.

"Me too." Robles rubbed the cross hanging around

his neck. "I want to be able to give my children their Christmas presents. You know in the old days we did not give presents on the twenty-fifth. We gave them later. Now we follow the custom of you *Norteamericanos.* I'm not sure if this is a good thing or not."

Neyhart fanned himself with his hand. "Well, the only thing I know about is that I want a cold drink." And he turned and headed back towards the hotel.

"You ever had Corona?" Robles asked as he joined him. "It is a very good beer."

Manuel looked at me pleadingly.

"Okay, go on," I told him. "I'll be along in a couple of minutes. But don't you dare have anything stronger than a soda."

"I won't," Manuel promised.

"And don't do anything else stupid."

"You're treating me like I'm five," Manuel said indignantly.

"You mean you're not?"

"Very funny." And he scurried after the two men.

I watched the three of them walk away. I wanted a beer but I wanted a last look around the murder site even more. One thing was for sure, I decided as I idly broke a small branch off the limb of a fallen tree and began poking around the grass where Johnson had been killed: Neyhart's appearance had been very opportune. Too opportune. And although I couldn't quite see him stalking us through the bush without making a sound, he certainly looked as if he had. And then there was his comment about Walker.

Neyhart didn't strike me as a man generous with information. So why was he telling me what he had? Why did he want me to speak to Walker so badly? And then I began wondering what kind of run-in Neyhart and Johnson had had. I prodded the undergrowth with my stick. Maybe Walker would know. Maybe he'd even tell me what it was.

I idly pushed an empty beer bottle aside with my stick. A light brown lizard scurried away. I squatted down to get a better look, but I was too slow. All I saw was the disappearing tip of its tail. Oh well. It was probably just a skink or an anole. Nothing unusual. On the other hand I would like to have seen what it was. I parted the grass hoping to at least get a peek and although I didn't get to see it, I did get to see something else. Two smallish square-cut canary yellow gemstones lay glinting in the sun. I hadn't seen them before because the bottle had shielded them from view. My heart was beating a little faster as I reached over and picked them up.

I felt foolish the moment I took a closer look. I don't know what I'd been thinking of. The stones weren't real. They weren't topazes, they were paste, the kind of thing you find in costume jewelry pins. Really. I'd been out in the sun too long. It was definitely time to go in and have a beer. I got up and tossed the stones back where I'd found them and started towards the hotel. I was just coming in the entrance when I overheard the Schmicks arguing. Or maybe arguing isn't the exact word I want.

The lobby of the Plaza Hotel is rectangular in shape. The walls are painted pastel, while the floor is made up of deep red Mexican titles. Clusters of seats and large potted plants dot the area. Because of the holidays, masses of poinsettias were massed on the counter. "Jingle-Bell Rock" was being piped in over the sound system. I was walking to the bar thinking how incongruous that song sounded down here in the tropics when I heard raised voices coming from behind a huge dumb cane.

"You really are imagining things," a man was saying.

"No I'm not," a woman cried. Her voice was muted. She sounded as if she was holding her hand over her mouth.

"I'm just trying to help," the man replied.

"You're not," the woman screamed. "You're trying to

make me think I'm crazy, but I'm not. I'm not," she repeated her voice throbbing with anguish.

And the next thing I knew Milagros had dashed passed me and out the door. George stepped out after her. His face was unreadable.

"I'm sorry you had to hear that," he said when he saw me. "My wife has been . . . having some problems lately. She seems to feel that I . . ." Schmick shook his head and gave a short bark of a laugh. "But you don't want to here about our marital difficulties." He straightened up. "Now if you'll excuse me, I need to see about a room," and he strode off toward the desk.

I took two steps toward the bar, then stopped, turned around and headed back out the door I'd come in through. Milagros had looked so distraught I didn't feel comfortable leaving her by herself. It took me a minute but I found her over by the van. She was crying and rummaging around inside for something.

"It's here," she kept on repeating. "I know it is."

"Milagros," I said.

She jumped around. Tears were streaming down her face. "Just go away!" she screamed.

I took a step toward her. "Can I—"

"Go away!" she yelled before I could finish my sentence.

A Madras-clad couple passing by stopped and stared. I took a couple of steps back. Maybe her husband was right. Maybe she was going around the bend. I was sympathetic, but I wasn't in my Mother Theresa mode. I turned and walked back towards the hotel. So much for being a good Samaritan. This time I walked straight to the bar and ordered a Corona. When it came I paid, picked up the bottle, and walked over to a table on the porch. Manuel was nowhere in sight.

I knew I should go look for him but I was too tired. I didn't even care that we were going to have to spend the night here. The day's events had finally caught up with me. The only thing I had the energy to do was sit down, sip my beer and watch an improbably bright red and green bird flit from one tree branch to another. Christmas colors, I thought. Then for some reason I recalled what my friend George had said to me once. He'd told me I had a karmic bond with trouble. I was beginning to think that maybe he was right. I yawned and closed my eyes. Suddenly I was very tired. It was cooler now—at four the sun had lost some of its ferocity, and it felt good to just sit and let my mind drift.

The next thing I knew a parrot was shrieking and I jerked awake. I looked at my watch. It was four-thirty. I'd been asleep for half an hour. I sat up and reached for my beer, then remembered that the bottle was empty. I was getting up to get another one when I spied Sam Walker over by the check-in counter. It looked as if he was arguing with the clerk. I remembered what Neyhart had told me and decided that the Corona could wait till after I spoke to Walker. But I wasn't fast enough. Walker had scooted out the door before I crossed the lobby floor.

"Problems?" I asked as I caught up with him outside the hotel entrance.

"Nothing that getting out of here won't cure," he snapped as he strode off towards the pyramids. I had to run to keep up with him. "What do you want?" he demanded three steps later when it was obvious I wasn't going away.

"I want to know about Johnson and the green tree boas."

Walker stopped and pirouetted around to face me. "Did Neyhart tell you about that?" he asked.

"Good guess," I replied wondering what he was going to say next.

Walker's face hardened. "That man has never forgiven me for Sophie, never has and never will," he muttered.

"Sophie?" I was puzzled. This was not the sort of answer I'd expected.

"His ex-wife. She and I had a thing going for a little while right after she left him."

I was surprised. Somehow I couldn't picture Walker with a woman. He was too contained, too cold, an ebony statue come to life. But maybe I'd misjudged. Obviously Sophie had seen something.

Walker looked down at his guidebook and back up at me. "Neyhart told you about the boas because he just wanted to embarrass me. It's old history anyway. The incident, if that's what you want to call it, happened a couple of years ago. It's all over with now."

"You want to tell me what it was about?"

He blinked. "Why should I?"

"Why shouldn't you?"

Walker's face seemed even more mask-like as he thought for a moment. "No reason, really," he said reluctantly. He put his hand up and resettled his sunglasses on the bridge of his nose. "It's just something I'd rather forget. I don't usually make errors in judgment and it grates to be reminded of them."

"I can imagine," I replied.

"I'm sure *you* can." He gave me a brief, humorless smile. I wanted to make a retort but I knew that's what Walker wanted so I kept my mouth shut and waited for him to continue. After a moment he did. "A couple of years ago the zoo wanted to start a breeding program for green tree boas and I was put in charge despite the fact that *Corallus canina* are not my area of expertise. Anyway I started making enquiries and the next thing I knew Johnson was on the phone. He told me he'd heard I was looking for some *Corallus* and it just so happened he had about five and that if I was interested he'd give me a good price.

"Well of course I'd heard about his reputation, but he was very convincing and besides, I heard people say some positive things about him too, so I said yes. To make a long story short the snakes turned out to be full of parasites and died. Then it turned out that Johnson didn't have the proper documentation for them, which was extremely embarrassing, especially since at the time the zoo was engaged in a mammoth campaign to enforce import laws. I should have checked more carefully, but I'd been dealing with a crisis in our rain forest display at the time and frankly my mind was on other things."

Walker's face had taken on a steely quality. Without realizing it he had balled his free hand up in a fist.

"You must have been very upset," I murmured.

"I was then. I'm not now."

"Are you sure? You know what the Japanese say?"

"No. What?"

I smiled. "Revenge is a dish best eaten cold."

"Are you implying that *I* killed Johnson?" Walker's voice rose a decibel. "Me?" He pointed a finger at himself. "I didn't come out of Harlem and work my way through college and graduate school and into a curator position to be brought down by some piece of white trash."

I took a cigarette out and lit it. "I'm not implying anything. I was just making an observation."

"An injudicious one. For your information, I've put what happened behind me." And he started to walk away.

"One last question," I called out.

Walker kept going.

"Why did you go on the tour with him?"

He halted and turned around. "I didn't know he had signed up and even if I had, I would have gone anyway. I'm not about to let my actions be controlled by the likes of someone like him. You want to talk to someone who was having problems with Johnson recently, talk to Neyhart. You can tell him I sent you." And with that he strode off towards the Tomb of the Chac-Mool.

As I watched Walker stride away, I wondered how deep his resentment of Johnson ran. Sometimes small humiliations rankle and fester more than big ones. For a man like Walker, coming from where he had and experiencing what he must have experienced, this might have been enough to tip him over the edge. Maybe Walker had spent the last two years brooding about what Johnson had done to him. And then he'd run into Johnson accidentally and Johnson had made some sort of gloating comment and Walker had gone berserk and killed him.

I clicked my tongue against my teeth while I thought. It was a nice theory, but it didn't explain a couple of things. It didn't explain the mutilations on Johnson's body. It didn't explain the snake skin. And as for the two men meeting accidentally, well, I wasn't too sure about that, either. After all, the back of the hotel was pretty out of the way. It wasn't a place most people would ordinarily go unless they had a reason. I sighed, tossed my cigarette away, and ground it out with the heel of my sneaker. Unbidden, a vision of Bill's face floated into my mind. I looked at my watch. Time was running out. I was no closer to the truth now than I was earlier. If I didn't come up with something soon I'd be stuck here for the night and maybe even longer. Maybe Neyhart could give me some answers. It was definitely worth a shot. But first I had to check on Manuel. It had been over an hour since I'd last seen him and I was beginning to get nervous. God only knows what he'd been up to.

Manuel wasn't in the dining room, he wasn't in the lobby, the desk clerk hadn't seen him, neither had the bellboys. The bartender told me he'd sold him two orange sodas but that been about an hour ago. I got more and more exasperated and more and more nervous. Where the hell was the kid? I'd told him to meet me in the hotel lobby and he wasn't here.

If it was anyone else I'd say he'd gone off to tour the ruins, but with Manuel you never knew. I had just stepped out onto the patio to get a view of the grounds, hoping I could spot him from there, when I heard snoring. I walked over to one of the chaise lounges that was hidden behind a big potted palm decorated with colored glass balls and there Manuel was—sound asleep. He'd probably been sleeping there all along and I just hadn't noticed. I laughed in relief. Then I walked over to one of the bellboys standing nearby, gave him two dollars, told him to tell Manuel I'd be back in a little while, and went off to try and find Neyhart.

It took me about twenty minutes, but I finally located him at the far side of the Great Ball Court. He was studying one of the bas reliefs engraved on the stone wall. As I drew closer I could see this one depicted the losing side being led to the sacrificial altar.

"Gives a new meaning to the phrase 'playing for keeps'," I said as I joined him.

"That it does," he agreed. "That it does." He pursed his lips. "So when do you think we're going to get out of here?"

"Whenever Lagartos lets us go."

"And when will that be?"

I ran my hand over the wall before answering. The stone was pockmarked with thousands and thousands of small holes. Age and pollution were eating it up. "When he finds Johnson's killer, I imagine," I finally said.

Neyhart's round face flushed. "That's absurd," he blustered. "I have to get back to Cancun."

"So do I," I said wistfully. I took my hand away from the wall and leaned against it. "Maybe you could speed the process up."

Neyhart cocked his head. "And how could I do that?"

"By telling Lagartos about your dealings with Johnson."

"Dealings? What dealings?" Neyhart asked nervously as his fingers pulled at the edge of his tee shirt.

I didn't say anything.

"Walker put you up to this didn't he?" he demanded.

"I think he felt a return favor was in order."

Neyhart's face took on a sly cast. "I just thought you'd find Walker's story amusing. I mean, he's always carrying on about how smart he is and here Johnson comes and fucks him over."

"You enjoyed that, didn't you?"

"Yes I did." Neyhart scratched at the bites on his arm. "I'm not afraid to say that. Walker is a pain in the butt. Always has been, always will be. It was fun seeing him taken down a peg or two."

Especially after Sophie, I thought. What I said was, "So what did Johnson do to you?"

"Nothing. He just owes—owed," Neyhart corrected himself, "me some money."

"How much?"

"Five thousand. It's not that big a deal. I've lost more than that in one night at Vegas."

"Earlier in the day I heard you call him scum."

"He is."

"And you still lent him money anyway? That strikes me as pretty odd."

"What can I say?" Neyhart threw his arms out. "He came to me with a sweetheart deal. He's trash, but who cared? It wasn't like I was sleeping with him, if you know what I mean. And anyway, sometimes he'd come through. That's what made dealing with him so tricky. You just never knew what you were getting. It could be good, it could be bad."

"I think I get the idea. So what was this deal?"

Neyhart started scratching his arm again. I tried not to look so I wouldn't start doing the same thing he was. "I don't know how Johnson did it," Neyhart continued as he dug into his flesh. I shuddered and jammed my hands into my pockets. "But somehow or other he got an export license for two baby Komodo dragons. He just needed a little extra money to close the deal."

"Those licenses are pretty hard to get, especially for individuals," I said dubiously.

"I know they are, but he did because I saw it before I gave him the check. I insisted. I figured the way the deal was set up I couldn't lose. First of all the check was made out to the Minister of the Interior so Johnson couldn't cash it. And if Johnson didn't pay me back, I got to keep the Komodos. They were my collateral. They were going to stay in my house out in Nyack."

"Are they there now?"

"They haven't arrived yet."

"When are they supposed to come?"

Neyhart's face flushed again. "They were supposed to arrive three weeks ago."

"What's the hold-up?"

"I don't know. Some sort of bureaucratic crap. The exit permits weren't right. They didn't have one of the stamps they needed. But Johnson said he fixed it. He said they'd be coming in next week." Somehow I didn't believe that and I had a feeling that as much as Neyhart wanted to he didn't either.

My thoughts must have showed on my face because Neyhart said to me, "Look, I know what you're thinking, but you're wrong. Those lizards *are* arriving next week."

"Well, I certainly hope you're right."

"I know I am." Neyhart started scratching his arms again. At the rate he was going he wasn't going to have any skin left.

As I walked back towards the hotel I wondered where he'd gotten all of his mosquito bites and then I wondered how much of the story he'd told me was true. After all, if it *was* true it provided him with a motive not to kill Johnson. With Johnson dead he couldn't get his money back.

Then I had another thought. Those lizards were worth something like twenty-five thousand dollars apiece, if I remembered correctly. If the lizards did come in, a big if, and if Neyhart was next in line to claim them, Johnson might be worth more to him dead than alive. I brushed a fly off my face. But where had Johnson gotten that kind of money anyway? And if he had, it why did he need Neyhart to put up five thou? The more I thought about it the less sense Neyhart's story made. I wondered what Walker would have to say about it. I spent the next fifteen minutes looking for him before I finally admitted defeat and went back to the hotel. I wanted to touch base with Manuel before I did anything else.

I didn't have to look far. Manuel was waiting for me in the lobby over by a large potted fern. He was impatiently fingering one of the leaves while *"Feliz Navidad"* played in the background. It was two days till Christmas but it didn't feel as if it were December to me. Despite the *piñata,* despite the signs urging guests to sign up now for a Christmas day meal it still felt as if it were the middle of July. I guess even if they had Santa and his reindeer sitting in the lobby I'd still feel that way. For me cold and Christmas are synonymous.

"Where have you been?" Manuel demanded the moment he saw me walking in.

"Talking to people," I replied. "Enjoy your nap?"

He shrugged. I started toward the bar. I was thirsty and discouraged. What I needed was something cold and wet and a place to sit down and put up my feet for a little while. I ordered a Dos Equis for myself and a Pepsi for Manuel.

"I got something to tell you," he said after the bartender had brought our order.

I moaned. I didn't think I could take any more of Manuel's revelations.

"No, no," he quickly assured me. "It's nothing like that. This is different."

"I certainly hope so." I took my glass and bottle and moved out to the patio. Manuel trailed after me.

The air was sweeter smelling now. The sound of the birds was louder. The trees threw shadows on the grass below. Even the colors seemed brighter out of the sun's glare. From inside the dining room came the constant chatter of the bellboys as they set the tables for dinner. Maybe being stuck here for a couple of days wouldn't be so bad.

"This is really interesting," he said after we'd both sat down.

I leaned back and put my feet up on the railing. "Go on, I'm listening," I said as I watched a moth-eaten ginger tabby slink across the open expanse of yard.

Manuel took a gulp of his Pepsi and leaned forward. "Well, after I woke up you weren't around so I wandered around a little and I got to talking with this dude."

I interrupted. "What dude?"

"One of the ones in the van," said Manuel impatiently.

"Who?"

"The skinny one with the squeaky voice."

"Percy Sorbus?"

"Yeah, that's his name."

"And?"

"And he told me he was really disappointed that Johnson was dead, cause now he wasn't gonna be able to get his snakes from him."

"Really?" My spirits started to rise. Maybe I could get back to Cancun tonight after all.

"That's what he said." Manuel twisted one of his earrings around. "I thought you'd be interested."

"I am. Thanks. By any chance do you happen to know where Sorbus is?"

"No. But I could find out for twenty bucks."

"Forget it." One thing about Manuel. He certainly wasn't shy about asking for what he wanted.

He shrugged. "Hey, it was worth a shot."

I put the bottle of beer up to my forehead. The cool glass felt good next to my skin. I decided to give myself five more minutes before I hunted down Mr. Sorbus. "Tell me, did you really lose all the money your mother gave you?" I asked Manuel. It was something I'd been curious about since I'd picked him up.

"Not exactly," admitted Manuel reluctantly.

"That's what I figured. So what did you do, spend it all on dope?"

"No," Manuel said looking shocked. "You know I don't smoke that much weed."

"Then what?"

He looked away. "I lost it in a card game."

I grinned. "You got scammed, didn't you?"

"They didn't look that good," Manuel protested.

I was about to say they never do when I saw Percy Sorbus walking across the lobby. I guess Grandma was right. Sometimes good things *do* come to people who wait. "Don't go away," I said to Manuel as I jumped up. "I'll be right back."

Sorbus was looking at postcards in the lobby gift shop when I intercepted him.

"I've bought specimens from Johnson for years," Sorbus said in answer to my question. Then he picked out a postcard of El Caracol and another of the Ball Court and went over to the cashier. "I think my mother would like these, don't you?" he asked as he counted out twenty pesos.

"I'm sure she will," I agreed as we walked out of the store.

"Johnson's always treated me fairly," Sorbus continued as he walked towards the desk.

"That's not what other people say," I replied.

Sorbus snorted. "That's because Neyhart is greedy and Walker is too stuck on himself to call for help when he needs it. I'm always careful. I always insist on seeing all documentation, I always examine any specimens I receive before taking possession, and even then I put them in isolation for six months just in case they're carrying a disease I don't know about. I follow common sense procedures. Johnson knew that and he acted accordingly."

"So what were you supposed to get from him?"

"I don't know."

"What do you mean you don't know?" I asked incredulously.

"He called me at the hotel and asked me if I'd be

interested in seeing something unique. Of course I said yes."

"And then what happened?"

Percy fanned himself with the cards. "He told me the specimen was down here at Chichen Itza and that he'd bring it back up. But since I was already signed up for this tour I suggested he come down in the van and I'd look at it here."

"And?" I leaned forward.

"And nothing," said Sorbus irritably. "Johnson told me he'd meet me around the back of El Castillo at eleven o'clock but he never showed up. Finally I left." He stopped fanning himself and slipped the postcards in his shirt pocket. "And now if you don't mind I think I'd like to go to my room and call my mother. She gets upset if she doesn't hear from me around this time every day."

"Did you tell Lagartos this?" I asked.

Sorbus looked at me in amazement. "Of course. Why shouldn't I have?"

"Why indeed," I said to myself as he left. I slumped against the doorway. Three strikes and I was out. I'd learned something from Sorbus all right, but it wasn't anything that put me nearer to solving who killed Johnson.

"Señora, you okay?" the woman behind the cash register asked.

"Fine," I said and walked off. This had been a dumb idea anyway. It was time to accept the inevitable and get a room.

"So?" Manuel asked when I returned. He was eating a chocolate bar. I reached over and broke off a couple of squares. "Do you think Sorbus killed Johnson?"

I put the candy in my mouth and licked my fingers. "More to the point, Lagartos doesn't."

Manuel looked puzzled. "I don't follow."

"Sorbus says he told Lagartos about his meeting with

Johnson. Since he's still walking around, I can only assume that Lagartos doesn't think he did it."

Manuel crumpled up the candy wrapper and slam dunked it into the ashtray over by the next chair. "Maybe Sorbus was lying to you. Maybe he didn't tell Lagartos. Ever think of that?"

"Sure, but do you want to ask Lagartos?"

"No."

"Me either." I straightened up. "I'll be back in a little while. I'm going to check us in."

"I'll wait for you here," Manuel told me.

The room turned out to be a little over a hundred dollars a night for the two of us, a fact that irritated the hell out of me since I was paying for something I didn't want. As I handed the clerk my credit card I wondered what would have happened if I hadn't have had the money for this. He made an imprint and I signed the slip and filled out a registration card. Then he pushed my card and a room key across the desk and directed me out the side door to a raised path on my left.

The path had so many twists and turns I began thinking that the person who'd laid it out must have been drunk when he'd done it. The farther I walked on it, the worse my mood got. Where was my room anyway? In the middle of the bush? This was ridiculous. For the money I was paying at least I could be in the main hotel. I was just on the verge of turning around and demanding another room when I saw a little Mexican girl leaning against a tree trunk. She was wearing a pair of red shorts and a Mickey Mouse tee shirt. Her head was down and she was watching something on her forearm. Then she looked up and smiled.

"Mira," she said and held up her arm to show me a large black beetle with one yellow stone glued to its shell. My heart started beating faster. The stone looked exactly like the two I'd found near the spot where Johnson had been killed.

"That's very pretty," I said kneeling down in front of her and touching the insect.

She didn't respond. *"Muy bonita,"* I said in Spanish this time.

She giggled.

"Where are the other stones?" I touched the spaces where the two other paste gems had been. *"Donde està?"*

She giggled again and said they'd been lost.

"Who gave you this pin?" I asked wondering if solving this case was going to come down to something this simple.

"I did," a voice behind me said.

I got up and turned around.

"Why do you want to know?" Hector Robles asked. He was furiously chewing on the tip of his mustache.

"It's unusual," I stammered.

"I have two more. I bought three for my daughter." From the beetle man, I thought. "But the stones fell out of this one so I gave it to this child." Then he said something I couldn't follow to the little girl and she turned and ran up the path. A minute later she was gone and there was no one but me and Robles. I started to get a really bad feeling. I should have known. He was the only one I hadn't suspected.

"Come, I show you the others," he said. "They're in my room."

"Maybe later." I took a step back. "Manuel is waiting for me."

"You know it is very unusual for a *gringa* to be interested in something like this. Usually you pale women hate bugs."

"I'm an unusual *gringa.*" I took a look around. The path was absolutely deserted. No one was in sight.

"Then why don't you want to come with me?"

"Because I don't want to end up like Johnson." And I started running.

Before I knew it I was lying face first in the dirt with Robles straddling me and holding a knife under my chin.

"I did not kill this Johnson," Robles hissed in my ear.

"Anything you say." This was not the time to argue.

Robles pushed the point of the knife a little farther into my neck. "Why were you so interested in the stones?"

It also didn't seem like the time to lie. "I saw two similar ones near where Johnson was murdered."

He pushed the knife deeper. Any further and the grass was going to be arterial red. "Where are they now?"

"They're still there. I threw them back."

"Show me," Hector commanded and he pulled me up and yanked one of my arms behind me.

Never underestimate those thin wiry guys, Murphy had once said. I decided he was right as Robles and I marched along. Robles had a grip of iron and every time I wiggled he pushed the knife tip in to remind me to be still. He also pushed it in every time I tried to talk. It was a quick, silent trip, but by the time it was over I had some sort of plan.

"So where are they?" Robles demanded once we got to the spot.

The truth was I didn't remember where I'd thrown the stones. Given the amount of trash and the grass and vines it could take days to find them. But naturally I wasn't going to tell Robles that. Red just isn't my color. Instead I pointed to the bush where Manuel had found Johnson's backpack.

"I think they're under there."

Robles pushed me over. "Go find them."

"Fine." I bent over and pretended to look.

"What's taking so long?" he demanded a moment later. He was getting more and more nervous. I could hear it in his voice. A bad sign. I didn't want to be around when he lost it.

"I know they're here. Wait." My hand closed on a beer can. "Yes. Here they are."

Robles's grip had relaxed a little as I straightened up, whipped around and bashed the beer can into his face. Blood ran from his nose as he staggered back. I picked up a broken chair arm and hit him over the head. Robles dropped to his knees, his eyes rolled back in his head, and he passed out. I ran to get Lagartos.

Unfortunately Robles was gone by the time Lagartos and I got back. I guess I hadn't hit him as hard as I thought.

"I'm sure they'll find him," Neyhart said as he ate another piece of roasted chicken.

"I'm sure they will." Actually I didn't even care.

I took a sip of my Margarita. I was in a very good mood. We were leaving Chichen Itza early tomorrow morning and that was all that mattered to me. That and the fact that I'd managed to change Manuel's ten o'clock flight to a late afternoon one. And then Bill and I would . . . do whatever we decided to do. I chewed on a piece of ice. Neyhart and I were the only ones left at our dining room table. Everyone else, including Manuel, had gone off to see the sound and light show at the ruins. The show was supposed to be spectacular but I was too tired to appreciate it and Neyhart had said he'd accumulated enough bug bites for one lifetime and he wasn't setting foot anywhere near the bush ever again.

"At least Lagartos believed you," Neyhart continued as he tucked into the rice.

"At least for that." For a while I'd been terrified that he wasn't going to. But then he'd talked to the little girl with the beetle and made some phone calls and when he'd come out of his office he'd told me I could go. He'd even apologized.

Neyhart put his fork down and took a sip of beer. "So Johnson was buying the snake from Robles?"

"That's what Lagartos said." I began shredding the tortilla into little strips. "I guess he was one of Johnson's suppliers."

"I wonder what he was selling?"

I leaned back. "Something restricted. Something rare."

"Except there are no restricted snakes down here."

"Then maybe it was a genetic anomaly. Something like that two-headed snake Fred has down in Dade. That thing is worth thousands, especially since it breeds."

"You may be right," Neyhart conceded. "In fact I think you are." He scratched his arm. "I have a vague memory of Fred having told me he got it down here somewhere. But why did Robles have to kill Johnson?"

"I bet Johnson tried to stiff him and Robles got mad and killed him. Then when he realized what he'd done he mutilated the body to make it look like it was the work of the MSM."

Neyhart cocked his head. "MSM? Is that a Mexican football team?"

I laughed. "No. The initials stand for the Mayan Separatist Movement."

Neyhart scratched harder. "How come I've never heard of them?"

"The government has been trying to hush them up. They don't want to scare the tourists away." I yawned again. I was having trouble keeping my eyes open. I shouldn't have had that Margarita. Too much excitement, not enough food, and too much alcohol is a bad combination.

"Maybe you should go to sleep," Neyhart suggested.

"I think I'm going to." I'd wanted to wait up for Manuel but it looked like I wasn't going to make it.

"You want me to walk you to your room?" Neyhart asked as I stood up.

"Thanks, but I'll be fine. I'm sure that Robles is long gone by now. If he's not he's stupider than I thought." I gave Neyhart a little wave and left. Funny, but he didn't seem like such a bad guy now.

I was almost out the door when I remembered I'd left my bag in the van. For a moment I thought about leaving it there, but then I decided that I really did need my hairbrush and my other pack of cigarettes. I only had one left in the pack in my pocket and that wasn't enough to hold me through the night. And anyway, the lot was just a short walk away.

I'd forgotten how velvety dark a tropical night could be. There were no street lights on the grounds, but I didn't have trouble seeing because the moon, an enormous silver globe hanging on the horizon, provided enough light to navigate by. I smiled at the fireflies darting around me. In Syracuse you didn't see that many on a summer's evening anymore.

I spotted the van over on the far edge of the lot. It was easy to see because most the cars were gone. The ruins closed at five. The only cars here now were the ones that belonged to the people staying at the hotel. I picked up my pace. I was anxious to get what I needed and get to my room. By this point I could almost feel the sheets against my skin. Then I thought, what if the van is locked? But then I remembered that Robles had specifically said he was keeping it open so we could leave things in it. And then I started thinking about Robles, which was a big mistake, because I started getting nervous. Maybe I was wrong, maybe he hadn't left. But that was crazy. Why the hell should he stick around? He hadn't. Period. Nevertheless I realized I was walking faster and looking around a lot more. Suddenly the night seemed a little less friendly.

For one crazy minute when I opened the van door I thought Robles was going to spring out at me, but of course he didn't. I breathed a sigh of relief and stepped in. My bag was right where I left it—wedged underneath the front seat. I grabbed it and was getting ready to go out when suddenly something flew in my eye. I blinked and brushed it away. My eye began to smart. Then it began to tear. I rummaged through my bag. No tissues. I emptied my pockets onto the car seat. I had candy wrappers, pesos, and the glasses case I'd picked up by the altar, but no tissues. Then I spotted a box of Kleenex on the dashboard above the steering wheel. I scooted over and took one out of the pack and held it up to my eye. I don't know why that made it feel better, but it did. I was sitting there wondering exactly what kind of bug it was that had flown into my eye when George Schmick stuck his head in.

"Didn't mean to scare you," he said when I jumped. "I just came by to get my backpack. Milagros needs her medicine. Hey." He reached over and grabbed the eyeglass case. "That's weird. I've been looking for these all day."

I froze.

Schmick looked at me, at the case, then back at me again. "You found it at the altar, didn't you?" His voice was flat and hard and his statement wasn't a question.

Suddenly before I knew it he was in the van and I had a gun pointed at the side of my head. It was only a .22, but if he shot me the bullet would do just as much damage as a .45 because it would bounce around in my skull taking out hunks of brain tissue as it went. I shuddered.

"Drive," he ordered.

"I don't have the keys."

"Robles left them in the dashboard ash tray."

I opened it up and felt around. Unfortunately they were there. "What about Milagros's medicine?" I asked as I turned the ignition key.

"She can wait." Schmick licked his lips. "This whole thing is her fault anyway. If she hadn't fucked around with Johnson none of this would have happened."

I glanced at him sharply. "You mean you killed a man because your wife slept with him? Why didn't you kill her instead. Or better yet, why didn't you just walk away?"

"I don't believe in divorce," Schmick said. "I believe in revenge. You know—an eye for a eye, a heart for a heart," he falsettoed and laughed. I felt a chill go up my spine. "And anyway," he continued. "I prefer to deal with my wife's betrayal at my leisure." He scratched at his cheek with his free hand. "You know, I might not have killed Johnson if he hadn't said what he had to me."

"And what was that?"

Schmick turned toward me. His face was half hidden in the shadows. His expression was impossible to read. "Everyone has quirks. He shouldn't have taunted me about mine. She shouldn't have told him what they were."

"So this has nothing to do with snakes?"

Schmick chortled. "Not on my part, it didn't. Now drive," he ordered. "And don't try anything funny."

"Where are we going?"

"To a *cenote* about thirty miles away. It's outside of a small village. I found it the last time I was down here. And while it's true it's smaller than the Sacred Cenote here, it's still at least fifty feet across and almost as deep, which makes it just fine for what I have in mind."

I tried not to panic. I tried not to think about the fact that nobody would ever find me. That I'd drown in the sinkhole and be held down by the roots and the mud. Instead I took a deep breath and told myself that we weren't there yet and that plenty of things could happen in the meantime. Then I looked down at the dashboard and almost smiled.

I pointed. "Too bad we're so low on gas."

"Fuck. All right, let me think for a minute." And Schmick began twirling the hairs of his eyebrows around with his free hand. A minute went by before he spoke again. "There's a pump in back of the hotel. Follow the road to the left once we get out of the lot. It'll take us down there. And don't try anything funny," he warned and pressed the gun against my temple for emphasis.

"So Robles had nothing to do with this?" I said as I headed for the gate. I was talking as much to give myself something to focus on as to hear the answers.

"No, he was just one of Johnson's suppliers. I saw Johnson heading out back and I followed. The opportunity was just too good to miss. But Robles was there, so I backed up and waited till he was gone. When he left I killed Johnson. He was quite surprised."

"With something of Milagros's?" I hazarded, remembering her frantic searching in the van.

"Her knife. It's got an onyx blade. It's very sharp, very strong, and very special. She's had it for years. It's one of the many items she always feels compelled to cart around. That's actually what gave me the idea of blaming the murder on the MSM. The Mayans used onyx knives too, you know."

"I know." I have the kind of mind that remembers trivia and forgets important things. Then I recalled the conversation I'd overheard. "She knows you killed him, doesn't she?"

"The problem with Milagros," Schmick said, "is that she always thinks the worst so she never knows what to believe. She was being treated for paranoia, you know. It must be hell not to be able to trust your own instincts."

"You must really hate her," I observed as I turned left.

"Hate is too strong a word," Schmick replied. "Tired of, is probably a more accurate phrase. Turn left again."

I did. A minute later we were at the gas pump. It was stuck out behind the kitchen. Nobody was there. The lights were off. Even the busboys had gone. This was not good.

"Now get out and fill up the tank," Schmick instructed.

Okay, I thought, now's my chance. I could run and hide in the bush. Even if Schmick did shoot me, I'd rather take my chances with a wound from a twenty-two than being knocked out and pushed into a water hole. But then my hope died because Schmick had slid over after me and was standing right next to me at the pump. Without taking his eyes off of me he reached over and unscrewed the gas cap.

"Let's go," he ordered.

I uncoiled the gas hose, put the nozzle in the tank and depressed the lever. Click. Click. Click. I could hear the gas going in. As I stood there listening I couldn't help thinking that with every click I was one more second closer to my death and that I didn't want to die here, like this. The more I thought about it the angrier I got at Schmick. What right did he have to do this to me?

"You can stop now," he said. "The tank is almost full."

And suddenly I knew what I was going to do.

"I don't think so," I replied as I turned the hose on him.

"What are you doing?" he screamed as I doused him with the stuff.

"You'd better drop the gun," I told him. "You shoot and everything is going to go up."

"Jesus," he cursed. "Fucking Jesus." And then he waved the gun in the air. For one awful second I thought he was going to fire it. But he put it on the ground instead.

I turned off the hose. Schmick stood there dripping from head to toe.

"You're crazy," he screamed. "You're a goddamned looney tunes."

"So I've been told." I stepped away from the gas on the ground and took out my matches. "Now the way I see it you have two choices—Lagartos or the morgue. Which is it going to be?"

Schmick got back in the van.

Even though I was riding with the windows open I still had a horrible headache from the fumes by the time I got to the police station.

* * *

I sat looking out the window of the taxi as the driver wove through the heavy traffic on Cancun's main avenue. Manuel, Sam Walker and I were on the way to the airport. The sidewalks were clogged with shoppers scurrying to buy last minute holiday items. Red and white tinsel stars and Santas strung between lampposts shimmered under the hot blue cloudless sky. Store window after store window was filled with pots of poinsettias tied with gold bows. As we passed by a large crêche standing in front of a monument on my right I was reminded of the first Christmas Murphy and I had spent together after we'd been married.

His mother, who was very Catholic, had come over early in the morning the day before Christmas to give us a 'special present', a small Nativity scene. Wanting to do the right thing, I set it up on the coffee table thinking Murphy would be pleased, but when he came through the door, he took one look and his face clouded. He told me to pack it up and put it away. We could have lights and eggnog and presents he said, but we couldn't have anything religious in the house over the holidays.

It reminded him too much of his family, and he didn't want to think about them—especially at a time when you were supposed to be feeling hospitable to your fellow man. When I'd protested, and to this day I don't know why I did since I'm Jewish and didn't really care, he'd gotten angry, which made me angry. We'd spent the next hour and a half in silence. It was only broken when Murphy lured me into the bedroom to show me the sprig of mistletoe he'd tacked over the bed. We disconnected the phone and spent Christmas Eve making love, finishing a bottle of Chivas, and inventing obscene lyrics to "Frosty The Snowman."

Our next Christmas wasn't bad either, even if I did forget to defrost the goose. By then Murphy's parents had moved down to Florida, which made things a whole lot nicer for us. We'd spent Christmas Eve decorating the apartment with strings of pepper-and-tomato shaped lights that I'd found at a thrift store, eating hash brownies, and giggling. Then we'd stayed in bed the next morning making love. Around one o'clock we decided that since our friends were coming over at three for dinner we'd better start cooking. Unfortunately I'd forgotten to defrost the bird so we had left-over black beans, rice, plantains, and salad for dinner. No one seemed to mind. It had been a good Christmas. After that they'd gotten more normal and less enjoyable. I sighed and turned towards Manuel.

"Happy to be going home?" I asked.

He grinned. "Yeah. I like the sun and all but it really doesn't feel like Christmas without the snow."

"That's for sure," Sam Walker chimed in. Since he was on the same flight as Manuel we'd agreed to share a taxi to the airport.

Manuel nibbled on his finger. "Can I ask you about something that's been bothering me?" he said to me.

"Sure," I replied.

"Tell me, would you have really set that guy on fire?"

"Schmick? No. I don't think I could bring myself to do that to anyone."

"So what would you have done if he'd decided to shoot?" Walker wanted to know.

"Run like hell. But I was almost positive he wouldn't have." The taxi was picking up speed. We were now inches away from the car in front of us. I closed my eyes briefly. Just don't let us get into an accident, I silently prayed. "Schmick wasn't suicidal, he was just mean."

"I think so too," Walker agreed. He clenched the edge of his seat as the taxi swerved into the other lane. "Did you hear Robles turned himself in?" he asked through gritted teeth.

I shook my head.

"This morning. The desk clerk told me when I checked out."

"So what's going to happen to him?" Manuel asked.

Walker gasped as our driver cut off another car. "Considering he's Lagartos's cousin I would suspect not much," he told Manuel when he'd gotten his breath back. "After all, he really didn't hurt anyone—except for the baby crocodile, of course."

"Crocodile?" I said.

"Yucatan crocodile. That was his surprise for Sorbus. I guess he wanted to sell me one of his brothers."

"But what about the shed I found?"

"That was probably from one of the constrictors Johnson sold at the show."

Manuel grinned at me, but had the grace not to say anything.

"What I don't understand," Walker continued. "Is why Robles attacked you."

"I think he panicked," I yelled as the driver leaned on his horn. "I think when he heard me ask the little girl who had given her the beetle he realized I must have known something. And then he realized the only way I could have known something is if I'd seen the stones and he wanted them back, because that was the only evidence that could tie him into the crime scene."

"So you don't think he would have killed you?" Walker yelled back.

"No. I think he would have knocked me out and thrown the stones away. Then it would have been my word against his and he was pretty sure who his cousin would believe." I was still yelling. This was ridiculous. I leaned over and tapped the driver on the shoulder. "Do you think you can hold it down?" I said.

"What you say?" he asked turning around in his seat to look at me.

I screamed and pointed. He turned back just as we rear-ended the taxi in front of us.

No one was hurt.

The cars weren't really damaged.

But according to our driver we had to wait for the police. He glanced at his watch and tsked. "Too bad you miss your plane," he told us sorrowfully. "The police can take many hours to come."

"I have to get home for Christmas," Walker shouted.

"Me too," Manuel yelled.

Our driver held up his hand to quiet us. "Fortunately," he told the three of us. "I have a cousin who can do the necessary paper work. Of course," he informed us as he studied his dented fender. "There are fees . . ."

"How much?" I demanded.

The driver smiled slyly. "A hundred American dollars each."

"That's blackmail," Walker snarled.

I grabbed him and dragged him away before he could say anything else.

"Look," I asked him. "Do you or do you not want to get home for Christmas?"

"That's not the issue."

"Yes it is. Either we pay him and you get on the plane or we don't pay him and you miss it."

Walker's mouth opened and closed in speechless outrage.

"Other places, other customs," I reminded him. "You should know that."

Walker narrowed his eyes and pressed his lips together. "If it weren't for Christmas," he finally said.

"I know. I know." I reached for my wallet. "But *it is* Christmas. So let's do what we have to do and get out of here."

"I still say it's blackmail," Walker hissed in my ear as we got back in the cab.

"No, it's Mexico," I replied as I slammed the door shut.

"Vamanos," the driver cried and we were off.

Manuel and Walker made the plane with exactly five

minutes to spare. Bill was waiting in the lobby when I got back to the Sheraton.

As he came toward me I wondered if you could buy mistletoe in Cancun. A sprig of that and a pitcher of margaritas and we'd have my idea of the makings of a very good Christmas Eve.

MARLEY'S GHOST

by Toni L. P. Kelner

The Walters family of Walters Mill might be Scrooges for most of the year, but when it came to the Christmas party, they really did it up right: fancy decorations, an open bar, plenty of tasty refreshments, and a disk jockey to play dance music. Even though I was there with my cousin Thaddeous instead of my husband Richard, I would have had myself a good old time if I hadn't been so concerned with trying to figure out who murdered Fannie Topper.

Instead of having fun, I was devoting my attention to the three men that could have killed her. I didn't really expect any of them to confess, of course. The idea was to try to figure out a motive for the killing.

First I chatted with Joe Bowley over plates of ham and roast beef. He looked like a man who enjoyed his food, but didn't mind talking while he ate. Of course I couldn't just casually bring up the subject of a murder that happened twenty-five years ago, so instead I got him talking about barbeque. I thought that it would eventually lead to Fannie Topper's barbeque place, but no such luck. I don't know if he avoided talking about Fannie on purpose or not, but he went on and on about Buck Overton's in Mt. Airy, which he hadn't even been to since before Fannie was killed.

Next I tried dancing with Bobby Plummer, and I had to admit that he was a real good dancer. He was light on his feet and smiled gallantly when I stepped on his toes. He didn't hold me so tight the way some men try to do, which made me wonder if the rumors about him being gay were true. Maybe he was just being polite. Bobby was in much better shape than Joe, so with him, I asked about exercise. Specifically, playing baseball. I thought that he'd mention the championship the Walters Mill team had won all those years ago, and the party afterwards, and the murder after that. Instead he talked about NordicTrack.

Finally I sat on the edge of the hall with Pete Fredericks. Getting him to talk about death was no problem, but it wasn't what I had in mind. It seemed that Pete was going to be leaving the mill soon to go work with one of Byerly's morticians. I learned lots about what happened to people after death, but nothing about how one particular woman came to die.

When the party ended, I didn't know a bit more than I had before I got there. And it was only two days before Christmas.

If I had had the sense God gave a milk cow, I told myself, I would have just bought Aunt Edna a sweater or a nightgown when I drew her name that Christmas. But no, I had to get it into my head that I was going to give her something she really wanted. That meant solving a twenty-five-year-old murder and laying Marley's ghost to rest.

I got the idea the day after Richard and I arrived in Byerly for Christmas, and I went to pay my duty call on Aunt Edna. If it had been Aunt Nora or Aunt Daphine, or almost any other Burnette, I'd have just tapped on the front door and walked on in. But this was Aunt Edna's house, so I rang the doorbell and waited for her to answer.

She opened the door so quickly that I knew she must have heard me drive up. "Hey, Laurie Anne. Come on in. Where's Richard?"

"He snuck off to finish his Christmas shopping." I

knew that the prospect of spending time with Aunt Edna had been the real reason my husband couldn't wait to shop, and given a choice, I'd have gone with him. It's not that I didn't like Aunt Edna, exactly, but she and I had never been close. Other than being related, we didn't seem to have a whole lot in common.

We hugged briefly in the hall, and then she took my coat to hang up.

"You're wearing an awfully light jacket for this time of year," she said. "Aren't you cold?"

"I guess I've gotten used to the winters up North." After several years in Boston, December in North Carolina seemed almost warm in comparison.

Aunt Edna said, "Why don't you go have a seat in the living room, and I'll go get us some hot chocolate."

"That would be nice."

It felt funny to be waiting in the living room like I was company. Any of my other aunts would have invited me into the kitchen instead of leaving me alone like that.

The room was chilly because it wasn't used often, but there wasn't a speck of dust anywhere. I never have understood the idea of keeping a room pristine for company, but obviously Aunt Edna did. Every chair was angled just so, and each sofa pillow was stiffly placed.

The only friendly touch was the row of Christmas cards taped along the mantel, and rather than disturb those pillows, I went to look and see who had sent them. There was the funny snowman that Richard and I had sent, a sweet-faced Madonna from Aunt Ruby Lee, a cheerful Santa Claus from Aunt Nora, and a pretty snow scene from Aunt Daphine.

There was a particularly elaborate card with a pear tree decorated with turtledoves, pipers piping, and representatives of the other days of Christmas. I looked inside and read the message: "Merry Christmas. I hope things have gone well for you." It was signed Caleb.

Caleb? I didn't know any Caleb. Did Aunt Edna have a new beau? I didn't think it was very likely. There was a photo of Aunt Edna on top of the mantel, and I couldn't help but compare the young woman in the picture to the older woman who had met me at the door. Somehow she had changed from slender to skinny, and the fine hair that had flowed over her shoulders was now tightly pinned into a bun.

Aunt Edna brought in two mugs of hot chocolate. "Here you go," she said.

"Thank you."

We sat down on the couch and sipped.

"How have you been doing, Aunt Edna?"

"Fair to middling. Yourself?"

"About the same. Have you got your Christmas shopping done?"

"Pretty much. How about you?"

"I have a few pieces to pick up yet." As a matter of fact, I still had to find a gift for Aunt Edna. Since there were so many Burnettes, we didn't try to buy gifts for everybody. Instead we drew names, and ever since Thanksgiving I had been trying to come up with something my aunt would want. "Every time I go into the stores, I keep finding things I want for myself instead of for the one I'm shopping for," I said subtly. "Don't you hate it when that happens?"

"I haven't seen much that interested me this year," she said.

So much for subtlety. I took a big swallow of hot chocolate, and wondered how long I'd have to stay before I could exit gracefully.

"Did you put your Christmas tree in the den?" I asked, since there wasn't one visible.

"I didn't bother with one this year. Just me by myself, it doesn't seem worth the trouble. Nora will have one for Christmas morning."

"A tree is a lot of work," I agreed, thinking of the live tree Richard and I had put up right after Thanksgiving so we'd have time to enjoy it before coming down for Christmas. "Your cards are pretty."

That got a little smile out of her. "I do enjoy getting Christmas cards," she said. "Of course, people don't send them like they used to. They cost so much now."

"That's true." I snuck a look at my watch. Only ten minutes gone.

"How's work?" Aunt Edna asked, and I gratefully launched into a description of my latest project. I know she wasn't really interested in the advantages and disadvantages of programming in Visual Basic, but I figured that anything was better than dead silence. I finally stopped when I saw her eyes start to glaze over.

"And Richard?" she prompted. "How is his work?"

That gave me a chance for another monologue. Then I asked about her son Linwood, his wife Sue, and their kids. That helped a little. Then she caught me up on her church activities, the real focus of her life.

Another look at my watch. We were now up to twenty-five minutes and had already exhausted our best topics. I'd have even welcomed her asking me when Richard and I were going to start a family, a question I usually dread. Instead, we fell into a strained silence. There are companionable silences where people just enjoy each other's company, but this wasn't one of them.

In desperation, I looked up at her Christmas cards again. "Who's Caleb?"

Aunt Edna started so hard that she spilled hot chocolate on her dress. "What?"

"That card is signed 'Caleb'," I said, surprised that the question had caused such a reaction. "I was just wondering who he is."

She stared at the card. "Just a friend. An old friend. Somebody I used to know."

That was the last time during that interminable hour that Aunt Edna seemed to know I was there. Oh, she said the right things at the right times and she offered me more hot chocolate, but I could tell that her mind wasn't in the same room as I was. It was a relief when enough time passed that I could politely leave.

* * *

After that, I couldn't wait to get to Aunt Nora's, where I walked right in, got enthusiastic hugs from Aunt Nora, Uncle Buddy, and cousins Thaddeous and Willis, and was promptly installed in the kitchen with more hot chocolate. Aunt Nora was shorter and rounder than Aunt Edna, kept her hair nicely styled and dyed, and she smiled all the time. Even her hot chocolate was sweeter.

After we had gone through the preliminaries of work and gossip, I asked, "Aunt Nora, do you have any idea of what I can get Aunt Edna for Christmas? I can't think of a thing."

"Well, you could get her a sweater. Or a nightgown is always good."

"Didn't Ilene get her a nightgown last year? And I know Carlelle got her a sweater the year before that."

"And I gave her a nightgown and robe myself three years ago," Aunt Nora said. "Edna's not easy to shop for."

"I'll say." Then I remembered that odd Christmas card. "Do you know somebody named Caleb? A friend of Aunt Edna's?"

She didn't jump like Aunt Edna had, but she did look mighty surprised. "Caleb? She used to know a Caleb. Why do you ask?"

"She got a Christmas card from him. When I asked her who it was, she acted real odd, and I just wondered why."

"Surely it can't be *that* Caleb," she said, more to herself than to me. "What did the card say?"

" 'Merry Christmas and I hope things have worked out all right.' Something like that. Who in the Sam Hill is Caleb?"

"Caleb is Edna's ex-boyfriend. One of them, anyway. She dated lots of fellows, but Caleb was the one she fell for. She's never been the same since they broke up."

"Aunt Edna dated around?"

"Oh yes. She was the most popular one of us sisters. Your mama was the smart one, just like you. Nellie was the dreamer, Ruby Lee was the pretty one, Daphine was the one with common sense, and I was the hard worker. But Edna—she was the one with spirit. You should have seen her. She was a pistol."

"*My* Aunt Edna?"

"You young people think the world didn't exist until you came along," she said, shaking her head. "You never knew the Edna I grew up with. All the fellows were crazy about her, and she broke half a dozen hearts before she decided just which one she wanted. And that was Caleb."

"So what happened?"

"Caleb left Byerly a long time ago. After Fannie Topper died."

"Fannie Topper?" That name sounded familiar. So did Caleb's, now that I heard it in that context. "You're not talking about Caleb *Wilkins,* are you? The one who killed Fannie Topper?"

Every kid in Byerly knew about Marley's ghost. Fannie Topper used to run a barbeque and beer joint in Marley, the black section of Byerly. One night her little boy Tim came downstairs looking for her and found a man standing by her dead body, covered in blood. They say Fannie didn't believe in banks and she had a lot of money hidden somewhere, and that the man came looking for it. When she caught him, he killed her. Since nobody but Fannie knew where the money was hidden, it had never been recovered. The story was that her ghostly figure appeared either to guard the money or to show somebody where it was, depending on who was telling it.

The man found over Fannie's body was Caleb Wilkins.

"He was found not guilty," Aunt Nora said firmly.

"I know, but everybody always said that the only reason he got off was because there wasn't enough evidence."

"Well, everybody saying something doesn't make it so. I never thought he did it then, and I don't think so now. More importantly, Edna never thought Caleb did it."

"The trial and all must have been awful for her."

"Well, it wasn't easy to get through, I can tell you that. Of course, all us Burnettes knew he didn't do it, and when he was found not guilty, we thought it was all over." She half-smiled. "I thought sure that he and Edna were going to live happily ever after."

"What happened?"

"What happened is that the people in this town drove Caleb away. They started walking by him on the street like he wasn't there, and whispering behind his back, and things like that. Oh, not everybody, but enough that he said he didn't feel at home here anymore. Can you imagine that? His family had been in Byerly for years and years."

"So he left town."

She nodded. "It was just about this time of year when the trial ended and Caleb saw how people were going to be treating him for the rest of his life. He came over to the house Christmas day and we sang carols and ate Mama's coconut cake and visited. That evening, we sisters played music on the record player so we could dance."

She looked up at me. "You were there, too. Just a little thing, and your mama and daddy were holding you between them so the three of you could dance together. Then Paw took you so they could dance." She smiled, remembering that night. I wished that I could remember it, too. My parents and grandfather were gone now, and I still missed them, especially at Christmas.

"Anyway, it got late and Edna went out on the porch with Caleb to kiss him good night. Then he left. The next morning Paw gave her a letter, said that Caleb had asked him to give it to her."

"What did it say?"

"It was Caleb saying goodbye to Edna. He said he couldn't stay in Byerly anymore, that he had to make a fresh start. He said he couldn't ask her to come with him, not when he didn't know where he was going or how he was going to make a living, so he thought it was best to just go alone. He said he hoped her life would be everything she had ever dreamed about."

Aunt Nora was quiet for a long time, and I finally asked, "Didn't she try to find him?"

"Lord no! She didn't *want* to find him. After she read that letter, she was so mad that she ripped it into little bitty pieces. Then she threw it and everything he had ever given her into the trash can. Every bit of it."

"I can't imagine Aunt Edna that angry."

"Laurie Anne, I'd never seen anybody so fired up. Here she had stayed with him all through his being arrested and in jail and on trial. When people stared at them on the street, she stared right back. She did all that for him, and then he up and left her. If he had come back that same day, I think she would have slammed the door right in his face."

"Do you think she would have gone with him if he had asked?"

"I know she would have. She loved him that much. But he didn't ask. It wasn't long afterward that she started dating Loman, and they were engaged within the month and married that summer. You know how things turned out with them."

I knew that Loman hadn't been much of a husband to Aunt Edna, and I was fairly sure that she was better off now that he was dead. As if guessing my thoughts, Aunt Nora shrugged and said, "Maybe Loman wasn't the best man in the world, but at least he was here. Still, I don't think Edna ever got over Caleb."

After that we talked about other things, but now I was preoccupied, just like Aunt Edna had been. Only I wasn't dreaming about a lost love; I was thinking that I had stumbled on something I could give Aunt Edna for Christmas.

* * *

"I never would have guessed that Aunt Edna had a past," Richard said after I got back to Aunt Maggie's house and told him the story.

Actually, first I gave my lanky, dark-haired husband a hug and a kiss. Then I asked him where Aunt Maggie was, and found out that after she made sure that he still knew where the kitchen and the bathroom were, she had headed out. Aunt Maggie sold collectibles at flea markets and auctions, and Christmas was such a busy time for her that we probably wouldn't even see her until Christmas day. That's one reason Richard and I liked staying with her when we came to Byerly. She went her way and let us do the same.

Richard asked, "Why do you suppose no one ever told you about Aunt Edna and Caleb Wilkins?"

I shrugged. "Maybe it's just something nobody wanted to talk about. You know how the Burnettes are. We talk about each other all the time, but we don't really say a whole lot."

" 'Full of sound and fury,' " Richard quoted, " 'signifying nothing.' *Macbeth*, Act V, scene 5."

Frequently quoting the Bard is the closest my husband has to a fault, at least as far as I'm concerned. I was used to it, but my relatives still wonder how a Yankee who teaches Shakespeare at Boston College ended up in our family.

"Wouldn't it be great if we could find Caleb and bring him back home?" I said. "Wouldn't that be a wonderful present for Aunt Edna?"

"May I assume that you want to investigate this murder?"

"No, I'm not interested in the murder. I just want to find Caleb Wilkins." Richard looked suspicious, but I went on. "The question is, is he the kind of man I want in Aunt Edna's life? What if he really did kill Fannie Topper?"

"I thought you said he was found innocent."

"He was found not guilty, and that's not always the

same thing. There just wasn't enough evidence to prove it beyond the shadow of a doubt."

"Aunt Edna is convinced."

"And look at Aunt Edna's late husband. He wasn't exactly a model citizen. No offense to her, but I want a little more to go on than her trust in her boyfriend."

"So you *do* want to solve the murder."

"No, I don't," I insisted. "I just want to make sure that it wasn't Wilkins."

" 'The lady doth protest too much, methinks.' *Hamlet,* Act III, scene 2." I started to object, but Richard kept going. "How do you expect to get evidence of Wilkins's innocence without solving the crime?"

"I don't need evidence. I'll settle for an objective opinion."

"And which aunt, uncle, or cousin shall we consult for objectivity?"

"Not a cousin, because they're too young to know any details, same as me. And not an aunt or uncle, either. They all knew Wilkins, so they'd be biased, too. I think I'll talk to Chief Norton."

"Junior?" Richard said, meaning Byerly's current chief of police and a good friend of ours.

I shook my head. "Junior was just a kid when Fannie Topper was killed. I mean her father, Andy Norton." He would have been in charge then, and he had been as good at his job then as she was now.

I looked up the Nortons' phone number and dialed it. Chief Norton himself answered.

"Chief Norton? This is Laura Fleming."

"Well, hey there, Laurie Anne."

I didn't bother to correct him on my name; it wasn't worth it. Instead we chatted about life in Boston and folks in Byerly for a little while before I got down to business. "Chief Norton . . ."

"You better not call me 'Chief'," he said with a smile in his voice. "Junior wouldn't like that. You can call me Andy."

"All right," I said, but I knew I wouldn't. In Boston

I call people of all ages by their first names, but I just can't do it when I'm in Byerly. "The reason I'm calling is to ask you if you remember when Fannie Topper was killed."

"Laurie Anne, do you think there's been so many murders in Byerly that I'd forget one? Especially a case that was never closed."

"I guess not."

"What are you asking about Fannie Topper for, anyway? That was twenty-five years ago."

"My Aunt Edna got a Christmas card from Caleb Wilkins, and I want to find him."

There was a pause. "Edna never did believe that Caleb Wilkins killed Fannie."

"Do you?"

"That's not an easy question to answer." Another pause. "Laurie Anne, my wife has gone Christmas shopping with the girls. Why don't you and your husband come on over here and we'll talk about it."

Chief Norton must have been watching for us, because he had the front door open before we got to the porch. "Come on inside," he said cheerfully. "It's colder than a polar bear's behind out there." He wasn't a tall man, but he had that same sense of presence that helped make his daughter a formidable police chief. His hair was all grey now, and he was dressed in slacks and a cardigan instead of the trim uniform he used to wear when I was young.

I introduced Richard, and once we got our coats hung up, Chief Norton led the way into the kitchen. Though I knew from previous visits that Mrs. Norton usually kept her kitchen spotless, this time every bit of counter was covered with sheets of decorated sugar cookies.

"Sorry there's such a mess. Daisy got all the cookie sheets ready so I can stick them in when the timer goes off." He grinned. "It was either do this or go along with her and the girls to carry bags. Sit yourselves down and I'll fix us some coffee."

We took seats around the kitchen table, cluttered with cookie supplies, and accepted the steaming mugs. "It smells heavenly in here," I said. It wasn't quite a hint, but I do love fresh sugar cookies.

Chief Norton held out a plate of broken cookies. "Help yourself. Daisy said I could have any that broke." He grinned again. "It's amazing how clumsy I can get if I work at it."

We spent a minute or two munching and complimenting the cookies before Chief Norton asked, "Now what do you want to know about Fannie Topper's murder?"

I explained my idea for a Christmas gift, and finished with, "I know Aunt Edna thought that Wilkins was innocent, but before I track him down, I want to hear the facts from somebody else."

"Don't you believe your aunt?"

I didn't want to admit to somebody who wasn't family that I didn't trust Aunt Edna's judgment, so I said, "It's not that I don't believe her, it's just that after what happened with Loman, the last thing Aunt Edna needs is to be hurt again."

Chief Norton nodded, and I guessed I had given him the right answer. "After what Junior has told me about your poking around in this murder and that, I might have guessed that you'd go after this one some day. What do you know about the case?"

"I know part of it just from hearing about it when I was young, but I don't really know the details."

Chief Norton settled himself down in that way that told me that a long story was coming, so I took another cookie and put on my best listening expression. Not only was it more polite, by you hear the most interesting stories that way.

"Fannie's Place was the most popular bar around Byerly at that time. Oh, there were fancier places, but hers was the best place to go to have a few beers and maybe a plate of barbeque. Fannie was just a little thing, and to see her you'd never have thought she could run a bar like that. Always a smile on her face, and as nice as she could be, but she was as tough as they come. She made it a good place for people to go and have some fun.

"It was late summer, and the Walters Mill baseball team had just won the mill championship. Big Bill Walters was so tickled at having something to brag on that he threw a party down at Fannie's the day they won. He paid for a couple of kegs and the barbeque, even came by himself to shake the boys' hands. He hinted that there might be a little something extra in their pay packets that week, but of course after what happened, he wasn't about to pay no bonuses.

"The party went on into the wee hours. I was there myself for part of it, and it was a good time. Loud and rambunctious, but not rowdy. Fannie didn't let things get rowdy. Her brother Eb watched out for her, and he was the biggest man in Marley. Plus she had a shotgun behind the bar if people didn't want to listen to Eb.

"Caleb Wilkins was on the team, and he and Edna were there, dancing up a storm."

I found it hard to think of Aunt Edna dancing. Then I remembered what Aunt Nora had said about her, and it wasn't so hard to believe.

Chief Norton went on. "As you might expect, the bar was one mess in this world after the party ended, so Caleb and Edna and a few others stayed on for a little while to help Fannie sweep up and take out the trash. I don't imagine they were much help, as high as they were, and Fannie finally chased them out, saying that she could get more done by herself. They all left at the same time, about two in the morning.

"Caleb took your aunt home, and your grandfather said they got there at about two-twenty and stayed out in Caleb's car for about twenty minutes before he turned on the outside light to let them know it was time for Edna to come inside."

I remember Paw doing the same thing with me.

"For the rest of the story," Chief Norton said, "all we have is Caleb's word to go on. He said that he was on his way home when he realized that he didn't have his baseball cap. He figured he must have left it at Fannie's Place, so he turned around to go after it."

Chief Norton shook his head. "I asked him why he didn't just wait until the next day, and he said that he wished he had. It's just that he was a bit drunk and so happy about winning the championship that he didn't want to take a chance on losing that hat.

"Anyway, he said he got back to Fannie's at around three in the morning. He figured Fannie would still be up cleaning, and sure enough, the front door was unlocked. When he got inside, he saw that the place was a mess, with the tables moved and everything pulled off of the shelves behind the bar. Then he saw Fannie lying on the floor in a pool of her own blood. He said he tried to revive her, but she was already gone. Supposedly that's why he had blood all over him when Fannie's boy Tim came in and saw them. Tim took one look and went running for help. He brought back his uncle Eb and Eb's wife, and they held the shotgun on Caleb while they waited for me to get there."

"It sounds pretty circumstantial to me," I said.

"It was circumstantial, all right, but the circumstances all fit the theory. Everybody in town knew that Caleb was saving up money to buy himself a house before he proposed to Edna, and everybody knew that Fannie was supposed to have a bunch of money stashed somewhere in the bar. The idea was that Caleb came back to look for it, and when Fannie caught him and threatened to call the police, he lost control and hit her. It looked like an accident to me. He pushed her or maybe punched her, and she fell and struck her head on the corner of the bar. He'd probably have gotten a light sentence if he had plea bargained."

"But he didn't."

Chief Norton shook his head. "He denied it to the

bitter end. Enough of the jurors believed him that he was found not guilty."

"What do you think?"

Chief Norton didn't answer right off, just reached for another cookie and took his time eating it. "I always liked Caleb Wilkins, but he had been drinking that night. And he was in an awful hurry to marry Edna. I didn't want to believe that he was guilty, and when the court said he wasn't, I was willing to treat him that way."

I could tell that there was more to it. "But . . . ?"

"Laurie Anne, there's nothing I can grab on to, but it just seemed to me that Caleb wasn't telling the whole story. At first I believed him, but after a while I got the feeling that he was holding something back." He shook his head regretfully. "I tried to get him to tell me what it was, but he just kept saying that he had told me everything he was going to."

"You don't have any idea of what he wasn't telling you?"

"I can't even be sure that there was anything, but I had this feeling."

Chief Norton's "feelings" were legendary in Byerly, so I took him seriously.

"That's all I've got," he said.

I asked, "Did you check on the other people who were at the party that night?"

"Of course I did."

"And?"

"A few of them had alibis, but most of them didn't. Pretty much everybody said they had gone home to bed. Either their wives and husbands verified it, which didn't mean a whole lot, or they went home alone."

"So somebody else who was at the party could have done it. Or somebody completely different."

"There weren't any strangers seen, and only people in town would have known about the money." He shrugged. "Now you know about as much as I do. What do *you* think?"

"I'm just not sure," I said honestly. I wanted to believe Aunt Edna and Aunt Nora, but the evidence was awfully compelling. Even so, Chief Norton hadn't been convinced Wilkins was guilty, despite the evidence, so maybe I shouldn't be either. "I guess that when we find Wilkins," I said, looking at Richard for confirmation, "we'll make up our minds then."

Richard nodded, and added, "If we can find him, that is."

"Finding him is no problem," Chief Norton said with a grin. "He owns a grocery store in Greensboro."

"How did you know that?" I said.

"I keep in touch with the police over there, have been ever since Caleb left Byerly."

"Why?" I asked.

"Fannie's money. We don't know that he found it because it wasn't on him, but we never found it anywhere else. I just wanted to see if he suddenly started spending more than he should have."

Richard said, "But he had already been tried once. You couldn't have arrested him again."

"Probably not," Chief Norton agreed. "Of course we only tried him for the murder, so we might could have tried him for the robbery if he had started spending Fannie's money. At least, that's what I told the police in Greensboro. That wasn't the real reason. I just wanted to know. There were a couple of other murders while I was police chief that weren't officially closed, but I had a pretty good idea of who committed them. I never was sure of what happened to Fannie, and it kind of stuck in my craw. It still does, even after all these years." He drank the last of his coffee and said, "If y'all will wait for a minute, I'll go find Caleb's address for you."

Mrs. Norton and Junior's sisters arrived just as Chief Norton gave us the address, and after a few minutes of chatting, Richard and I took it as an excuse to leave. The last thing we heard on our way out the door was Mrs. Norton fussing at Chief Norton. "You made them eat broken cookies with all these nice ones fixed? What on earth were you thinking of?"

It was too late in the day to drive to Greensboro, so Richard and I headed back to Aunt Nora's for dinner. She wasn't really expecting us, but she knew we were in town and that meant that she'd cook about twice as much food as usual, just in case we showed up. I wasn't about to let any of her good cooking go to waste, especially not her biscuits.

This time I didn't mention Caleb Wilkins. Aunt Nora isn't the best woman in Byerly to keep a secret, and I wanted to be sure that Wilkins was worth bringing home before the word got out.

Instead we talked about the family: whether I knew that Sue was pregnant again and how Arthur was doing as city councilor and did I think that Ilene was serious about her new boyfriend. After all, that's why I come home for Christmas.

The next morning, Richard and I got up bright and early to make the two-hour drive to Greensboro. Since Wilkins owned a grocery store, our plan was to go to the store and see if we could spot him there. If we didn't get a chance to talk to him at the store, we'd go to his home address.

We got to Greensboro at around eleven and after consulting a map, found the store pretty quickly. It was a small place, but the number of cars in the parking lot showed that Wilkins had his share of customers.

I pulled out a shopping cart as we walked in the door.

"What's that for?" Richard asked.

"We can't just browse in a grocery store," I said. "It would look funny." We glanced around, but didn't see anybody old enough to be Caleb Wilkins, so we started slowly going down the aisles.

The shopping cart really had just been for camouflage, but I did find a few things to put inside.

"Pork rinds?" Richard asked, with a look of distaste.

"I like them," I said. And the country ham would keep for us to carry back to Boston, and you can't get Cheerwine, my favorite cherry soda, anywhere but in North Carolina. Fortunately, before I could fill the cart, we saw an older man with a name tag on that said, "Mr. Wilkins."

"There he is," I whispered.

"Looks decent enough."

Not like a murderer, Richard meant. I know you can't tell a book by its cover, but I certainly wouldn't have picked out the round-faced man with salt-and-pepper hair as anybody sinister.

I suddenly realized that this whole trip might be a waste of time if he were already married. Just because Aunt Edna was lonely didn't mean that he was. I took a closer look, and was relieved to see that there was no wedding band on his finger.

We were trying to be surreptitious, but I guess he could tell we were watching him, because after approving a check for one of the cashiers, he came over to Richard and me.

"Can I help y'all with something?" he asked with a smile.

I said, "Mr. Wilkins? Mr. Caleb Wilkins?"

"Yes."

"From Byerly?"

The smile seemed to freeze. "I used to live there, yes."

"Mr. Wilkins, my name is Laura Fleming, and I'm from Byerly. This is my husband Richard."

There was a pause as we all tried to decide whether or not handshakes were appropriate. Good manners won out, and we briefly clasped.

"What can I do for you, Mrs. Fleming?"

"My aunt is Edna Randolph." Then I corrected myself. "Edna Burnette Randolph."

He nodded and looked a little more at ease. "The Christmas card I sent."

"Yes, sir. Do you think we could talk for a few minutes?"

He glanced around the store. "I think I could leave for a little while, and my house is just around the corner. Why don't we go there?"

We agreed, though I did wonder if going to a suspected murderer's house was a good idea. He spoke to his assistant while Richard and I paid for our groceries and loaded them into the car. Then we all walked to Wilkins's house. None of us spoke along the way.

Wilkins had a nice house, and I couldn't help but think that it was similar to Aunt Edna's. It was just as neat, just as well-tended, just as empty. He let us into the living room, offered us a drink, and when we declined, gestured us toward the couch and sat opposite us in a wing chair.

Wilkins said, "I thought that it might be a mistake to send Edna that card. It's just that I was thinking of her and I wanted her to know. Is she doing all right?"

"She's fine."

"And the rest of your family?"

"Just fine."

"I remember that Edna's sister Alice had a little girl named Laurie Anne. Is that you?"

"Yes, sir." Then I added, "My mother passed away many years ago."

"I knew about that. I did try to keep up with things in Byerly for a while, but I hadn't heard anything in a long time." He thought for a minute. "How's Edna's family? I know that she married Loman Randolph. They just had the one son, didn't they?"

I nodded. "Linwood. He's married himself now, with three children and another on the way."

"Is that right? I can't imagine Edna as a grandmother. She and Loman must be very proud."

"Actually, Uncle Loman has been dead for about a year and a half now."

"I'm sorry to hear that. I didn't know."

I asked, "How about you? Did you ever get married?" It was probably rude to ask, but I had to be sure. I was pretty sure he hadn't, both because there was no ring on his finger and because the house didn't show any signs of a woman.

He shook his head slowly. "No, I never did." Wilkins went on to ask a few more questions about people in Byerly, and I answered them as best I could. Finally he asked, "Did Edna have a message for me or anything?"

"Not exactly," I said, feeling awfully awkward. "Mr. Wilkins, we'd like you to come back to Byerly."

"Did Edna send you?"

"Not exactly," I said again, which was a polite way of saying not at all. "I thought that seeing you would be a nice surprise for her, sort of a Christmas present."

He leaned back, closed his eyes, and took a deep breath. I couldn't even guess at what he was thinking. Then he opened his eyes again and said, "I don't think that would be possible."

"I know about Fannie Topper, Mr. Wilkins," I said, "but it's been over twenty years. And you were acquitted."

"Edna must have told you how people in Byerly acted. I don't think that they've forgotten."

"But if you were innocent . . . ?"

He smiled very sadly. "That's what I mean. You're Edna's niece, and you're not even sure, are you? That's why I can't go back to Byerly. I've made a life for myself, and I'm happy enough. Nobody here knows anything about my past, so I don't have to worry about people whispering behind my back."

This wasn't what I had expected. I had thought that he'd want to renew his lost romance, that he'd jump at the chance to come home. I briefly considered bringing Aunt Edna to him, but then I thought about how angry she had been when he left. After all of that, I just knew she wouldn't come to him. The Burnettes have a lot of pride, and a lot of stubbornness. I know, because I'm as stubborn as a mule myself, which was why I wasn't ready to give up yet.

I said, "What if the real murderer was found? Would you come back then?"

"I don't think that's very likely."

"But if he was?"

He looked at me funny, but he said, "I suppose I might."

I looked at Richard, and he nodded slightly. "My husband and I have had some success in investigations before, and we've been looking into the case."

"Are you two private detectives, something like that?"

"We've worked with the police in the past, both in an official and unofficial capacity." Richard's face showed the strain, but he didn't say anything. Before Wilkins could press for any more details, I said, "Do you think you could answer some questions for us?"

He agreed, and I asked him what had happened that night. What he said didn't add anything to what Chief Norton had told us, other than a list of the other men on the championship ball team. Richard dutifully jotted the names on a pad he produced from his pocket.

After Wilkins had gone through the story, he said, "That's pretty much what I told Chief Norton all those years ago, and it didn't help him."

As delicately as I could, I said, "Chief Norton said he always thought you were holding something back. Is that true?"

He didn't answer for a long time, and I wondered if he was about to throw me and Richard out. Finally he said, "There was something, but it probably doesn't mean anything."

I just sat and waited, hoping that he'd go on.

"I never told anybody, not even Edna," he said slowly. Then he took a deep breath, and I guess he had convinced himself. "You know that when I went back to Fannie's Place, I was looking for my ball cap."

"Yes, sir."

"Well, that hat was the first thing I saw when I came in. It was lying on the floor next to Fannie's body. With blood on it. Chief Norton took it as evidence."

I nodded.

"A week or so later, after they let me out on bail, I dropped my keys onto the floor of my car and I had to reach up under the seat to get them. I found my hat under there."

I cocked my head. "If your hat was under there, then whose hat was it at Fannie's?"

"I don't know."

"So it must have been left by one of the other players." I didn't see why this was important.

"You don't understand. That hat wasn't there when I left the bar after the party. Edna and I stayed to help Fannie clean up, even swept up for her, and I know it wasn't there when we left."

"And the team members were the only ones with hats like that," I said, starting to get more interested.

Wilkins nodded.

"Couldn't somebody else have had one?" Richard asked.

"There weren't any more. Big Bill Walters would only pay for enough for the team members. If he had had his way, he'd have only had enough made for the fellows on the field at one time and made us trade back and forth. We talked him out of that idea, but you can be darned sure that he didn't get any extras."

"So what you're saying is that one of the other team members killed Fannie," I said.

"I'm not saying anything of the kind. All I'm saying is that the hat on the floor at Fannie's Place wasn't mine."

"Why didn't you tell Chief Norton? Maybe he could have found out who it was that was missing his hat."

Wilkins shrugged, and wouldn't quite meet my eyes.

"Was it loyalty? Did you think that it would be a bad thing to turn in a team member?"

He shrugged again.

"How could you be loyal to a murderer? The murderer didn't care anything about you. You could have been sent to prison."

"But I wasn't. If one of them killed Fannie, I know that he'd have come forward if I had been found guilty."

"He let you get chased out of Byerly without speaking up."

Wilkins was shaking his head. "You don't understand how it was. Every one of the fellows came to see me in jail. They raised the money for my bail, and they paid for my lawyer, too. How could I go to Chief Norton and tell him that one of those men was a killer? It would have looked like I was trying to save myself by dragging them down."

"Of course you realize that one of those men only helped out because he felt guilty," I pointed out.

"But the others did it because they were my friends," he shot back. "Chief Norton would have questioned all of them, stuck his nose into all kinds of places where it didn't belong."

I suppose I should have left it alone, but I just couldn't. "So you let a murderer go free?"

"I don't think it *was* murder. Even Chief Norton said it looked like whoever it was didn't mean to kill Fannie."

"What about Tim Topper? Don't you think he deserves to know what really happened to his mother?"

Wilkins looked down. "I felt bad about Tim, I really did. He was a good boy. But I couldn't bring his mama back no matter what I did."

"What about afterward, when the people in Byerly treated you so badly? Didn't you think about telling Chief Norton about the hat then?"

"I thought about it, but that's all I did. I felt like I had made my decision and I'd have to live with it."

"What about Aunt Edna?"

Again he wouldn't meet my eyes. "In a way, Edna is the reason I had to leave Byerly. I could have stood it if it had just been me people were talking about. But I couldn't put Edna through that. She deserved better."

What I thought was that what Aunt Edna deserved was a chance to make her own choices, not have them made for her. I wanted to tell him that, too, but he looked so sad that I just couldn't. "Aunt Edna still cares for you," I said softly.

He nodded. "I care for her, too."

Richard touched my shoulder then to tell me that it was time to go.

I had to make myself drive slowly on the way back to Byerly because I was so mad that I wanted to drive like a Boston cabbie. "Can you believe that man?" I demanded of Richard. "If Wilkins had told Chief Norton the truth all those years ago, the real murderer would have been found out instead of getting away with it, and Aunt Edna would have married him instead of Loman. And she'd be happy now!"

"Don't you think you're laying an awful lot of blame on poor Caleb?" Richard said mildly.

"No, I don't," I said, but I didn't really believe it. I just couldn't help but think of how things might have been. "All right, I don't really blame Wilkins for everything that's happened, but I do think he should have told Aunt Edna what he was going to do. Aunt Nora said that she'd have gone with him."

"He didn't want to drag her down with him. He was trying to do the honorable thing."

"Honor!" I snorted.

"Since when is honor so distasteful? 'Mine honor is my life, both grow in one; take honor from me, and my life is done.' *Richard II,* Act I, scene 1."

"And they did take Richard's life away from him, didn't they?" Before he could respond, I said, "Do you remember Robert E. Lee?"

"The patron saint of the South?"

"Not to me! You know he was against secession? He was even asked to head up the Union army before he took over the Confederate forces. The only reason he fought for the South was his honor."

"This makes him a villain?"

"In a way it does. You know that the Confederacy

never had much of a chance. They just didn't have the infrastructure they needed. The war should have been over almost before it started. But Lee was a genius. With him in charge, the war dragged on and on. How many people died for Lee's honor?"

"Aren't you simplifying it a bit?"

I ignored him. "Then there's Reconstruction. If the war hadn't lasted so long, the North wouldn't have been so hard on the South. Lincoln would have been alive well into the process and made sure of it."

"Unless Booth decided to attend an earlier show at Ford's Theater." I started to object, but Richard raised his hand. "All right, I'll concede that honor isn't always the best motive. But you can't play this kind of guessing game after the fact. Unless you're watching *It's a Wonderful Life*, that is." He looked at me suspiciously. "Which you watched last week, if I recall correctly."

I had to grin. "Actually, I watched it twice."

"Ah hah!"

As usual, Richard had dispersed my foul mood. "Well, since we don't have an angel to call upon to go back, we'll just have to go forward."

"Agreed, but first I want to remind you that I told you that this would happen."

"You don't mind, do you? Spending your Christmas vacation tracking down a murderer?" I could easily have added, "Again."

" 'At Christmas I no more desire a rose than wish a snow in May's new-fangled mirth; but like of each thing that in season grows.' *Love's Labour's Lost,* Act I, scene 1."

It took me a minute to worry the meaning out of the quote. "Are you implying that murder and trips to Byerly go hand in hand?" He opened his mouth to speak and I could tell that another quote was coming. "All right, you have a point."

"Then I think I'm entitled to one I-told-you-so."

I sighed. "I suppose you're right. Go ahead."

He shook his head. "No, I think I'll save it for later. When you're not expecting it."

"That's mean."

He grinned. "So now that you've bowed to the inevitable, what shall we do next?"

I thought for a minute. "How many men did Wilkins say were on the baseball team?"

He pulled out the list and counted. " 'So Judas did to Christ: but he, in twelve, found truth in all but one.' *King Richard II*, Act IV, scene 1."

"So we have twelve men to track down."

"Actually, only eleven. Wilkins himself is one of the twelve, but the quote was so obvious that I had to use it."

"Of course," I said, though I couldn't imagine how it could have been *that* obvious. "Maybe we should talk to Chief Norton again and see if any of them had alibis. I'd hate having to do the groundwork again, especially after all this time. Eleven men are a lot. Although if they're still working at the mill, they should be pretty easy to find." So many members of my family worked at Walters Mill that it would just be a matter of picking one to ask for help. "As soon as we get back, we'll give Chief Norton a call."

We were nearly back to Byerly when I thought of something else. "Richard, are you hungry?"

"Planning to tackle some of those pig rinds?"

"That's pork rinds. Or pork skins, if you prefer."

"I don't prefer either."

"Good. That leaves more for me. I wasn't suggesting them anyway. I was suggesting that we go to Pigwick's."

"I beg your pardon?"

"Pigwick's Barbeque. That's the name of Fannie Topper's old place. It might be helpful to scope the place out."

"It's still open?"

"Yes and no. They closed the bar after Fannie died, but her brother and sister-in-law kept the barbeque part going, just for take-out. Fannie's son Tim took over after a while, and I guess it was doing well enough that he decided to try it as a restaurant. So he opened Pigwick's a few years ago."

"Do I dare ask about the name?"

"From Dickens, of course."

"Of course."

"The napkins even have 'Pigwick Papers' printed on them."

"Of course." Richard was quiet for the rest of the drive, and I had a feeling that he was just glad that nobody had decided to honor Shakespeare in the way that Tim Topper had honored Charles Dickens.

It was mid-afternoon when we pulled into the parking lot at Pigwick's, which explained why there weren't many other cars there.

"Have you eaten here before?" Richard asked as we walked to the door.

"I've eaten their food before, but only take-out."

He raised one eyebrow. "Afraid of the ghost?"

"Not hardly. At least four Burnettes have died in Aunt Maggie's house, and you know that never bothered me." The reason was a different specter, one that still haunted Byerly. Marley was the "black" part of town. Getting food to take home was one thing, but actually going there to eat was something else. I felt a rush of liberal smugness that I was going inside, admittedly tempered by knowing how long it had taken to get me there.

The only other customers were a party of three men and a woman, all dressed in business suits. A big man with dark hair and caramel-colored skin was at the register by the door, and I recognized him as Tim Topper.

"Two for dinner?" he asked, picking up two menus.

"Yes, please," I said.

"We must be early," Richard said as Tim took us to a table.

"Just a bit," Tim said. "I expect the place will be filling up later." He handed me my menu, started to give

Richard his, and then looked back at me. "Do I know you?"

"I think we've met once or twice. I'm Laura Fleming."

He shook his head, not knowing the name.

"Laurie Anne Burnette," I said in resignation.

"That's right, now I remember. We talked at your cousin's victory party when he was elected to the town council."

I nodded. "This is my husband, Richard."

They shook hands and Richard said, "I take it you're an admirer of Dickens."

Tim grinned and shook his head. "No, that was my mama. She used to read me stories from Dickens when I was little, and the names were so funny that I used to get them mixed up. I could have sworn that she was saying Pigwick, and I thought that it would be a good name for a barbeque house." He took our orders, managing to talk us into getting large plates of pulled pork barbeque instead of the small ones we originally asked for.

As soon as he was out of earshot, Richard asked, "Aren't you going to ask about his mother's murder?"

I wrinkled my nose. "I don't think so. He was only ten when it happened, and I'm sure that Chief Norton must have questioned him pretty thoroughly. Besides, I can't just ask him about something like that out of the blue."

"You're not going to tell him that we're looking for the murderer?"

"If we find him, we can tell Tim then. I don't want to go dredging up memories like that, especially not at Christmas. It must have been awful for him, finding his mother dead like that."

"And this is where it happened?" Richard said, looking around the room.

I nodded, reminding myself that I didn't believe in ghosts. "Of course, it probably looked a lot different." From what Chief Norton had said about Fannie's Place,

I didn't think it would have had big picture windows and gingham curtains and tablecloths. The floor would probably have been wood or tile, not carpet. The fireplace looked old enough to be original, but there was no sign of where the bar had been.

"And they never found Fannie's money?"

I shook my head. "Every once in a while, some of the kids would plan to sneak over here at night to search for it, but I don't think anybody ever did. Either afraid of the ghost or afraid of Tim's Uncle Eb. They just talked about how great it would be to find the money. Hidden treasure holds a certain appeal, doesn't it?" I looked at him, and from the gleam in his eye, I could tell that it certainly held a lot of appeal for him. "Richard, don't tell me that you want to look for the money."

"Just speculating."

"A lot of people have looked for that money over the years."

"True," he said.

"Of course," I added, "none of them were as brilliant as you are."

Richard grinned. "Is that so?"

We were turning around in our chairs to look for likely hiding places when Tim came back with our order. "Don't tell me that you're looking for my mama's money?" he said.

I didn't know what to say. It did seem pretty tacky. "I'm sorry—we didn't mean to be rude."

He held up one hand. "Hey, don't apologize. If you can come up with a place I haven't already looked, I want to hear about it."

Richard said, "If you don't mind my asking, why did your mother keep her money here? Why not in a bank?"

"For one, we didn't have a car, so getting to the bank would have been a problem. For another, Big Bill Walters was still running the bank then and Mama just didn't trust him."

I could believe that. I didn't think that Big Bill was

actively dishonest, but he was smart enough to think up ways that he could be honest and still get his hands on other people's money.

"She never told anybody where the money was?" I asked.

Tim just shook his head again, like he had been asked the same questions many times before. "You've got to remember, I was only a kid then. If I had known where it was, I'd have been into it every time I wanted a new toy."

"What about the people who worked for her?"

"There wasn't nobody but her, my Uncle Eb, and Aunt Fezzy. She wouldn't tell Uncle Eb because he'd been known to drink more than he should, and she wouldn't tell Aunt Fezzy because she might have told Uncle Eb." He shrugged his shoulders. "I know it sounds funny now, but things were different then. Mama was alone, and she had to think about the future. She had her heart set on my going to college, so she wanted to be sure that the money would be there for me."

For a minute he looked over toward the center of the room, and I hoped he was remembering his mother in life, not in death.

"I'm sorry," I said again. "We *are* being rude."

"Don't you worry about that. I imagine a lot of people have come in here because of curiosity. Maybe I should have called the place The Curiosity Shop." He grinned, and left us to our meal.

"I wish he wasn't so nice," I said to Richard. "I feel like such a heel."

"He said he didn't mind. And don't forget that we're doing this to find the person who killed his mother."

I nodded in agreement, but I still felt like a heel. Tim must think that we were like those people who slow down on the highway when passing a wreck. My parents had died in a car accident, and I had always hated the idea of people staring at them.

I didn't much feel like eating, but I took a bite of the

barbeque anyway. And another. And another. "You know," I said to Richard, "people might come here because of curiosity, but they come back for the food."

As Tim had predicted, the restaurant started to fill up soon after that, so we didn't have a chance to talk to him further other than to compliment the barbeque on our way out.

When we got back to Aunt Maggie's house, I headed straight for the telephone.

"Hello?" Chief Norton said.

"Hi, this is Laura Fleming."

"I was hoping that you'd call. Did you go see Caleb Wilkins?"

"Yes, sir. We sure did."

"Did you find anything out?"

"As a matter of fact, he told us what it was that he wouldn't tell you."

"Is that so? Well, don't leave me hanging."

I explained about the baseball hat, and why Wilkins had never told him.

"Well I'll be darned. It never occurred to me that it wasn't his hat. I appreciate his loyalty to the other fellows, but it sure would have helped if he had told me the truth."

"I know. You don't happen to remember if any of the other ball players were missing alibis, do you?"

"It just so happens I dug up my files after we talked yesterday. I just had a hunch that I'd want them. Have you got a pencil?"

I made gestures at Richard, and he handed me a pad and pen. "Go ahead."

While I waited, Chief Norton looked up each of the other eleven members of the team to check their alibis. As it turned out, two of them had ended up at a different party, five had gone to work the late shift at the mill, and one was seen to arrive at his home by a nosy neighbor.

"That leaves three," I said. "Joe Bowley, Pete Fredericks, and Bobby Plummer."

"That's what it sounds like to me, too," Chief Norton said. "None of them have ever been in any serious trouble, but then again, neither had Caleb Wilkins."

"They shouldn't be hard to track down."

"I expect not, but you do realize that by rights we should hand this new evidence over to Junior and let her deal with it."

"That's true." I should have been glad to let Junior take over. As long as it was solved, did it really matter who did the solving? But like I said, the Burnettes are stubborn. I was bound and determined to do this for Aunt Edna. Besides, Caleb Wilkins had trusted me. I wanted to finish it myself.

"Of course," Chief Norton said, "Junior's awfully busy this time of year. I hear that she's had a lot of trouble with shoplifting."

"Really?"

"This being such an old case, she probably wouldn't have a chance to get to it for a while. Until after Christmas, at least. And she hates it when I stick my nose in, so I can't do a thing."

"You're not suggesting that I withhold evidence, are you?" I said in mock surprise.

"Of course not," he said, in equally mock reaction. "In fact, you can let me tell Junior, just as soon as I get a chance. You and your husband go ahead and do whatever you usually do on vacation. Now if you should happen to hear anything interesting, you be sure and let me know."

"I certainly will."

"Well?" Richard asked when I hung up.

"He's going to let us take a crack at it," I said. "If we can't figure it out by Christmas, Junior can take over."

"That gives us what? Three days?"

"Three days, and three suspects."

"But no motive other than this cache of money."

Richard thought for a minute. "Laura, who was Tim's father?"

"I don't think Fannie was married, but if she was, he wasn't around anymore. Why?"

"It occurred to me that Tim has fairly light skin."

"Are you thinking that his father was white?"

"It's a possibility, isn't it?"

"I suppose, but I don't know how dark Fannie was."

"Wouldn't that have been a terrible thing to have happen in North Carolina? Don't people around here look down on mixed relationships?"

"Mixed relationships are looked down on in most parts of the country!"

"Sorry. You're right."

I nodded, somewhat mollified.

Richard said, "The point I was trying to make was that Fannie might have threatened to make the father's identity public."

"Blackmail? I don't think she'd do that. Chief Norton seemed to think a lot of Fannie, and he's an awfully good judge of character."

"But she did want to send Tim to college. Maybe she asked the father for money, and he refused. She could have gotten mad and made the threat, or maybe he misconstrued what she said as a threat. Remember, Chief Norton didn't think the murder was premeditated."

"True. I suppose that one of our three suspects could be Tim's father." Then I thought of a complication. "So why the search for Fannie's money?"

"Maybe he wanted it to look like a robbery. Or even better, maybe Fannie had some proof that he was the father, and he was looking for that."

"It's possible," I admitted. "I was planning to talk to Aunt Nora to get some background on our three suspects, so I could ask her about that, too."

"You mean you don't already know all of the suspects? Angels and ministers of grace defend us!"

"Cut that out! I don't know *everybody* in Byerly." I looked questioningly at him. *"MacBeth?"*

"*Hamlet.* Act I, scene 4."

"I was close." Before he could argue the point, I said, "Shall we go talk to Aunt Nora?"

"We could, but if we go over there now, she's going to try to feed us and I'm still stuffed from the barbeque."

"Me, too." I checked the clock. "They've probably already eaten, but I'll use the phone this time. Just in case she's got leftovers."

After a few minutes of preliminaries, including my fending off an offer of Uncle Buddy coming by to deliver food, I said, "Aunt Nora, I need to pick your brain."

"Still trying to come up with a gift for Edna?"

I avoided answering directly by saying, "Richard and I went to Pigwick's Barbeque today, and we were wondering about Tim Topper. Who was his father?"

There was a long pause. "Does this have something to do with Caleb Wilkins?"

So much for my surprise. "Yes, ma'am." I explained about Caleb Wilkins and what Richard and I were trying to do. "Do you think it's a good idea?"

"Laurie Anne, that is the sweetest thing I've ever heard of," she said. Darned if she didn't start sniffing.

"Well, I don't know if it's going to work yet," I said, feeling embarrassed.

"I know you'll do it, Laurie Anne. I just know it. Now what was it you wanted to know?"

"Tim Topper's father?" I prompted her.

"I'm sorry, Laurie Anne, but I don't have any idea."

I was surprised. "There must have been some talk at the time. I mean, her not being married and all."

"Of course there was, but she never would say. I hear that when the doctor asked her what to put on the birth certificate, Fannie just said, 'His daddy doesn't want him, and I do, so you can put me down as mama and daddy, because that's how it's going to be.' "

"Does Tim look like any of the fellows she dated?"

"Not to speak of. Now, she spent some time with her

aunt in Saw Mills the summer she got into the family way, so it might not even have been anybody from Byerly."

I wasn't sure if the next question would shock Aunt Nora or not, but I had to ask. "Was there any talk about Tim's father being white?"

"I thought that's what you were getting at. Of course there was some talk, on account of his coloring. She was right much darker. Of course, that happens sometimes. There's probably not a black person in this country who hasn't got some white blood in him."

The converse was probably true of white people, but I didn't think that Aunt Nora would appreciate hearing that.

"Is there anything else I can help you with?" she asked.

"There's three men I need to talk to: Pete Fredericks, Joe Bowley, and Bobby Plummer. Do you know them?"

"Just to speak to. Do you think that one of them killed Fannie?"

"Maybe." I explained why. "Do they all still work at the mill?"

"I believe so."

"Then maybe I could go talk to them up there. Do you think Thaddeous could get me in?" Uncle Buddy and Willis worked at the mill, too, but as quiet as Uncle Buddy was, he wouldn't be nearly as good at introducing me to the men, and Willis worked the night shift.

"I imagine he could. I'll ask." She moved her mouth from the phone, but I could still hear her as she called, "Thaddeous! Laurie Anne needs to do some detective work at the mill." I cringed. "Never you mind what it's about. Can you get her in to see some men?" She named them, and he said something I couldn't quite make out. "I didn't think of that. Let me check." She came back to the phone. "Laurie Anne? The mill's Christmas party is tomorrow night and Thaddeous says you can go with him. That way he can introduce you."

"Doesn't Thaddeous have a date?"

There was a small sigh. "I'm afraid not."

"Then I'd love to go."

After that, I asked her for background on the three men, and had to write like crazy for nearly half an hour to keep up with her. And this for men she said she barely knew.

She finally stopped to take a breath. "That's all I know."

"That's plenty," I said. The F.B.I. should have such detail.

We talked a bit longer after that, mostly about what I should wear to the party. Once I hung up, I explained the arrangements to Richard. "When I talk to them, I'll be looking for a family resemblance."

"Which you will no doubt be able to spot instantly."

"You're just jealous because I can see these things and you can't."

"Is that so?"

"It is."

"So tell me—do you think Rudolph looks more like Donner or Mrs. Donner?"

After that, I had no choice but to chase him through the house with a sofa pillow.

Thaddeous picked me up at seven o'clock the next evening, and after Richard kissed me and told Thaddeous not to keep me out too late, we headed for the party. It felt odd to get kissed before a date instead of after.

"You look real nice, Laurie Anne," Thaddeous said as he handed me into his pickup truck.

"Thank you," I said, smoothing down the skirt of my deep red velvet dress. "You look pretty sharp, too." It was a shame he didn't have a real date. Poor Thaddeous was tall and nice-looking, and like his mama, he always had a smile on his face. Despite that, he had the worst luck with women of any man I had ever met.

We pulled out of the driveway and Thaddeous asked, "What's Richard going to do with himself tonight?"

"He thought he'd go over to the mall in Hickory and do some last-minute shopping."

"He's a brave fellow. That place is a madhouse this time of year." There was a short pause. "Mama told me what you and Richard are up to. Is there anything I can do to help?"

"Just taking me to the party is a big help."

"I know you want to talk to those men, so I figured I'd point them out to you and maybe introduce you to them. Then I'll leave you alone so you can see what you can find out."

"That's perfect."

"Now I don't want to see you going out into any dark corners with them. If one of them did what you think he did, you don't have any business being alone with him. And if you get into any trouble, you holler for me. Mama and Daddy are going to be at the party, too, and so is Willis. So somebody is going to be watching you the whole time."

I suppose it wasn't very liberated, but they meant well. And Thaddeous's advice was good. "I'll be careful."

The party was being held in the Byerly High School gym, because there really wasn't anyplace else in Byerly big enough, but the decorations committee had outdone itself in making it look nice. It was still early, so after Thaddeous and I checked our coats, we headed for the refreshments table. It was but a few minutes before Thaddeous said, "There's Joe Bowley now. Are you ready?"

"You bet." While we waited for Joe to fill his plate, I remembered what Aunt Nora had told me about him.

"Joe is Burt Walters's second-in-command, thanks to Joe's daddy," she had said. "Don't get me wrong—Joe's a right smart fellow, and he'd probably have that job even if his daddy wasn't Big Bill Walters's best friend. The Bowleys had some money, though not nearly as much as the Walters, and Joe's daddy made sure Joe went to the same college as Burt. Joe always was a good community man, but since his wife died, he's really thrown himself into charity work."

Joe turned out to be balding and plump, and shook my hand enthusiastically when Thaddeous introduced us. When Thaddeous then came up with an excuse to leave us alone, he seemed perfectly happy to keep me company.

"Now you live in Boston, don't you?" he asked.

"Yes, sir."

"Now don't you 'sir' me," he said, wagging his finger. "You'll make me feel old. Call me Joe. Everybody does."

"All right, Joe." I took a bite of baked ham while trying to figure out how I could move the conversation in the direction I wanted to go. "They certainly laid out a nice spread."

"I bet you don't get good cooking like this up North."

"That's the truth." That gave me an idea. "It's the barbeque I really miss. There's a couple of places that sell barbeque, but it's more Texas-style than North Carolina-style."

"That's one reason I could never live up there. I don't know what I'd do without good barbeque and hush puppies."

"I just try to get as much as I can when I'm home." Now for the subtle part. "I ate over at Pigwick's the other day. Tim Topper's place." I watched him closely for a reaction.

"They fix some good barbeque," Joe admitted without blinking, "but I think I like Fork-in-the-Road a mite better."

I suppose I shouldn't have expected him to turn white at the mention of Tim Topper, because surely he had heard him named any number of times in the past twenty-five years. I tried something a bit more direct. "My Aunt Nora says that the barbeque there was better when Fannie Topper was cooking it. She said Fannie had a real knack for it."

Maybe he winced a little at that, but really no more than anybody would when reminded of an old murder. Then he launched into a list of recommendations for other barbeque houses across North Carolina, from Bubba's Barbeque in Charlotte to Buck Overton's in Mt. Airy to the Barbeque Lodge in Raleigh.

I guess he could tell that I was losing interest, because he finally said, "I guess you can tell that I enjoy my food." He patted his stomach with a grin. "You'd never know that I was the star player of my baseball team in high school."

"Oh, it still shows," I lied politely.

"My daddy thought it was important to play sports. Teamwork and all that. He always said, 'Even if you can't be an athlete, be an athletic supporter'."

It was an ancient joke, but I joined in when he chuckled.

Then I asked, "Didn't I hear you played for the mill, too? On the championship team?"

He puffed his chest out a bit. "One of the proudest moments of my life, winning that game. Nothing like playing sports to make friends. I still keep in touch with all those men." Then he looked down at his plate. "Well, most of them."

I knew he was talking about Caleb Wilkins, but then he said that after talking so much about good food, he had to go refill his plate.

Thaddeous came up to me once Joe was gone. "How's it going?"

"Not much yet." I looked around, and saw that the place had pretty much filled up. "Have you seen either of the other two?"

"I just saw Bobby Plummer over by the dance floor. Come on."

When Aunt Nora told me that Bobby Plummer was said to have lace on his underwear, I had to stifle giggles. I hadn't heard that particular euphemism for being homosexual in years. She had gone on to say, "He was married for a year or so, but after the divorce, he moved back in with his mama. Now that she's gone, he lives by himself. He goes down to Charlotte a lot on the weekends, and somebody I know swears he saw him in one of those gay bars, dressed in leather pants." Damning evidence to be sure, but I had to wonder what Aunt Nora's friend had been doing at that bar.

Bobby was one of the better-dressed men at the party, both because of the quality of his suit and because of the style with which he wore it. Unlike Joe, he had a full head of dark hair and a trim build. Once again Thaddeous introduced me, and then remembered that he was needed elsewhere.

We chatted, but I couldn't help noticing that Bobby was tapping his feet to the music.

"They're playing good music," I said, intending to somehow lead this to the celebration party at Fannie's.

But then Bobby asked, "Would you like to dance?"

I said, "I'd love to," but added the warning, "I'm not very good."

He smiled and said, "I'm sure you're wonderful."

Soon enough, he learned that I hadn't been exaggerating, but he was good enough to make me look competent. Unfortunately, I had never been one of those people who could carry on a conversation while dancing, and from the way Bobby was going, he'd have been happy to keep dancing all night long.

Finally I said, "I think I need to catch my breath."

"Of course." He lead me to a table. "Can I get you a drink?"

"That would be very nice," I said. It would also give me a chance to come up with an approach. By the time Bobby returned with two glasses of punch, I was ready for him.

"I think I've been a desk jockey too long," I said. "I just don't have your stamina. You must be active in sports."

"Sometimes," he said. "I prefer working out on my own. I have a NordicTrack in my basement."

"I thought I heard something about your playing

baseball. I was talking to one of your old team mates earlier. Joe Bowley."

"That was years ago," he said. "The year we won was the last time that any of us played for the mill."

"Really? Why is that?"

"You're too young to remember, but it was after our victory party that Fannie Topper was killed, and one of the team members was arrested for the murder. A fellow named Caleb Wilkins."

"Oh?" I said, hoping I sounded interested enough to make him keep talking, but not so interested as to make him suspicious.

"Big Bill Walters fired Caleb right after he was arrested, saying that he couldn't keep a murder suspect on the payroll. We team members didn't think that was fair. After all, Caleb hadn't been convicted. We talked about quitting, but since we couldn't do that, we decided we'd at least quit playing baseball. If Walters wouldn't stand by Caleb, we weren't going to play baseball just so he could have a trophy."

"So you turned in your hats?" Maybe I could find out who hadn't turned in his hat, the one who had lost it at Fannie's.

But Bobby's next words dashed that hope. "Actually, no. We burned them. We set a fire in a trash can on the parking lot during lunch and tossed in every single cap. Big Bill was furious, but there wasn't anything he could do. He couldn't fire all of us."

I had to grin, even if it had ruined my half-formed idea. Unless . . . "That's great. Whose idea was it to burn them?"

"Oh, I think we all agreed on it. It was the sixties, and the revolutionary spirit had struck, even in Byerly."

By now I had my breath back, and Bobby asked me to dance again. In other circumstances, I'd have been happy to, but I declined with thanks and went looking for Thaddeous.

Instead I found Aunt Nora. "Are you enjoying the

party?" she asked in an obviously innocent tone of voice.

"I'm having a wonderful time," I said.

Then Aunt Nora lowered her voice. "Have you talked to them all?"

"Two out of three. I still need to find Pete Fredericks."

"You come with me, and we'll find him." Aunt Nora wasn't as efficient a guide as Thaddeous was because she had to stop and say hello to just about everybody we saw, but eventually we made our way over to a tall, thin man with short, greying hair and dark eyes. He was standing alone near the edge of the room, smoking a cigarette.

"Hey there, Pete," Aunt Nora said. "Pete, do you know my niece Laurie Anne? She lives up in Boston."

We made the obligatory small talk about how different Massachusetts was from North Carolina. Then Aunt Nora excused herself to go powder her nose, leaving me alone with Pete.

I try not to have any illusions about my feminine charm, but from what Aunt Nora had told me about Pete, I was halfway expecting him to make a pass at me once we were alone.

She had said, "Pete has an eye for the ladies. I think he's gone out with every woman in town, or at least with any of them that would. He wanted to date Edna once, but she wasn't about to put up with his roving. He had to get married about fifteen years ago, but Martha knew what she was getting into and she seems pretty happy. He's probably still running around, but at least he's careful."

I had to wonder if he had dated Fannie Topper, but I could not for the life of me come up with a way to gently broach that subject. The best opening gambit I could devise was, "What do you do at the mill, Pete?"

"Supervisor of dyeing right now, but I gave notice just this week."

"Is that so? Are you going to work for a different mill?"

"No, I'm going to work with my wife's uncle. Maybe you know him. Harry Giles."

"Over at Giles Funeral Home?"

"I like to say that I'm moving from dyeing to dying." Darned if he didn't already have that solemn, restrained smile down pat.

I suppose I should have been able to easily move the conversation from death to a particular death, but I just couldn't do it. I even asked about how they made bodies presentable for open casket ceremonies, specifically when the deceased had died by violence, but the answer was far more graphic than I had wanted and left no room to ask about Fannie Topper.

Trying to change the subject, I mentioned playing baseball, and he told me about a grisly case when his uncle had a client who died from a blow to the head from a baseball. I don't even want to think about what he told me when I mentioned barbeque.

By the time Aunt Nora came to rescue me, I didn't know whether or not Pete was the murderer, but I was pretty sure that he wouldn't be fooling around on his wife anymore. Not if that was his idea of pillow talk.

The party went on for hours, but I could have left right after talking to Pete Fredericks for all the good it did me. I hadn't learned anything useful. Still, I didn't want to make Thaddeous miss anything, so I stuck around and tried to have fun. I even danced with Bobby Plummer some more.

It was around one o'clock when Thaddeous and I finally headed for the parking lot.

"Sorry I wasn't much of a date for you, Thaddeous," I said.

"That's all right. Did you get what you were after?"

"Not really," I said.

"Don't you worry. I know you'll puzzle it out."

I was glad somebody had confidence in me. At that point, I sure didn't. We were all the way to Thaddeous's pickup before I saw the man leaning up against it.

"Richard!" I said. "What are you doing here?"

"Were you afraid I'd keep her out too late?" Thaddeous said with a grin.

"Just couldn't stand being away from her any longer," Richard said, and gave me a big hug.

Thaddeous snickered. "I suppose that you're going to steal my date."

"You've got it."

I thanked Thaddeous again for his help and got into the car with Richard while he drove away. "If you came to get me to find out what I learned, you wasted your trip," I said.

"That bad?"

"Just about." I told him everything I had learned from the three men, and concluded with, "I didn't get the first hint of a motive, unless Fannie was blackmailing Bobby Plummer because he's gay."

"Is he gay?"

"I don't even know *that* for sure."

"What about family resemblances? Could any of the three have been Tim's father?"

"He doesn't favor any of them. I had wondered if Pete could have been the sower of wild oats, but the way he is now, he'd be more interested in Fannie dead than alive." I threw my hands up. "It was a complete waste of time."

"Not complete. The part about the hats was significant. Burning them couldn't be coincidence. Now we're sure that the murderer was one of the team members."

"True," I said, "but we were pretty sure of that before."

Richard patted my leg comfortingly.

We drove a few minutes longer, and finally it dawned on me that we weren't headed for Aunt Maggie's house. "Richard, where are we going?"

"To Pigwick's."

"At this time of night? I imagine they're closed." Richard didn't answer. "What are you up to?"

"Nothing much," he said. "I just figured out where Fannie hid her money, that's all."

"You what? Where?"

He pulled a paperback book out of his jacket pocket. "The answer is in here."

I read the cover. *"Oliver Twist?"*

"Tim said that his mother loved Dickens, and I've read a little Dickens myself. Contrary to popular opinion, I do read things other than Shakespeare. All that talk about Tim's father reminded me that Dickens used more than one case of disputed parentage or illegitimate birth. I thought I remembered something about a hiding place, too, so I went to the Waldenbooks at the mall and looked at Dickens books until I found what I was looking for."

I was impressed. Dickens wrote long books. "And?"

He handed me the book, and switched on the car's dome light. "I've got it marked."

There was a slip of paper sticking out near the end of the book, and when I opened it, I saw that Richard had circled a passage. "You wrote in a book?"

"Desperate times call for desperate measures."

Clearly he thought this was important. I read the passage out loud. " ' "The papers," said Fagin, drawing Oliver towards him, "are in a canvas bag, in a hole a little way up the chimney in the top front-room." ' What papers?"

"The papers that proved who Oliver's parents were. And I remembered a fireplace at Pigwick's. Of course in Fannie's case, I'll bet the papers are green with numbers and presidential portraits on them."

"And maybe something that proves who Tim's father was?"

"That's what I'm hoping." He looked toward me, obviously expecting expressions of delight.

I didn't disappoint him. "Richard, you're brilliant!"

He tried to assume a modest expression. "Well, we

should probably wait until we find out if I'm right or not." Still, he couldn't help but break into a huge grin, like a cat who had just swallowed a particularly plump canary.

It was almost two in the morning, so we weren't surprised that Pigwick's was dark when we drove into the parking lot.

"Drive around back," I told Richard. "There must be a stairway up to Tim's place. I was right, and we climbed up to knock at the door. When that didn't work, we progressed to pounding with our fists.

Finally Tim opened the door, wearing a pair of jeans he must have just pulled on and rubbing his eyes. "What's going on?"

"Sorry to wake you up, Tim, but we think that Richard's figured out where your mother's money is."

That woke him up. "Are you serious?"

"Richard, read him that piece from *Oliver Twist.*"

Richard complied.

I asked, "Is it possible?"

"Well, we sure never looked in there," Tim said. "I know Mama had read *Oliver Twist,* but she was only halfway through reading it to me when she died. I never had the heart to finish it." He stepped back from the door. "Come on in, and we'll go look."

Stopping only to put on a sweatshirt and pull a flashlight out of a drawer, Tim led us through his apartment, down the stairs, through the kitchen, and into the dining room. He flipped on the lights and said, "I'll turn the heat up."

I guess it was cold in there, but I was too excited to really notice. All I could do was stare at the brick fireplace that nearly filled one wall.

"Well," Tim said, "let's see what we can see."

All three of us started tugging on the bricks that made up the fireplace. We must have spent an hour, and I know that no brick escaped our attentions. Tim even pulled out a step ladder so he could get to the highest bricks.

"Did y'all find anything?" Tim finally asked.

I shook my head.

Richard pulled out *Oliver Twist* again and said, "The books says the money was on the inside of the chimney."

"Then let's try that." Tim got down on his hands and knees and hunted up inside, using the flashlight to light his way. Richard and I watched eagerly at first, but as the minutes passed, it was obvious that he wasn't finding anything. Finally he crawled back out. "Nothing!"

"Let me try," I said, reaching for the flashlight. I was both shorter and smaller around than Tim, so I could get a little further in. Not that it did me any good. All I found was soot. I knew I was ruining my coat and my dress, but I just didn't care. Finally Richard tugged on my foot, and I gave up and came away from the fireplace.

"I'm sorry, Tim," I said, feeling foolish. "We really thought this could be it. Here we got you out of bed and everything."

"No, that's all right. It sounded like a good idea to me, too. I don't really need the money anyway. Pigwick's is doing fine. I just thought if I could find it, maybe I could go to college part-time, and get that degree Mama wanted me to have."

Now I really felt awful for raising his hopes for nothing. "I'm sorry," I said again.

Tim shrugged, and looked at the clock. It was almost four. "I may as well stay up and get the meat ready to cook. I'm supposed to cater a lunch in Hickory today. Your car's in back isn't it? Come on out to the kitchen, and I'll let you out that way."

He didn't even wait for an answer before going into the kitchen.

Richard looked even more forlorn than Tim had. "It *was* a good idea," I said, and rubbed his back.

He said, " 'The attempt and not the deed confounds us.' *MacBeth,* Act II, scene 2."

It was when I heard Tim rattling around in the kitchen that something rattled loose in my brain. I pulled at Richard's sleeve. "Hold on just one minute! You may have solved it after all!"

Tim had pulled out a big pan, and was opening the walk-in refrigerator. The kitchen was all stainless steel and tile. There was an oven, but it looked brand-new. Besides, it wasn't big enough to cook a whole hog in.

"Tim, you don't cook the barbeque in here, do you?"

He said, "No, I've got a stone oven out in a shed. Mama said she had to put it out there or it would have been too hot in here in the summer."

"So it's the same one that your mother used?"

"Of course." Then he caught onto what I was talking about. "You don't suppose . . . ?"

"Where's the shed?" Richard asked.

Again Tim led the way as we went outside, cut across the parking lot, and into a wooden shed that held a few shelves and a huge oven. I looked up at the stone chimney rising up from the oven, and saw Richard and Tim doing the same.

I asked, "Is it possible?"

Tim said, "The only thing is that we keep this going most of the time." Even at this hour, I could feel low heat rising from it. "I don't see how Mama could have put anything inside without burning herself. She'd have had to climb right into the oven."

I said, "What about on the outside?"

Richard went to one side and Tim to the other, and started pushing on the stones at eye level. After a few minutes, they shook their heads.

"Maybe it just needs to be pulled harder," Richard said. "It's been a long time."

"Maybe," Tim said doubtfully.

I said, "Tim, how tall was your mama?"

"About your height, maybe an inch or two shorter," he said, catching on. "We were looking too high up."

This time I squeezed in and started pushing and tugging. Long minutes went by, with Tim and Richard watching anxiously, and I think I would have given up if it hadn't been for the hopeful light in Tim's eyes. Even with that encouragement, I was just about ready to admit defeat when I felt a rock give a little. "That one moved," I said.

"Can you pull it out?" Richard asked.

I tried, but couldn't get a good grip.

"Let me," Tim said, and reached around me. I guess cooking ribs is better hand exercise than punching keys at a computer all day, because he had it pulled out in a second. Or maybe he just had a stronger motive than I did.

Once he had the rock out of the way, I stuck my hand into the hole and felt a piece of cloth. "There's something in here." I yanked and pulled out a canvas drawstring sack. It was about as big as my biggest pocketbook, and looked about half full. I was tempted to open it myself, but that wouldn't have been right. Instead I handed it to Tim.

He swallowed visibly as he pulled the string. It came partway loose, then disintegrated. "Rotted through," he said, and pulled on the bag itself. The canvas held for a second longer, then came open and Tim looked inside. A yell burst out from him, and he grabbed an enormous stew pot from on top of the stove and spilled the contents of the bag out into it.

Neatly banded parcels of money poured into the pot.

"It's Mama's money!" He reached his arms around both me and Richard and clutched us to him in a bear hug.

The three of us danced around and did our best to recreate the lost Rebel Yell. Eventually I remembered the other reason for our treasure hunt, and pulled myself free. "Is there anything else in there?"

Tim laughed, handed me a slotted spoon, and said, "Just stir it up and see!" Then he danced around some more with Richard.

I took the spoon, but used it to rummage around the bills. A couple of stacks came loose because the rubber bands containing them had given up, so I didn't find it right off. Besides, I was looking for papers or an envelope. What I found was a badly tarnished box.

"Tim, was this your mother's?" Not knowing how long fingerprints could last, I didn't touch it, just pointed with the spoon.

Tim finally stopped dancing. "What is it?"

"I think it's a cigarette case," I said. I still had on my coat, so I reached into my pockets to find my gloves, and only picked it up after I had my hands covered.

Tim took a look. "I don't think so. Mama didn't smoke. And that looks like silver."

I flipped it open. It was filled with cigarettes, but they didn't look mass-produced. "I don't think these are tobacco."

Richard and Tim nodded.

"I know my Mama didn't smoke pot," Tim said firmly. "She didn't even like Uncle Eb drinking because she didn't want me picking it up."

"Maybe this was the reason she was killed," I said slowly. Possession of marijuana might be a misdemeanor now, but twenty-five years ago, it could have led to a long jail sentence. "What if the murderer was looking for this, not for the money?"

Tim looked confused, but then, he didn't know what Richard and I had been up to. "Caleb Wilkins was a junkie?"

"I don't think it was Caleb Wilkins," I said. "I'll explain it all later, but right now I think we ought to call the police. Maybe they can still find fingerprints on this, and figure out who it belonged to."

"We won't need fingerprints," Richard said. "Hold the case up to the light again."

I closed the case, and took a closer look at the front. The inscription was obscured by the tarnish, but after a minute I read the initials out loud. "JB."

* * *

"Well, Joe," Andy Norton said. "Do you want to tell us what happened?" He hefted the cigarette case, now encased in a plastic bag.

Joe Bowley wasn't smiling now. His chubby face had gone slack, and he wasn't meeting Chief Norton's eyes.

It was around nine o'clock in the morning by then. Neither Richard nor I had gone to bed after finding Fannie's cache. Instead we had called Junior Norton and her father to come take charge of the cigarette case, and told them all we knew. After that, we had all gone to the police station to wait until it was late enough that Junior could go get Joe Bowley.

Junior even deputized her father so he could lead the questioning, since it had been his case originally. "It's an early Christmas present," she had said with a grin. An odd present, maybe, but no odder than what Richard and I were trying to give Aunt Edna.

Now Richard, Junior, Tim, and I were waiting for Joe's answer. He had already waived his right to have a lawyer present, and even agreed to let Tim, Richard, and me listen in.

Joe took a long, ragged breath, and started to speak. "I didn't even like pot much at first—that's the crazy thing. I only started smoking because some of the guys liked it, and I always carried it around in case somebody wanted to smoke with me. Nobody did at the party, but I went around back of the shed to smoke one anyway. To celebrate winning. That's where Fannie found me. Lord, she was mad. Said she didn't need drugs around her bar.

"I probably shouldn't have offered her one, because that just made her madder, and she snatched the case away from me. She said she wouldn't call the police, but I was going to have to tell my daddy or she would. She said she'd give him the case back when he came to talk to her.

"I was going to tell him, I was going to tell him that

night. Only when I got home, he kept saying how proud he was of me for playing such a good game. I couldn't tell him then.

"So I went back to Fannie's late that night, after everybody else had gone home. I just wanted more time, but she said I had to tell Daddy right away. I offered her money to keep quiet, but she said that she was going to call Daddy first thing in the morning." He shook his head, not so much in regret as in complete lack of understanding. "She just wouldn't listen to me."

"Is that when you hit her?" Chief Norton asked.

Joe looked shocked. "You make it sound like I meant to hurt her. What happened is that she wanted me to leave, and I wouldn't go without my case. She said she was going to get her shotgun, was even heading for the bar to go get it. I just wanted to stop her, so I tried to catch her arm. She wriggled away, so I had to grab her. She kept moving, trying to get away, and she pushed herself away from me and lost her balance. That's when she hit her head. It was an accident."

"If it was an accident," Chief Norton said quietly, "why didn't you call for help?"

"I didn't think she was dead—I thought she had just knocked herself out. I had to find my case. I knew it was there somewhere, and I didn't want anybody else to find it."

I wasn't supposed to talk, but I couldn't help asking. "What about the blood? Didn't you even check for a pulse?"

He didn't really answer me, just said, "I would have called for help once I found the case."

Chief Norton said, "Didn't you stop to think that if Fannie had been alive, she could have called your father when she woke up? Maybe even the police?"

"She wouldn't have done that, not without the case as proof. It would have been her word against mine, and Daddy wouldn't have believed a ni—" He looked at Tim and stopped. "She knew that."

"But you didn't find the case."

I pictured him ripping up the bar while Fannie lay there bleeding, and shivered. Richard took my hand.

Joe shook his head. "I looked everywhere, and then I heard a car drive up. I didn't know it was Caleb. I thought it was Fannie's brother, and he might have been drinking. He'd have killed me if he had found me in there with her like that. So I went out the back door and drove away."

"You must have thought that I'd come looking for you pretty soon," Chief Norton said. "Why didn't you try to run?"

"I didn't have anywhere to go. This is my home, my family is here."

Byerly had been Caleb's home, too, I thought.

Joe went on. "The next day I heard about Fannie being dead and Caleb being arrested, but nobody mentioned my cigarette case. I was sure that Caleb would get out of it. He was innocent, after all."

I didn't find his trust in our legal system very touching.

Chief Norton said, "What about your hat?"

Joe looked surprised that he knew that part, but answered anyway. "I saw I didn't have mine a couple of days later, and that's when I thought about getting the team to burn them all as a protest. Like burning flags and bras the way people did then."

I didn't think that anybody had ever burned a bra to hide evidence of a murder.

Finally Joe met Chief Norton's eyes. "I did what I could for Caleb. We paid for his bail and his lawyer, never asked for a penny of it back. Walters would have hired him back eventually. He didn't have to leave town like that."

Easy for him to say when he hadn't been the outcast.

He looked down at his hands. "I tried to make up for it."

I remembered what Aunt Nora had said about Joe's charity work, and I couldn't help but wonder how much of his life had been spent trying to make up for Fannie Topper. He had done everything but the right thing.

"So Joe murdered Fannie," Aunt Nora said after Richard and I had told her about it.

"It wasn't murder after all," Richard said. "Joe told us it was an accident, and I believe him. Even Tim said he couldn't hate him."

I wasn't quite so forgiving as Richard and Tim, but I had to admit that Joe had looked right pitiful sitting there, knowing that he was finally going to have to tell his father the truth.

"Did Junior put him in jail?"

I shook my head. "She let him go home for now. She's not sure what the district attorney is going to want to do."

"Have you called Caleb?"

"First thing. I had to get Andy Norton on the line to convince him that it was true, but he said he's going to meet me and Richard at Aunt Maggie's on Christmas morning. Then we'll bring him over here." The Burnettes always gathered together on Christmas morning, and this year Aunt Nora was the hostess. "I can't wait to see Aunt Edna's face."

Then I thought of something. "Aunt Nora, do you suppose you could throw some hints around that Aunt Edna might want to dress up a bit?" After all this, I didn't want Caleb to be shocked by her appearance.

"I think I can handle that. Why don't you two go get yourselves some sleep. You look like you've been ridden hard and put away wet."

"That sounds like an excellent suggestion," Richard said, and pulled me out of the chair before I could fall asleep right where I was.

We slept most of that day to catch up, and since the next day was Christmas Eve, we stayed busy wrapping gifts and visiting. Chief Norton brought over a platter of

Christmas cookies, and Tim Topper delivered enough sealed bags of barbeque to feed my habit for a year.

Christmas morning dawned bright and clear. Richard and I were up early to exchange gifts before joining in on the official Burnette celebration. Then we ate breakfast with Aunt Maggie and sent her along to Aunt Nora's house so we could wait.

Caleb showed up right on time, dressed in what had to be a new suit, and grinning from ear to ear. He kept trying to thank us, but I finally got him into his car by telling him that we were going to be late.

The plan was for him to follow us, and let us go inside first. After a few minutes, he would ring the bell and we'd make sure that Aunt Edna answered.

Caleb looked nervous, but no more than I was. As we drove to Aunt Nora's, all of a sudden I was wondering if this had been a good idea. What right did I have to meddle this way? Aunt Nora had said that Aunt Edna had been furious at Caleb when he left. What if she didn't want to see him?

"It's going to be fine," Richard said. "Even if they don't get together again, I'm sure they'll enjoy seeing each other."

"What if they don't get along anymore? Aunt Edna has changed an awful lot." I kept remembering the picture of how she used to be. If that was the woman Caleb was expecting to see, he was going to be disappointed.

"It's going to be fine," Richard repeated. "Don't get your shorts in a bunch."

I had to giggle. "Where did you hear that?"

"Aunt Nora, of course. You didn't think *that* was Shakespeare, did you?"

Finally we were there. Richard and I parked on the street, and I made sure Caleb had parked behind us before we went inside.

Aunt Nora's house was filled nearly to the bursting point with aunts, uncles, and cousins, and it took me a few minutes to spot Aunt Nora. I called her name, and she bustled over to me.

"Is he here?" she whispered.

I nodded. "He's outside. Where's Aunt Edna?"

"Ruby Lee took her to freshen up." She looked up the stairs. "Here they come now."

I looked up that way, meaning to wish Aunt Edna a Merry Christmas, but I never did get the words out.

Aunt Edna was wearing a dark green dress that flattered her slim figure, and matching pumps. Her hair had been released from its bun, and trimmed and curled around her face. She had on a pearl necklace and earrings, and even eye shadow and lipstick.

"Merry Christmas, Laurie Anne," she said, smiling shyly.

I looked at Aunt Nora, and she grinned. She and the other aunts must have spent the past two days remaking Aunt Edna.

Before I could say anything else, the doorbell rang. Aunt Nora must have prompted everybody, because even though there were several people near the door, nobody moved.

"Edna, would you get that?" Aunt Nora asked innocently.

Aunt Edna looked curious, but went to the door and opened it.

From over her shoulders, I could see Caleb holding a bouquet of roses and a wrapped box. "Hello, Edna," he said.

I held my breath for her answer.

"Caleb Wilkins," she said. "I was wondering if you'd ever show up again. What do you want?"

My heart went right through the floor. She *didn't* want to see him.

"I'm sorry, Edna," he said. "I've regretted leaving you like I did every day for the past twenty-five years."

"I hope you don't think I've been sitting around waiting for you to come back!"

"No, I didn't think that. I just hope you'll let me come back now."

"For how long this time?"

"Edna, I swear that the only way I'll leave again is if you want me to." He paused. "Are you telling me to go?"

They stood there for what seemed like an eternity, both so filled with pride that it hurt to watch them. Aunt Edna's head was held high in a way I had never seen before, and I finally knew why Aunt Nora had called her the one with spirit.

Finally Aunt Edna said, "No, I'm not telling you to go, Caleb. I'm asking you to stay." She reached out a hand, and Caleb took it. Then suddenly she was out on the porch with him and they were in each other's arms, kissing with twenty-five years' worth of passion.

After a few stunned seconds, Aunt Nora closed the door behind them and wiped her eyes.

Richard put his arms around me, and we kissed, too.

"Merry Christmas, Richard."

"Merry Christmas, Laura." Then in a voice loud enough for everybody to hear, he added, "God bless us, every one!"

Too Little Room at the Inn

by J. Dayne Lamb

A swag of holly draped around the doorway like a green and red picture frame. Teal Stewart registered the scene and skidded to a stop. This was not what she expected.

Not at all.

Teal sighed, the sound pressing from her diaphragm, twisting out of her lungs to expel the breath in a rush through her nose. The entire physical reaction, claiming no more than a nanosecond, had been as involuntary as the next step she knew she must force herself to take through the opening and into the dining room. She closed her eyes for a moment.

As always these days, she had left her office too late last night into the dark and bitter cold. The kind of Boston cold where the stars remained sharp in the sky and the dusting of early snow lay over patches of ice to confuse the traction on the sidewalk or road. Even last-minute shoppers had long gone home, the downtown stores empty and locked. No Salvation Army bell ringers stood on the corner.

Santa's elves continued to busy themselves in stirring the same batch of cookie dough, wrapping the same present and skating over the same artificial pond in the window of the Jordan Marsh department store, but no children stood outside to watch, noses squashed to the glass, lost to reality in a fantasy moment.

No, the parents and children, the nuclear and extended and broken families, and those who traversed life alone, all were off the city streets. Most, Teal had imagined, were snug in a festive home, sipping eggnog in front of a fire or stringing popcorn around a Christmas tree bright with shining balls and colored lights. Somewhere someone was retelling the traditional and the religious stories of Christmas Eve.

And where was she? Running across the Public Garden, past the worn crèche with the infant ever lost or stolen, over the ice-encrusted path heading to where she had parked the rental car on Charles Street on the flat of Beacon Hill.

At least she had been smart enough to arrange to pick up the car from Hertz this morning. The reservationist had warned her the counter would be closing early the afternoon of Christmas Eve. Why she hadn't driven to work was inexplicable. The habit of walking to her office at the international accounting firm of Clayborne Whittier, maybe. A stupid decision, in any event, with how her day had dragged on and on, until everyone else had departed and the deserted office cooled to frigid with the heat turned off.

She wanted to think that the client matter which kept her late represented a crisis, an imperative, a necessary reason to stay. She didn't want to consider why she needed such a fiction this particular evening. She couldn't help thinking about it, though—couldn't help but ask herself why she had said no.

She had refused Hunt's invitation to join him and his parents for the celebration out at their place in the Berkshires. She'd been to more than one Huston family Christmas, but she hadn't known what she would say this year when Hunt's mother and father asked her about her plans with Hunt, hinted at marriage, spoke too fervently about the joys of having a baby. She had not wanted to craft an answer or address her own feelings.

Teal had not hesitated, not even to work out an excuse. She had said no. Flat no.

Hunt had shrugged in that tight movement which

meant he would not fight, not about this, not when he wanted her to come. He didn't argue and say he could deflect the pressure from his family. He didn't remind her she liked the contour of the Berkshires, enjoyed his parents, would be left for time on her own. He had said fine, and skipped further niceties and turned with Argyle from her door. Two weeks ago and he had not called or stopped by to see her since.

Only Argyle sent her a Christmas card, his paw print in festive colored ink. The elegant and dignified Scottish deerhound belonged to Hunt now. At least more than sort of, if not entirely. Huntington BG Associates did not object to Argyle hanging around the office. Hunt, a famous architect with his own two-partner firm, claimed a flexibility Teal could not enjoy. Clayborne Whittier had nineteen or more partners in Boston and hundreds in the US alone and frowned on individual displays of lifestyle like bringing a dog to the office.

Anyway, Hunt had taken Argyle with him at the time of the break-up those many years ago. Argyle never understood, not to this day, but considered Hunt and Teal to belong to him as they had before. Hunt did not offer to leave Argyle with her this Christmas, and foolish pride had constrained her from making the request.

Hunt's back disappearing through her door that afternoon had made her turn to punch out a string of numbers on the telephone.

The River Bank Inn in Bath, Maine, had answered in two rings with Hawley's fine, Yankee voice, and he was delighted to take her reservation. All she wanted, she had decided, was Christmas away and in privacy. She took care to warn Hawley and May she likely would be arriving late.

"Don't worry about that," Hawley had said, the inflection of his native state taking *that* up and down and up through the drawn out *a.* "Key'll keep under the stone. Come in and make yourself at home in the room to the back of the stairs. The one you like. Don't have but one other booking, father and daughter, so you can expect quiet. And prob'ly snow. Don't be driving that car of yours."

Teal had accepted his advice and made the next call to Hertz for the rental. Her classic 190SL sportster was a great automobile, but its 1959 rear wheel traction and an underbelly adverse to salt and sand was not made for a Maine winter. She would leave the old companion at home.

The rental handled as well as she could expect from an automatic. The empty roads let her fly, but it was a good thing she'd warned Hawley she might be late, she had realized when she pulled in beside the Inn. Past one in the morning. Christmas Eve turned to Christmas morning.

She found the key and her room laid out with the three pillows she needed. One to go under her knees, one for under her head and one to cover her head. She had heard nothing. Not a hint of what she saw before her outlined by the festive decoration of the door.

The River Bank Inn could boast many fine points. A rural setting above the banks of the Kennebec River. Acres of tall growth woodland. Generous rooms and numerous fireplaces in a Federal era mansion adapted to modern expectations. Hawley and May. Hawley's breakfasts.

Hawley always set down the first course; maybe his tart, homemade yogurt swirled with Washington County, Maine, blueberry compote. Hawley could talk anyone into a plate of his buckwheat ployes, the French Canadian pancake of the state. May accepted morning bragging rights to the coffee only, and made up herbal tea especially for Teal.

Teal had not been about to miss a Hawley breakfast, no matter how sleep deprived she'd be. Thus the rush through a shower and throwing on clothes. Maine clothes. Duck boots from L. L. Bean. Worn dungarees. She drew the line at plaid flannel or wool shirts, but did choose her old waffle cotton thermal top to go under the sweatshirt from the Patagonia outlet store in Freeport.

No bothering with pinning up a small chignon today. Her chestnut hair hung loose to frame her oval face, curtain the feelings in the gray-blue eyes she wanted to hide away. Teal never considered make-up optional, but used a flick of blush and lick of navy mascara. Waterproof in case of snow.

The morning smelled like snow was in the forecast.

Teal sighed again at the dining room door, the taste of precipitation at the back of her nose as she forced open her eyes. The view had not changed. She identified the father and daughter. Hawley hadn't been wrong on that score. But he hadn't predicted quite right, either.

Seven more people were organizing themselves to sit to breakfast around the length of tables pushed together across the middle of the dining room. The one leftover stood beside the window, the father and daughter each in a seat, but the silver and napkin showed a place for number three. Her place.

The picture did not promise solitude.

Not at all.

"Teal!"

Hawley's voice caught her considering her feet. Working out how to make them move forward or maybe turn fast for the front door. Would a MacDonald's be open on Christmas morning?

"Teal!"

Too late. She lifted her face and smiled. She couldn't help smiling. She loved Hawley, at least in his persona as innkeep. In the same way, she loved May.

"You're here with these nice folks," Hawley was saying. "Up from Florida to look at Bowdoin. Fine college."

Hawley set a dish of stewed Turkish figs and a dab of his yogurt at each of the three places.

The father was watching her while the dark-haired daughter blushed into her place setting. Teal walked into the room and sat, working to keep her ire at the surprising number of guests to herself.

Perhaps father and daughter felt the same way,

because after the minimum of introductions all around—he was Abe, she Rachel—they let silence take hold.

A relative silence. A silence at their table. The group of seven made enough noise to fill the room. Enough to let Teal indulge in a favorite restaurant pastime, listening to the lives of strangers unfold.

Well-timed glances at the bigger group let her establish its composition and pecking order.

The matriarch, and no other word would do justice to the woman's position, age and grace, headed the table. Teal could cock her neck and see her straight-on.

Opposite this mother sat the son. His profile was substantial, shaped by a nose like a blade, lips strong and mean. His hair shone with streaks of the same silver which colored his mother's head. If the matriarch held the position of honor, he held command of the family. Furtive expressions among themselves showed how much the remaining five deferred to his control. His mother appeared or had chosen not to notice.

A tenuous flutter of a hand to the son's arm identified the woman on his left as his spouse. Sufficient conversation ensued to untangle the identity of the man beside this wife. He was the brother-in-law, married to the matriarch's daughter, the son's sister, who sat between him and her mother. Wife, brother-in-law and sister, three backs to the burning fire, fronts to the windows.

Two grown children faced the line of adults, a young man and young woman. The young man, Teal decided, belonged to the matriarch's son, the young woman to her daughter. Otherwise, all Teal really could see of these two were strong, broad shoulders.

Hawley returned to clear as May followed with three bowls of steel-cut oatmeal, cream and honey for Teal, Abe and Rebecca.

"May," Teal whispered in the small woman's ear. "Who are they?"

"Nicholses," May whispered, easing her body to set her face away from the long table. "Big house down the road. Whole family's together for the holiday. First time since the wedding years ago."

May cocked a discreet bob to the daughter and son-in-law.

"Surprised us. Filled us solid. She's not one for staying in the big house." Here May flicked her elbow to the matriarch. "Never did care for her husband's brother. She as good as raised those children without his help after Mr. Nichols died. Tragedy."

May stopped speaking. Her lips had not relaxed, but remained taut. There was more to say and nothing more to say to a stranger, even a stranger accepted as a sort of friend. Teal understood. Certain secrets stayed in Maine. Period.

"So," Teal whispered. She tipped her chin at the big table. "Do they have names?"

"Hawley!" May called across the room. "You introduce these folks!"

Mrs. Nichols, the matriarch, accepted the introduction with the poise of a woman in her late seventies. She was a beautiful woman, the silver hair brushed into a heavy french braid, her skin fine and luminous, her eyes a reflective, deep brown.

She took over from Hawley, motioning to her son Robert and his wife June, her daughter Meredith and her son-in-law, Dennis. Dennis looked to be Robert's age, mid-fifties, his hair still light brown where it hadn't gone to a yellow white. Where Robert's posture set him square at his place, Dennis hunched over down in his chair.

Introduced by name, Robert nodded to Teal, Abe and Rachel. Dennis squirmed and slid his eyes away. Meredith's curt acknowledgment exuded the strength and confidence of a Nichols. No doubt she ran her marriage, as no doubt Robert ran his. June's faded blond hair was pulled back by the teeth of a hair band from her worn and unadorned face. Weary eyes watched Teal without interest or shame.

The children, both, showed Nichols vitality. Lise had

her father's light brown hair, but on her it glowed the color of polished teak. Jamie's grin showed fine white teeth and raised a sparkle in his sea-green eyes.

Abe had stood to shake hands all around. Teal saw him to be dark eyed and tall, almost gawky if the description could suit a man over forty. Rebecca, no more than seventeen, was bright and shy, the blush again burning at her fair cheeks when Jamie allowed as how he'd gone to Bowdoin.

The singular groups turned back to their community and Teal returned to eavesdropping.

Presents had been going around the Nichols table since the start of breakfast. Lise's was the last to come out.

"Oh Nana," she said, her voice breathless with joy after she shed the foil wrap and long box. "You shouldn't have—an Anschutz."

Lise's compact hand stroked the metal barrel extended past one side of her body. Her fingers grasped the curve of the butt on the other. Then Lise had the rifle sight to her eye.

"This will make all the difference in the world—"

"Move your biathlon ranking up from fourth to first?" Robert asked. "With the money Mater expended, it should."

June forced her eyes over to give him a *please don't* look.

"Things aren't going that well in real estate these days, Dennis? Need Mater to pull out the gun? Ha-ha," Robert said.

He didn't laugh, but repeated "Ha-ha."

"Shut up, Robert!" Meredith snarled. "Let Lise enjoy her gift, let Mother enjoy making the present."

"Been shooting much, yourself?" Dennis asked Robert in a voice used to appeasing the furies.

"A little skeet," Robert said. "Jamie here took first in the region for 12 gauge."

Dennis turned to Jamie. "How'd it feel to beat out the old man for a change?"

"Fine," Jamie said.

Teal understood the monotone, the prayer not to upset the balance of power.

"I continue to whip his pants off in 20 gauge, 28 gauge and 410 bore." Robert snorted.

"You smoke the targets, Dad," Jamie muttered to the old cue.

Robert shrugged at his prerogative. "How've you been coming in, Dennis?"

"He switched this year. He comes out with me after deer," Meredith said.

"Gives Bambi better odds. At least a deer doesn't drop every shot." Robert laughed at his joke. "How about you, Mater, going for those squirrels?"

The whole table laughed, now, at the in-joke.

May was beside Teal to clear.

"She hunts squirrel?" Teal whispered, though she didn't need to—the big table had produced an effective screen of noise.

"Did, for su-ah. All of us down here went for squirrel during the war. And woodcock and deer and any darned thing to make a change from picking mussels. Can't stand the sight or smell of any of those creatures for food. Except as mincemeat," May said.

"Mincemeat?" Teal repeated.

May stared. "Yes, mincemeat. Real mincemeat is made with meat. Deer meat here in Maine. What did you think?"

Teal didn't know what she thought, except she'd never connected the meat in mincemeat with, well, meat. May turned to look over to Meredith.

"Hawley and I sure do appreciate that neck. You or June or Lise want to help me make the mince?"

June mouthed a yes. Lise and Meredith wrinkled their noses up in a no.

"Well then, June, you come out to the kitchen when you have time and Hawley will set you to chopping the apples, and stirring in what applejack we don't fancy drinking while he grinds the meat!"

Everyone grinned with May except for Robert, who glared at June.

"I don't know," June said, her voice evasive, her glance to Robert fast and as fast away. "Sounds like work."

"And you're welcome to do it," Hawley drawled. He had the main course on a tray. Omelets turned over goat cheese for each diner, a basket of his bran muffins for each table. "How's the biathlete?" he asked at Lise's place.

"Great! See what Nana gave me?" She held up the sleek rifle. "Ammunition, too. The best. Fiocchi."

"Oh my," Hawley said. He laid a palm to the gleaming wood. "That's some Christmas present."

The matriarch shifted her attention to the window table.

"I understand Jews hate this Christmas business," she said in a voice as open and clear as a bell.

Teal expected Rebecca to flame up red, and the girl did. Teal expected Abe to act annoyed or angry, but he did not. He stretched his congenial grin, big knuckled hands laid flat to the table cloth.

"It's not an easy day," he said. "Not an easy season."

Mrs. Nichols nodded. "I don't blame you."

"Mother!" Meredith's voice rose, embarrassed and shrill.

Her mother raised hooded eyes. "I had a best friend before the war. My German friend. We met the summer I traveled to Berlin. She was Jewish. The Nazis took her away on Christmas Day. My best friend. What do you think God made of that?"

No one tried an answer. Mrs. Nichols regarded Abe. "Abraham, did you light your candles this year?"

"Yes," Abe answered. "Every night of Hanukkah."

"Abraham, keep your faith."

"Thank you, Mrs. Nichols," he said. "I do."

Rebecca's black eyelashes brushed her cheeks. Being seventeen and singled out was not easy, even if her father had absorbed the shock.

"It is a beautiful menorah," Rebecca offered to no one, her soft voice shaking.

"How are you finding Maine?" Teal asked. There was a reason for topics like the weather. "I think it will snow today."

Rebecca raised her eyes a cautious quarter inch. She shifted her arms around and stabbed at the omelet.

"It's too cold," she said.

Abe was concentrating on Teal over Rebecca's bent neck.

"Mother usually gets me over the Christmas holiday," Rebecca said.

Abe bit his lip.

"But Maine's okay, except it's too cold. Right Dad?"

Abe's face eased to a smile as Rebecca raised her head.

"Not for me," he teased. "I grew up in Brunswick."

"Just down the road," Teal said. "Sure, home of Bowdoin College—and is that where you went?"

"No, but my father, Becca's grandfather, was a professor there. I went to Princeton and teach at the University of Florida. Becca's not used to this."

"Did you know the Nicholses?" Teal dropped her low, resonant voice.

"Nope. Knew of them, of course."

"Of course?"

Abe finished with separating the raisins from his muffin. They made a little black pile of shot on his plate, like wrinkled baby bullets.

"Nichols about owned the Phippsburg peninsula and a good chunk of Brunswick. Powerful folks. She was a summer girl." He edged his head to Mrs. Nichols. "My father knew every detail, the whole area did. Robert Nichols senior was supposed to marry a Sewall, but he chose an outsider, instead."

Mrs. Nichols could have spent every summer of her youth on the Phippsburg peninsula, could have walked Morse Mountain every morning, sailed the Kennebec and the Atlantic Ocean and yes, she would have been a stranger to a family like the Nicholses. Teal may not have grown up in New England, but she understood where summer people stood. Same place they did in every other part of the country.

Rebecca was interested in this story.

"So, could you have married a Nichols, Daddy? Being from Maine?" she asked.

Abe rolled his eyes. "Not exactly, honey. Your grandfather wasn't born here—"

"Germany," Rebecca said. "Like her friend."

"Right, so I wouldn't be considered a real Down Easter by the people who weren't happy when one of them married her." Abe rolled his eyes at the matriarch.

The background recording of the *Messiah* stopped. Robert Nichols's voice rose, loud in the void.

"—beat some business sense into the government."

"You're right," Dennis said.

Robert turned to his brother-in-law. "How would you know? Huh? How would a failure like you know?" He chuckled at his malice before he addressed the table. "I meet with the governor tomorrow."

"Isn't it too early?" June asked. Teal watched the woman's head swivel from her husband to her mother-in-law.

The matriarch smiled with calm indulgence. "Let's not forget Robert understands the land is mine until I die."

"Let's not," Robert agreed, staring at his sister.

Forks scraped on porcelain plates and china cups clattered to rest on matching saucers. Someone coughed. A throat cleared.

"For unto us a child is born, unto us a son is given . . ." burst from the speakers to proclaim the promise and joy of the Christ child's birth.

The Nicholses' conversation resumed. Robert arbitrated the ebb and flow, locked in on his sister's eyes when she spoke, ignored his wife, snorted with derision whenever Dennis's mouth opened. Jamie and Lise exchanged the glances of cousins long accustomed to the family dynamic.

Robert surprised Teal with a transfer of his attention to her.

"Hawley said you were from Massachusetts." he said. "Boston."

"Yes," Teal allowed, wondering what could come next.

"City is a mess." He crinkled his face in a mean smile.

Gotcha, it said.

"Honestly, Robert." Meredith fanned a hand in her brother's direction. "Ignore him. Boston wouldn't let him develop his high-rise complex beside the Common a few years ago and he's still—"

"Oh, be quiet," Robert pounced on his sister's words.

Meredith looked murderous.

"The Friends of the Public Garden worked hard to defeat your proposal," Teal said. She could feel the desire to pick a fight. Robert Nichols brought it out in everyone. "They had my support. I don't believe anything made by man should be allowed to shadow the country's oldest public park."

Robert colored up a choleric purple. Tension rippled the Nichols table like the snap of towel. The pearl stud earrings and circle pins on the women, the camel hair sports jackets over crew neck sweaters on the men, the matriarch with her high-boned face and elegant wool challis dress, all these details accumulated into such a white and Anglo Saxon portrait of position and success. Whatever any individual family member thought of Robert, they did not welcome Teal's criticism.

No.

Lise broke the stiff silence. "So, Auntie June, when do I get to take you out to shoot?"

June giggled then, the most inappropriate, hysterical sound. She fought for her composure.

"I haven't held a gun in I don't know—"

"Since you refused to shoot because Dad—" Jamie

Nichols held his mouth open for a beat before he pressed it shut.

The matriarch rustled her bright shawl tighter around her shoulders. She stood. "Church in ten minutes, children. We shall meet in the hall."

She led the procession, her sharp brown eyes meeting Teal's for the moment she took to pass the windows.

"That's a contentious gathering of crack shots," Abe said as Lise, the last Nichols to clear the doorway, disappeared cradling her new weapon. Abe enjoyed the accuracy in his joke.

"The deer, targets and clays around here can't feel too safe," Teal agreed.

"Clays?" Rebecca asked. She squinted her eyes at her dad.

"Clay disks are used as targets in skeet," Teal said.

"What's skeet?" Rebecca asked.

"I'm no expert," Teal said, "but skeet started in Massachusetts early in this century. The clays are thrown from low and high trap houses to simulate the flight of a live bird."

Hunt's partner, BG, called himself a "middling fair wingshot" in the sport. Teal had seen BG compete. She had never pulled the trigger on a shotgun, herself. Never would.

"Skeet." Becca rolled the word through her mouth. "Sounds funny."

"Skeet is an old form of a Scandinavian word meaning 'to shoot'. Some woman suggested the name in a contest," Teal said. BG had told her the story.

"And biathletes cross-country ski to shoot at stationary targets, I know that," Rebecca said. She squinted at her father. "We aren't a gun family, are we."

"No," he said and shut his mouth.

Teal wondered what this discussion of sport shooting had become about, but she could not ask.

Hawley and May were back in the dining room.

"What's the word on the weather?" Teal asked.

"They're saying snow," Hawley said, the word *snow* rising and falling and rising in the accent of Maine.

"My joints are saying blizzard," May said. "Don't you go listening to him."

"We'd better get moving, Becca, if we want any time to explore," Abe said to his daughter.

"Isn't Bowdoin's campus closed?" Teal asked.

"The buildings, yes, but Becca's grandfather arranged an interview for her Monday morning when admissions is back. We thought we might get comfortable with the lay of the land today. What do you say, Bec?"

"Let's go, Dad!" she agreed enthusiastically.

"Excuse us," Abe said. Father and daughter left the table.

"Nice family," Hawley said as Abe and Rebecca went through to the stairs.

"Like the Nichols?" Teal offered.

"Uhmph." May raised her eyebrows and lowered them down. "She's a lovely woman, but that—"

"Robert still owns a good bit of hereabouts, May," Hawley warned his wife.

"What land is his mother's until she dies?" Teal asked, quoting the Nichols matriarch.

"One hundred twenty-five acres down to the Small Point area. Abuts the mountain and the state park," Hawley said.

"And goes right to the ocean?" Teal asked. "Part of the beach where the Piping Plovers nest in the summer?"

"A-yah," Hawley nodded. "Bit part. Least Terns, too. Heard he's thinking about doing some building—"

"But I thought it belonged to his mother," Teal said.

"It's a tangle of family trusts," May said, "and nothing Hawley and I understand. Could be it belongs to Robert is one of the rumors I've heard."

"Think I have time to get down to the peninsula to walk the state beach before the blizzard comes in?" Teal asked.

Hawley laughed. "You can try."

* * *

Teal's room, her favorite, was positioned on the first floor behind the stairs. It was actually an addition, the norm for New England houses of the vintage when another family member meant a new room built. The hall to get to it ran behind the staircase and across with a back connection between the front hall and the large common sitting room on the other side of the stairs. She could crack her door and hear, unseen, a good part of what went on in three locations: front hall, grand stairway, common room.

The perverse curiosity of someone who had hoped to be alone and found she was not prompted her to leave her door ajar as the Nichols clan gathered to attend their church service.

Robert came down first and ran into Abe on the stairs.

"Don't think you can talk my mother into a donation." Teal heard Robert say.

She eased closer to the open door. Abe's chuckle came relaxed and slow.

"You remember my father."

"Can't say he wasn't a man to try hard," Robert said in a good humored voice.

"Dad?" There followed the squeak and squeal of ancient stair treads as Rebecca bounced down the stairs. "Ready to go?"

"You bet, honey."

Teal could imagine Abe's skinny arm wrap around Rebecca's waist for a moment before his daughter squirmed away.

"Have a nice morning," Robert said.

"And you a Merry Christmas Day," the innocent Rebecca rejoined. A draft blew in with the jingle and bang open and close of the front door.

Teal heard more footfalls from above in the hall.

"Think you'll try your rifle out today?"

Teal recognized Jamie as the source.

"But you could go over to the skeet field, it's as good as owned by the family, you know," Jamie persisted. Lise must have shaken her head no.

The skeet field was across the road and maybe a quarter mile up, Teal remembered. She'd walked it in late summer, turning the stroll into a treasure hunt for intact orange clay pigeons. Argyle had been indifferent to the game; Hunt had been amused. That day the field had looked deserted, the signs and the trap houses shot with dents and holes.

"Dad!" Jamie's surprised voice interrupted Teal's thoughts.

"Planning to get your cousin in trouble?" Robert called up. "You know we're expected at the big house for a Christmas dinner after church."

"But I just thought," Jamie started, the tread of his feet on the stairs as he came down.

"You just thought wrong, son. Dead wrong. If you want to stay in business with me, you'd better start showing common sense. How do you think your grandmother would feel about you and Lise disappearing? Go find your mother!"

Thumps accompanied Jamie's return journey to the second floor.

"Why do you have to be so hard on everybody?" Lise asked.

She had guts, Teal decided.

"What do you mean, hard?" Robert demanded.

But Teal could imagine a satisfied smile on his face. Robert liked his reputation.

"Picking on Jamie, fighting with my dad, arguing with Mom—I don't know."

"Spoken like a true Nichols, Lise. Jamie needs to toughen up and get some sense kicked into his fool head," Robert responded.

"But Dad and Mom—"

"What about your mother and father, Lise, dear?" The matriarch's light, controlled footfall disturbed the stairs.

"Lise is chiding me for being hard on Dennis and my sister," Robert said.

"P-l-e-a-s-e," Lise moaned in an undertone.

"Well, where are they? And your wife, Robert?" The imperious voice gave no indication of her interest in the niece and uncle squabble.

"I'm here," June called down and followed her message at a trot.

"Robert James the Third! Meredith! Dennis!" The matriarch's voice penetrated the walls.

"Coming!" chorused from above.

"We shall take three cars to church," the matriarch instructed. "To make things easier at the big house if anyone needs to come back here early."

"I'll take you in my Jeep, Nana," Jamie offered.

"And me," Lise cut in.

"No darlings, I'd rather the Jaguar with Robert."

That must have settled the discussion, because a draft of cold air swirled around Teal's feet and the hall went quiet when the sleigh bells stopped ringing after the door slam.

Finally, Teal thought, as though the Nichols could be held responsible for her self-created delay. She'd wanted to hear every word, and more, she wanted to understand the spaces, the words unsaid.

Some people might have been appalled by this behavior from a certified public accountant and partner in a major international firm. Like Hunt. But Teal considered his lack of curiosity a human abnormality.

She added a scarf, watch cap, earmuffs and gloves to the pile with her down jacket. She found the sitting room fire no more than glowing ash, but she still enjoyed suiting up for the outdoors in the residual warmth. Hawley's old black and white pointer lay on the hearth, happily absorbing heat from the slab of granite. His thin tail thumped the stone as Teal approached. She knelt to scratch his splendid head. "How's it going, old boy?" she murmured.

Hawley had told Teal endless stories of hunting with

this dog, best he'd ever owned. Now the pointer enjoyed the life of the semi-retired, Hawley having given up hunting and the pointer having grown older.

Teal waved to May and Hawley through the windows to their private living rooms as she left the house. No snow had started to fall, and Route 209 through Bath and onto the Phippsburg peninsula was clean. Trees and house eaves were strung with Christmas lights and Santa with his reindeer decorated many front yards. The general store by Phippsburg center had a hand lettered sign, "Open Until Noon," propped against the gas pumps. Teal took the left there on Parker Head Road, the scenic route to Popham Beach State Park.

The state parking lot stood empty and the wind was whipping off the ocean with a howl when Teal got out. She pulled earmuffs over her watch cap and wrapped her face with the thick, cashmere scarf. No other soul braved the beach.

The tide was low, leaving the sand bar between the peninsula and small offshore islands exposed. Teal tucked her head down and started out. From the granite island, she could see what must be the Nichols property on the other side of the Morse River and past Seawall Beach.

Too far to walk, and impossible in any event with the river to cross. She'd done it twice in the summer, waded in and found herself waist deep, the current deliberate and strong, the other side more white sand, more Atlantic swells breaking. Further up the river was the landscape of an estuary and Morse Mountain. You could see land and ocean for miles from the top.

Today the view of the ocean would be snow gray, the sky a growing fog, but in the summer Teal had seen the ocean shine back sapphire under a cloudless day. Once, she and Hunt rented a canoe to paddle, not the famed Kennebec, but the gentle Morse. They had discovered a world of birds and reeds edged with trees and the mountain. This was a beautiful spot, open, undeveloped, accessible to naturalists for study and the unscientific to enjoy.

Teal hoped Robert Nichols would not find a way to ruin his family's companion land with hideous summer estates. What perverse impulse drove human beings to build for escape houses more suburban, more elaborate and more audacious than they often inhabited at home? She'd asked Hunt at least one hundred times and as many times he had shrugged.

No. Robert Nichols should not win. Teal wished the matriarch good health and a long life.

The bitter wind carried the damp of the ocean. The cold invaded Teal's fingers and joints, her flesh and bones. Her ears ached and her cheeks froze. A gust of spray hit her with frozen pellets of the churning Atlantic. The clouds coalesced into snow. One flake became one hundred, one thousand, one million, and Teal realized it was time to return to the inn.

A glaze of slick ice had formed on the road forcing her to take the ride north slowly. Impulse made her detour to get lunch at Ernie's Drive-In in Brunswick on Route 1. She and Hunt had discovered the drive-in, with its neon lit sign board hawking "CLAMS HADD SHRIMP SCALOPS" in abbreviated spelling, on their first trip to the area.

A thick ice cream shake and lightly battered clams in a basket under the car-port overhang wouldn't be much like the Huston family goose today, but it might make her feel at home. She found the lights on the sign board dark, and the flat roof crusted with a foot of old snow over an unploughed lot. No car-hop would be running out for her order. Teal did not stop the car.

She stayed with the road through Bowdoin Pines, the College's evergreen forest. She pulled over and gazed at the lovely scene of trees in the storm, trying to rouse some holiday emotion. Failing, she pulled a U-turn and headed back to where a McDonald's she had passed was open. Teal ordered a McLean without cheese and tea.

"Merry Christmas, dearie!" slid across the counter with her meager order.

The room was otherwise empty. She did not linger to enjoy the decor, but ate and left. The Inn welcomed her with an outside light and its picture-perfect look in the falling snow.

She kicked the snow from her boots at the front door, and slipped them off as she stepped inside. The sitting room was quiet—even the pointer gone from the fireside. She searched for a book and laid a new fire. The sounds of Hawley and May at the other side of the house drifted to her ears from time to time.

The warmth may have been the culprit, or her choice of reading, but she drifted into a pleasant nap on the old couch. The bang of the door and ringing sleigh bells jerked her awake with a shivering bump. The Nicholses were returning.

Jamie and Lise came in first. Jamie punched up the fire to a crackling roar while Lise broke out the cards.

"Hearts?" she invited Teal.

Teal shook her head and smiled. She loathed organized games and playing cards, another point of friction with Hunt. He would have said yes in an instant. Lise didn't seem to mind, but began the shuffle.

June startled the group by sticking her head around the door jamb from where she stood on the stairs. She must have been up above and napping herself since before Teal returned.

"Cards?" June said. "May I join you?"

"Sure, Mom," Jamie said and pulled another chair to the coffee table across from the couch.

"Have a nice time?" June asked.

Teal caught the glance between the cousins, the flicker of secret smiles before both said yes.

"Are you feeling better?" Lise asked.

"Thank you, dear, yes," June replied.

Rebecca came down the stairs next. The house was full of surprises, Teal realized.

"Would you like . . . ?" Jamie began to ask as Rebecca's eager assent cut him short.

"Hearts! I love Hearts!" Becca wriggled a chair to the table and flopped to the seat.

Ten minutes or more passed before Dennis, Meredith and the matriarch entered, scraping snow off their boots and shaking flakes from their coats. Lise was up and helping her grandmother settle into the wing back.

"Nana, you gave me the best present today," she said and added a hug.

"And where is it?" the matriarch asked, eyes bright and brows arched to match her smile.

"Where I left it." Lise took off at a trot and was back with the rifle before Teal had a chance to finish reading the sentence.

The matriarch stretched out both hands for the gun. "Lovely," she said, and from her the judgment did not sound wrong. The rifle was a piece of craftsmanship, the wood oiled to a fine polish, the metal well cast and precise. Still, a chill climbed Teal's spine. The gun represented a deadly art.

"Let me," Jamie said and reached to his grandmother.

She let the rifle pass to his hands. Dennis took it next to stick a thick finger through to the trigger. Meredith assessed the sights, then demonstrated her technique for felling a deer in one shot. June shivered and shook her head, but still grabbed the stock to pass the gun to Abe, who asked to see it.

The round of asking, passing and holding had Teal's stomach in a knot. All those muddle of hands, she thought, the wood and metal instrument going fingerprint to fingerprint, palm to palm. How silly of her, she chided herself, and listened in shock to her own voice pipe in.

"May I?" she asked.

"Sure!" Lise acted delighted by this new interest, and carried the gun from Abe to Teal. "No, no," Lise corrected, "hold it like this."

She adjusted Teal's right and left hands, smoothed the twist from Teal's shoulders and set Teal's near elbow. The rifle re-balanced to an easier fit. Teal could appreciate the difference. She was handing the gun back to Lise when they heard the pointer whine.

Jamie was the first to the back door. It opened into the room from a path out of the woods. The dog flashed through the room to find the only person he knew. He dropped his game in her lap and waited, tense with pride.

Teal touched the stiff edge of the red woolen cap. Her fingers came back smeared with blood. Teal raised her head.

Lise. Jamie. June. Rebecca. Dennis. Meredith. The matriarch. Abe. Hawley's voice raised to join May's in laughter from the kitchen. That accounted for ten.

Teal could do the math. She needed eleven.

"Where's Robert?" Teal asked. She turned to Jamie, to the matriarch. "Where's your father? Your son?"

Blind heads shook back, mouths slack in dread. Teal knew how to move fast.

"No, you stay here. Abe, don't let anyone leave the room until we . . . I come back."

Her duck boots were laced by the end of the sentence, her coat zipped to her chin. She pulled on gloves and fished Hawley's flashlight from out of the desk drawer.

"Come," she commanded the pointer, and he wagged his tail and dashed ahead of her out the back door.

Late afternoon held the woods in a dark shroud. The snow was coming faster now, a small drift growing larger at the turn in the road. The dog led with his sleek, dark head down and vivid against the snow. He understood where she wanted to go. His muscular body pushed through the pine forest until he stopped beside the body. Teal stopped short.

Blood foamed out of Robert Nichols's mouth, the bubbles frozen. She could see where the bullet of death had ripped into his chest.

The pointer knew something about this hunt was wrong. He sat on his haunches and stared at Teal with an expression of alert sadness. She did not need to search for a pulse. The woods were too dark and the snow too thick to follow any set of tracks but her own and the dog's, and they were being buried fast.

The conversation at breakfast, the tensions and hostilities overheard in the hall, Abe's joke about the contentious family of crack shots—the killer wasn't just somewhere. The killer was back there, waiting for her return to the house.

There was something else. When Teal had held Lise's new firearm, she had noticed the smell. This morning's pristine rifle had been fired.

"Teal? You thay-ah?" she heard Hawley's voice lift under the whistle of wind. The loyal hunter sprang from her side, his white body blurred into the storm while his dark head merged into a stand of dusky of tree trunks.

"Good boy!" Hawley's anxious voice affirmed. "Teal? I'm coming."

Her friend was beside her. "Jesus Christ!" he breathed.

"On Christmas," Teal said. "What do you think?"

Hawley understood. "Could be a .22 gauge."

"Like Lise's?" Teal asked to reinforce the question in her eyes with words.

"Mebbe. Mebbe not," but Hawley said it without faith.

"We need to call the police from the house," Teal said.

Hawley raised his head to squint into the sky. "It's coming down."

"So?" Teal said.

"So if some damned liquored-up fool's got in an accident, could be hours. Happens every time." Hawley snorted.

"Then we can't let any one of us out of our sight," Teal said.

"A-yah."

Teal stretched out her gloved palm. Flakes had it dusted with cartwheels of ice in a second.

"How will we ever find the body?" she asked.

Hawley tipped his head at the dog. "He won't forget."

The walk back was different from the way out. The walk back held certainty. No hope. No comfort. No joy. The day to rejoice in one son's birth had brought another son to a violent end.

May had joined the group in the sitting room, her hands busy working a skein of wool. Nine curious, apprehensive faces greeted their return. Hawley knelt to dry the pointer. Teal found the matriarch's eyes and spoke.

"I am so sorry, Mrs. Nichols. Your son."

The matriarch rose from her chair, her refined facade suddenly inelegant and contorted.

"Please," she said. "Where—"

"Nana! I'll go." Jamie rushed to the door.

Hawley's restraining arm barred Jamie's exit. "No, boy."

June swung her head to work the row, Hawley to Teal to Jamie. "But why not?" she said. "Let him go."

"Robert can't use Jamie's help. Robert is dead," Teal said.

"How can you know?" June asked, her skin as ashen as her hair, the words like dirt in her mouth.

"June's right. How can you be sure? Robert could need our help!" Dennis added a bullying voice.

Teal regarded mother, sister, son. Wife. Brother-in-law. Niece. The unrelated father and daughter. The innkeepers. Grief, shock, horror and curiosity remodeled the relaxed or bored or tense expressions of moments before. If only she could remember how each visage had greeted her return at the door. Too late.

"Too late," Teal said.

"But how can you know?" Dennis persisted. "Are you a doctor?"

"There's no mistaking murder," Teal said.

"Murder?' Lise gagged the word, her communication internal.

"How," Meredith asked, her voice a bark.

"Bullet to the chest. One shot." One shot accuracy, Teal realized, was nothing new for this crew.

Everyone was on his or her feet, shuffling like restrained dogs at the end of a leash, pointed toward Hawley still at the door. The pointer could not settle on the hearth, but quivered with excitement beside his master. Rebecca kept her eyes on her dad, the red climbing to stain her white cheeks crimson.

"We have to do something," Meredith instructed in a voice as strong as her brother's.

The family gravitated to the force she exerted, all but the matriarch who had dropped back down into her chair, hands clasped and head bowed in private prayer. Silent tears etched a trail of grief down each cheek. The shining drops splattered onto veined hands.

Teal took in these and other details as Hawley spoke.

"Have to call the sheriff," he said.

The gathered bodies parted when he stepped forward. No one spoke or coughed or fidgeted. Teal wondered if they had been as still in church.

Hawley's side of the discussion on the telephone held the attention of the room. You could have heard a pin drop, Teal thought. A log popped like a gun's retort. It took a moment to hear again, for the edgy group to settle.

"No sir, we didn't. Left him where he went down. Can't do much of a thing about critters—"

Here gasps sucked into every mouth. Teal had not thought of what could happen to a body left in the woods.

"—won't let a soul out. Understand about the pile up. Count on us." Hawley hung up the receiver. "Jaws of life," he said to explain the conversation.

Dennis broke first. "What's that supposed to mean?" he bullied.

So quickly free of his brother-in-law, Teal thought. So quick to assume Robert's style and position. Robert's demise offered Dennis a terrible release.

"Four car spin-out on the bridge to Georgetown," Hawley said.

"Too narrow, I always said, and dangerous in the cold." May continued to wring her skein of yarn to a snarl. "Anyone local?"

Hawley did not answer what he did not know, but finished his prepared statement. "Sheriff will try to get here before midnight, but you never know when it's bad. We're to stay together until he arrives."

"Are we suspects?" Lise asked. She darted her eyes from Hawley to the Anschutz rifle and back to Hawley. Her palms scrubbed across her pants. Up and down, up and down.

"Sheriff asked that we stay together, is all," Hawley repeated.

"Well I'm damned well sick of cards," burst from June. She threw her hand to the air, the stiff paper rectangles gliding to spread across the floor. Jamie took his mother in his arms. June's sobs were horrible to hear. Jamie's jaw clenched and tears leaked from his eyes. Meredith pulled a handkerchief out and laid her face down in cupped palms. Dennis rubbed her back in circular sweeps.

Rebecca moved to stand close beside her father, Abe's arm around her waist as she bit at her lips.

Teal did not want the group to stay in the sitting room or any part of the house they may have been in and out of today. Crucial evidence could be shifted, hidden or destroyed before the sheriff arrived. She wanted an opportunity to speak with each of them alone, and yet she hoped to keep everyone together.

Robert Nichols, Jr., murdered, had not been a festive sight.

"We have to do something to keep occupied," Teal said.

"Not cards." Lise looked down at her aunt's mess.

"Let's make May's mincemeat recipe," Teal suggested.

Heads whipped around and up, expressions of grief changed to shock, mouths opened and groaned.

"How could you?" Meredith jerked out of her mouth. "When my dear brother—"

"Your dear brother? Don't make me sick," June said.

"Please." The matriarch loosened her body from Jamie's support. "Ms. Stewart has a point. We need to keep busy. Can we help with the mince, May?"

May laid her jumbled wool on the table. "Yes. Help is always appreciated."

Hawley did not waste time with maintaining pleasantries. He bolted the sitting room exit and, like a good shepherd, circled the group, easing them across the hall and through the dining room into the big, open kitchen. The pointer, not being a sheep dog, was indifferent to herd duty. He trailed the group and settled beside the wood stove.

May fetched the deer neck from the refrigerator and laid it on the counter for Jamie to bone.

"Gross," Rebecca whispered to her father. The word carried through the room.

"Not a bit, my dear. Genuine deer neck mincemeat is ambrosia, if a treat of the past." The matriarch spoke through rigid lips, game to carry out the pretense.

She knew, Teal realized. The matriarch knew one among them was a killer. Perhaps they all knew.

"Chop tonight," Hawley said, "pie tomorrow."

He must have read her mind, Teal thought, as he set to organize the gathering into individual work stations. Easy one-on-one conversing places. Jamie already was pulling the boning knife across the wet stone.

Hawley set out two old-fashioned crank grinders and a food processor in a row. May moved Dennis to the first and showed him how to feed the hopper and rotate the handle to pulverize Jamie's strips of venison to hash. Two turns and blood was running down the crank shaft. May handed Teal a list of ingredients for Lise to fetch out of the cold pantry. Teal read the paper, first, herself.

Two quarts of winter apples (Baldwin, Cortland, Golden Delicious, Ribston, Florence, Red Siberian, among others), 1 quart of sugar, 1 cup cider vinegar, 1 teaspoon black pepper, 1 teaspoon salt, 1 cup molasses, 1 whole nutmeg grated, 2 teaspoons cinnamon, 1 tablespoon allspice, 1 teaspoon cloves, 1 cup suet pressed through the grinder. The nutmeg alone would keep Lise occupied.

Rebecca and June accepted the task of grinding or processing the apples. May had Meredith half fill one pot with water and bring it to a simmer for the venison. Abe placed a second kettle on the wood stove for cooking the mince. He prepared to travel between the counter and the kettle and stir in the ingredients as each became ready.

The matriarch held the place of honor in the rocking chair. Hawley and May busied themselves with guiding and instructing. The cooking project was in process.

Teal caught Lise alone in the pantry. She placed herself as an effective blockade to moving freely into the kitchen.

"Did you sing your favorite hymns in church this morning?" Teal asked. She'd had favorites.

Lise, surprised, smiled. "Yes. Some of Jamie's and Mom's, too. We're considered the family chorus."

"Good party at the big house?"

"Okay," Lise said, more uncomfortable now. She occupied herself with getting the molasses down, pulling a measuring cup out.

"Need help?"

Lise pursed her lips to a no, but her eyes blinked with less certainty. Teal seized the moment.

"Jamie told me you snuck away. Had to try the new .22 today. It's a beautiful piece of craftsmanship."

Teal watched her gamble pay off. Lise's hand trembled, and a thread of molasses pooled on the floor. The looks the cousins had exchanged in the sitting room had meant what she thought.

"Did he tell you he went next?" Lise mumbled into her knees where she bent to wipe up the mess.

"No, he didn't," Teal answered with honesty.

"Well, if he wants to go ratting on me, he could at least confess himself," Lise spit out. "You really think one of us killed my uncle?"

"Did you like him?"

Lise straightened. She was taller than Teal, maybe 5'9" to Teal's 5'7". She was younger by a good ten years. Her training and discipline as a biathlete made her stronger and tougher. But she was much, much angrier, and lost her caution.

"He was a perfect bastard to everyone, including me sometimes, but I didn't count that much. Not like June or Dennis or Jamie. That's why he was relatively nicer to me today."

"What about your mother?" Teal asked.

"Mother could handle Uncle Robert's mean streak. I don't know how—she has it herself maybe. Anyway, Uncle Robert never teased or humiliated Mom to the same extent as he did the rest of us on a bad day."

"How did you like the rifle?"

Lise lifted the cup of molasses. "It shoots straight."

"Did it shoot straight into your uncle?"

Lise lowered pale lashes over her fawn eyes to hide their shift from Teal's face. "I wouldn't know. I left it in the hallway for Jamie where we had agreed and went back up to the big house."

Jamie, finished with separating the flesh from the bone, was cutting the meat into manageable strips. The whine of the food processor and May's CD player crowded the kitchen with noise. Teal stood by Jamie's ear, the one away from Dennis.

"Enjoy taking a few shots at the clay today? What's

the difference when you use bullets instead of shot?" she asked.

Jamie turned his head to stare at his mother.

He had some elements of his father's face. The prominent nose, the chiseled lips, but where Robert's had curled with malice, Jamie's were soft like June's.

"Did she go with you to throw up the clays?"

Teal knew the trap houses weren't set up to work in the winter, but she'd found unbroken disks in the skeet field. Argyle, being a sight hound, never could be engaged in a game of run-fetch. She had settled for hurling the disks at a tree to watch them break into smithereens. How much more satisfying it must be to shoot up puffs of orange dust.

Jamie might have thought so.

"Isn't shooting clay a sacrilege with a target gun?"

Jamie moved his shoulders.

"Did your mother go with you to throw disks?" Teal repeated.

Jamie gave up catching June's eye.

"Yes."

"Have fun?"

He shrugged. "It's really a biathlon rifle."

"Did your mother try it out today? After you?"

"Mom?" Jamie sounded surprised. "No."

"Why not?" Teal asked.

"Because she doesn't shoot anymore. Dad humiliated her during competition at our club and she finally stood up to him, wouldn't take it," Jamie said, the words coming hot and fast. A shadow dimmed his face like he realized this was not such a great answer.

"Did he humiliate you?" Teal asked. "Did you still take it?"

Jamie jerked the blade through the venison and a fillet fell free.

"Yes."

"Any chance you tried the gun out on him, a live target?" Teal suggested.

Jamie stabbed the knife at the meat. Another slice

dropped from the bigger piece. Jamie's mouth closed. The interview was over.

The smell of spiced and sweetened ground apples growing warm filled the kitchen. Steam rose from the venison water to fog the windows. Here and there condensation turned to spider webs of frost on the panes of glass. Hawley broke out a glass gallon of applejack, his home brew, from the garage. A good measure went into the apple kettle and another into one of the glasses May put on the counter. The matriarch took him up on the offer. June and Dennis and Jamie said yes, while Meredith compressed her lips to a line and declined.

Teal accepted a glass. The applejack burst with flavor and a fearsome kick.

Lise stirred a handful of currents and citrus into the kettle. May added shots of rum and brandy.

Despite the bustle of group activity and the delicious smells, no Christmas cheer lightened the atmosphere.

June wasn't hard to ease aside by herself. She wanted to enjoy her drink away from family eyes, may have wanted to enjoy one ever since this morning, Teal decided.

"How was dinner?" Teal asked. "Does the big house serve good wine?"

June's small tongue flicked a topaz drop of liquid from the glass rim.

"Not to me." Her eyes challenged Teal to ask why.

"Did you find anything to satisfy you here when you came back early?" Teal asked, instead. The why was evident in the web of broken capillaries beside June's nose.

Teal knew Hawley and May kept their liquor cabinet locked. It had to do with all their various liabilities as inn-keepers. June must have been disappointed coming back after throwing clay for Jamie. No wonder she had chosen sleep. Or had she?

"Robert hated your drinking—"

"My weakness." June curled her lip at unpleasant memories.

"Did he cut you off this Christmas with the family?"

"Yes." June laughed, emboldened by the burn of Hawley's blend. "Clever Robert, out to save me from myself."

"He'd be furious at you right now."

"But he's dead," June observed, her smile up to her eyes now. "He's not here to stop me. Never will be again." Her voice ended with a satisfied sigh.

"Did you use Lise's rifle to get rid of your husband?" Teal asked. "Let Jamie drop you off here with the gun, then turn around and go back out alone?"

June's pupils squeezed to the size of a pin. Her expression went sour. She gulped the last liquid from the glass.

"You can't prove it," she snarled. She scurried her body past Teal and back to Hawley for a refill.

What a family, Teal thought.

Dennis's hands dripped with blood. He handed the last grind of meat to Abe and moved to the sink.

"Was this Meredith's deer?" Teal asked as he scrubbed.

"Mine," Dennis said. His jaw worked at milling his teeth.

"So all the joking of this morning aside, you aren't a bad shot."

Dennis turned a pugnacious face to Teal. "No."

"Do you think Robert meant to develop the peninsula?" Teal asked.

"Not without Meredith and me, he wasn't," Dennis said.

"Could you have stopped him from cutting you out?"

Dennis dried his hands on a linen towel dotted with jolly Santas. He rubbed each finger and both palms twice before he draped the towel over its rack.

"We won't have to find out, will we?" he said.

"Did you leave the big house this afternoon to come down early?" Teal asked.

"Why would I tell you?" Dennis asked.

He blew wet breath into her face. He edged his groin closer to her hips. She knew the type—a secret pinch on the subway, a covert rub on a crowded street. The first to protest, "Not me." He thought he was enticing, sexy.

"I bet Robert didn't appreciate you," Teal said, her voice smooth and provocative. Why not use his vanity?

Dennis nodded, eager. "That's what I told him in the . . ."

Dennis let his mouth sag before it snapped closed. Teal dropped her attention to his feet, the duck boots he wore. Mud lined the seams. A leaf stuck out from near his right arch.

"Woods? Before the snow?" Teal asked. He should have taken them off at the door.

Dennis's piggy eyes flared.

"Ask him no questions, and he'll tell you no lies," Meredith said behind Teal.

Teal spun around and gave a good imitation of a laugh. "And is the advice as true for you?"

"Tut-tut," Meredith chided. "You're asking a question. And I can guess the next one. Where was I when my dearly beloved brother died?"

Meredith qualified as a handsome woman. Her brother's strength, her mother's poise, a head of sable hair swept off her face, her mahogany eyes deep with secrets.

"He was an absolute, total prick. Would have screwed his own grandmother. No, no, I'm lying. Would have screwed me. He tried once, to tell the truth. I was nine, he was fifteen. Father took him to the woodshed on that one."

Teal waited for the pause to settle Meredith. "And your mother?"

Meredith looked at the upright figure in the rocker. "Mother did not know."

"Tell me about the land in Phippsburg," Teal suggested.

"Beautiful, isn't it? Nicholses possess so many things of beauty, except our souls. Poor mother, marrying into this. She sure confused the home folks. She had studied art in Germany, wanted to take in a German Jew during the war. The friend she mentioned this morning. You can imagine the reaction."

"Yes," Teal said. She wanted to think her family would have been different, she would have been different.

"But you want information on the land," Meredith said.

"Yes," Teal said with more ease.

"We are a family of trusts and distrusts, nothing ever inherited outright, nothing possessed individually. The land on the peninsula has belonged to the Nicholses since we arrived here in the 1600s. Mother, through Father's will, has an interest during her lifetime. She wants to donate it to the Preserve." Meredith snickered. "Protect the birds."

"What did Robert think?" Teal asked.

"Robert thought he wouldn't burden her with the truth. She couldn't give the land over. She really is more a conservator than an owner, not being born a Nichols. Robert hired lawyers. There is a chance he had a legitimate claim to overturn her control." Meredith blinked. "I rooted for her to give it away when I knew Robert would stop her."

Teal did not need to say what both of them were thinking. Meredith's reality was not pretty.

"Were you out alone in the woods today?" Teal asked.

"As a matter of fact, yes. I drove down here to get my pills. Nothing life threatening, but required daily. Anyway, Lise's gun and the box of Fiocchi ammo was in the hall." Meredith opened her dusky eyes to Teal. "How could I resist such perfection?"

"Did you kill your brother?"

"What an ugly suspicion." And Meredith laughed. Roared, actually, and swung away from Teal.

The buzz of activity in the kitchen reduced to a dull hum as the assigned tasks were done. May added a few tablespoons of thick boiled cider and the cooked venison to the apple mix. Twelve hours at a slow simmer on the wood stove, and tomorrow they'd be making pies.

Not all of them, though, Teal thought. Not the killer.

Lise cleared the kitchen table and organized another game of cards. Teal drew a free chair to the matriarch's side. The cherry rocking chair did not slow.

"I am terribly sorry," Teal said.

"Do you have children?" the matriarch asked from a stiff mouth. "A son?"

"No," Teal said.

"A husband?"

"No."

The rocker made the knock of wood on wood. Voices raised in playing at Hearts. The kettle hissed with a gentle bubble.

"Will it be hard?" the matriarch asked.

Teal inhaled and spoke as she let the breath go. "Yes. The gun—all that passing around—fingerprinting will not help. The motive—" Teal dipped her head toward the players. "Everyone in the family seems to have a good one. They all left the big house—"

"Even me," the matriarch interrupted. "I came down to escape my husband's brother for an hour."

Her brown eyes were as still as a pond, and as wet.

"Did you love your husband?" Teal asked.

The matriarch stopped rocking. She leaned forward. Teal could not explain her response, but she took the older woman's dry, warm hand into her own.

"Too much, perhaps," the matriarch said. "He was my world."

Her laugh came soft and fast with an edge of bitterness and a measure of sorrow.

"His family hated me. I brought ideas and notions from the outside to stimulate his mind. He loved me enough to fight and win. You cannot imagine how happy we were . . ."

"How did he die?" Teal asked this woman who had lost father, husband, son.

"Off the peninsula in Phippsburg. I fussed with the

picnic on the shore. He and Robert sailed in the new boat. She had a shallow draw and when they were done with the race, a race just for fun against friends, they planned to pull up the centerboard and join me on our beach. I waited and waited. Darkness fell before Robert arrived alone and fighting a broken boom. He told a terrible story of when the boom swung free of the mast and lifted my husband off the deck."

The matriarch held Teal's hand in a vise grip.

"Robert was fifteen. He'd spent an extra hour trying to find his father's body, bring it home to me. Two weeks later, my husband washed up on the sand on our beach. What was left of him. He's buried on that land. He wanted to be."

The rocking resumed. The hand pulled free. The tears flowed.

"Please ask Abraham to come sit with me," the matriarch said in a quiet and controlled voice.

Teal did as she'd been told. Abe replaced her in her seat and she settled into his beside the kitchen window. The sky still poured with snow. Wind howled in the chimney. Hawley stoked the wood stove to last a few hours. May played cards. The pointer waved his feet, a prince of hunters in his dreams.

Teal did not need to wonder what the matriarch was saying to Abe. The pair did not talk, but sat in a silence more companionable than speech. Hawley laid out a short buffet of Christmas's remains. Cold turkey, crusty rolls, lettuce. He found two bags of chips in the pantry. The group approached the spread in waves, hungry enough to eat and guilty enough to show remorse. The matriarch and Abe stayed away.

Rebecca brought her sandwich and sat with Teal.

"What are they doing?" Rebecca whispered.

"Mourning what is dead," Teal said.

"Robert?"

"Yes, and his father and your mother."

"My mother? But she's alive," Rebecca said in alarm.

"Yes," Teal reassured the girl. "But sometimes the

end of a relationship cuts as deeply as death. I think for your father, that is how the divorce hurt."

Becca held her breath and stared at Teal. "Is that why he refuses to ever see her, even when she comes for me?"

"Could be," Teal said. "I'm only guessing from what I saw in him this morning, how I've felt myself.'

One thing she never had felt. Hunt never overtook her life, her identity. He brought her joy and happiness, caused pain and anger, yes, but had total devastation come with his withdrawal? Teal observed the matriarch and Abe locked in their dark and personal sorrows. No. Not that.

"I think it makes him crazy, that Mom remarried. It makes me crazy," Becca said with the candor of seventeen. "Her husband doesn't want anything to do with me. He doesn't like kids. He wanted this Christmas to be me-free." Rebecca sighed.

"Some people are better at being half a couple than a member of a family," Teal said.

"Think that was true of Mary and Joseph?" Rebecca asked.

She took a bite of her sandwich. This girl would survive Abe and her mother and Mom's new spouse just fine, Teal decided.

"That's a question I never asked about the Christmas story," Teal said, and they both grinned.

May's cookies on the kitchen table lured Becca back to the card game. Hawley got to the telephone on the first ring.

"Ay-yah," he said to the unheard voice. He put a palm over the mouthpiece. "Sheriff."

"May I talk to him?" Teal said.

The electricity in her words circulated like a jolt of current around the room. Hawley motioned to her to take the extension in the front hall. Her conversation did not last long.

"He'll be here within the hour," Teal said as she returned to the kitchen.

"Well, I'm not staying cooped up with the rest of you until he comes," Dennis said. "I'm going to my room."

Try and stop me read his expression. But Teal didn't want to. There was nothing to stop. What had been done was done, if not yet finished.

With Dennis out, the game broke apart. Lise and Jamie stooped to kiss their grandmother before they slipped away to the stairs. Meredith and June helped May tidy up.

"Will Lise get her gun back now?" Meredith asked. She had the dishtowel strangled in her hand, fist to hip.

"Eventually, I should think," Teal said. "Not in time for competition this winter."

"Maybe I'll suggest Mother give her another. Lise's a damned good shot."

"You all are," Teal said.

"Kind of makes laying blame difficult." Meredith's smile carried a chill as she hung the towel and walked out.

June poured herself another measure of rum. The applejack had been the starter, not the finish. She drank and cried at the empty table. Swallows and snivels. The matriarch rose with a gesture of impatience.

"Go to your room, June. A public display is in—"

"Bad taste?" The red lines curled like tendrils through the whites of June's eyes. "I'm a widow. I don't have a father for my son. I don't know what I'll do tomorrow." June progressed to hysterical gulps. Nothing was going to move her away from the supply of kitchen rum. Abe lay a kind hand on the matriarch's back.

"You could go to the sitting room," he said. "None of us will bother you."

Her dignity did not erode with anguish. "Thank you," she said. "To wait alone will suit me." She stopped to address Teal. "You won't tell me? His mother?"

"It isn't my place," Teal said. "I could be mistaken. The police will have science on their side, a plan for their investigation . . ."

The matriarch's touch brushed her cheek as light as the wing of a dove. "You are right, my dear. I should not have presumed—but my family . . . is destroyed. I'm not sure I can take more."

Teal wished she could change the outcome for everyone today. Wished Robert Nichols had been a different kind of son, a better husband, a loving father, an affectionate brother, a compassionate brother-in-law, an indulgent uncle. But Meredith had summed the truth of him to a different total. He'd been none of the above.

He had been a human being, though. An individual with an individual death. Civil society demanded someone be charged, the murderer convicted. Even for a Robert, someone must pay.

June carried her glass and bottle up the back stairs. Abe and Rebecca took the route through the dining room. Hawley and May went to the section of the house they called their own home. Like the matriarch in the sitting room, Teal needed the time alone. She shut off the kitchen overhead and watched the shadows cast by the wood stove flame where its light leaked around the door.

Outside, the blizzard faltered as the clouds broke and moved north. One star shone in an open patch of sky. The Kennebec River caught the reflection of broken light. Ice crusted the banks, but the swift river flowed.

Robert had been scheming to sell the land his forefathers once settled as home. The land of his father's headstone. He was a man to cut his sister and brother-in-law out of the deal. He badgered and harassed his wife and son. Fawned over and ignored his mother with a calculated hypocrisy. Murder became his judge in the end.

Who would judge his murderer?

The clouds continued to dissipate although dark patches remained to veil the road and obscure the path to the river bank. Teal heard the siren before she saw the flashing light, the cautiously proceeding police car. A minute or less would bring the rule of human law to the Inn.

The pointer stirred and sighed and did not follow Teal from the kitchen. She worked to keep her footfall light across the dining room, past the grand stairway, over to the common sitting room. Teal did not want to consider her motive. Earlier, when the matriarch had asked for knowledge, Teal had refused.

The wing chair faced the dwindling fire, away from Teal in the doorway. The matriarch did not show at all except in the drape of her bright shawl over one chair arm. Teal hesitated, then pressed out her right foot and moved on tiptoes. The matriarch did not evidence an awareness of Teal's careful approach. Teal stopped before she had to look into the chair. Into the face of woe.

"I had hoped I would not find you here," Teal said in an undertone, but her voice echoed and reverberated in the still room.

The shawl moved, the chair creaked as its occupant stood.

"I entered with the same hope."

Abraham extended his hand to Teal and she grasped it, the fingers cool and strong. Together they walked to the back door to watch the police pull into the drive. The matriarch's small boots had left childlike dents in the snow. Some prints were blown over, but Teal could read the faint trail to where the path which ended at the river entered the woods.

The pressure of Abe's compassion held Teal close.

"I thought, at first, she shed tears of mourning," Teal said. "Not the tears of memory and the terrible release for a mother who killed her son. Killed him deliberately."

The police climbed out of their car and started for the front door.

"Do you think he pulled the wings off butterflies when he was young?" Teal asked. Abe's wool shirt scratched her cheek, kept her focused. "He was going to sell his father's grave."

Abe rocked his head. "Her husband's brother told her the truth today. That Robert had legal rights under the trust, that he could make the sale."

"And that was too much," Teal said. "How long had she suspected, I wonder? Held off the taint of knowledge that her son had killed his father? She knew why, though. She had been filled with guilt for years for loving her husband too much and her children too little. She had not protected her daughter, had ignored the cruelties of her son. He brought her punishment."

"With a terrible result," Abe said.

The police were banging on the front door. Teal heard Hawley's foot step, the shake and clatter of jingle bells as the door opened and shut.

"What will you tell them?" Abe asked.

"The truth," Teal said. "But I plan to take my time."

Abe sighed and turned from the back door, his back to the footsteps filling slowly with the last of the storm's snow.

"Think she'll be found?" he asked.

Teal had her nose against the glass. Her breath fogged the distant river until it no longer glittered.

"The river should take her to the sea. She'll wash up on the peninsula in a few weeks. On her beach."

"Like her husband."

"Yes," Teal said.

One son had brought the hope of salvation and rebirth to the world. The matriarch's son had brought iniquity.

Abe pulled Teal around to face him.

"She was at peace. She told me she was done with second guessing. None of us can be sure of the outcome when we start a life."

"Not even Mary?" Teal asked. "With the Messiah?

Abe smiled. "We Jews still wait. She advised me to be patient."

Deep and Crisp and Even

by James R. McCahery

For Three Lovely Ladies at Christmas:
Kathleen Anderson, Mary Connaughton, Mary Ottino

Five inches weren't too bad. Not considering the snowfall they had predicted.

In her still-darkened living room Lavina London peered out the picture window that faced what in better weather was clearly the side lawn of her lakefront home. The partially drained lake off to her right was already frozen some three or four feet around its bank. Fortunately, the narrow road that surrounded it had already been plowed, the blacktop ribbon the only color now against the pervasive sheet of white. That, and the area immediately outside her two-car garage on the opposite side of the road. The only problem she'd have at this end would be making it out of the house and up to the road. The feeder road leading out to old Rt. 17, she knew, would be cleared as well, as would the highway itself into Monticello.

She pulled back her short-cropped steel-gray head from the icy window pane and padded over in her white furry scuffs to the wall thermostat, which she proceeded to turn up a few notches from its nightly sixty-four. Fortunately, the members of her family who had been at her home since Christmas Eve for her annual holiday festivities were still all asleep. If her daughter knew she intended going out in weather like this to Mass, the woman would have one of her conniptions. But, then, that was Tracey. What the woman didn't know wouldn't hurt her. And would certainly save Lavina an unnecessary argument that she would have won anyway. Her son-in-law, Damian, and granddaughter, Susanne, on the other hand, would understand completely. Even at seventysomething, Lavina had her priorities. Starting her day off with Mass and Communion was one of them. She smiled now at the thought as she went back through the dimly lit kitchen up to her bedroom above the kitchen and back porch. It was the last thing Ken had added after converting their summer home to an all-year-round residence. He had died shortly after, of a cerebral hemorrhage.

Once upstairs, she looked out her bedroom window in the rear of the house toward the lake. The picture-card winter scene brought a smile to her lips. The white-clad evergreens glittered in the moonlight. It was a shame the snow hadn't come a day earlier, providing the proverbial White Christmas. As far as she could see from the surrounding darkness, she was the only one up and about. Not that that surprised her any, of course. At five-fifteen in the morning, most of her neighbors would probably just be smacking their snooze alarms in annoyance in an attempt at putting off the start of another day for as long as they could. Precisely what day that was, however, suddenly dawned on her. The feast of St. Stephen, the first martyr. She'd have to remember to wear something red in appreciation of the occasion. As she pulled away from the window, she began to hum the carol that unconsciously entered her mind:

Good King Wenceslas looked out
On the feast of Stephen,
When the snow lay round about,
Deep and crisp and even . . .

The snow was that, all right. She smiled at the all-round appropriateness of the carol as she headed for her bath, untying the corded belt of her lavender chenille robe as she went along.

Once she was showered and dressed she went back

downstairs to work her feet into the rubber Totes boots she had dug out of the hall closet, then shrugged into her insulated brown carcoat. She returned to the kitchen, grabbed her keys off their hook on the wall, and after turning out the light, headed back to the front door. If she was lucky, the rest of the family would be up by the time she got back, with coffee already made.

The engine of the blue Tempo turned over without the slightest hesitation and within five minutes it was out on the highway, its low beams the only light on the deserted highway. The snow had obviously been dry enough to facilitate the early-morning plowing, leaving no wet, icy residue. Damian would be glad of that when it came time for him to clear the paths around her home. The poor man. Here he was up from the city for the holidays stuck with having to do her shovelling, a chore he always boasted of avoiding by living in an apartment. She shook her head at the thought as she kept her eyes firmly on the road.

As expected, the trip was safe and uneventful, and she tossed up a thankful prayer to her guardian angel as she pulled up to the mounded deposit of plowed snow alongside the curb in front of the church. She could have parked in the cleared church parking lot, of course, but she always preferred the street; it required less walking on her part once she got out.

She was headed toward the front entrance of the church when she heard the light banging down past the rectory and grammar school in the vicinity of the parking lot. Dull, resonant, and at regular intervals, like a hesitant drummer trying to keep in cadence with his fellow instrumentalists. She walked back out toward the sidewalk to see if she could get a better view of the area down to her right. Once she spotted the tractorless van that had been set up in the lot for the collection of used newspapers, she knew what it was. Someone had left the rear door unlatched and it was now swinging on its hinges, alternately slapping open and closed in the wind.

Maybe it was a sign of things to come. Weatherwise, that is.

Lavina sighed. So much for saving steps. She turned and headed in the direction of the stationary vehicle. Once she reached the area just beyond the brick school building and turned in off the sidewalk, she found herself in snow again. Whoever had left the door unlatched obviously had been here before the snow ended because the impressions of footprints were almost completely covered over again by fresh snow. They recalled later lines of the Wenceslas carol:

In his master's steps he trod,
Where the snow lay dinted;
Heat was in the very sod
Which the saint had printed.

She smiled as she deliberately set her booted feet in the earlier imprints that led her up to the long, low white van. When she reached the banging door, she held it partially open and looked inside. People, she noticed, were still leaving their bundled-up stacks of old newsprint directly on the floor inside the door instead of taking the time and effort to go up the little set of steps into the van and stack them up toward the front. She was about to excoriate whoever was guilty in her mind when it dawned on her that many, if not most of them, were probably not quite as agile as she was assuming they were. After all, she probably wouldn't have ventured the feat herself if she were of a mind to drop off papers for recycling. Which, of course, she wasn't. She always rolled her own weekly collection of *The Record* for use in her fireplace during the long, cold months of winter. "Killing two birds" is what her neighbor and best friend, Winnie O'Kirk, always called it, however mixed the metaphor might have been.

She closed the tall unwieldy door now, and then, going up two of the steps outside, carefully fastened the metal latch, making it impervious to the wind. It was when she turned to come down again that she noticed it for the first time. A stretch of snow at the bottom of the steps off to the side of the van was not quite as the St. Stephen's Day carol would have it. Deep and crisp, yes, but hardly even. It looked as if someone had just dropped stacks of papers outside as well, not even bothering to hoist them up into the van. The ensuing snow had whitewashed the careless sin of omission.

Lavina realized she was in the process of passing judgment again—more fodder for Father Cernac at her next confession—when the shape of the uneven snow sidetracked her. It was something she couldn't have seen as well at ground level, certainly; it was the aerial sort of view that did it. The hilled-up snow below had a strange if familiar shape. Almost like a person lying under the snow in a fetal position. *My God! Had some poor homeless soul fallen asleep out here? Or gone to sleep in the van and then fallen out and knocked himself unconscious? Ended up blanketed by the fallen snow? Maybe even suffocated by it?* The thought frightened and unnerved her. She looked around to see if any of her fellow parishioners were yet in sight. Unfortunately, there was no one. She checked her watch. It was still only six-fifteen. Father Cernac probably wouldn't even have the church open yet. He usually did the honors around six-thirty. This morning, of course, Lavina had left a little earlier than usual because of the weather, figuring she might be delayed on the roads. She always liked to get to church in time to say her rosary before the beginning of Mass.

She made her way gingerly down the steps in a sideward fashion, wishing there were a handrail. When she was on ground level again alongside the odd-shaped mound, she bent down. With her gloved right hand she brushed lightly at the section of the heap she took to be the head. It wasn't long before the dry snow was whisked away, exposing what she had feared. Her gasp was loud and clear, even to her. It was like watching herself in a movie. She could feel her heart speed up and pound as she continued to brush away at the now-exposed head.

It was that of a man, a young man, mid to late thirties, his grayless hair a rich, dark brown, parted in the middle. The gaunt face was white, obviously drained of blood in the cold. Or was it just a question of lividity? There was no way of knowing by mere appearances whether or not he was still alive. She bent closer to see if she could detect any movement, any sign of life at all. Nothing. Nothing visible to her, at least. The breath she saw against the cold morning darkness was obviously her own. Unfortunately, her reading glasses were still tucked inside her jacket on their chain so her vision at that close range wasn't all that good to begin with.

She removed a glove and with trepidation felt under the turtleneck sweater along both sides of the young man's neck for the carotid arteries and signs of a pulse. If there was one, she certainly couldn't find it. Maybe her hands were just too numb from the cold, or maybe she was just too nervous. Somehow, she didn't think either was the case.

Still down on her haunches, she pulled back and uttered a deep sigh. When she finally decided to rise again, it took a real effort. There were some aspects of her age that even she had no control of. Not that she would have admitted it in public, of course. She looked down again to the exposed portion of the body beneath her. From the looks of what she could see of the man's clothing, he wasn't your stereotypical homeless at all, if indeed that's what he was. Come to think of it, maybe he was a regular parishioner, one she simply didn't know. Maybe he had simply taken a nasty fall after dropping off his bundle of papers. After all, she could hardly be expected to know everyone at St. Michael's, even though most of them probably knew her. Over the years Lavina London, retired actress, had been on radio and television broadcasts too numerous to mention. For that reason alone it was nigh impossible not to recognize her name, if not her face, if you lived anywhere within the news range of Sullivan County. Not to mention the notoriety she had received of late as a result of the help she had given the county Sheriff's Office in solving a few of its recent murders. Sheriff Tod Arthur, of course, might not put it quite that way.

Shoving her bare hand into her glove again, Lavina turned and made her way back in the direction of the rectory for help, thinking that maybe there was an even better reason why she hadn't recognized the young man. Maybe he was the newly ordained transitional deacon St. Michael's had been expecting. She knew he was due sometime Christmas night because Father Cernac had announced it only yesterday at Christmas Mass. The man was originally supposed to have arrived sometime back in mid October for an assignment that was to have extended into mid May, at which time he was to be ordained to the priesthood. Unfortunately, he had been taken ill; it was only recently that he had been pronounced well enough to assume the assignment. Perhaps he had suffered a relapse of some type. She stabbed a gloved finger at the buzzer outside the rectory door. She had no idea of the nature of the man's illness to begin with, so there was no way of telling. The more she thought of it, though, the more unsure she became. What would the seminarian be doing down at the newspaper van in the first place, she wondered, looking back again in the direction of the accident. It probably wasn't him at all.

As she waited for some sign of life inside the dark rectory, she began to stamp her feet against the cold. It was the first time she had noticed it since she left the house. Maybe her blood wasn't circulating properly as a result of the unexpected shock, or maybe the cold was somehow affecting her old pump. She peered past a thick rhododendron bush with its now heavily curled leaves through the unlighted front window. The only thing she was able to make out on the other side of the flimsy white ninon curtain was a blooming Christmas cactus on the window sill.

More impatient than ever, she reached over and stabbed again at the buzzer, this time holding her finger down longer. She could hear the strident ringing inside. If the priest didn't answer soon, she could only assume he had gone to the hospital on an early call. The pastor, she knew, was away for the remainder of the week, having left yesterday after the last Mass. Father Cernac was alone in the large house, and as such, responsible for carrying out the daily routine, whatever that might entail.

Alone in the house. She turned and looked down again toward the partially exposed body at the foot of the van. What if the priest were inside, a victim of something that, until then, she hadn't even considered? The flood of thoughts that rushed now unbidden through her mind was enough to make her actually stagger. She reached for the wooden porch railing nearby to steady herself. It felt as if the blood had left her head entirely. She just hoped she wasn't going to pass out. She couldn't recall ever having experienced such a sensation before, and it frightened her. As much for herself as for the priest whose life now seemed to hang in the balance—in her admittedly overactive imagination, if nowhere else. Fortunately, the spell passed as quickly as it had come. She gave a deep sigh of relief and sat back on the railing until she was sure.

After a moment she straightened up and turned to see if anyone else had arrived for Mass, but her car was still the only one out front. A glance in the direction of the parking lot told her that it was still empty as well. Except for the van and its silent visitor, that is. *Where was everyone this morning, anyway?*

She tried the buzzer once more, praying with all her heart that her suspicions were wrong.

It was then that she spotted him out of the corner of her eye. He was headed across the driveway that separated the rectory from the church, obviously having left by the rear kitchen door. His head in its dark blue Greek fisherman's cap was down, his chin buried in the upturned collar of his World War II Navy pea jacket. He hadn't even seen her.

"Father! Father Cernac!" she half shouted, aware of the early hour. There were private houses a short distance down the street and she didn't want to disturb anyone unnecessarily.

The priest glanced sideways without actually raising his head and beamed a broad smile, then continued on in the direction of the front of the church.

Lavina was sure he hadn't recognized her, even given the short distance that separated them. "Father!" she called again, this time proceeding to run after him, totally oblivious of the snow on the rectory lawn, as well as her earlier spell. When she reached the blacktop driveway, she almost slipped on a patch of black ice.

Before she even had a chance to look up, Father Cernac was at her side, a sturdy grip on her elbow. "You all right, Lavina?" he asked in obvious concern. "I didn't even recognize you." His hands, out of his side pockets now, were bare, already reddening in the cold.

"I'm fine," Lavina protested, forgetting herself completely again. She grabbed his helping hand in one of her own and all but pulled him in the direction of the newspaper van. "But there's someone hurt down in the parking lot." Just as they were about to pass the rectory, she stopped in her tracks. "No, we've got to go back inside first. You've got to call emergency. The man may be dying, if he isn't already dead. I couldn't find a pulse, but then I wouldn't want to be the one to make such a pronouncement anyway." She wasn't sure she was making much sense at that point and just hoped he was getting the gist.

Father Cernac knew Lavina London well enough from past experience to know he wasn't dealing with some kind of hysteria. He kept up the pace at her side, and when they reached the little rectory porch, stepped around her to unlock the front door.

"I've been ringing and ringing for the past five minutes," she said as she watched him insert the key. "I thought you had gone to the hospital on a sick call or something. Or maybe even worse."

"Worse?" The priest threw her an inquiring glance over his shoulder as he pushed in the door and stepped aside to let her precede him inside.

"I'll explain later," she said with a dismissive wave of her gloved hand. "Right now we've got to get to the phone."

"The closest extension is in the kitchen," he said, pointing off in the darkness toward the rear of the house as he closed the door behind them. "Which is where I must have been when you rang the bell. I can't always hear it in there—or at least not when I don't have my hearing aid on, I suppose I should say. I still can't seem to get used to the thing."

She had forgotten about that. "I couldn't see any lights, either."

"I only had the light on over the stove. Got to watch those electricity bills, you know, Lavina. With the summer crowd gone back home to the city, we're back to our regular weekly contributions. I've got to keep a tight grip on the purse strings." While she couldn't actually see his face in front of her as he led the way now through the darkness of the rectory, she knew from the tone of his voice that he was smiling. Now that she knew he was safe, she felt like smiling too. She could well do without scares like this at this hour of the morning. Or at any hour, for that matter. This priest meant too much to her. Not only was he her confessor and spiritual advisor, he was also a dear friend of long standing. That something might have happened to him—especially something violent—was more than she wanted to think about.

Once they were in the kitchen in the back of the house, Father Cernac made the call from the wall phone, handing the receiver to Lavina once he got through. It was she who actually filled them in at the other end of the line, doing much the same for the priest as well as he followed her brief explanation.

The light in the ventilator fan above the stove was still the only source of illumination.

"Who is he, do you know?" Father Cernac asked, following her out the door again when they were through. They proceeded out to the sidewalk and then down toward the newspaper van. He didn't even bother to relock the door.

"I don't know, Father. I thought he might be either a parishioner I don't know or a homeless person who was sleeping in the van for the night." She was speaking now without looking over her shoulder. When they reached the school building, she stopped and turned. "For a while there I even had the idea he might be our new deacon." She didn't know how else to broach the possibility in case it later turned out to be true.

"It can't be Andrew," Father Cernac said, his hands shoved back into his deep pockets again. "He's back at the house. Upstairs getting ready to assist me at this morning's Mass, as a matter of fact." He lifted one hand out of his pocket and consulted his watch. "He came up from Yonkers late last night, early this morning. A bit later than expected because of the snow. I wanted him to sleep in his first day here, but he'd have no part of it. He's already offering to do things around the place, if you can believe it. Even before he gets settled in. He'll be a great help, Lavina, believe me. And it will be nice to have a younger man around the parish, too, even if it's only until May."

Lavina let out a sigh of relief. "I'm certainly glad to hear that, Father. As you'll soon see for yourself, this is a young man, too. Which is probably what put the idea in my head in the first place." She was pointing now in the direction of the body as they neared the stationary van. With Lavina in the lead, they trudged through the already formed imprints in the snow. They had begun to ice up, Lavina was quick to notice. For some reason, she looked around to see if there were any others that she might have missed earlier. There weren't. Was she still unconsciously looking for something sinister?

Maybe, as some of her friends liked to tease from time to time, she had been playing the role of amateur sleuth too long after all. She dismissed the thought as quickly as it had arisen. As far as she was concerned, she had never done anything she hadn't felt it necessary to do. If some people found that difficult to accept, that was their problem.

Once the two of them actually reached the foot of the van, they both crouched down alongside the body, the priest the closer this time.

"Do you recognize him?" Lavina asked, watching Father Cernac's careful scrutiny of the man's face. "Is he a parishioner?"

"Not one that I know," Father Cernac said, slowly shaking his head as he proceeded to brush aside the remaining snow that was hiding the body.

"Do you want my gloves?" Lavina asked when she saw the bare red hands at work in the snow.

"No, Lavina, I'm fine," Father Cernac said as he continued his chore. It was when he reached the area of the chest that the white turned first to pink, then, deeper down, to red.

"Oh, my Lord!" Lavina uttered, suddenly pulling back and crossing herself. "Is it—?"

"So it would seem," the priest said, answering her unfinished question in an oblique manner that satisfied them both.

Actually, the blood couldn't have been clearer, contrasted as it was against the freshly fallen snow and the whiteness of what looked to Lavina like an Irish cable-knit sweater. The hoarfrost on the face and hair gave the head the strange appearance of something only partly human emerging from its cocoon. It reminded her of the film *Invasion of the Body Snatchers*. "Do you think he's dead?"

"I can't tell for sure, of course, Lavina. The body's too cold. If I had to bet on it, though, I'd say yes. But then, as you yourself said a little while ago, we'll just have to wait for the professionals to be sure." It was at that point that the priest bent over closer to the young man's exposed head, his ungloved right hand on the forehead, and formed the sign of the cross with his thumb. Lavina could make out a few barely audible words which sounded like Latin. It wouldn't surprise her if Father Cernac occasionally reverted to the earlier Church formula. She knew that he was praying, giving a blessing. Maybe even a form of last rites, what they used to call Extreme Unction in the days before Vatican II, even if he didn't have any holy oil.

"Can you tell what caused the bleeding?" she asked when the cleric finally sat back on his haunches and emitted a long, drawn-out sigh that seemed to originate in the depths of his very soul.

"No," the man said softly. "And I don't want to start probing at this point to find out in case I might make things worse."

"No, of course not." If there was one thing Lavina had learned during the course of her occasional investigations it was that you never disturbed anything at a possible crime scene. It was just the helplessness she felt that prompted her even to ask. She thought again of St. Stephen and his horrible death by stoning. To this day people had been striking out at what they didn't understand, ever eager to harm those who were different, those who spoke a truth they didn't want to hear. There would always be martyrs of one type or another, she knew.

It was then that it dawned on her. She *had* disturbed something. The footprints. She looked back at the now heavily trodden area behind them. They had messed it up royally. She shook her head in dismay; not that there was anything they could do about it now, certainly. But there was something else about it too, something that puzzled her. There had only been one set of prints to begin with, even when she had first seen them. She was sure of it. Then she remembered the carol again:

In his master's steps he trod,
Where the snow lay dinted;
Heat was in the very sod
Which the saint had printed.

That had to be it, then. Someone had trod in the victim's footsteps, then just as carefully retraced his steps backward to make it appear that there had been only one set. Which meant that the crime had to have been premeditated. If, of course, they were dealing with a crime. She still didn't know that for sure. The blood could have been from some other cause.

She turned to see if there was any sign of life yet in the area besides their own. The volunteer ambulance crew, she knew, didn't have far to come. And, of course, the Monticello Police Department would radio one of its cars directly.

"I can't feel anything in his pants pocket," Father Cernac was saying, interrupting her musings and causing her to look back again. In spite of what he had said about not probing, the priest was rummaging now under the man's heavy woolen pullover. "No wallet or anything, I mean. And he doesn't seem to have any others as far as I can tell, either. Pockets, I mean."

"You mean he has no identification?"

"Nothing that I can see."

"Did you try his back pocket? Can you reach it?" The man was lying, as she had noted earlier, in the classic fetal position, in this instance on his right side.

"I did, yes. Nothing. Not even a handkerchief."

Something else that was premeditated, maybe? she wondered. Had someone wanted to hide the man's identity for some reason?

"There are holes in the sweater, Lavina," the priest added, his bare fingers feeling around now in the man's clothing. The red Lavina saw on them now was not from the cold. "It looks like the poor man's been stabbed. Or shot."

"I was afraid it was something like that," Lavina admitted. It was something she had felt in her gut, all her hopes to the contrary notwithstanding. She was glad to be out with it, and to hear that someone with credibility agreed with her.

"Why? Because you were the one who found him?" In spite of the unfortunate situation confronting them, the priest began to laugh. "Sorry, Lavina, I couldn't help myself," he quickly added by way of amendment.

"I'll bet you are," Lavina said, giving him one of her mock withering scowls.

"You feel up to solving this one?" he asked, the smile still on his lips.

"I'll do anything I can to help the police, of course, but I don't see myself going out of my way this time, if that's what you mean."

Father Cernac shrugged. "More's the pity."

"Why?"

"Nothing really, except—"

The flashing lights from the top of the patrol car, followed by the slamming of doors, cut him short.

"The police," Lavina said, stating the obvious.

"And the EMS folks right behind them," the priest added, pointing in the direction of the emergency vehicle entering the farther entrance to the parking lot.

The two uniformed policemen were alongside them even before the ambulance had a chance to pull up behind the patrol car out in the street.

" 'Morning, Father," the older of the two policemen said, touching the visor of his cap by way of greeting. He was still only in his early thirties, Lavina decided.

"Officer," Father Cernac acknowledged with a nod.

With an additional hand-to-hat salute to Lavina, the policeman crouched down to examine the body.

Lavina looked out toward the sidewalk to the official vehicle. The Monticello Police department, as expected. In a way, she wished it had been the sheriff or his deputy. Them at least she knew. And vice versa. Not that it really mattered, of course; she had no intention of becoming any more involved than she had to, even if the man's death *was* something other than accidental.

"It's Mrs. London, isn't it?" the policeman said, rising to his feet.

"That's right." He had probably been given that much information from their phone call, Lavina decided.

"I recognized you right away," he added with a smile, taking her totally by surprise.

It was Lavina who now smiled. Maybe it wouldn't be quite so bad after all. When she turned to share her comfortable feelings with Father Cernac alongside her, the priest was already grinning. "I hope that's good," she said, looking back.

"Oh, you bet. You've got quite a name for yourself up here in Monticello. A good reputation, I mean. Both as an actress and—" The word seemed to fail him all of a sudden and he reddened visibly on the spot.

"Amateur sleuth?" Father Cernac suggested, coming to his assistance.

"Well, something better than that, certainly, Father," the policeman protested, yet still not supplying an apt description of his own.

"How about concerned citizen?" Lavina offered with a little tongue in cheek of her own.

The volunteer paramedics arrived in time to interrupt a situation that had nowhere to go but downhill as far as Lavina was concerned. She and Father Cernac stepped aside to let them get at the body, then, at the officer's request, moved out to the sidewalk. On the faroff horizon to the east she was happy to see the beginnings of an orange-sherbet sky. It would soon be daylight.

"Well, finally!" Lavina said, turning and looking beyond the priest's shoulder. Father Cernac turned his head to follow her gaze. "Ernie," she added unnecessarily. Ernie Holmdel was a St. Michael's parishioner who regularly attended the daily seven-o'clock Mass along with Lavina and some twelve to fifteen others. Where the others were today, Lavina could only guess. Religious snowbirds.

"Late, aren't you?" Lavina said, teasing.

"We've had a bit of snow, Lavina," Ernie added in all innocence. Sometimes Lavina worried about the man's dwindling sense of humor.

"Not to mention a possible assault," she added, gesturing toward the van. She proceeded to fill him in, repeating as necessary at the arrival of some of the other regulars. By the time she was done, there were seven of them all told, herself included.

"Where's your car, Ernie?" she asked, looking off to the front of the rectory where he usually parked it.

"You don't think I drove in this weather, do you?" the man answered. "I walked." She didn't quite know where that placed her in the man's estimation of things and didn't bother to pursue the point. Ernie, she knew, was only in his early fifties. She couldn't imagine what he was afraid of.

"Where's your hat?" the man asked, in seeming retaliation.

He was right, of course. She should have remembered it. "I know. I should be wearing one. I just forgot when I left the house. Force of habit, I suppose. With all this hair I didn't even notice it." "All" was a close-cropped feather cut that would completely have exposed her neck to the cold had she not been wearing a warm woolen scarf and turned-up jacket collar.

"Will there still be Mass, Father?" Ernie asked, turning his attention to the priest. "I mean, the church is still locked and all."

"Good heavens, yes," Father Cernac said, checking his watch again. It was, Lavina noted, checking her own as well, almost quarter of seven. "Here, let me give you the key," the priest quickly added, digging into his jacket pocket. "You can go open up and get things set up for us. I'll be along as soon as I have a word with the police."

"Right," Ernie agreed, taking the proffered keys and moving off in the direction of the church.

"I might as well go give him a hand as long as I'm not doing anything," Frank Straub said. Frank was one of their weekday lectors. He and Millie Edwards. Millie wasn't here this morning. Arlene Dawson was, though. Arlene was a newcomer to St. Michael's. She and her six-year-old son had recently arrived from Pittsburgh after a separation from Mr. Dawson. How permanent the situation was, Lavina didn't know. With her expertise in computers, Arlene had been a welcomed addition to the parish office where she had already begun to update church records. She had even offered to teach Lavina word processing once she learned of the reminiscences the actress was working on. Lavina still hadn't given her an answer. If the truth be known, computers scared her, and she was the first one to admit it. To herself, that is.

"Where's our new deacon, by the way, Father?" Lavina asked, when the two men had moved off. "Shouldn't he be down by now?"

"Good grief! I forgot all about him. He's probably gone in through the side entrance to the sacristy. I gave him the key before I left the rectory."

"So he probably has things set up already," Lavina said, referring, of course, to such items as the cruets, chalice, wine cups—items regularly used at Mass.

"If he can find everything," Father added.

"You want me to go over and make sure?" She was eager to meet the new deacon anyway.

"No, I think you'd better stay put a while. The police will undoubtedly want to question you, seeing as you're the one who actually found the body." She had expected as much, and nodded agreement. "I'd better go ahead myself. Whatever we have here can keep till after Mass. Right now prayer is more important than anything else anyway, for the young man and his assailant both." Father Cernac shook his head. "I just hope Andrew doesn't ask for a transfer already after he hears what's happened here."

With that, Father Cernac moved off toward the front of the church, the small knot of early-morning worshipers in tow behind him, leaving the police and medical authorities behind to do their thing as they in turn went about theirs. Lavina felt temporarily trapped somewhere in the middle. She looked first toward one group, then the other, her toes fast becoming the target of the morning's frost.

It wasn't long, however, before the young officer was back facing her on the sidewalk, his small notepad palmed now in his ungloved left hand. His name, she learned, was Tim Franco. His younger partner was Sid Something-or-other. He seemed to be overseeing the medical team at the van. "I'd like to ask you a few questions, if I may, ma'am," Franco said with a pleasant smile. "Won't take long."

"Of course," Lavina agreed and proceeded to fill him in accordingly as his questions prompted.

She learned the young stranger had been pronounced dead by the ambulance team, the victim of multiple stab wounds, the weapon as yet to be determined. His identity, of course, was still unknown, as was the motive and time of death. The weather had thrown that off completely. The ambulance crew had since called for the medical examiner and was just waiting around for his arrival. There was obviously nothing else they could do. The rest was up to the police authorities, in this case the Monticello Police Department and the county medical examiner's office.

"Will there be a regular investigator along as well?" Lavina asked after Franco had completed his preliminary questioning and replaced his notepad in his hip pocket. She was sure she wasn't about to be let off quite this easy.

"Yes, ma'am. Now that we're pretty sure we're dealing with a homicide, there'll be a whole slew of professionals along. They should be on their way already." In time to meet the break of day, she thought, looking again to the east. The sun was almost up.

Which reminded her. She checked her watch. "Is it all right for me to go on into Mass, do you think, Tim? I mean, that's why I'm up here in the first place. I live down on Hemlock Lake in Boulder."

"I don't see why not, Mrs. London," he said, becoming less formal now that the questioning was over. "We'll know where to find you if we need you again before we pack it in. I'll tell the lieutenant when he shows up." He looked back to what was now officially a crime scene and shook his head. "Not quite our idea of Christmas, is it?" he said, almost nostalgic. "Peace on earth, good will to men, I mean?"

"Hardly that, no," Lavina agreed, still sorely aware that it was also the day on which the Church celebrated the death of its first martyr.

"Say a prayer for me while you're at it, will you, Mrs. London?" the policeman said, taking her somewhat by surprise.

"I'll be glad to, Tim." She left the young officer standing on the sidewalk near his police car and proceeded in the direction of the church. She was about to go in when, out of the corner of her eye, she caught a glimpse of two more vehicles arriving at the lot. The second police car was undoubtedly that of the detective lieutenant Tim Franco had mentioned, the other probably that of the medical examiner—or more likely at that hour of the morning, his substitute.

A blanket of warm air embraced her as soon as she was in the vestibule, and even more so when inside the church proper. She wished she could have taken off her boots and shoes and just wiggled her toes to get the blood flowing again. Unfortunately, that would have to wait until she got back home.

As always at this time of the year, the church had been totally transformed, the predominant color white, flecked here and there by the reds and greens of the seasonal plants. After the somber if meaningful blue-violet of Advent, it was especially brilliant and welcome. A mass of red poinsettias in red foil pots stood like silent sentinels surrounding the base of the central altar facing the congregation, with others marching boldly up the marble steps of the pre-Vatican II altar against the wall behind it where the tabernacle still retained its place of prominence. Here the poinsettias were white, fronted by lower silver foil pots of cascading red Christmas cactus. The walls of the sanctuary were all but hidden by tall, dense pines, their rich fragrance filling her nostrils even as she walked up the left aisle, summoning up in her mind a lifetime of Christmases past. After a brief prayer at the manger set up before the left side altar, she proceeded across the front of the church to the opposite side and her usual place in the third row where she moved in toward the middle of the pew.

She knelt down and unzipped her red crocheted bag and was about to take out her rosary when she realized she wouldn't have time to complete it before Mass. She zipped up the bag again and placed it on the wooden bench behind her, following it up with a few impromptu prayers of her own. She knew that the distractions this morning were going to be worse than ever, given the situation outside. With that in mind, she made a firm resolve to try to keep her mind on the holy sacrifice that was about to take place before her, at the same time fully aware that she would fall short of her intention.

She sat back in her seat and lifted out the missalette from its holder in the back of the pew in front of her. Locating her place for the day's Mass, she then set it face down on her bench, ready for use. Directly ahead of her, just beyond the marble communion railing, was the children's Christmas tree that had been adorned by the youngsters at the ten o'clock Mass the day before. The ornaments were either homemade or individually bought and hung by the children one by one. The ornaments, of course, were intended as gifts for the Christ Child, and hung with loving care "In hopes that the Baby Jesus soon would be there." She smiled, remembering how Father had worded it for the youngsters, basing it, of course, on Clement Moore's *A Visit from St. Nicholas*. As she examined the ornaments now from the distance of her pew, she found that she especially liked an elongated silver swan that seemed to be swimming effortlessly in midair, its metallic finish reflecting the myriad of tiny colored lights strung on the tree.

As Lavina watched, almost mesmerized by the display, Arlene Dawson suddenly appeared as if from out of nowhere to crouch down at the base of the tree, a clear long-necked wine bottle in her hand. Lavina smiled. Who else but a mother would think to give the poor uprooted tree a drink of water to quench its thirst? The maternal thought made her wonder who stayed with the woman's youngster on those mornings when his mother came to early Mass. She certainly wouldn't leave a six-year-old home alone. She'd have to remember to ask her when she had the chance. Her motherly task finished, Arlene returned to the sacristy via the side door, only to return again a few moments later with a fresh sanctuary lamp, which she proceeded to substitute in its chain-supported brass holder for the one that had burned out. As she watched her finally return to her pew nearby, Lavina suddenly realized that she had never seen the woman quite so active before in church.

The tinkle of the tiny bells stirred her from her reverie. She glanced up to see one white-clad altar boy complete with crucifix, followed by a man she took to be their new deacon, and Father Cernac bringing up the rear. She smiled. Father was wearing a red-on-red silk chasuble and stole she had made earlier in the year. It was shot through with fine silver thread with the capital letters *alpha* and *omega* on either side of the cross. Red, of course, was the liturgical color for martyrs. Father's vestments had their match today in the deacon's stole, which was now draped over the man's right shoulder and crossed and fastened at his left thigh. It and the white alb, of course, were his only vestments. Seeing her chasuble and stoles now, she was happier than ever that she had made them, even though it had taken her the better part of three months.

She looked carefully now at the new deacon who was to be with them until his ordination to the priesthood next May. He followed the celebrant at the altar at the priest's right-hand side. Lavina was a little surprised that he wasn't wearing the deacon's dalmatic, especially during the Eucharistic celebration. Not that most people would notice, of course; it was only by accident that she had learned about the garment herself while reading up on the role of the deacon once she heard they were to have one. And, of course, it would be just like Father Cernac to forget to purchase one himself, seeing that the parish wasn't accustomed to the luxury of its own deacon. All things considered, though, it was an honor to have him, she thought, even if only temporarily. And who knows, in time maybe they'd have their own permanent lay deacon. The diaconate was one of the holy orders that was making a fast comeback in the Church, and one that was sorely needed.

Somehow she found it difficult now to take her eyes off him. Maybe because she was still subconsciously sizing him up. Physically, he was a good six inches taller than Father Cernac, and well over six feet. The full hair was dark blond and somewhat curly, the sides combed back neatly into what her two brothers used to call a DA way back when. Needless to say, she was too far away to distinguish the color of his eyes, though she was sure they were blue. He seemed somehow awkward now as he attempted to follow the celebrant, almost at times unsure of himself. Lavina smiled again. He was obviously self-conscious in the presence of his new congregation, however small. Time would change all that, she was sure. Once he got to know them, all it would take was a little encouragement. Well, he had the right group for that here at St. Michael's, that was for sure. She'd have to spread the word—as well as have a chat with Deacon Andrew himself, of course. She wondered what his last name was. She couldn't remember actually having seen it in the church bulletin.

From an overhead lateral stained-glass window, one of the many in the sanctuary, the early-morning sun suddenly sent shafts of ruby light onto the altar below, bathing altar and faces in a misty red glow. Like martyr's blood spilled out upon the land, she thought, remembering St. Stephen again. Like the blood of the unknown young man lying dead outside in the sullied snow. For the first time now since she had come into church, she offered up a prayer for his departed soul. As she thought of him again, she realized how much older he actually was than their deacon. By as much as ten years maybe, she figured. The man assisting at the altar looked closer to twenty-eight.

By the time Father Cernac finished the opening prayer and the congregation sat down for the readings, she remembered her resolve and picked up the missalette still face down on the bench where she had set it earlier. She held it partially closed now in her hand over one long, slender finger, then caught Frank Straub out of the corner of her eye as the lector proceeded up the aisle from his pew and approached the lectern.

"A reading from the Acts of the Apostles," he intoned, following the prescribed formula for the opening of the First Reading. Lavina followed along as intently as she could, her eyes on the middle-aged lector standing before them. Somewhere between his pew and the lectern he had slid on his black-framed reading glasses. They made him look like an owl, she thought, not for the first time. She liked Frank. He was down to earth.

". . . As they were stoning Stephen, he called out, 'Lord Jesus, receive my spirit.' Then he fell to his knees and cried out in a loud voice, 'Lord, do not hold this sin against them'; and when he said this, he fell asleep."

The death of St. Stephen. And the death of the stranger outside. Somehow the two were intrinsically linked in her mind. How or why, she didn't know. And here they were yesterday celebrating birth, the birth of the Christ Child, who was to bring life into the world. How incongruous it all seemed. Yet she knew it wasn't. Nothing happened without a reason. Nothing. Even the evil that the Lord permitted. She wondered why that poor man had been killed, tried to make sense of it all. And why the single set of footprints? What was someone hiding by removing his identification? And more importantly, why?

"Into your hands, O Lord, I entrust my spirit." The Responsorial Psalm. How fitting in the case of Stephen. She repeated it now aloud along with the rest of the congregation at the end of each verse read by the leader. She only hoped the poor stranger outside had had time to make peace with his Lord as well if, indeed, they were not already one together. Who was he anyway? And why had he come to St. Michael's? She just couldn't get it out of her mind now that it had taken a hold. It was like a leech intent on draining her mental faculties.

In view of what Father Cernac had told her outside about their overly zealous new deacon, she more than half expected to see the man mount the pulpit after Frank had finished to read the Gospel and give the homily. It was one of a deacon's special privileges. One of many, as a matter of fact. In a way she was disappointed when he turned instead and sat down on the bench nearby, allowing Father Cernac to do the honors himself. He probably wasn't ready after his trip, unless, of course, he was just still too nervous. Either that or Father Cernac had insisted on his taking a breather. Well, there would be plenty of time ahead to hear him. Five months.

Frank Straub was back at his usual place in a pew somewhere behind her, Arlene in the second row center, a little to her left. Ernie Holmdel was up in the front pew on the opposite, Gospel side of the altar—or what used to be known as the Gospel side, anyway. He looked stiff as a board even sitting. When it came down to it, she thought, the man probably needed more help at relaxing than anyone she knew. She couldn't imagine how anyone could be so serious all the time. But then, of course, she couldn't say that she really knew the man—either him or his problems.

The Gospel was from St. Matthew, and like the first reading, spoke of death and giving final witness to the faith: *"But beware of people . . . Brother will hand over brother to death, and the father his child. . . .*" The prediction Christ had foretold had come true more than once over the course of history, Lavina knew. She thought again of the stranger outside in the snow. Where exactly did he fit in?

Her resolve at self-recollection was surprisingly well kept during the Consecration, the central portion of the Mass, even if only by comparison. Well, her intentions at least were good. That, after all, was what really counted when you came down to it.

When it came time to distribute communion, Lavina was surprised to see Arlene Dawson accompany Ernie up to the sanctuary. Obviously she was going to help with the distribution of the wine. Lavina hadn't even known the woman was an extraordinary minister. Another first for Arlene.

Father Cernac was already into the *Agnus Dei* when she realized she wasn't paying attention as she should have been. Again. Not that she could really help it. There was something gnawing at the back of her mind. Something she couldn't quite get hold of. It had to do with the scene there in the church, that she was sure of. Exactly what, though, was another question. She looked around from the sanctuary to the pews nearby, then back up to the altar. What was wrong with this picture? She sighed. Winnie would have said the actress in her was working overtime again. Maybe so. But still . . .

Communion progressed as usual, with Father Cernac distributing the bread and the two lay ministers the wine, one at the head of each side aisle. Deacon Andrew remained seated in the sanctuary, his strong hands folded in his lap. From time to time he brushed at the red silk stole that stretched diagonally across his broad chest as if it were a form of fetters restraining him in his seat. He seemed miles away—probably, Lavina finally decided, in his post-Communion meditation. It was good to see a young man so thoroughly absorbed with his God. Now if only a septuagenarian she knew could do half as well . . .

It wasn't another five minutes before Father was giving the final blessing and dismissal, after which he left the sanctuary in the same manner in which he had entered, with the altar boy and deacon preceding him.

Lavina made her way up to the front of the church to light a candle for Ken beneath the statue of St. Anthony, after which she knelt down on the blue leather cushion at the communion railing and said her usual series of prayers. The smell of pine was even stronger here than it had been in her pew. She closed her eyes and inhaled deeply, trying at the same time to picture the first Christmas at the manger in Bethlehem.

When she finally finished and turned to see whom she could entice into the sacristy with her to meet the new deacon, she was faced with an empty church. They had all flown the coop. Not that she could blame them, of course—not on a morning like this. They were probably all eager to get home before the additional snow that had been forecast for later that morning had a chance to change its mind and sweep in early. Oh well, looked like it would just be her this time around. She'd just have to make sure to see them all tomorrow morning before Mass. After all, she didn't want to prolong the newcomer's anxiety any more than necessary. That would hardly be Christian.

She pushed herself up from her knees with the help of the communion rail, then went out through the side door into the inner alcove where she mounted the short steps leading up to the sacristy. Since the door was closed, she knocked as she always did, waiting for Father Cernac to tell her to come in. Instead, the door was opened by none other than Arlene Dawson, a broad smile on her youthful face.

"I told you she wouldn't leave without coming back to do the honors," the younger woman said, addressing someone behind her without actually turning around.

"Father has you tending the door now as well, has he?" Lavina said, hoping it didn't sound sarcastic. She certainly hadn't intended it that way—at least not consciously. She followed it up with a little laugh just to make sure.

"I thought I'd surprise you this morning," Arlene said, stepping aside for Lavina to enter the narrow confines of the small, square-shaped room. "About being made a minister, I mean."

"You certainly did that," Lavina admitted. "When did all this happen?"

"I've been attending instructions since the last call went out in the bulletin," the woman said, letting the door close shut on its own. She sauntered over as gracefully as she could considering her knee-high white rubber boots to stand alongside the new deacon. The man was smiling now at the exchange between the two women.

"I'm very happy for you," Lavina said, joining her and planting a kiss on the woman's cheek.

"Now all we have to do is get Lavina into the fold," Father Cernac said from the large wooden sideboard against the wall that housed the sacred linens. He was depositing a folded linen purificator into one of the small side drawers in the upper portion of the piece of furniture. Lavina could hear the smile in his voice even thought she couldn't actually see his face.

"The day you see the likes of that will be the day the earth stands still," Lavina said with a little laugh. "I'm afraid that's just not my thing. I'll leave it to the younger members of our congregation." She was a simple servant of the Lord and that she would remain; ministry was someone else's job.

"You should at least consider becoming a lector, Lavina," Ernie said, serious to a fault. "What with that professional voice of yours and all, it's almost a sin not to. It sounds like a special charism to me."

"Don't tell her that, Ernie," Father protested, turning around from the sideboard to face the group. "She's liable to take you seriously. About the sin part, I mean." He gave Lavina a conspiratorial wink, as if to reassure her he was only teasing. Not that she would have thought otherwise, of course. They knew each other far too well for that after all these years.

"Now that's something I might actually consider," the former radio actress said, at the same time raising a halting palm to forestall any further enthusiasm on their part. "If and when I personally feel the time is right, that is." She had, as a matter of fact, already given it some preliminary thought.

The group laughed at her outspoken inflexibility, causing her to smile in spite of herself. Age, she had learned during the course of her recent investigations, had been a decided asset in dealing with people—especially possible suspects. They either didn't take you seriously or thought you were headed down the path to second childhood and, as such, completely harmless. In the case at hand today, seeing her as adamant as she was, they just backed off with a laugh.

"So this is our new deacon," Lavina added, quick to change the subject, just in case anyone in the group should suddenly decide to pursue the subject further. She turned to the young man in question who was standing between Arlene and Father Cernac and extended an ungloved hand. "Lavina London," she said, introducing herself.

"Andrew Bonavic," the newcomer said with a bright smile that brought forth two deep dimples on either side of his mouth. He took the proffered hand in his own warm yet firm grip.

"Rhymes with 'rich,' in case you all didn't catch it," Father Cernac added. "Like our dependable young altar server here." The priest turned to look for the youngster who had braved the snowy morning to serve Mass. "Rich, where are you?"

"He's gone around to the other side of the sanctuary to hang up his alb and get his coat," Frank said, gesturing with his head to the semicircular passageway that led around the rear of the apse behind the sanctuary. "He's probably still over there reading his magazine waiting for me. I'm his ride home."

"Anything to stay clear of the adults," Ernie observed, as if the boy had made a poor choice.

"Can you blame him?" Lavina said, siding completely with the youngster's decision.

"It's a good thing my name isn't Rich, isn't it?" the deacon said with another smile. "Can you just picture having to answer to Rich Bonavic for the rest of your life?"

"Bonavic." Lavina repeated it aloud as if just to hear it on her own lips, to get the taste of it, so to speak, in her mouth. "Croatian?"

The young man merely nodded.

"We have a number of Croatians in the parish, don't we, Father?"

"I don't speak the language," Andrew was quick to add, as if Lavina were setting him up for something he was unable or unwilling to handle.

"No need, Andrew. They all speak English, and very well, I might add. Even the ones who've been here only a short time."

"Great."

"Any news from the police outside?" Lavina asked, the morning horror in the parking lot never far from her thoughts. She gestured to the closed sacristy door.

"I haven't heard anything so far," Father Cernac said. "But I'll be going out to see as soon as I can get out of my vestments."

"Mrs. Brogan told me the ambulance people were just leaving when she arrived," Frank added.

"They didn't take the body though, did they?" Lavina said, a statement more than a question.

"She didn't say."

"Ernie says no one even knows who the dead man is," Arlene said, slipping an arm into her fur-fringed overcoat. The tiny bells on her charm bracelet set off a chain of little tinkles. She must have left the coat hanging in the sacristy before Mass, Lavina thought, remembering that the woman had been wearing only her white woolen dress outside.

"As far as we know," Lavina said, nodding. "Or at least Father couldn't find any identification on him."

"You searched him, Father?" Andrew asked. "Was that wise? I mean, with the police outside and all? You might have gotten youself in serious trouble."

"I didn't disturb anything, Andrew, if that's what you're getting at. Just felt in the normal places for his wallet to see if he had any ID."

The deacon merely nodded.

"I thought Lavina here was our local sleuth," Frank said, beaming a pleasant smile. Lavina could hardly take offense at something said with no deliberate malice. Especially by someone like Frank Straub. "You trying to usurp her job, Father?"

Unless Lavina was mistaken, the priest actually blushed. "Hardly that, Frank," he said, dismissing it with a wave of his still vested arm. Then, obviously catching sight of the puzzled look on the newcomer's face, added, "Mrs. London has been involved with the police on a number of local homicide investigations, Andrew. Believe it or not, she has a knack for that sort of thing."

Now that he mentioned it, Lavina wondered if that would be considered a charism too. She'd have to remember to ask him when they were alone.

"Really?" The deacon smiled as he turned his gaze on the former actress. Lavina wasn't quite so sure how to interpret it. It somehow seemed more amused than anything else. Or was she subconsciously on the defensive all of a sudden?

"Don't pay any attention to the lot of them," she said. "I just happened to be in the right place at the right time, that's all."

"I see."

Lavina watched as both Father Cernac and Deacon Andrew Bonavic proceeded to remove their vestments, the subject apparently put on the back burner. At the same time, the something that had bothered her outside in the church was back again, teasing her brain, something she couldn't quite zero in on. "Catch me if you can," it seemed to say, defying her to take up the challenge. She was smarter than to take the bait. Leave it alone, as they say, and it will come by itself; try to force it to the fore and you'll lose it for sure.

"Do you usually wear the alb at Mass, Deacon?" she asked, having noticed the fact outside. It was something that interested her since her reading. "I thought the dalmatic was more in keeping for a Eucharistic celebration." She looked around at the others to see their reactions. She hoped they didn't think she was showing off her newly acquired knowledge. She wasn't.

"It is, Lavina," Father Cernac said, answering for his new assistant. "But, as I told Andrew here earlier, I'm afraid we just can't afford one for every set of vestments right now. This is the first time we've had a deacon up this way, don't forget. We're lucky to have chasubles and stoles. If it weren't for generous people like yourself, we wouldn't have. This red set is just gorgeous." He raised one side of the chasuble on the hanger held up now in his other hand, displaying the expanse of silk.

Lavina merely smiled. Now that it dawned on her, she was glad no one had asked her to make a dalmatic as well when she donated the set of vestments. To begin with, she wouldn't have had a pattern.

"What's a dalmatic?" Arlene asked, fastening the top button of her soft wool coat just under the gray fur collar. While Lavina did not believe in fur for decorative purposes, she was not one to make a point of it either. Regardless of their feeling on the subject, most people, she was sure, did not believe in causing animals pain.

She smiled at the woman's question. "Why don't you explain it to her, Andrew? I can call you that, can't I? I'm not sure I can describe it myself just from my reading." It was true. She had seen pictures, of course, and would definitely recognize one, if and when she saw it.

Andrew looked from Lavina to Father Cernac, then back again. "I don't think I'd be much better at it myself," he said with a little laugh. When no one offered any help on the subject, he shrugged. "What can I say? It's just a garment worn by a deacon."

"And a bishop," Lavina was quick to add.

"Yes, that too, of course," Andrew said. "Why don't you try your hand at it, Paul?" he said, turning to the priest standing alongside him. "You've been at this longer than any of us."

So it was Paul already, Lavina noted, not really surprised. She was one of the few people in the parish, she knew, who didn't address Father Cernac as Paul or Father Paul. For her, he was always "Father." It would have been the same with any man of the cloth. Another example of her upbringing and lifelong habits.

Father Cernac grimaced. "Well, let's see now. It's an outer garment to begin with—much like the chasuble in that respect, but cut differently. With short, wide sleeves as I recall. I think there are different styles even today. And what else . . . ?" He looked around as if subconsciously looking for help from anyone capable of offering it.

"It's the same color as the chasuble, too," Lavina said as an afterthought.

"It's not white linen like the alb then," Ernie said, obviously trying to create a mental picture for himself.

"Oh, no," Father added.

"Another difference, of course," Lavina added, remembering, "is that the deacon would wear the stole under the dalmatic rather than over it as he does with the alb. As you saw Andrew do this morning."

"And the bishop wears it under his chasuble as well," Father Cernac added. "During his consecration and pontifical masses."

"Right," Andrew agreed.

Lavina looked around their little group standing there in the sacristy. It was then that it happened. Like watching a dense fog slowly rising from in front of her mind, exposing a previously hidden vista. She mentally squinted as if to see it even more clearly. Yes, there it was, finally out in the open, unmistakable. What it might mean, of course, she didn't even dare to imagine. It was too frightening, too incredible. But she had to make sure she was right. There was no point in going off half cocked making accusations based on unsubstantiated facts.

"Do you happen to have a copy of the latest *Catholic Almanac* in here, Father?" she asked. "Actually, it doesn't have to be the latest one. Any recent edition will do just as well."

"There won't be a picture of the dalmatic in the almanac, Lavina," Father said, shaking his head. "I'm sure of it. You'd have to check the *Catholic Encyclopedia* for something like that, I should imagine. It probably has at least a sketch of some kind. And maybe even in a regular large dictionary as well."

"That's not what I want it for," Lavina said, looking around to see if she could spot the annual reference book for herself.

"In that case, sure," Father Cernac said, turning and opening a door in the wall cabinet above the sideboard. After checking one area, he closed the door again and opened another. He took out a soft-covered yellow book. "Here you go," he said, handing it to her. "Is this all right? I didn't get this year's edition yet."

Lavina took it from him and, raising her clear-framed glasses hanging on the chain around her neck, read the cover. "This will be just fine," she said, slipping on the glasses. She checked the table of contents in the front of the book, then went over and sat in the straight-backed chair against the wall opposite the sideboard. She opened to a page and ran a slender finger down the left-hand column. It was right there toward the bottom of the page. So she hadn't been wrong after all. She could almost feel a fresh surge of blood coursing through her body—or was it adrenaline? Whatever it was, it felt good. Made her feel more alive than she had all morning. It was her first positive clue to the possible identity of their killer. Not to mention of the dead stranger outside.

"As long as I've got you all here together, I might as well tell you the news," Arlene suddenly said, causing Lavina to look up from her reading. She closed the book over her finger and listened. "Bobby and I will probably be moving back to Pittsburgh," the woman added. Bobby was her son. Another unexpected surprise. Looking around, she found the other parish regulars to be just as amazed as she was.

"But you just became a minister, Arlene," Frank protested. He almost seemed hurt. "How come now all of a sudden?"

"Robert just called last night. He wants us to get back together. He's been away in rehab for help and is sure he . . . well, that things will work out for us now." Did she actually not want to discuss it, or was she just afraid someone would try to talk her out of her decision? Lavina couldn't say. "Maybe my turning myself over to the Lord here like I did—becoming a minister and all—made the difference. Maybe that's what He was waiting for from me. Who knows? The Lord works in strange ways." Who knows, indeed, Lavina thought, closing the book and replacing it on the shelf from which Father had taken it. She pushed in the cabinet door.

What followed could only be described as a mixture of congratulations and reservations, all relating to Arlene's impending departure from parish and town. When everyone had put his two cents in, the woman made her final move toward the sacristy door.

"Aren't you going to stay around to find out more about our poor victim outside?" Lavina asked as the woman was about to open the sacristy door again.

"What's to find out?" Arlene said, halting in her tracks and half turning around, her hand still on the doorknob.

"Who he is, for one thing," Lavina said. "And who killed him, for another." She adjusted the slipping crocheted red bag on her jacketed shoulder and smiled.

"Don't tell me you know, Lavina," Frank said,

amazement lighting up his face. "Not that I'd really be surprised, of course."

All eyes turned to stare at her.

"I think I might," Lavina said simply, not wanting to overstate the fact at that point. There was always the off chance that she had made a miscalculation somewhere along the line.

"You'd be outdoing even yourself if you did," Father Cernac added with a little laugh as he went over to the clothes tree near the straight-backed chair and lifted off his old-fashioned, faded black overcoat that he then proceeded to put on over his clerical garb.

"When did you get in, Deacon?" she asked, turning back to the newcomer.

"Here at St. Michael's?" the man asked.

"Yes."

"Early this morning sometime. About one or so, wouldn't you say, Father?"

"Five after, to be exact," Father Cernac said. "I had fallen asleep in front of the television waiting for you, if you recall."

Andrew smiled. *"Mea culpa,"* he added. A little Latin. *My fault.* Why she was surprised by it, Lavina didn't know, but she was.

"And had you driven straight up from the seminary in Middletown? Without stopping, I mean?"

Father Cernac shot her a puzzled look, as if he didn't know where she was going with her questioning. She just hoped he didn't decide to interrupt her and throw a monkey wrench into her little plan.

"Yes," Andrew said. "I got a much later start than I intended because of the weather, of course. It had finally stopped down there at the time I started out, but then started in again while I was en route. That's why I arrived so late. It took me forever. But, then, I took my time, too. A dead deacon would be of no help to anybody." He laughed.

"That's for sure," Frank agreed, reaching for his own

coat on the tree, at the same time passing over Andrew's black leather jacket to its owner as well.

"You wouldn't get me out in weather like that," Ernie added. "In a car, I mean. That's asking for trouble, if you ask me."

"I see," Lavina said, ignoring the other man's interruption. "And where's your car now?"

"I had him put it in the rectory garage, Lavina," Father said, answering again for his deacon. He was in the process of buttoning his overcoat with one hand. And had obviously put on a great deal of weight since he bought it, Lavina noted. "It was still snowing at the time and I didn't want to leave it out in the driveway in case it got any worse. I also didn't want it blocking the snow plow that I knew would be along."

"No, of course not," she said.

"What's all this got to do with the body outside?" Arlene asked, her hand off the doorknob now, waiting for Lavina to fill her in. "Do you think Deacon Andrew might have seen something and not realized it? The murderer, maybe?"

"Andrew here knows, don't you, Andrew? Or whatever your name is. Maybe you'd care to tell us that, as well."

For the second time that morning, all eyes turned in Lavina's direction and just stared.

"I'm afraid I don't know what you're talking about, Mrs. London." The sweetness act again. Well, it had worked so far, she thought, why not now?

"We're talking about your seminary, for one thing."

"What about it?"

"It's not located in Middletown."

The young man laughed as he slipped his black wool scarf out of the arm of the leather jacket he was holding and then tossed it around his neck with his free hand. "Is that what this is all about? I know that. I knew when you mentioned it, Mrs. L. It's just that my mother taught me never to contradict my elders, that's all."

Father Cernac shot him a scolding look.

Lavina let the obvious sarcasm pass. There was something else in his voice that bothered her far more. The last person who had addressed her as Mrs. L was a murderer intent on burying her alive in a mausoleum crypt. She shivered now just remembering it. Was this young man's unfortunate turn of phrase an ominous foreshadowing of what lay ahead? she wondered. She certainly hoped not. She had promised all concerned, herself included, that she would never let herself be caught in a predicament like that again.

"If that's the case," she continued, "then you won't mind telling us where the seminary *is* located." She canted her head to one side, eagerly awaiting his answer. The only sound in the little room at that point was the hum of the furnace, which had just gone on again.

The man was obviously growing restless now, shifting as he was from one foot to the other. He turned the black leather jacket around in his hand until he found the opening for his arm, then stuck it in. When he finally had it on and zippered up, he looked up and shook his dirty-blond head, the earlier smile now more a smirk than anything else. "You're hardly making me feel welcome with questions like that, Mrs. London. As a matter of fact, you're making me feel downright uncomfortable."

"Can you answer it?" Father Cernac asked, staring at him more intently, as if seeing him now for the first time.

"Sure. It's in New York."

"Would you care to try a little farther north?" Lavina said. "Like Yonkers, maybe?"

"Right. Just outside the city," the younger man agreed, as if he had known all along. "So what's the problem?"

If the man thought he had gotten himself off the hook with that one, he hadn't. Not as far as Lavina was concerned. "And it's not just a question of the seminary, either," she added.

"Oh?" The smirk again. He shoved both hands down

deep in the pockets of his leather jacket. He looked more like something out of a B movie than the deacon he was supposed to be. Lavina was leery about the pockets now, too.

"Tell me about the stole," she said.

"The stole?"

"Yes. Tell me how the deacon wears his stole."

Father Cernac gave her another quizzical look, as did the others in their little group. For whatever reason, they had all managed to pull away from the newcomer and were standing now on the sidelines.

Andrew shrugged. "What's to tell? Over the shoulder. Like you saw me outside. And in here until I took it off." He turned to gesture with his head in the direction of the long drawer where Father Cernac had neatly deposited the two red silk stoles.

"If that's the case, maybe you did study somewhere in Middletown. Because you certainly never learned to wear a stole that way at St. Joseph's." The name was out even before she realized it. It had originally been part of her trap about the seminary. Oh, well . . .

"If you'll excuse my saying so, Mrs. London, I really think you should stick to your knitting." The irritation was beginning to show now in his voice as well as in his nervous movements.

"I have never knitted a stitch in my life," Lavina said, almost good-humoredly, knowing it had nothing to do with anything. "I crochet, though," she added, partially raising the red crocheted bag she was still toting on her shoulder. Right now, though, she wouldn't have minded giving him a jab or two with a nice sturdy knitting needle.

"You know what I mean, Mrs. L. So what do you think was wrong with the stole?"

"Just that you wore it over the wrong shoulder, young man. That's all. It should be worn over the left shoulder and fastened down on the right side of the body. You had it over the right shoulder."

"Is that all?" He laughed again. "This is almost the

twenty-first century, Mrs. L. The church is changing. Or haven't you noticed? It doesn't make any difference what shoulder I wear it over."

"Young man, that will be quite enough!" This from Father Cernac. Lavina couldn't remember ever having seen the priest quite so upset.

"I should think so," Frank added.

"And Mrs. London is correct," Father Cernac added. "It certainly does make a difference how you wear your stole. You should know that. Your ideas about liturgical propriety are completely off the wall. If they're any indication of your other ideas on the Church, you've got a lot of soul-searching to do between now and next May. I for one certainly don't need a deacon around here fostering ideas like that, let me tell you."

"As I was trying to indicate before, Father, I don't think he's our deacon at all," Lavina said, her eyes narrowed, watching the man's every move. "Are you?" This to the newcomer. Maybe she should have waited until they were outside again with the police before having thrown down the gauntlet. Well, it was too late now. She just hoped it wasn't another example of fools and angels.

The young man smiled. "I used to be an altar boy," he said, slowly removing a switchblade from his right-hand jacket pocket. An altar boy. Of course. Just enough to enable him to fake it, she thought. No wonder he had been so hesitant at times at the altar. She could hear the intake of breath around her at the sudden appearance of the knife, her own included. Weapons of any sort always frightened her. Now, as she heard the rapid switch of metal as the knife opened, she knew why.

"What's this all about?" Father Cernac asked, his narrowed eyes on the newcomer who had obviously played him for a fool.

"Your Christmas collection, Father—that's what it's all about."

"Our—"

"You took it in yesterday and won't be able to get it to the bank until this morning. I just thought I'd pop along and save you the trouble." One of the difficulties of Sunday collections, Lavina realized. Since yesterday was also Christmas, it just added to the problem. "It would have been so easy if we didn't have all this nonsense to deal with." He darted visual daggers in Lavina's direction to indicate the source of the nonsense in question. "I simply would have offered to take the money down to the bank for you and you wouldn't have seen hide nor hair of it or me again once I left the rectory."

"You don't think I would have given it to you, do you?" Father asked with a little snicker of his own. "That's one thing I do myself. Deposit the money, I mean. Either me or our pastor."

"In that case, I simply would have had to deal with you alone then, wouldn't I?" the newcomer said, the smirk back again.

"We're not a rich parish, you know, young man, whatever your name is."

"Come off it, Father," the would-be deacon said, obviously not willing to satisfy the priest's curiosity in regard to his name. "This is Christmas we're talking about. People came to church here yesterday that didn't come all year long. You know that as well as I do. Christmas and Easter. And maybe Palm Sunday. Happens every year without fail."

Lavina couldn't fault him there. Father Cernac didn't even try.

"So you can't tell me you didn't take in a nice haul," the young man added when no one contradicted him. That he used the Christian fisherman image, Lavina was sure, was entirely accidental. After all, he certainly wasn't talking souls.

"Is that our real deacon lying out there in the parking lot, then?" Father finally asked, anger visible now in his voice and face alike. Lavina just hoped he didn't try anything foolish. After all, he certainly wasn't a young man anymore.

"I'm real sorry about that, *Padre,*" the stranger admitted. "Honest I am. But he didn't give me any choice. I had to let him have a few jabs in the gut." He stabbed now in the air with his knife to illustrate his meaning. He seemed to enjoy it. "He wouldn't sit down like a good boy and let me tie him up in that van like I wanted to. What else could I do? How he landed outside there like you described to me, I have no idea. I left him on the floor inside with the door closed tight. He must have come to after I left and tried to make his way out and fell. Is he dead?"

"As if you needed to ask," Father Cernac said very simply, all signs of anger gone now. "So that's the real Andrew Bonavic." He was looking past them now in the direction of the sanctuary. After a moment he made the sign of the cross, his lips mouthing silent words. Lavina remembered the man's earlier comment about a dead deacon and closed her eyes.

"That he is," the stranger said. "Or was, I should say." He smiled as he shifted the knife into his left hand and reached under his jacket into his pants pocket. He took out a folded brown leather wallet and tossed it across onto the sideboard. "There's his wallet. I just needed it for the temporary masquerade. And thanks, by the way, for pronouncing the last name for me when I first arrived. I never would have guessed that it rhymed with Rich." He laughed.

"I had spoken with him on the phone earlier," Father said, still in a low voice, obviously remembering now. "I thought your voice sounded different. But then, who would ever have guessed . . . ?"

"Before the two of us go back to the rectory to conclude our little financial transaction, Paul, suppose we just tie the rest of these nice people up here to keep them out of harm's way." The first name took on a completely different cast this time around. Lavina felt like smacking his smug little face.

"I have a young son at home to think about," Arlene protested, tears beginning to well up in her eyes.

"Then you'd better start thinking about him, lady," the pseudo deacon said, impatient now. "It's either sit and get tied up, or this." He waved the knife in front of her face. "Don't forget what happened to your stubborn deacon out there." When Arlene didn't offer any further protest, he added, "Now all of you—down on the floor." He waved the glistening blade of the knife around again, making a wider arc this time, making sure he took them all in.

Out of the corner of her eye, Lavina suddenly spotted movement at the end of the passageway behind the apse. Richie. Their own altar boy. Her mind started racing. She didn't want to take any chances on the boy's getting hurt. On the other hand, he might be their only chance. Tied up or not, there was no way they could be sure this maniac was going to let them go free. They had, after all, seen his face, would be able to recognize him again. And he had admitted killing their deacon out in the parking lot. Chances were he'd feel he couldn't afford to let them go. There was no question about it now—she should have waited until they were outside with that nice policeman before she had made her foolish accusations. She could already hear Sheriff Arthur bawling her out for her stupidity. She deserved every bit of it. Her only concern now was whether she'd ever be around to hear it in person.

"How do you expect to get by the police outside when you eventually decide you want to leave?" she asked, making no attempt to get on the floor. Not that she saw any problem for him, of course; she was just stalling for time. Or trying to. Which is why she remained standing in spite of his order. She was still trying to figure out the best way to handle the situation. Her eyes kept darting back and forth between the stranger and the passageway. Richie was still there, as if trying to figure out what he could do himself. She offered up a little prayer that he didn't try anything foolish before she had a chance to think more clearly for both of them.

The stranger smiled. "I'll just drive out," he said, taking the question at face value. "If anyone stops me, I'll tell them I'm on my way to the hospital on a sick call." He reached across to the top of the sideboard with his left hand. "Come to think of it, maybe I'd better hold on to this for a while longer," he added, picking up the wallet again and shoving it down into his back pants pockets. The knife had switched hands again. "You never know. It's not like old Andrew will be needing it anymore." He laughed again, clearly enjoying his idea of humor.

"How did you know when the deacon was going to arrive at the rectory here in the first place?" Lavina asked. "I'm assuming, of course, that this robbery of yours was planned in advance."

"Well in advance, Mrs. L.," he said. "And to answer your question, you people announced it in the bulletin last Sunday. Not to mention the nice follow-up article that appeared in *The Record* later during the week. Not that I was going to go entirely by that, of course. I also called the rectory yesterday morning when I knew Father was at Mass to make sure—and, of course, to get the ETA. That nice housekeeper told me he was expected at ten last night. So I just parked across the way from the rectory and waited. A little longer than I expected, I might add. The snow did delay things a bit. I had a good three-hour wait before he finally showed up. About twenty to one, as a matter of fact."

"And you just followed him when he got out of the car?" This from Father Cernac. "Followed him and killed him?"

"Well, it wasn't quite that simple, Paul," the stranger said. "I had to get him over to the van, don't forget, so I could eventually stow him away inside. I told him I needed help. That I was having a problem with the van door. Being the nice Christian gentleman that he was, he obliged." He tossed up his open palms. "The rest, as they say, is history."

"And, of course, you already knew about parish banking procedures," Father added. "Pretty clever."

"I thought so," the newcomer agreed with a smile. "Like I said, I used to be an altar boy. Things haven't changed all that much. Not as far as collections are concerned, anyway."

"Now I know why you didn't want to read the Gospel and give the homily," Father said, shaking his head. "And here I chalked it up to nerves on your part."

The newcomer laughed. "That did work out nicely for me, didn't it?"

"The only thing you didn't figure on was Mrs. London here," Frank added. Lavina could have done without that little accolade at the moment. Well, at least Father's questions had given her time to consider a suitable course of action. For that at least she was grateful.

"Ah, yes. Mrs. London." The stranger started to make little circles with the blade of the knife. "I do owe you a little something for that, don't I, Mrs. L?"

Lavina didn't say anything. She couldn't even if she'd wanted to. She was too frightened. Anyone who thinks he'd be otherwise has obviously never been on the wrong end of a switchblade.

The movement was back in the passageway again. Richie was getting restless. It was now or never. She just hoped she was doing the right thing. She offered up another quick prayer, this time to the Holy Spirit for guidance. "You know, it would serve you right if someone really put you in your place," she said, thinking as fast as she could on her feet. The actress in her again, she supposed. She'd often had to improvise in the course of her long career. As it was, there was only one thing that had come to mind; she didn't have time to pick and choose. She only hoped it worked. It was a long shot at best, but what other choice did she have?

"Oh? And who do you think might do that, Mrs. London?" the intruder asked. "You?" Another laugh. "You know, I'm actually beginning to enjoy this. It's a shame it has to come to an end so soon."

"You would," Frank Straub said, immediately setting off a scowl on the face of the newcomer.

"What we really need right now," Lavina added, shifting her feet to distract the man's attention, "is a knight in shining armor." She was speaking now a little louder than normal to make sure she was heard in the passageway. "One with one of those long lances like you see in the movies. Like they have at that Renaissance Festival they hold in New York every year. That would knock you off your feet for a while." Father Cernac, she knew, had taken the altar boys to the festival earlier that fall as a reward for their faithful service during the year. Richie had been talking about it ever since. He and his young friends played Knights of the Round Table every chance they got. The question now was, would he realize that she was talking directly to him? Would he get the message and follow through? She darted another glance in the direction of the passageway, careful again that the impostor didn't notice. The lad was gone. She could only hope.

It wasn't ten seconds later before he was back, both hands wrapped tightly around the shaft of the four-foot crucifix pole, the one he had used earlier leading the little procession in and out of the sanctuary. He had removed his outer jacket, Lavina noticed, and was now in his blue-and-white school pullover. He seemed hesitant for a moment, but then, lowering the pole to a horizontal position, crucifix forward, he charged, like a knight of old without his study steed—or perhaps more aptly, like a Crusader behind his standard, the Cross of Christ. *In Hoc Signo Vinces,* she recalled from the life of Constantine the Great. *In This Sign Thou Shalt Conquer.*

It wasn't until she heard the screaming and general commotion around her that Lavina realized she had inadvertently closed her eyes against the impending charge. Opening them she saw their mutual enemy down on all fours trying unsuccessfully to regain his balance, one finger-splayed hand planted squarely on the tiles, the other reaching behind him for the area of his kidney where Richie had obviously planted the tip of his Christian lance. The switchblade had slid across the tile floor and was already in Frank's hand. Thank God he was wearing his gloves, she thought. The fingerprints would have been invaluable.

Young Richie was still basking in his glory long after the Monticello police had taken their suspect into custody. Not only had he gotten the gist of Lavina's message and saved the day, running their assailant to the ground with a charge of the church staff crucifix, but he had also run out to summon the police once the man was subdued. The murderer was now outside waiting to be officially escorted to the station.

"I caught what you meant about the lance right away, Mrs. London," Richie said, his adrenaline still flowing. "Especially after our trip to the Renaissance Festival and all. Gee, who thought I'd ever have a chance to do something like that?" Lavina was sure the story would be milked for all it was worth far into the coming year. As well it should be.

"I wasn't sure you knew I meant you," she said.

"I saw you look at me when you mentioned it."

"I wasn't sure if you did or not. I didn't want our assailant to see me looking in your direction so I had to be careful."

"Set an altar boy to catch an altar boy, is that what it was?" Frank Straub said, summing it up succinctly. He, Lavina, and Father Cernac were the only adults left now in the sacristy.

"It certainly looks that way, doesn't it?" Lavina said with a smile, the fact dawning on her now for the first time.

"How did you like my charge?" Richie asked, still milking. "Cool, huh?"

Lavina didn't have the heart to tell him that, with her eyes shut, she'd missed the actual attack. "It couldn't have been more strategically planted if you'd practiced it in advance," she said with a laugh.

"You knocked him for a loop is what she means,

Richie," Father Cernac translated with a laugh of his own.

"Exactly," Lavina agreed. "The White Knight to the rescue."

"I think with today being what it is and all," Richie said, "I should be the Red Knight, don't you?"

The three adults laughed again, together this time. "St. Stephen!"

It gave her cause to remember again. Stephen, one of the first seven deacons of the Church chosen by the Twelve to attend to the secular needs of the Hellenic Jewish Community in Jerusalem. "It's strange, isn't it?" she added. "To think that our new deacon should be murdered on the feast of St. Stephen, himself a deacon."

"Apropos is more like it, wouldn't you say, Lavina?" Frank said.

"That's what I mean, of course. The first martyr a deacon and now another one following in his footsteps." She recalled the footprints outside in the snow. They had certainly been made by a holy man, as the carol said. His assailant had just sullied them. Well, maybe in time he too would come around. After all, hadn't Stephen begged God's forgiveness for those who stoned him? Maybe Andrew Bonavic was in heaven now as well pleading his killer's cause. Somehow she was sure of it.

"You're forgetting something else that was special about the original deacons, Lavina," Father Cernac said, herding his three remaining parishioners in the direction of the door and reaching for the wall switch to douse the light.

"What's that, Father?"

"The reason deacons were formed in the first place. Or don't you remember?"

Lavina narrowed her eyes. "You'll have to refresh my memory on that one, I'm afraid, Father."

"It's nice to think you leave something for me to do," the priest said with a little grin. "I was the one who should have recognized the fact that our imposter was wearing the stole improperly."

"You would have if you had given it any thought," she said, reassuring him.

"Maybe."

"It didn't come to me right away either, if you really want to know. In the beginning, I just knew something was wrong that I couldn't put my finger on. It took a while before it finally dawned on me. That's why I asked to check the almanac. I knew they described how the deacon's stole was worn in there. The first time I looked it up was when I made the stoles to match the red chasuble. I had to see how it differed from the priest's stole. Then again later when I learned we were actually getting a deacon here."

"That bit about the seminary in Middletown was just to set him up then, right?" Father said.

"Right. Wearing the stole incorrectly might have been a simple mistake—odd as it would have been—but not knowing *where* he had supposedly studied, well, that would be a bit too much."

Father Cernac laughed.

"Now, what's all this about the original deacons?" Lavina asked lest he forget. "Why did the early Church use them?" They were through the inside door now and on their way down the short flight of steps to the side door leading outdoors.

"The twelve apostles—there were twelve again at the time, don't forget—chose them because the Hellenists complained that their widows were being neglected in the daily distribution."

Lavina laughed. "Widows like me, you mean."

Father smiled. "Maybe what you've done here this morning is to help repay the debt."

"As a widow helping to solve Deacon Andrew's murder, you mean."

"Precisely."

Maybe he was right. Maybe this lone widow had filled her God-given role after all, she thought, as she preceded the others out the side door into the cold morning air. After all, wasn't she, with the Church, a firm believer that nothing ever happened without a reason? That one way or another, everything was God's Will? She smiled. So maybe her sleuthing savvy was a special charism from God after all.

Slayride at Spirit Mountain

by J. F. Trainor

I came over the rise like a spooked whitetail, knees flexed, raven hair streaming, Dynastar Elle skis churning up a thigh-high spray of powdery snow. I got maybe a split-second glimpse of spruce treetops and the distant St. Louis River, then the trail veered sharply to my right, plunging downslope into a grove of white birch.

No problem, though. Just lean into the fall line. Stab with the downhill pole. Turn gracefully at the waist and slide both skis to the right. And do it all quickly, unless of course you really want to end up plastered to the bark of a trailside spruce.

So there I was, plummeting down the steep corkscrew trail they call Juggler Joe, stirring up clouds of champagne powder. Birches streamed past on either side, a blur of slender white trunks. My downhill plunge exploded a snowdrift, sending me careening into the next turn.

Mild fussbudget face. Almost lost it there, Angela!

I couldn't really blame the trail. Not this time. Last night's storm had left the twin ports of Duluth, Minnesota and Superior, Wisconsin smothered in four inches of what my people call *ishpate jakagonaga.* Deep dry powdery champagne snow. Perfect for the downhill.

Nope! The problem was yours truly—Angela Biwaban. I hadn't donned a pair of skis in over three years. Meaning I probably shouldn't have tried to tackle Juggler Joe first time out. Then again, I'd been skiing Spirit

Mountain since Daddy taught me to snowplow at the tender age of seven. Surely my downhill savvy would compensate for any rusty skills.

I gave it my best shot, staying loose and limber, keeping my spine arched, letting my Elle skis shoom over the powder. But it was no good. As my speed picked up, my leg muscles failed to compensate. I began throwing myself into those forty-five degree turns, steering with my knees instead of my upper torso. So intent on anticipating upcoming turns was I that slowly, imperceptibly, I began leaning back, shying away from the line of fall. And then, all of a sudden, I became the passenger, not the driver, shanghaied into a steep creekbed by my runaway skis.

"Shit!" I muttered, aiming for a four-foot drift ahead. Hit the boot release. Bailout Biwaban.

Splashdown! The impact splattered the featherbed drift, bathing me in a shower of crystalline snow, knocking my Polaroid goggles askew, turning my hair the same shade of white as my grandmother's. I rolled another twenty feet and came to rest beside one of my ski poles. The other slinked away in the direction of downtown Duluth.

Galumphing through knee-deep snow, I retrieved that pole and then went hunting for my skis. Quick examination of the tips. No dings or cracks. ESS bindings in good shape. Jabbing both poles in the snow, I seated myself. Grimace of embarrassment. Sure hope nobody witnessed that!

A woman's light contralto laughter dashed all my hopes. Turning, I saw a lean lady in a sleek cranberry Nordica ski suit zipping down the slope. Expertly she slid to a halt, kicking up a fine spray. The face beneath her mirrored goggles was chocolate brown, and that broad smile looked awfully familiar.

"Angie Biwaban! What on earth was *that!?*"

Embarrassment gave way to sudden delight. I hadn't heard that voice in nearly ten years. *Yvonne Pryor!*

"Oh, just looking for a shortcut back to Grand Avenue!" Grinning, I wiggled my ski boot into the bindings.

"I'll bet!" Yvonne's expression turned serious. "Are you all right? That was quite a spill."

I put on my other ski. "No, I'm okay, Yvonne. Nothing hurt but my pride."

"So what are you doing back in the Twin Ports?" she asked.

Planting my poles, I boosted myself up. Ladylike grunt. "I'm home for the holidays."

"You're rusty," Yvonne observed, brushing the snow from her knitted cap. "Don't they have good downhill runs in the Black Hills?"

Sheepish smile. "Uh, I'm not living in Cameron any more."

Yvonne's dark eyes gleamed. "Oh?"

Muted sigh. "It's a long story, dear."

She levelled her pole at the wooded trail. "Listen, Angie, we've got lots to talk about, and chatting is best done at the lodge. Come on, I'll spot you the rest of the way down."

Showing a tart smile, I pushed off with both poles. "Maybe I should have stayed on the *beginner's slope.*"

Trilling contralto laugh. "Don't worry, Angie. I'll watch out for you—like always!"

Although it sometimes seemed as if Yvonne had been looking out for me forever, our friendship only stretched back a dozen years. We met at Duluth's Central High School, Yvonne and I. She was a year ahead of me, a celebrated athlete, the most feared outside hitter in Class AA volleyball. She put our team, the Lady Trojans, at the top of the league her first year at Central. And, with a little help from me and the former Mary Beth McCann, the Lady Trojans took the state championship three years in a row.

It's a long winter in the Northland, stretching from the first snows of Halloween to ice-out in April. We spent many a snowy afternoon at Spirit Mountain, then operated by Mary Beth's father. Although I qualified as a hot dog on the downhill, no way could I ever match Yvonne. On skis, she made us all look as fumblefooted as Tahitians.

The chairlift returned us to the summit in exactly four minutes. After shedding our poplin ski jackets, ski pants and Dolomite boots, we put in our orders for hot chocolate and found a pair of cozy chairs beside the vast fieldstone fireplace.

As we talked, I daintily sipped cocoa and marvelled at the changes in my old teammate. Cornrowed braids had given way to a stylish wedge that covered Yvonne's ears and forehead. She'd put on five or ten pounds since graduation. But on her it looked good, softening the angularity of her features, adding more pronounced curves to her lean, athletic body. Yvonne finally had an ass. Quite a change from a decade ago!

Peering out the lodge's oversized window, I saw the ski runs cloaked in mountain shadow. We were rapidly running out of daylight. Streamers of thin cloud stabbed eastward into Lake Superior. Late afternoon December sunshine glimmered on the silvery trestles of the Bong Bridge. Further east lay the rust-colored taconite docks, the lofty shoreside grain elevators and the far-off sandspit of Park Point—my old neighborhood.

Swallowing a mouthful of cocoa, I turned Yvonne's way and asked, "So what brings you here on a workday afternoon?"

Knowledgeable feminine smile. "Business."

"Ski instructor?"

"Afraid not." All at once, Yvonne's smile turned cold and brittle. "I tried that right after graduation. Made all the rounds—Lutsen, Eagle Mountain, Copper Peak. No luck!" Bitterness hoarsened her lovely voice. "Maybe I should've dyed my hair blond and changed my name to Heidi, eh?"

I let the subject drop. Yvonne's African ancestry hadn't mattered that much during the glory years at

Central. Quite a different story, though, the day after graduation.

"What are you doing these days?" I asked.

"Office manager." She held the steaming mug in both hands. "I kicked around the Twin Ports for a bit. Then the Job Corps got me into Ridgeline Realty as a clerk-typist. I've been there seven years now." Sour smile. "Polaris kept me on when they took over."

"Polaris?"

"Polaris Development Corp. New company, Angie," she explained. "Actually, it's more of a one-man band . . . Derek Sjolund. Ever heard of him?"

I shook my head.

"From Brainerd. He quarterbacked that new big shopping center off Route 371. Derek hopes to do the same thing here. Which is why he bought out Ridgeline." Her lips puckered in wry amusement. "Derek yanked us off Superior Street and dropped us into this brand-new office building on Anderson Road. Said we had to be where the action was. Well, at least he had the good grace to hold onto me and Greg Halstead."

"Sjolund is thinking about another mall?"

"Uh-huh!" Decisive nod. "There's been a real boom in retail development since Gander Mountain and ShopKo moved in. Derek wants to put ours in about a mile west of Trinity Road. He even has the name all picked out—*North Star Mall.*"

I winced. "Don't you think it's getting a little crowded up there on the Miller Trunk Highway?"

"That's where the Northland loves to shop. Or so they say."

"Right! And where are we going to get all our shoppers from? North Dakota!?"

"Careful, dear!" She stifled a giggle. "You're starting to sound like one of those merchants on Superior Street."

"How far along is the big project?"

"Well, we've got Trautmann's lined up as a flagship store," Yvonne said, snuggling into the sofa cushions.

"There is opposition, though. The Superior Street merchants, of course. They see every new store up there as a mortal threat to downtown. And Derek's drawing flack from the EPA."

"How come?" I took another sip.

"Our original plan called for a two-hundred-space parking lot," she explained. "But with Trautmann's coming in, we're going to need a lot more parking. The redesign proposes five-hundred spaces within a fifteen-acre commercial lot. The EPA says that will endanger the wetlands bordering Miller and Chester Creeks." Sudden dispirited sigh. "Now the damned Planning Commission won't grant the zoning change until we've settled with the EPA."

I could see major problems for Polaris on the horizon. "How will that affect your financing?"

"Well, it certainly won't help, that's for sure! Banks like to see a quick start on new construction. Fact is, Angie, that's why we're here today." She glanced toward the mezzanine. "Derek's meeting with some people from Minneapolis. I did my dog-and-pony show this morning. Now he's up there alone. Top level stuff. Very hush-hush."

My gaze soared up to the polished cedar railing, catching a glimpse of a fortyish blond man in one of the glass-walled conference rooms. Receding hairline, blunt-tipped nose and narrow chin. Well-tailored woolen suit in heather gray. His wire-rimmed glasses gave him the look of a fanatic accountant.

My thumb tilted skyward. "Is that him?"

"Uhm-hmmmmm. Derek Sjolund, man on the move."

I detected an undertone of disapproval there, but before I could comment, my former teammate frowned and put her empty mug on the polished chestnut coffee table.

"You know, I ran into Mary Beth recently."

"You did? Where?"

"The Soo. The Ojibway Hotel. Derek sent me out there for a regional Realtors' conference six weeks ago."

Thinking of my recently-widowed friend and her lively four-month-old son, I grinned. "Is baby Jim sleeping all the way through the night yet?"

Yvonne didn't smile. "Mary Beth told me what happened to you in Cameron."

No comment from Angie. Really, there was nothing I could say. My mother had suffered a recurrence of cancer, and, to pay for a lifesaving operation, I'd embezzled money from my employers at Town Hall—a crime which resulted in my three-year stay at the South Dakota Correctional Facility for Women at Springfield.

"Angie . . ." Yvonne rested her elbows on her knees, her face tensing with a strange anxiety. "Uhm . . . if you don't mind a personal question . . . uh, what was it like in prison?"

Cool but gracious smile. "That's kind of a depressing topic for Christmas, don't you think?"

Yvonne looked as if she wanted more than anything to drop the subject, but something prodded her on. "Please! I—I've got to know. Is it, uhm, as bad as they say?"

"Worse!" I snapped. "Your life is controlled by this little electric bell. Whenever it rings, you have to do something. Eat, sleep, shit, whatever! There are a lot of people in there determined to screw you every way they can—physically, mentally, sexually. But that isn't the worst of it, Yvonne. The worst comes in the middle of the night when you wake up and listen to the screams reverberating up and down the cellblock. Screams of loneliness and rage. Incarceration is hell for women. I've heard that men can take it a little better, but I really don't see how!"

Yvonne's brown eyes widened in absolute fright. Knuckles bulged as she clutched the cushion. For a moment I thought she was going to faint.

Okay, so resentment hadn't exactly turned me into Diplomatic Angie. Still, I felt guilty about upsetting her. After all, it wasn't Yvonne's fault that I'd spent the last three Yuletide seasons in the Big Dollhouse. Seeking to make amends, I patted her forearm and murmured, "Sorry. I didn't mean to snap at you like that. It—well, it's a difficult subject for me, Yvonne. And . . . say, why are you so interested in—?"

Just then a male voice drifted down from the mezzanine. "Yvonne!"

Looking up, I saw Derek Sjolund peering over the rail.

Instantly Yvonne glanced his way, fighting to regain her composure. "Yes, Derek?"

"Give me a hand with the slide show, would you?" His blond head tilted toward the conference room. "Ornell and Dahlberg want to see those subcontractor cost estimates again."

"I'll be right there." Showing a regretful smile, she rose from the sofa. "Duty calls, I'm afraid. We'll have to continue this another time."

Not wanting our conversation to end on such a sour note, I remarked, "Tell me, what are your plans for Christmas dinner?"

"It depends on whatever my sister Kendra has in mind, I guess."

Holiday Angie smile. "You're welcome to stop by and try some of Grandma Biwaban's celebrated Christmas goose."

"I—I don't want to intrude, Angie."

"Listen, Yvonne, we've got plenty of food. Half of Fond du Lac reservation usually drops by. Just grab a knife, a fork, and a plate, and join the line." Giving her hand a gentle squeeze, I added, "We'll have a chance to *really* talk."

Languid smile. "I'll think it over, Biwaban."

As she sauntered away, I added, "If you're not there by noontime, I'll come looking for you!"

With a gust of laughter, Yvonne waggled her long fingers in farewell. Skier's legs, sheathed in black denim, carried her swiftly upstairs to the mezzanine.

As for me, I grabbed our cocoa mugs and carried

them over to the snack bar, completely unaware that my former teammate had just under three hours left to live.

Wednesday morning found me at Grandma Biwaban's, my temporary home in Duluth, diligently working out in expectation of a second crack at Spirit Mountain. Exercise gear had turned the Queen Anne parlor into an impromptu health club. I carry that gear with me wherever I travel. Step-by-Step foam pillow. Exer-Slide workout pad. And the Door Thing, perfect for doing all those forearm curls and rowing motions.

So there I was, clad in my blue-and-white biketard, long black hair confined by a terry headband, nylon booties covering my Reeboks, finishing up my hip flexor routine. Both hands on the end ramp, fanny pointed at the ceiling, I slid my feet one at a time down the pad. Anishinabe princess getting in shape for the downhill.

Just then, Aunt Denise appeared in the dining room doorway, busily stirring a yellow mixing bowl. She shook her head, frowning. "Are you still exercising your buns off?"

Sassy grin. "I *like* being a size six."

Her hand stirred more vigorously. "Can't be a spoiled princess all your life."

Perspiration dampened my face as I turned her way. My grin widened. "I'm setting a longevity record."

"You wouldn't have time for all those calisthenics if you had a *husband.*"

"See? I *knew* there was a reason why I haven't taken the plunge." Squatting on my haunches, I lifted both arms in a glorious stretch. "By the way, Aunt Denise, what size slacks would *you* like for Christmas?"

Anishinabe lips compressed in frustration. Denise Giashko was my father's younger sister, a matronly lady with a soft mouth, a high forehead and Daddy's aquiline nose. Substantial gray frosted her shoulder-length hair. "Wrap it up, eh? Mother and I could use a little help in here."

After mopping my face with a towel, I shed my booties and slithered into a fresh T-shirt. My shower could wait. Carving and boning can be messy work, indeed.

Nearly everybody in our extended family celebrates Christmas as a religious holiday. Both the Biwabans and the Blackbears are Roman Catholic, converted by the *mekatewikwanaiag,* the Jesuit black robes, back in the Seventeenth Century. However, among our Giashko, Maingan and Attikameg kin, we have Baptists, Methodists, Latter-Day Saints and more than a few who follow our ancestral Anishinabe faith, *Midewiwin.*

For us, Christmas is *Niba-anamiaygijigad,* the occasion for a grand winter feast. Since my grandmother's roast Canada goose, with its succulent cornbread-and-wild-rice stuffing, is known to every member of the Bear clan from Duluth to Saskatoon, she always has plenty of visitors on Christmas Day—most of them relatives stopping by on their way to the big New Year's powwow at Lac Courtes Oreilles (pronounced *Lah-koo-der-ay*), Wisconsin.

Entering the kitchen, I watched my grandmother, Juliette Maingan Biwaban, butcher the hindquarters of a moose. She's a gaunt, birdlike woman in her mid-seventies, two inches shorter than me, with high cheekbones, a narrow chin and fine hair the color of newly-fallen snow. Wrinkled copper-brown hands expertly wielded the saw, transforming moose haunch into top and bottom round steaks.

I had a bad feeling about this, and it worsened when I spotted the rack of antlers in the sink. Sickish expression. "You're expecting the Gwawabanowes, aren't you?"

"Eyan, Noozis," she replied, with a nod. She prefers to speak Anishinabemowin in her own home. "They know we always eat traditional on *Niba-anamiaygijigad.* And you know how much they love jellied moose nose. Get to work!" She shot a quick glance at Aunt Denise. "When you finish stirring the lard, *Indaanis,* put it in the refrigerator."

My aunt chuckled. "I just hope there's some room!"

Grabbing a long curved *migoss,* I stepped up to the sink and set to work. I inserted the razor-sharp tip three inches in front of *Moozo*'s dark sightless eyes, then carefully cut away the upper jawbone. Another lengthy slice separated the pulpy nose meat from the bone. I boiled the bulbous nose in a stovetop kettle for forty-five minutes, slapped the warm meat on an oak cutting board, grabbed a short-bladed knife, and did some skinning. Then, while the trimmed meat soaked in cold water, I prepared the stewpot for boiling, adding chopped onions, sage and wintergreen berries.

Grimacing, I ran the back of my hand across my damp forehead. Whew! All this work for *hors d'oeuvres* that would disappear in less than five minutes!

Just then, I felt a wintry gust on the seat of my biketard. A husky male voice boomed, *"Watchiya, Biwabanikweg.* When do we eat?"

"Uncle Walter!" Turning, I saw two elderly Anishinabe men removing their snowboots. The shorter was Grandma Biwaban's kid brother—my father's uncle—Walter Biwaban. Sixtyish fellow with thinning white hair, low eyebrows and the trademark Biwaban aquiline nose. At his side stood my mother's father, Charlie Blackbear, whom I kiddingly call *Chief* because of a slight resemblance to old Rain-in-the-Face. He is my grandmother's age, a rugged, white-haired trail guide with deepest obsidian eyes bracketed by wrinkles and small, flat ears.

I hugged each of them in turn. Then, with Uncle Walter holding me at arm's length, I asked, "Any trouble getting here?"

"Not a bit, Angie." He nodded in the direction of my grandfather. "Charlie was waiting right there on the Bayfield dock." Muted chuckle. "That windsled ride gets bumpier every year."

Chief ruffled my hair. "This girl been behavin' herself, Julie?"

Grandma went right on smothering moose steaks in

white flour. "Up to a point. Does she always jump around that way up at Tettegouche?"

"It's called aerobic exercise, *Nokomis,*" I added, using our people's affectionate term for "grandmother."

"Is *that* what it is?" Chief chuckled. "And all this time I thought I was living in a Pringle's commercial."

"Oh, ha-ha-ha," I groused, then spotted the newspaper tucked beneath my uncle's arm. "Is that today's *News-Tribune?*"

"Sure is, Angie," he said, handing it over. Affectionate squeeze of Grandma's shoulders. "Is that hot coffee I smell, *Nimissay?*"

Since I still had tons of Christmas shopping to do, I decided to check out the ads for the Glass Block. As I snapped open the paper, however, a front-page headline caught my eye.

WOMAN KILLED AT SPIRIT MOUNTAIN

A local woman perished yesterday evening in a skiing mishap on Spirit Mountain's Blue Ruin trail.

The body of Yvonne Pryor, 29, of 5304 Ramsey Street, Duluth was discovered by ski trail groomers shortly after 9 p.m.

Police believe the woman skidded on one of Blue Ruin's hairpin turns, lost control and collided with a tree. The impact killed her instantly.

A lifelong resident of the Twin Ports, Ms. Pryor was employed as the office manager at Polaris Development Corp. She had attended a business meeting at the lodge earlier yesterday.

Grandma Biwaban was the first to sense my distress. Tone of concern. "What is it, Angie?"

"Y-Yvonne Pryor!" Tears blurred my vision as I lowered the newspaper. "She—She's *dead!*"

Chief stepped forward. "Yvonne . . . that black girl you played volleyball with?"

Blinking tears away, I nodded. "She was killed last

night at Spirit Mountain. I—I saw her there a few hours earlier."

Aunt Denise sought to comfort me. "Angie, perhaps you'd better sit down—"

"No!" I waved her off, then quickly shed my apron. "Look, I've got to go out for a while. Okay? I—I'll be back."

"Angie . . ."

"Let her go, Denise," Chief advised. Expression of deep sympathy. "You want a ride downtown, girl?"

"Gawiin, Nimishoo." I shook my head, handing him the newspaper. "I'll be all right."

Reaching Duluth's lakeshore proved to be an adventure in itself. It had snowed again the previous night, smothering the Zenith City in a good four inches of fresh powder. Fortunately, my trusty 1969 Mercury Montego, Clunky, was all decked out in brand-new B.F. Goodrich snow tires. *De rigeur* for Duluth's vertical hillside streets in the wintertime.

My grandmother's restored Queen Anne house sits on just such a street. It's right up there at the summit of Goat Hill, on a gabbro promontory offering a panoramic view of the Twin Ports. The ten houses up there on 18½ Avenue West are separated from the rest of Duluth by lofty gabbro bluffs. The only way up there is via the city's cliff-hugging wooden stairway, which probably explains why Grandma has stayed so slim.

So distraught was I at Yvonne's unexpected death that I reached I-35 before I realized that I had no idea where her sister lived. The Pryor family used to reside on Second Street East, in the Central Hillside district, but there was no guarantee that Kendra had remained in the neighborhood. And then I remembered the address listed in the newspaper.

So I took the long bend from Piedmont Avenue onto the expressway, zoomed along in the westbound lane, past crowded neighborhoods and distant waterfront grain elevators. Overhead passed the coal-black trestles of the Duluth, Missabe and Iron Range Railroad. Then the expressway levelled out a bit, and I spied the 40th Avenue exit.

Within minutes, I was cruising down Grand Avenue, the section of town we call Spirit Valley. Aging brownstone office buildings, cafes and small shops. Not to mention baroque Denfeld High School, where Mother had taught history, with its decorative towers and wide, newly-shovelled walkways. I drove past the snowdrifts of Memorial Park and that miniature fortress of dark red Minnesota sandstone, the American Legion Hall, slowed to a crawl in front of West Duluth News, hit the blinkers and hung a sharp left into the K-Mart lot. Clunky came to rest grille-first against a tall mound of plowed snow.

Back down Grand Avenue I sauntered. Anishinabe princess in her plum-colored down parka, woolen toboggan hat, light gray ski pants and black dress boots. Snow-clad mountains, their slopes dusted with evergreens, rose on three sides, giving the neighborhood a distinct alpine air. You never would have guessed that the lakefront lay a hundred yards to the south, just beyond the huge paper mill.

Spirit Valley brimmed with holiday cheer. Imitation silver bells dangled from the streetlights. Plastic Santas, candy canes, winged angels and red-nosed reindeer cluttered the storefront windows. There was no need for artificial frost. One thing about Duluth—you can always count on a white Christmas!

Remembering the address given in the *News-Tribune,* I turned left in Ramsey Square and headed for Yvonne's apartment house. I'd planned on asking her landlady for Kendra's address. That notion faded, however, as I spied the commotion in front of Number 5304.

Two brawny uniformed patrolmen were struggling with a stunning and strangely familiar black woman. Others streamed through the front entrance, directed by a bareheaded man in a woolen topcoat. The lady had a surprisingly imaginative vocabulary. Ignoring her tirade, the cops wrestled her down the steps and into the back seat of a curbside cruiser.

Of course, I could have walked over there and asked what was going on. Having served a prison term, I wasn't too keen about wandering onto a crime scene and chatting with the cops. They might put handcuffs on me, and, boy, would that play havoc with my parole!

So I waited until the three cruisers had departed, then headed for the front walk. Yvonne's landlady stood in the doorway. Elderly Swedish lady with her white hair in a bun. Slightly lidded blue eyes and a thin, downturned mouth. She shot me a wary look as I stepped onto her front walk.

Bright Angie smile. "Merry Christmas!"

"God Jul!" She seemed dwarfed by her wool blend anorak. Thin denim-clad legs protruded into unclasped snowboots.

Tilting my head slightly, I asked, "What was that all about?"

Pinched frown. "The police arrested one of my tenants—Nikki Slater. Arrested her for drugs." Mild shake of the head. "I might have known."

"Drugs?" I echoed.

"Cocaine." Blue eyes flashed fire. "I warned them right off! I told Yvonne and Nikki I wasn't going to put up with that. Hmph! Should've known better than to rent to a couple of ni—*those* people!"

Ignoring the comment, I prodded, "Cops came here looking for Nikki?"

"No, no!" Her veined hand waved impatiently. "They came here looking for the money."

Surprised blink. "Money?"

"The money Yvonne stole! Lord, I just about died when Detective Keegan showed me that search warrant. Cops found Nikki's cocaine while they were hunting for the money."

"How much money?"

"Four hundred grand." A breathy tone softened her harsh alto voice. "See, Yvonne got killed in a skiing accident last night. When her boss opened her desk this morning, he found a whole other set of accounting files—"

"Her boss at Polaris Development?"

"That's right." All at once, the landlady's expression turned suspicious. "You a friend of Yvonne's?"

"Long time back. We grew up on the Central Hillside," I lied, my dark eyes guileless. "I read about the accident in today's paper."

Fond Scandinavian smile. "The Hillside?"

"Uh-huh! Lived right down the street from Hilma." An easy lie. Everybody on the Central Hillside knows Mickey Fedo's Aunt Hilma.

She let out a wry chuckle. "Boy, that Hilma sure is a character, isn't she?"

Seeing the lady laugh, I eased her back into interrogation. "The police think Yvonne embezzled the money?"

"You bet! It didn't take Judge Drossel more than fifteen minutes to issue the warrant. That Sjolund fella is a real big shot. Kitchi Gammi Club. He was fit to be tied when he found those watchacallem—computer things."

"Accounting software?"

"That's it." Thin features brightened momentarily, then saddened. "I still can't believe Yvonne took that money. She seemed okay to me . . . you know—for one of *them*. Not like that Nikki." Loud harrumph. *"She* dances at the Club Oriskany—if you want to call it that!"

I made a mental note of Nikki's workplace.

The landlady rummaged in her coat pocket for a key. "Listen, I'd love to stand here and chitchat, but I've got a *grofarbraud* in the oven." Reddening fingers wiggled it into the door lock. "Merry Christmas!"

"Debia Niba-anamiaygijigad!"

I flashed a holiday smile, taking care to conceal my true feelings, then strolled briskly back to the square.

* * *

Wednesday night. Ten minutes past seven. I stood at the edge of my grandmother's yard, hands in my parka pockets, watching the silvery moon ride high above Wisconsin. To my left, the blunt spire of the Enger Tower loomed above the trees, its green lights twinkling.

Crusty snow crunched beneath the weight of a man's foot. I turned instantly. Chief lifted a hand in greeting. "It's only me. Had enough fresh air?"

I shrugged. "I guess."

"You know, you haven't said more than fifteen words since you got back this afternoon." Wrinkled features softened in sympathy. "What's got you so upset? Yvonne?"

Nodding, I took a long swallow, then began my tale. Chief listened in respectful silence. When I finally finished, he shook his head. "It could all be coincidence, girl."

"Coincidence!?" I blurted. "Chief, the winter after she graduated, Yvonne drove down to the U.P. to compete in the Olympic trials. She came this close—*this close*—" I held my thumb and forefinger a quarter-inch apart. "to making the U.S. team! There's no way she could've skidded off that trail. Yvonne could ski Blue Ruin with her eyes shut!"

"Could be she had a lot on her mind," Chief pointed out. "If she did steal all that money, she might've been worrying about getting caught."

"We only have Sjolund's word for it that anything was even stolen!"

"Then why did Yvonne ask you what prison was like? Sounds to me like a woman really worried about going to jail."

No reply from Angie. The thought had crossed my own mind—and more than once! I had to wonder if my own brutally frank comment had contributed to Yvonne's inattention on the ski trail.

But to believe that, I also had to believe Yvonne

Pryor guilty of embezzlement. And I didn't. Not for one moment.

My obsidian eyes flashed. "Do you really believe Yvonne hid four hundred grand in her apartment?" Chief opened his mouth, but I beat him to the punch. "An apartment she shared with Nikki Slater. And how did she keep Nikki from finding it? Nikki works nights at the Club Oriskany. She's home all day."

"Maybe Nikki didn't know about the embezzlement."

"Roommates have few secrets from each other, Chief. And four hundred grand will buy a lot of cocaine."

"Yvonne could have hidden it elsewhere."

"And left the incriminating software in her desk drawer where Derek Sjolund could conveniently find it?"

Chief's mouth curled at the corners. "*Nandobani* time again, eh?" Rueful chuckle. "I've got a granddaughter who thinks she's the Lone Ranger."

"I think Yvonne was set up, Chief."

"Aren't you taking a real risk, missy? The FBI is still out hunting for *Pocahontas.* Do you really want to draw that much official attention to yourself?"

"Sooner or later, the Duluth P.D. is going to find out about my chat with Yvonne." I sighed. "When they come calling, I'd like to be able to give them more than a simple confirmation of accidental death."

"Could be that's all it is."

"Let's find out for certain, Chief."

"What do you have in mind?"

Turning to the right, I let my gaze wander up the shoreline. Spirit Valley was a basket of lights huddled at the foot of the snow-clad mountain. I smiled at my grandfather. "I always wanted to see the inside of the Club Oriskany."

Deep chuckle. "You're still too young."

"You can be my chaperone."

The Club Oriskany occupied a two-story building on Grand Avenue, easily within walking distance of the mill. Red neon signs advertised Pabst, Schlitz and Iron City beer. Hand-painted placards proclaimed *Sexy Coeds, Exotic Dancing* and *No Cover!* No cover—right! Somehow they neglected to tell prospective customers about the ten-dollar entry fee.

And so, Alexander Hamilton won my grandfather and I admittance to the varnished elm lobby. Faint bluish smoke gave the bar a dreamlike haze. I could almost taste the beer fumes tinting that hot, moist, smoky air. The big Wurlitzer jukebox belted out the Billie Jane Baxter version of "Jingle Bell Rock." The lady's Oklahoma twang competed with a raucous masculine undertone.

Flanking either side of the bar's entrance were life-sized cardboard mockups of two gorgeous black women in Las Vegas garb. Ostrich feathers, sequinned G-strings and fishnet pantyhose. The club's two stars—Foxy Doxy and Bahama Mama.

"What now?" my grandfather whispered.

Before I could reply, I felt a chilly breeze on my spine. The club's door boomed shut behind us, and the bartender hollered, "You're late!"

"Cut me some slack, Mac." Sexy contralto voice. "Bondsman didn't get there till seven. They don't spring the jailhouse door right open, ya know."

Turning, I got a close-up glimpse of Bahama Mama, a.k.a. Nikki Slater. Slender black woman three inches taller than my five-foot-four. Short hair, large golden loop earrings, chestnut eyes and the lovely sculpted features of a Yoruba princess. That face seemed awfully familiar, and then I remembered. I'd seen Nikki at Central, usually smoking funny cigarettes in the ladies room.

A furious scowl spoiled the lines of Nikki's mouth. Looking past us as if we weren't even there, she marched down the side corridor, heading for the dressing room.

I set off in quick pursuit. "Ah . . . Nikki?"

Graceful dancer's pirouette. Recognition gleamed in

those chestnut eyes. "I know you!" Her slender forefinger jabbed at my collarbone. "Park Point, right? Angie something."

"That's right," I purred, pacing her to the dressing room door. "Could I talk to you for a minute?"

"Sure, honey!" For a second, she was the same old giggly Nikki I remembered from high school. But that silly smile failed to alter the hard set of her eyes. "We can talk while I get dressed."

Nikki's dressing room, formerly the broom closet, measured sixty square feet and somehow managed to hold two vanity tables and a pair of closets. Brightly-colored Miami travel posters covered what little wall space there was. Taped to Nikki's bulb-rimmed mirror were snapshots of herself in scanty dance outfits. A miniature Christmas tree occupied the far corner of her vanity table.

Actually, Nikki did all the talking. The lady kept up her nonstop monologue as she shed her street clothes, donned her sequinned costume, smothered her face with foundation makeup and pasted on her curling false eyelashes. I received a complete summary of the showbiz career of one Nichole Jeannette Slater, which consisted mostly of bump-and-grind routines at Northland watering holes.

" . . . lot of great bars in Hurley, Wisconsin. Usually I dance at Cousin Jack's, but Tony DiLuglio's been after me to work at his place in Ironwood. Trouble with Tony is he's too bossy. Insists I work the weekend. Shit! I could be Triplicate Girl and dance my ass off at Cousin Jack's, Tony's Bar *and* the Come-On Inn in Ontonagon and still come up short. Nothing beats dancin' weekends in the Twin Ports, gal—*nothing!*" Putting down the mascara brush, she gave her eye makeup a critical stare. "Except maybe Miami! Yeah, that's where I'd love to be spendin' Christmas. Right down there in Miami, Florida. And I would be, too, if that no-good Chango hadn't—" Biting off the remainder, she snatched her lipstick off the table. "I'm tellin' you, hon,

I've seen enough snow to last me the rest of my life. So when are we goin' to Miami, Chango honey? 'Soon, baby, soon.' *Shit!* I should live so long!" Uncapping the tube, she aimed a quizzical glance my way. "Say, you used to be a dancer, didn't you? What brings you here, Angie? Lookin' for a job?"

"Not quite." Folding my arms, I leaned casually against the closet door. "I heard you were rooming with Yvonne Pryor."

"Uh-huh!" Artfully she applied her lipstick. Then, capping it once more, she added, "What's it to you, gal?"

I fell back on my cover story. "I heard what happened to Yvonne. I thought maybe you could give me her sister's address."

"Kendra? She still lives on Second Street. Couple of blocks up from Fitger's." She gave me the number, picked up her lip pencil and let out a mild grunt. "Don't expect me at the funeral, though."

Her anger startled me. "Why not?"

"Uppity bitch got me busted, that's why not!" Nikki's voice rose sharply. "Cops come crashin' in with a warrant, lookin' for the money she stole, and there's my coke sittin' on the night table. Now *I'm* the one lookin' at eight months in Shakopee!" The lip pencil quivered in her hand. "I'd better get probation, that's all I've gotta say. No way am I doin' laundry with a bunch of women. No way, no how!" Flustered, she slapped the pencil down hard. "Then Miss Goody Two Shoes went and got herself killed. Ohhhhh, I wish that bitch had lived. I would've loved to have seen her black ass down in Shakopee. All her fault, ya know? Miss Goody-Good Pryor! It all woulda been different if she and Chango hadn't—" Her fist thumped the tabletop, making her creme jar clatter. "God damn it all! If it weren't for that bitch, I'd be in *Miami!*"

So there'd been friction between the roommates, eh? That was interesting. But I had to know more.

"Who's Chango?" I asked innocently.

"Son of a bitch!" Sudden tart smile. "Or *hijo de puta*, like they say down there in Cali, Colombia."

"Did you go out with him first?" I inquired.

"I go out with a lot of guys, honey." More than anything else, that sudden nonchalant pose revealed the depths of her jealousy.

"Then he became Yvonne's boyfriend," I added.

"Boyfriend!?" Nikki's teeth clenched. "Surely you don't think Miss Goody-Good Pryor would let herself be seen in public with a Colombian . . . sports promoter! Why, if that rich cracker she worked for knew she was bumpin' Chango, he'd have tossed her out on her little black ass. Whitey don't like sharin' the wealth, Angie gal."

I blinked. Nikki had just thrown me a curve. "Are you saying—"

"Yvonne had a taste for white meat? I surely am!" Carefully she adjusted her rhinestone tiara. "He drives a mighty fine car, too. A big white Connie. Seen it with my own eyes."

"When?"

"October. He come by one mornin' to pick up Yvonne." She reached for the lip pencil again. "See, I usually hit the sack around four. I was asleep maybe three or four hours when I heard this horn honkin'. Went over to the window to see what was goin' on. There's this big white Connie parked out front and Yvonne comes dancin' down the front steps with this shit-eatin' grin on her face. Happy as a meadowlark. She got in, and they drove away." She paused to touch up her mouth. "Later on, I asked Yvonne about it, and she told me she'd gone to some business meetin' in Minneapolis. Business meetin', my ass! I got a good look at her face. That gal was itchin' for it."

"How do you know he was white?" I asked.

Snort of laughter. "How many Duluth homeboys you know ridin' around in a brand-new Connie?" She pursed her lips at the mirror. "Shit, that Yvonne was no end of surprises. Liftin' her skirt. Rippin' off the Man."

Nikki's expression changed suddenly, turning craftier. Or, to be more precise, an unintelligent woman trying to look sly. "You wouldn't know anythin' about *that,* would you?"

"About what?" I replied. The question came at me too abruptly. My answer sounded much too contrived.

Nikki's dark eyes gleamed with avarice. "You don't fool anybody, gal. You'd like to get your hands on all that cash money."

"And set myself up for a lengthy tour of laundry duty at Shakopee? No thanks, Nikki."

"Help me find it." She swiveled in her chair, her sexy voice breathless with excitement. "I got friends in the mob. It's hot money, sure, but we could fence it easy. I'll split it with you fifty-fifty." Delighted chuckle. "With that kind of money, I'll buy myself Christmas presents and wrap them in mink!"

Just then, Nikki's gaze travelled past me to the doorway, and her jovial expression vanished, replaced by one of hellish surprise.

Glancing over my shoulder, I spotted a well dressed, hawk-featured man with slicked back raven hair and deepset ebony eyes lounging in the doorway. Sharp nose, mild overbite, thin eyebrows and an Errol Flynn moustache. The suit came straight from *Caporegime's.* Pale cream woolen blazer and slacks, glossy black shirt and spotless white tie.

He levelled a stubby Hispanic finger at me. "Out!"

Instant Angie retreat. From the corridor I watched a very nervous Nikki rise from her chair. "Ch-Chango . . . *querido* . . . I—I thought you w-were in M-Minneapolis."

"Hank called me." All business, he strolled into the dressing room. "He told me you were in jail."

"I—I'll pay it all back, honey. The b-bail money—every penny, I swear!" Nikki's hands fluttered in apprehension. "Just don't—don't get mad, okay!?"

"You've got it all backwards, *puta!*" Chango's voice raised gooseflesh on the back of my neck. "Your ass is supposed to *make* me money—not *cost* me money. Maybe we'd better have a talk, *verdad?*"

"Uh . . . uh . . . Chango, I got a show at nine."

"This won't take too long."

He slammed the door in my face.

I found my grandfather at the bar, nursing a small beer. As I sidled up beside him, he murmured, "Learn anything?"

"Plenty!" I groused. "Yvonne's roommate cordially hated her. Seems Yvonne made a play for Nikki's main man, who, incidentally, is also her pimp. Before that, she was going out with one of the big boys at the Polaris office."

"Big boys?" he echoed.

"Big enough to afford a white Lincoln Continental." My expression soured. "Sure doesn't sound like the Yvonne I knew."

"The Yvonne you knew is ten years older," Chief replied, and seeing my scowl, added, "What is it, Angie?"

So I told him about the encounter between Nikki and Chango, how their quarrelling voices had chased me down the corridor.

". . . Look, I'm a grownup, okay? I know she probably chose the life. I mean, you don't get to be Bahama Mama by attending Sunday school. Still, when I think about leaving her with—"

"There wasn't much you could do about it, Angie."

My memory was stuck on a single image. Teenaged Nikki goofing off in the ladies room. Prolonged sigh. "She wasn't a *bad* girl, Chief . . . just messed up."

Tilting his head to one side, my grandfather whispered, "I'd be more concerned about *him* if I were you."

Peering over my shoulder, I watched Chango move through the crowded bar, his hawk face swiveling from side to side. No need to guess who he was looking for. Grabbing my purse, I murmured, "I'll meet you at the truck."

Frigid air stung my face as I stepped into the night. Pulling on my fleece mittens, I headed straight for Chief's Bronco. Footsteps crunched the snow behind me.

Run for it, princess!

I almost made it, too. My hand actually touched the Bronco's passenger door. Then a firm grip snagged my parka's hood and slammed me against the cold metal.

I swung at the masculine arm. "Let go!"

"Not yet, *chiquita!*" Chango kept his grip. Small feral smile. "What did Yvonne tell you, eh? Did she put you up to this?"

Blinking in confusion, I muttered, 'What?"

Chango's wiry hand squeezed my chin. "Did that bitch send you to Nikki?"

"Of course not!"

"Then why were you talking to her, eh?"

Defiant glare. "I needed Kendra's address."

Dark eyes reflected surprise. "What for?"

"Don't you read newspapers, Chango? Yvonne's dead."

The news took him by surprise. There was no mistaking that sudden wide-eyed expression of shock.

"You shitting me?"

"She was killed at Spirit Mountain last night. But I forgot—you were in Minneapolis, weren't you?"

He didn't appreciate the reference to his whereabouts. It was a hard shove, hard enough to thump the back of my head against the truck door. "Nikki has got to learn to keep her *boca grande* shut. I see you got the same problem, too, bitch."

"You'd better get your alibi squared away, *amigo.*" I tried without success to ignore the painful lump sprouting beneath my scalp. "When the police find out Yvonne was your girl, they'll want to talk to you."

"It won't do any good. I don't know where that money is."

Well, well, I thought, he didn't know Yvonne was

dead, but he knew about the money stolen from Polaris Development.

My stomach began to squirm. Had Yvonne really embezzled that four hundred thousand? Had Chango put her up to it?

"But maybe *you* know, eh?"

His grip tightened on my chin.

I kicked hard. My boot tagged him just above the ankle, where the skin is thinnest and the nerves most sensitive. Chango let out a baritone howl. Doing a one-legged hip-hop, he clutched his bruised shin with both hands.

At that moment, the Bronco's window slid down, and a long blued shotgun barrel poked out. My grandfather's Remington 870 twelve-gauge. Its muzzle captured the tip of Chango's nose.

Nikki's pimp turned as white as Spirit Mountain. *"Caramba!"*

"Don't sneeze!" warned Chief. "This piece makes a helluva mess at point-blank range."

I grinned. Boy, my grandfather sure is quiet. I didn't even hear him slip into the Bronco from the driver's side.

"Now why don't you wave to the moon, boy? Both hands. That's it. Nice and high." Chief's stern face appeared in the window. "And the next time my granddaughter tells you to let go, you do it. Understand?"

"Claro que si!" Chango nodded vigorously.

"Hop in, Angie."

"One minute." Stepping forward, I unbuttoned Chango's blazer and gave him a thorough frisking.

His nose still lodged in the Remington's barrel, he peered down at me. *"Que—?* What are you, cops or something?"

"Vigilantes," I replied, resisting the naughty urge to tickle his ribs. "I'm the Lone Ranger. Great disguise, eh?" I found an automatic pistol huddled in a hideaway holster on the inside of his waistband. My mittened hand plucked it away. Hmmmm—nine millimeter

Makarov. Serial number filed off. Probably smuggled out of the Caribbean.

Hawkish features tensed in fury. "Bitch! You can't—!"

"Chango," I said, all business. "I'm going to call the club tomorrow night. If I find out Nikki isn't dancing, or if I see her face with any bruises . . ." I held the pistol aloft. "The BATF will be getting a little surprise package from Santa Claus. I'm betting this piece isn't registered. And I just know your fingerprints are on file with Uncle Sam."

I tossed the Makarov to my grandfather. Slowly he withdrew the shotgun, leaving me just enough room to open the door and climb aboard. The pimp stood there, hands upraised, cursing us both in *colombiano* Spanish.

As we drove away, my grandfather shook his head. "Was that fun, Angie?"

I replaced the Remington on the cab's varnished gunrack. "Hey, I had to do something to help Nikki. What's the matter?"

"Have you noticed we seem to be getting nowhere fast?"

"Got a better idea, Chief?"

"Yeah! Let's have a look at the crime scene."

My grandfather and I arrived at the Spirit Mountain lodge just before eleven. A handful of cars filled the spaces closest to the snow covered chalet. The wind pushed tendrils of loose powder across the moonlit slopes.

We timed it just right. The snowmakers had gathered their equipment and were about to make their nightly gun run. Rugged, outdoorsy people in their early twenties, clad in face masks, ski pants, mountaineer boots and a firefighter's black rubber coat. As we approached the lodge, they were lugging water hoses and wheeling snow cannons out of the pump house.

One groomer loitered behind. Tall blond guy. Early twenties. Corduroy ballcap and ruddy cheeks. He squatted beside his small, pinch-nosed water cannon, using a wrench to tighten its skinny metallic legs.

Flashing a friendly smile, I made my approach.

"Woman who got killed?" he echoed, brushing the snow from his knees. "Sure! Over there on Blue Ruin. Yvonne Pryor. She did a lot of skiing up here, you know. She was usually one of the last ones off the slope at nine."

"Did many people stay that late, Eric?" I asked.

He shook his head. "Only the hardcore hot dogs. Ms. Pryor was *definitely* one!"

"Did she ever come here with other people?"

His lips puckered thoughtfully. "Couple times, I guess."

Remembering Nikki's story, I asked, "Did you ever see her arrive in a big white Lincoln Continental?"

"Well, no . . ." Uncertain look. "But there was a white Connie here the other day, though."

"The evening Ms. Pryor was killed," Chief prodded.

Swift nod from Eric. "I got here a couple hours early. My girl was working cocktail waitress in the lounge. Car pulled out just as I arrived." Sudden grin. "I thought some rich guy had hosted a private party or something."

"Had you ever seen it here before?"

"I might have. Once or twice, maybe. I—I really can't say." He looked up suddenly, then showed us both an apologetic expression. "Listen, I'd love to talk, but I see my partner stamping his feet out there, and I've really got to get going. Scissor Bill's a long trail." He stooped and picked up the snow gun. "And we've got plenty of these to plant."

After thanking him, Chief and I returned to the Bronco. We gave the Spirit Mountain snowmakers forty-five minutes to descend their assigned trails. Then my grandfather opened the truck's toolchest.

Minutes later, Chief and I were shuffling down a snowy side trail in our bearpaw snowshoes. Stars littered the sky like diamonds on black velvet. The wind chill had pushed the mercury down past thirty below on the

Fahrenheit scale, but I was dressed for it. Two insulating layers of rabbit fur warmed my sturdy moosehide moccasin boots, and I had shed my stylish winter coat in favor of a hooded anorak trimmed with *ojeeg* fur. What's that? Well, *Ojeeg* is better known to you new people as the fisher. Like his *Mustelidae* cousins, the weasel and the otter, he positively thrives during our Northland winters.

Of course, no Anishinabe princess goes out on a December night without her *mindjikawanag*—fur-lined mitten-style gauntlets with drawstrings that tie just below the elbow. New people call them *choppers*.

So there we were, humping along, with Chief well out in front. He gets around as easily on snowshoes as I do on high heels. Then again, he's had nearly fifty more winters to practice. He led me down the powdery trail, through groves of slim white aspen and stands of dark blue spruce. Then, all at once, he halted, stood erect and gestured at a sharp curve with a two-fingered jab. "There, *Noozis.*"

My reply was a whisper. Sound carriers far at night, and I didn't want us overheard by the snowmakers. "Are you sure?"

Leading me over to an aspen, he pointed out the scraped bark near the roots and a trio of broken twigs just beyond.

"Yvonne's ski made the scrape," he whispered. "She was already out of control when she plunged through here."

I glanced back upslope. Thirty feet of Blue Ruin straightaway led into this sharp turn. Mild scowl. How could Yvonne have lost it back there?

As if in answer to my question, Chief patted my shoulder. "Poke around in the snow. I'll do the same over there."

"Poke around!?" Blink of utter confusion. "What am I looking for?"

Chief grinned. "You'll know when you find it."

For a moment, I thought my grandfather had lost his mind. He shuffled along at the edge of the woods, periodically halting, squatting on his bearpaws, and sifting snow with his mittened hands. On the other hand, I thought, he *is* the best tracker on the shores of Lake Superior. So he must know what he's doing.

Hunkered down, I thrust both hands into the loose powder. Cold tickled my fingertips. It was like moving my hands through dishwater. Again, Angie. White frosted my choppers as I raised my hands. And again.

This was the loose powder snow that had fallen the previous night. Our people call it *jakagonaga.* There are eight different kinds of snow, and we Anishinabe have a word for each and every one.

Just then, my choppers made contact with a crusty solid lump. I fished it out of the snow, holding it up to the pallid moonlight. It was a teardrop-shaped snow fragment, firm and sandpapery. The kind of snow we call *onabanadonaga.*

Frowning in puzzlement, I hissed, *"Nimishoo!"*

Chief's snowshoes made *whisk-whisk* noises as he hurried over. Obsidian eyes gleamed in triumph. "Poke around some more, *Noozis.*"

Together we excavated a half dozen such snow fragments, ranging in size from chestnut to softball. Each new trophy drew a muted grunt of satisfaction from my grandfather.

Hefting my original find, I whispered, "You *knew* this would be here."

"Let's just say I had my suspicions."

"What have we found, *Nimishoo?*"

"The way he killed Yvonne," he explained, *sotto voce.* "I suspected as much when I saw those snow cannons. The killer borrowed one from the pump house and set it up right alongside the trail. When Yvonne came over that rise, he opened the nozzle and let her have it. The snow spray knocked her off-balance. There's no way she could've stopped, not at the speed she was moving. She skidded off the trail over there, struck another tree and got killed."

"And these lumps?" I inquired.

"Leftover man-made snow. It froze in the nozzle the last time the groomers carried the snow gun back to the lodge."

Scowling, I visualized the hardened snow erupting from the nozzle in a shotgun pattern—the stream of man-made snow arching upslope, splashing into a horrified Yvonne. Clever fellow, the murderer. The police had found Yvonne's snow-covered body among the trees and snow fragments littering the trail. And who on the Duluth P.D. could tell the difference between man-made snow and the powder that had fallen from the sky?

"Can we find the spot where he set it up?" I asked.

Chief nodded. "Sure!" He gestured downslope. "Move into the trees. Slowly, *Noozis*. Look for snow plastered to the tree trunks."

I found a dozen trees in there wearing vertical snow stripes. My path converged with my grandfather's about fifteen feet from the ski run. Doing a pert about-face, I had a flawless view of the moonlit straightaway.

Chief peered over my shoulder. "This is it, all right. Here's where he set up his snow cannon."

"That tells us something about Yvonne's killer."

"Like what?" he asked.

"He's very familiar with ski slopes, particularly the runs here at Spirit Mountain." I shivered as the icy wind buffeted my anorak. "He's worked as a snowmaker in the past. He knew exactly where to go for a snow cannon, how to set it up, and how to turn on the nozzle. And he knew Yvonne would be coming down Blue Ruin sometime that evening."

Chief's gaze met mine. "Meaning he was at the lodge after you left. He must've spoken to Yvonne. Found out she was planning to ski Blue Ruin."

"Or he was there *when I was,*" I replied. Instantly I thought of Yvonne's boss—the victim of her supposed embezzlement—Derek Sjolund.

* * *

After skulking around Spirit Mountain, I had hoped to sleep in on Thursday morning. Just snuggle beneath Grandma Biwaban's hand-sewn comforter and snooze.

No such luck! Just after eight a.m., my cousin Laura showed up to help with the Christmas cooking, and, the moment her back was turned, her two giggling preschoolers tiptoed upstairs to sound reveille.

I awoke to find the bedsprings pinging and two warm bundles squirming atop my thighs. Toddler shrieks and a unison cry of "Wake up, Aunt Angie!"

So I got up, kissed the kids, pulled on my terry bathrobe and headed downstairs to greet my grandmother. The house was rapidly filling up with relatives. Aunt Denise and her daughter, Laura. Plus another cousin, Carolyn Wadena, down from Two Harbors with her children. Grandma was busily planning our mammoth Christmas dinner, an event requiring the timing of the Normandy invasion. The minute my grandmother's Canada goose was done, Aunt Denise would arrive to warm hers in the oven. Twenty minutes after that, Carolyn would arrive with the third goose. And then . . . *Wissiniwin!* Let's dig in!

Grandma's butcher shop was still open. She was busily trimming deer tongues and washing them in salt water. Aunt Denise and Laura filled the countertop with jars of wild potatoes, wild onions, Jerusalem artichokes, pumpkin blossoms, powdered cornsilk and sun-dried cranberries.

While looking for tomato juice in the refrigerator, I spotted my jellied moose nose on the middle shelf. The dark meat had been cut into rigid strips vaguely reminiscent of straight pretzels and sat cooling in its own aromatic juice.

By ten-thirty I was on the road again, heading downtown on I-35. I got off at the Lake Avenue exit, admired the immense Christmas tree in the plaza, stopped for the red light, and then turned right onto Superior Street. Crusty snow lined the sidewalks, and a mock silver bell dangled from each lamppost. Ahhh, Duluth—Christmas City of the North!

Down Superior I drove, past the antique shops and electronics stores, the brash new casino and the venerable Hotel Duluth. Fitger's slid by on my right, once a red brick nineteenth century brewery, now a luxurious shopping center. The green wreaths and holly gave the aged building a distinctly Dickensian air.

I had planned to quiz Yvonne's old boss at the Polaris office, but their receptionist informed me that Mr. Halstead was at Glensheen for the day. Reason enough to put me into a Corporate Angie outfit. Woolen taupe jacket and slit skirt to match. Opaque black tights and high-heeled pumps.

When I arrived at 3300 London Road, the wind skidding off Lake Superior made me wish I'd worn some long johns under those tights. Teeth chattering, I dashed across the parking lot into the lee of the elegant lakeside mansion, then made a beeline to the door.

Glensheen was the dream of one Chester Adgate Congdon, lumber baron and mining magnate, an elegant three-story Jacobean manor house. Hundreds of Italian and Croatian and Finnish immigrants had labored to erect its red brick walls and install its breathtaking hand-tooled pilasters and leaded stained-glass windows. The house had taken three years to build and had cost Mr. Congdon just under a million dollars. That was back in 1908, when bread still sold for a nickel a loaf.

The Congdon family donated the mansion to the University of Minnesota-Duluth back in 1968, and since then it's been open to public tours. Every Christmas, the Friends of Glensheen decorate each of the thirty-nine rooms in the holiday style of the early 1900s.

Steamed heat washed over me as I stepped into the foyer. A Christmas tree laden with Victorian glass and handmade ornaments brushed one of the ceiling's stout oak beams. Candy canes, ribbons, garlands and poinsettias from the Glensheen atrium littered the evergreen's branches. Off to the left, a hand-carved cedar stairway, trimmed with red ribbons and holly garlands, rose along the panelled wall. An antique grandfather clock stood sentry on the landing.

Just then a slender brunette wearing a geranium-colored surplice dress drifted into the foyer. Brown eyes and forty-something laugh lines. "May I help you?"

"Yes." Polite Angie smile. "I'm here to see Mr. Halstead. His office told me I could find him here."

"Really?" Hostility chilled her tone. "He isn't here right now. He is expected for brunch, though. Would you like to leave a message?"

I had the strangest feeling the lady was toying with me. "I'd rather wait . . . if you don't mind."

"Oh, he'll get the message." Her brown eyes flashed fire. "You see, I'm *Mrs.* Halstead."

Ah, that explains the hostility. Somehow I had to convince this woman that I wasn't making a play for her husband. Erasing my smile, I came on like a police sergeant. "I'm afraid this is official business, Mrs. Halstead. My name's Nichole Slater. I'm with the state treasurer's office in St. Paul."

"Oh!" Her hands suddenly clenched. "This isn't about . . . that business with Ms. Pryor . . . is it?"

"I'd prefer to discuss the matter with your husband, ma'am."

"He'll be here any minute. We have the Christmas Choral Pageant at one o'clock and—" The door slammed behind us. Mrs. Halstead's face reflected sudden welcome. "Gregory!"

I turned. Standing before the door was a tall man in his late forties. Deepset dark green eyes, sparse low eyebrows, a blunt nose with the tip tilting downward, thin lips and large, protuberant ears. Wavy brown hair rimmed those ears, but he was going a little thin on top. His hairline started a full seven inches above his eyebrows. Give the gentleman credit for style, though. He wore a dark gray woolen topcoat over a crisp heather gray suit. Its unbuttoned cleft gave me a glimpse of his white shirt and diamond-pattern Geoffrey Beene silk tie. Only his gloves didn't match. They were suede and camel-colored, reminiscent of the gloves worn by Grand Prix drivers.

Leaning over, Halstead gave his wife's extended cheek a perfunctory kiss. His gaze flitted in my direction. "What's going on, Margaret?"

"This is Miss Slater. She's with the state."

"Slater?" he echoed, offering his gloved hand.

"Nichole Slater. Treasurer's office." I kept my handshake brief and professional. "This is just a routine inquiry. I understand your firm was hit by an embezzler."

"Hold it, Miss Slater!" He lifted his hand suddenly. "I think you'd be better off talking to Mr. Sjolund."

"He's a hard man to see, Mr. Halstead."

"Tell me about it." He showed me a mild grimace. Like Yvonne, he wasn't too keen on working for Derek Sjolund. Peeling off his gloves, he asked, "What can I do for our friends in St. Paul, Miss Slater?"

"You can call me Nichole." Pert smile. Angela Biwaban, woman of a thousand aliases. "Basically, my office is interested in how the embezzlement was done. The nuts and bolts, so to speak." I extended my smile to Margaret. "You see, we publish advisories from time to time, hoping to help other businesses guard against embezzlement schemes."

"You must understand something." Features troubled, Halstead removed his jacket. "Yvonne . . ." Wary glances toward his wife. "Uh, Miss Pryor was a friend as well as an associate. She worked for me a long time."

"When the company belonged to you?" I added.

"That's right." Decisive nod. "Seven years. Lord, I get sick to my stomach every time I think of it. I still don't understand why she did it—why she turned on us that way."

"How did she get along with Mr. Sjolund?"

"All right, I suppose. Their relationship was very cool. I'm afraid Derek has a low opinion of the original staff. He seemed to think they were responsible for the firm's big slide during the recession."

Greg Halstead sounded so neutral that you never would have suspected that *he* was the original owner.

"How exactly was the money taken, Mr. Halstead?"

Hushed sigh. "Well . . . Miss Pryor was the office manager. She reviewed the accounts payable on a weekly basis." His hand brushed the sparse blond crown. "Apparently, she concocted some accounting software and used it to show accounts paid when they hadn't been. She diverted the money into a bank down in Ashland, Wisconsin and wrote checks out to cash. The auditors are still running it down. Ballpark estimate of the loss looks to be about four hundred grand."

"The police tell me you found the software, Mr. Halstead."

"That's right. I was boxing Yv—Miss Pryor's personal effects so they could be turned over to her sister." His handsome face seemed to sag. "I wondered what was on those diskettes. And when I turned on my computer . . ." Thin lips tensed in misery. "Well, that's when I discovered the theft."

"Who else had access to the accounts payable?" I asked.

"Derek and myself, of course. Wanda McKellar—she's our fiscal officer. That's about it."

"The bookkeepers had no direct access?"

Halstead nodded. "Derek wanted it that way. One of us had to open the general ledger every morning. Usually, it was either Miss Pryor or Mrs. McKellar."

"How did Miss Pryor get along with the staff?"

"Very well! She was the best aide I ever had."

Thinking of the white Lincoln Continental, I added, "Did she have any boyfriends at the office?"

"Not that I know of." The question irritated Halstead. "Miss Pryor kept her office life and her social life completely separate."

"Sure about that?"

Green eyes reflected puzzlement. "What do you mean?"

"I understand Miss Pryor was an expert skier."

His grin showed perfect teeth. "Nichole, I'd say eighty percent of our employees are skiing enthusiasts. You'll find them on slopes all over the Northland."

Coy Angie smile. "Are you a skier, Mr. Halstead?"

"Not anymore." He gave his wife a sudden one-armed hug. "The little woman won't let me. I'm getting too old, she says. It's strictly snowmobiles for me now."

I thought of Eric the snowmaker. "Do any of your employees happen to own a white Lincoln Continental?"

"White—!?" Touching her husband's sleeve, Margaret blurted, "Greg, isn't that one of Derek's—?"

Halstead cut her off. "The company owns a number of cars, Miss Slater. And, yes, one of them is a white Lincoln. They are for company business only, however, and *are not* used for skiing jaunts!" His tone grew angrier. "If you'll check with the police department, you'll find that there are *dozens* of white Lincolns here in the Twin Ports."

My eyes narrowed. "Why are you getting so angry, Mr. Halstead?"

"I don't like your insinuations, Miss Slater," he snapped. "Unless I'm very much mistaken, you're suggesting that Yvonne *had help* embezzling from those accounts." Hostile glare. "From now on, you'd better do your talking directly to Mr. Sjolund."

With that, he ushered the missus into an adjoining room, showing me the rear of his dark gray topcoat. The breeze of their passage made the glass ornaments tinkle. I watched them depart, wondering why mention of the Lincoln had upset him so, and I stood beside the Christmas tree like an anxious toddler awaiting Santa's imminent arrival.

* * *

Shortly after noontime, I wheeled Clunky into the Fitger's parking garage. A quick call to the Polaris office had pinpointed the whereabouts of Derek Sjolund. Now I had to nab him before he started gallivanting again.

After securing my trusty dark green Merc, I darted across Superior Street and strolled up the walkway of the staid and venerable Kitchi Gammi Club.

Life magazine once described the Kitch as "Duluth's swank country club." Some country club! It's right there in the heart of downtown, an English Gothic manor in dark red brick, with limestone window frames, tall chimneys, arched doorways and triangular gables that rise above the steeply pitched roof. The Kitch is the oldest private club in the state, founded in 1883 and including such luminaries as Chester A. Congdon, Luther Mendenhall, C.H. Graves, A.B. Wolvin and Pentecost Mitchell. Steel, lumber and shipping barons whose names have graced many an oreboat. The building itself went up between 1911 and 1913, courtesy of the McLeod and Smith construction company. Joe Blackbear, Chief's father and my great-grandfather, came down from Lax Lake and worked on the Kitch during the summer of 1912, for which he was paid thirty-five cents an hour, the going rate for a master carpenter in those days.

Once inside, I admired the plush maroon carpets, polished white oak woodwork and gently arched ceiling with golden plaster-relief designs. An anxious *majordomo* hurried over and questioned my presence there. Showing him my prettiest smile, I identified myself as *Nikki Slater*, apprentice anchorwoman for Channel 6 KBJR-TV, and asked to speak to Mr. Sjolund. Looking even more anxious, he escorted me to the library and suggested that I make myself comfortable.

So I did. A very easy task, I might add, considering the library's opulence. Plush leather chairs flanked either side of the huge recessed brick fireplace. Among the bricks appeared diamond-shaped tiles, each one depicting a scene from the city's history. Garlands and Christmas stockings dangled above the andirons. Carved woodwork enclosed the fireplace, rising to meet the stout oaken ceiling beams. Wandering past the heavily decorated Christmas tree, I studied the Kitch's collection of rare books. One caught my gaze. *The Ghastly Ghost of Gravesend* by Prudence Anne Clively. Took it off the shelf and glanced at the flyleaf. Hmmmm—1876. The year Jill Stormcloud's Lakota relatives sent Custer to that Big Bivouac in the Sky.

Just then, a familiar balding blond man in a dark gray pinstriped suit strode into the room. Blunt-tipped nose, narrow chin and wire-rimmed glasses. And a very uncooperative frown.

"Mr. Sjolund?" Showing a media princess smile, I extended my hand. "Nikki Slater. KBJR News—"

He cut me right off. "I'm afraid I don't have time to talk to reporters."

"Make time, Mr. Sjolund."

Green eyes bulged. He wasn't accustomed to backtalk. Harsh swallow. "Why should I?"

"You're out four hundred thousand dollars," I said, folding my hands very demurely. "The money allegedly stolen by Yvonne Pryor—"

"There's no *alleged* about it, Miss Slater." He just wouldn't let me finish a sentence. "I saw the software with my own two eyes. Yvonne was keeping a double set of books. She'd been tapping those accounts for over a year."

"Did you work closely with Miss Pryor?"

"On occasion." His thin shoulders shrugged.

"How would you characterize her work?"

"Competent, I suppose. She was recommended by Greg Halstead, the former owner. I bought the business from him. Yvonne really wasn't my choice at all. Greg persuaded me to keep her on. He was very fond of her. She was sort of a protégé, I guess. Greg took a personal interest in her career." His scowl dipped even lower. "Why all the questions about me and Pryor?"

"I'm just wondering what her motive was," I explained. "Wondering if she had some kind of grudge against you."

"I don't see why." Aggrieved expression. "If anything, that woman should've been grateful I kept her on. The original staff ran Ridgeline right into the ground."

"Does that assessment include Mr. Halstead?"

"To be perfectly candid, yes." His eyes glittered behind those wire-rimmed glasses. "Don't get me wrong. Greg's a good salesman, and he really knows the real estate trade, but he's too soft. He lacks the killer instinct you need to succeed in this business."

Intrigued by his choice of words, I remarked, "Still, you kept most of the old staff."

"I really didn't have a choice, Miss Slater. I had to get my Duluth operation up and running. I would've preferred to have used my own people. They're trustworthy—reliable." Derek seemed obsessed by the notion of employee loyalty. "This never would've happened if I'd brought in someone from Brainerd."

Time to ask him about that white Connie, princess.

"What were you and Yvonne Pryor doing at Spirit Mountain Tuesday afternoon?" I asked.

Derek stiffened. "I've already given my statement to the police. I really don't see where that's any of your business, Miss Slater."

"You didn't get the money, eh?"

Emerald eyes blossomed in anger. "I beg your pardon!"

"Let's not bullshit each other, Derek." My own smile turned frosty. "You were at the lodge making a pitch to some big money boys from the Twin Cities. To get your proposed North Star Mall off the ground, you need upfront funding. Lots of it! You and Miss Pryor gave a spirited presentation, but they didn't buy the concept."

"I don't know where you heard that, but—"

Now it was my turn to interrupt. "Stands to reason, guy. Your lot isn't zoned commercial. All you've got is fifteen acres of rural land, plus a whole lot of opposition from merchants, residents and environmentalists. Too risky, Derek. That's why Ornell and Dahlberg turned you down."

An angry crimson flush crept up his face. "I will thank you not to repeat that to anyone at your station. My business dealings are *not* legitimate news items!"

"They are when they're part of a murder case, Derek."

Expression of disbelief. "Miss Pryor was killed in a skiing accident—"

"At Spirit Mountain less than three hours after she last spoke to you, Mr. Sjolund."

His eyes narrowed. "And what is that supposed to mean?"

"Let's try this on for size, Derek." My hands outlined a rectangular shape. "You paid out big bucks for that rural acreage on Miller Creek. Now it turns out the lot is a white elephant. You can't get your zoning change, and the Minneapolis bankers won't bite. When you add the current real estate slump to the equation, it's got to hurt. Maybe that mall was supposed to keep you from going the same way as Ridgeline Realty."

"You'd better keep that big mouth *shut*, Miss Slater!"

Ignoring his threat, I murmured, "You know, for a guy who just lost four hundred grand, you seem awfully chipper."

"Are you suggesting that I—!?"

"Yvonne Pryor wasn't the only one with access to your general ledger, pal. There's no proof that she's the one who concocted that accounting software."

I made no mention of Chango's knowledge of the theft. Or Yvonne's troubling questions about prison. I wasn't all that certain she hadn't embezzled the money. My needling, however, had an unexpected effect on the great man's composure.

"Shut your mouth!" Up came his white-knuckled fist. "If so much as one word of that goes out over the air, I'll sue the station for every damned cent!"

"Well, you must admit, Mr. Sjolund, it was rather

convenient—Yvonne dying *just before* you discovered the theft."

"It was an accident—*an accident!*" Rage turned him into a tenor. "I had absolutely nothing to do with it!"

"You brought her to Spirit Mountain, didn't you?"

"I told you to *shut your mouth!*"

Derek's angry bellows brought the *majordomo* on the run.

"What seems to be the problem!?" he asked.

I aimed my thumb at Sjolund. "Got a man here who doesn't like your horseradish."

Sjolund exploded in fury. While the majordomo tried to calm him, I made a swift and graceful exit.

You know, I'll bet that's the most excitement the Kitch has seen since the day old man Congdon dropped his fork!

Two-thirty found me back in Grandma Biwaban's kitchen, preparing the stuffing for Christmas dinner. My taupe suit had given way to a black raspberry mock-turtleneck cardigan, flannel-lined jeans and knee-high moosehide moccasin boots.

Margarine curdled in a saucepan on the stove. I poured in a tablespoon of flour, added pinches of sage and wild onion, and did some stirring. Then I lifted the lid on the neighboring pot. The wild rice was coming along very nicely. Stepping over to the counter, I reached for a small knife. My grandmother had left the cornbread out overnight, letting the air harden it. I reduced the loaves to bite-sized chunks. Then, holding each one above the mixing bowl, I reduced them to crumbs.

So many questions, I mused. Did Yvonne steal that money? Did she have some kind of grudge against Sjolund? And if she *didn't* steal it, then how had boyfriend Chango found out about the theft?

Pursing my lips, I kept on crumbling cornbread.

Let's assume for a moment that my old friend isn't

guilty. What if she had *discovered* the theft before Halstead?

In that case, Yvonne must have known she would be a logical suspect. She knew the theft might be pinned on her. That would explain why she was so worried about prison.

And it might also explain Chango's knowledge of the theft. Yvonne might have confided her worries to him. Which leads us to the next question. Namely, why hadn't she confided in Sjolund or Halstead?

Fussbudget frown. Because she suspected *one of them* of stealing the money?

Possible, Angie. After all, access to the general ledger was restricted to Yvonne, Derek Sjolund, Greg Halstead and that McKellar woman. Maybe the Polaris boys knew the North Star Mall project was doomed from the start. Maybe one of them decided to grab the cash and run.

There's another possibility, too. Yvonne really did steal the money, and then Chango found out about it. After that, all he had to do was find a new hiding place for the loot, then murder Yvonne before she could skip town.

My frown deepened. On the other hand, Yvonne's murder might have absolutely nothing to do with Sjolund's money. In which case the logical suspect is Yvonne's roommate, Nikki Slater.

I remembered the edge in the dancer's voice when she mentioned Yvonne and Chango. Could she be lying about Yvonne's corporate boyfriend and the white Lincoln?

Shaking my head, I continued stirring. Unh-uh! The white Connie exists. Snowmaker Eric saw it in the lodge parking lot. Margaret Halstead recognized the description. And her husband admitted that it was a Polaris company car. Hmmmmm—maybe it's time for another trip to Spirit Mountain . . .

Just then, Grandma came bustling into the kitchen,

carrying two half-gallon cartons of Arrowhead Milk. "How are you doing with that stuffing, *Noozis?*"

"Mino!" I put down my wooden spoon. "Hey, the roasting pan is empty. Where are the hunters?"

"Charlie called at noontime. Says they're headed up to Gander Lake." Somehow she managed to wiggle those milk cartons into the crammed refrigerator. "They'll be back soon."

"In the meantime, *Nokomis,"* I said, untying my apron. "Do you mind if I take a quick run up to Spirit Mountain?"

She glanced quickly at the darkening window. "It's kind of late in the day for skiing, *Noozis."*

"There's a man I've got to talk to, *Nokomis.* It's very, very important."

"All right." Smiling, she checked the contents of the boiling rice pan. "Don't take too long, though. I'll need help plucking that goose!"

"No, I don't think anybody'd mind if you had a look at it," Eric said, tromping downslope through the powdery snow. He aimed a puzzled glance over his shoulder. "Why are you so interested in that accident?"

"I'm not too sure it was an accident," I replied, trying to keep up with his long-legged stride. Ahead stood the pump house, topped by a layer of thick snow.

"Amateur detective, eh?" Grinning, Eric removed his mitten and fished a keyring out of his parka pocket. "Well, make it fast, Angie."

"I will," I promised. Of course, I'd really lucked out, running into Eric and his blond girlfriend at the lodge cafe. Hinges creaked as I pushed the frozen door open. A white plume swirled away from my lips. The shed's interior was just as cold as the shady side of Spirit Mountain.

Eric pointed at one of the frost-covered, tripod snow cannons. "That's it—number nine. We usually mount her out there on Blue Ruin."

Kneeling beside the cannon, I scanned it from its tapered nozzle to the snow-covered baseplate. Patches of ice clung to the smooth metal. It hadn't had much chance to melt in this frigid shed.

Just then, I noticed something odd. Four tiny frosted mounds on the underside of the tube. Leaning closer, I brushed the frost away from the top mound. Dark gray leather peeped out at me.

"Eric!" I waved him over. "What do you make of this?"

"Uh-oh!" He squatted at my side. "Somebody screwed up."

"What do you mean?"

Pointing at the leather patch, he added, "He must've forgotten his choppers. He was wearing ordinary leather gloves when he grabbed it. Fingertips froze to the metal!"

"Is that possible?"

"You bet. That cannon gets pretty cold sitting up there on the mountainside." He stood erect, showing me a knowledgeable smile. "That's why we always wear choppers on the job."

Thoughtful Angie frown. "Whoever grabbed this tube tried to pull his gloves free—"

"And tore off the fingertips, right!" Pulling his woolen cap over reddening ears, he added, "Seen enough?"

"More than enough, Eric. Thanks!"

We parted company back at the lodge. I rounded the corner, heading for the guest entrance. Excitement quickened my stride. I had to alert the Duluth P.D.—let them know that Yvonne's killer had left physical evidence at the scene.

Dark gray leather driving gloves. Well, that let Nikki off the hook. The frosted mounds were too large for her dainty fingers. Meaning the killer had to be either Derek Sjolund, Greg Halstead or Chango.

All at once, my mind jumped back to Glensheen, riveting onto my first glimpse of Yvonne's mentor, Greg Halstead. Debonair businessman in his dark gray woolen topcoat and camel-colored suede gloves. Grim smile. I *knew* they didn't match!

Mind telling us what happened to your dark gray gloves, Mr. Halstead?

Spotlights illuminated the beginner's slope. A party of skiers shoved off from the rim, hooting and laughing as they slalomed downhill. I rushed into the lobby, stamped my snowy boots on the mat, and headed straight for the pay telephone. My hand lifted the receiver, and then something hard and metallic nudged my spine.

"Hang up," muttered the familiar masculine voice.

I dropped the receiver back in its cradle. Greg Halstead stood right behind me, with the dark gray topcoat draped over his right arm. Barely visible beneath the coat was a snub-nosed .38 revolver.

"Who are you?" His whisper tingled with menace. "And don't give me that St. Paul routine. I've met the *real* Nikki Slater!"

"You put on a good act at Glensheen," I murmured.

"I was wondering what your game was. I still am."

"Just asking a few questions."

"Friend of Yvonne's?" he snapped.

Decisive nod. "Why did you kill her, Halstead?"

"I had my reasons." He tilted his head toward the door. "Outside."

So I made my exit, keenly conscious of Halstead's pistol. The *apres-ski* merrymakers took no notice of the departing couple. Yelling for help was definitely out. Halstead could get off a couple of point-blank shots, then escape in the confusion. No, I'd have a better chance for escape outdoors.

"How long have you been stealing from the firm?" I asked, as we stepped into the frigid night air.

"Just over a year." He gestured downslope, pointing out a black snowmobile. "I took a real bath in the commodities market. I thought selling out to Sjolund would cover my losses. It didn't."

"So you began tapping the accounts," I added, moving very slowly. Believe me, I was in no hurry to get there. "Why pin it on Yvonne?"

"She *betrayed* me!" Tone of outrage. "She threw me over for that Colombian bastard!"

So Nikki had been right about Yvonne's office boyfriend.

"Yvonne wouldn't wait," he complained, the gun nestled in his fist. "She wanted me to divorce Margaret. Be patient, I told her. Give me some time. I needed time to make money—to hide it from Margaret and her lawyer. But Yvonne refused to wait. She gave me an ultimatum: her or Margaret. And then that idiot Nikki introduced her to *him!*"

"Making it a bit easier when it came time to choose a patsy, didn't it?"

"A bit!" Halstead's gun pointed out a pair of Kastle skis mounted behind the saddle. "Put those on."

I did as I was told, adding, "Cops don't fall for the same gag twice, Halstead."

"That's assuming they find the body!" And he handed me the ski poles.

A cold moist shiver glided up my spine. My feet fumbled their way into the grips. "Don't be a fool, Halstead. I'm not the only one Yvonne talked to." I noted his sudden expression of surprise. "She knew somebody had been embezzling, and she suspected that she was being set up. I know she told Chango."

"Really?" He flashed a feral smile. "I can see we're going to have an interesting chat out there. Say, what *is* your name, anyway?"

Suddenly, as if in answer to Halstead's query, a male voice rang out. *"Angie!"*

Looking back upslope, I saw a furious Chango descending the snowy trail. He must have spotted me in the lobby. No doubt he wanted his pistol back.

Halstead's features blanched in alarm.

Taking instant advantage, I hollered, "You were right, Chango. Halstead did it!"

Snarling in fury, Halstead swiveled the snub-nosed pistol in the pimp's direction.

"Madre de Dios!" Chango skidded on the loose snow.

As Halstead's forefinger tightened, I twirled my ski pole like a majorette's baton. The pole smashed his wrist, driving the gun muzzle downward.

Blam! The Colt's muzzle flash lit up the snow. Halstead's numb fingers lost their grip on the weapon, and it vanished into the powder. He plunged in after it.

And she's off! One scared-shitless Anishinabe princess, angling her lengthy skis toward the run, pumping away with both ski poles. I had to get over the crest before Halstead retrieved his pistol.

I had a very simple escape plan in mind. Over the edge, down the slope, out onto Grand Avenue, and head for the nearest telephone. The first part seemed to be working quite well, too. I rocketed down the well-lit ski run. Crouching, I tucked the poles beneath my arms, kept my eyes glued to the trail, and listened to the hushed hiss of waxed skis on powdered snow.

Blam! The shot kicked up a snow spray at my side. Snapping a quick glance over my shoulder, I saw Halstead astride the black snowmobile. The sleek machine came tearing down the slope, kicking up a billowing snowy contrail. Halstead rode low in the saddle, gun hand extended like a pursuing Western sheriff.

Blam! Friction heat from the passing bullet warmed the flannel lining of my jeans. Gasp of alarm. Instantly I stooped, offering a smaller target. Angie the Skiing Midget.

I was safe . . . but only for the moment. Fifty miles per hour was a skier's top speed on this slope. Halstead's snowmobile could match that with ease—going *uphill!* It wouldn't take him more than a minute to catch up with me.

Unless . . .

I veered toward the fresh snow along the rim, picking up speed. Halstead saw what I was doing and stayed on my left. Perhaps he was trying to cut me off—I don't know. My first concern was putting a stop to his shooting.

Fixing the fall line in my mind, I dug in my poles, pulled up my feet and cut to the left. Then, repeating the motion, I jigged to the right. Within seconds, I had a good rhythm going. Feet up—push to the side—pull up—push to the other side. In no time at all, my antics stirred up a miniature blizzard, a billowing cloud of white powder that spread outward in my wake.

Instant snow screen!

Originally, I'd planned to brake and let Halstead go speeding right on by. But, as I started my wedge, I noticed a snow-covered rise dead ahead. Blink of confusion.

I don't remember a hill . . . Obsidian eyes goggled wide. *Oh, shit! I went too far to the right! The ski jump!*

The snow-draped ramp rocketed toward me. Tossing my poles away, I hunkered down and unsnapped my safety grips. Bailout Biwaban strikes again!

Head down, I hugged both knees and rolled off my skis. Spinning like a demented hockey puck, I skidded kittycorner up the snowy ramp. Suddenly I was airborne, sailing through the night sky on my back, wreathed in swirling snow.

All at once, snow walls rose miraculously all around me. That deep snowdrift made a handy cushion. Oh, sure, the impact knocked me breathless, and my back felt as if I'd landed on asphalt. But I was luckier than I had any right to be.

Rare, indeed, is the woman who survives a fifty-mile-per-hour plunge into hillside snow!

Dazed, I heard the snowmobile's engine roaring at full throttle. Then the vehicle itself burst into my field of vision, corkscrewing skyward, looking like one of those loop-de-loop roller coasters. But there was no steel track beneath those skis, just the night and the stars and the swirling flakes of snow. The machine completed a perfect barrel roll, with Halstead shrieking and waving his arms. Then gravity tugged at its trim nose, and it plunged earthward in a furious tailspin, like a World War Two fighter plane shorn of its wings.

Head throbbing, I feebly clawed my way through the snow—just in time to see the crash. The snowmobile exploded upon impact, and pieces of smoldering machinery went tumbling down the run, trailed by Halstead's sliding loose-limbed form.

Groaning, I collapsed on the broken snow, oblivious to the shouts of approaching skiers and the distant ululation of a police siren.

"Did the police ever find the money?" Aunt Denise asked.

We were seated at the dinner table, my aunt and I, along with twenty-nine Biwaban relatives. Chief occupied the seat at my other elbow. Three golden-brown roast geese occupied platters on Grandma Biwaban's immaculate white tablecloth.

"You bet!" Carefully I laid the linen napkin across my lap. I was wearing one of my Christmas presents—a pair of wine-colored silk palazzo pants—and I didn't want any gravy stains. "They found the four hundred grand in a safety deposit box in Minneapolis, along with a duplicate diskette for the accounting software."

"Will you have to testify at the inquest?" my aunt asked, unfolding her own napkin.

I nodded. "Don't worry, though. It shouldn't take more than a couple of days. They've got their proof. Lieutenant Monaghan told me their search turned up Halstead's black gloves . . . *minus* the fingertips."

Chief rearranged the knife and fork to suit himself. "Quiet, you two. Walt's about to offer the prayer."

Uncle Walter occupied the seat at the head of the table. As he stood erect, Laura's toddlers shook their turtleshell cymbals. It's an old custom in *Midewiwin*. The sound summons the good spirits.

Turning his palms upright, my uncle began his prayer.

> *"Mino daeshowishinaung.*
> *Chi mino inaudiziwinaungaen.*
> *Nanaukinumowidauh matchi daewin.*
> *Zaugoochi tumowidauh matchi dodumowin."*

Defend our hearts against evil—Against evil prevail, I thought, watching my uncle fill his calumet bowl with tobacco.

And I thought of Yvonne, dead these past few days, and the sorrow in her sister's home.

Chief's hand touched my shoulder. Gravelly whisper. "When it gets dark, we'll go up to Hawk Ridge. Walt can say a prayer for Yvonne."

I nodded. My old teammate would've liked that.

The KBJR weatherman had forecast another cold snap for the Twin Ports. Sub zero temperatures and a chilling starlit night. I hoped for a bright aurora.

Why? Well, the *Mideg* believe that the spirits of our Anishinabe ancestors live in the far north. The aurora is the glow of their torches as they lead the dead to the Path of Souls.

My glance flitted toward the window. Spirit Mountain loomed on the horizon, its snowfields glistening in the midday sun. And I thought once more of Yvonne, clad in her Nordica suit, skiing to an expert stop on the trail.

Have a safe journey, my friend.

Patting my grandfather's hand, I smiled. "You're one in a million, Chief."

He grinned like one of Santa's elves. *"Debia Niba-anamiaygijigad, Noozis!"*

ON THE CASE WITH THE HEARTLAND'S #1 FEMALE P.I. THE AMANDA HAZARD MYSTERIES BY CONNIE FEDDERSEN

DEAD IN THE WATER (0-8217-5244-8, $4.99)
The quaint little farm community of Vamoose, Oklahoma isn't as laid back as they'd have you believe. Not when the body of one of its hardest-working citizens is found face down in a cattle trough. Amateur sleuth Amanda Hazard has two sinister suspects and a prickly but irresistible country gumshoe named Nick Thorn to contend with as she plows ahead for the truth.

DEAD IN THE CELLAR (0-8217-5245-6, $4.99)
A deadly tornado rips through Vamoose, Oklahoma, followed by a deadly web of intrigue when elderly Elmer Jolly is found murdered in his storm cellar. Can Amanda Hazard collar the killer before she herself becomes the center of the storm, and the killer's next victim?

DEAD IN THE MUD (0-8217-156-X, $5.50)
It's a dirty way to die: drowned in the mud from torrential rain. Amanda Hazard is convinced the County Commissioner's death is no accident, and finds herself sinking into a seething morass of corruption and danger as she works to bring the culprits to light—before she, too, ends up 6-feet-under.

Available wherever paperbacks are sold, or order direct from the Publisher. Send cover price plus 50¢ per copy for mailing and handling to Kensington Publishing Corp., Consumer Orders, or call (toll free) 888-345-BOOK, to place your order using Mastercard or Visa. Residents of New York and Tennessee must include sales tax. DO NOT SEND CASH.

THE MYSTERIES OF MARY ROBERTS RINEHART

SNAPSHOTS IN HISTORY

The Indian Removal Act

Forced Relocation

by Mark Stewart

The Indian Removal Act

Forced Relocation

by Mark Stewart

Content Adviser: Greg O'Brien, Ph.D., Associate Professor of History, University of Southern Mississippi

Reading Adviser: Katie Van Sluys, Ph.D., School of Education, DePaul University

Compass Point Books ✦ Minneapolis, Minnesota

COMPASS POINT BOOKS

3109 West 50th Street, #115
Minneapolis, MN 55410

Visit Compass Point Books on the Internet at
www.compasspointbooks.com
or e-mail your request to
custserv@compasspointbooks.com

For Compass Point Books
Jennifer VanVoorst, Jaime Martens, XNR Productions, Inc.,
Catherine Neitge, Keith Griffin, and Carol Jones

Produced by White-Thomson Publishing Ltd.

For White-Thomson Publishing
Stephen White-Thomson, Susan Crean, Amy Sparks,
Tinstar Design Ltd., Greg O'Brien, Peggy Bresnick Kendler,
Will Hare, and Timothy Griffin

Library of Congress Cataloging-in-Publication Data
Stewart, Mark, 1960–
The Indian Removal Act : forced relocation / by Mark Stewart.
p. cm. — (Snapshots in history)
Includes bibliographical references and index.
ISBN-13: 978-0-7565-2452-4 (library binding)
ISBN-10: 0-7565-2452-0 (library binding)
ISBN-13: 978-0-7565-3179-9 (paperback)
ISBN-10: 0-7565-3197-9 (paperback)
1. United States. Act to Provide for an Exchange of Lands with the Indians Residing in any of the States or Territories, and for Their Removal West of the River Mississippi—History. 2. Indians of North America—Relocation. 3. Indians of North America—Government relations. 4. Forced migration—Government policy—United States—History. 5. Land tenure—Government policy—United States—History. 6. Jefferson, Thomas, 1743–1826—Relations with Indians. 7. United States—Territorial expansion. 8. United States—Race relations.
9. United States—Politics and government. I. Title. II. Series.
E98.R3S784 2007
973.04'97—dc22 2006027084

THE INDIAN REMOVAL ACT

Contents

The Trail Where They Cried

Chapter 1

The soldiers arrived without warning on a spring day in 1838. They moved from home to home, rounding up Cherokee women and children and forcing them toward the main road. In the surrounding fields, more soldiers, their bayonets fixed, gathered up the men and instructed them to join their families.

This was not an attack on the Cherokee farmers. It was a removal. The Cherokee people, who had lived side by side with white settlers for decades, were being forced to move from their lands.

Eight years earlier, the U.S. government had passed the Indian Removal Act of 1830, a law requiring the Native American groups living in the Southeast to leave the rich land they had tilled for generations. The population of the

United States was growing, and more room was needed for new Americans to settle and farm. For these settlers, the native people of the Southeast were simply in the way, and they no longer wanted them to remain there. Cherokee leaders had tried every way they knew how to fight this new law. But they lost their battle, and now the soldiers had come to enforce the removal law.

White settlers wanted to live on Native American lands in the Southeastern United States.

The soldiers' instructions to the Cherokee people were simple: Take whatever you can carry, and leave the rest. The Cherokee were escorted to temporary holding areas called stockades. From there, they would be taken to their new home, west of the Mississippi River. The soldiers assured them that everything they would need for the journey would be given to them when the time came. However, for a number of reasons, including bad weather and poor planning, this would not be the case.

Through the summer of 1838, the camps holding the Cherokee people slowly swelled as each new group was marched in. They came from the western parts of North Carolina and South Carolina, from the northern parts of Georgia and Alabama, and from sections of Tennessee. Disease took many lives in the stockades while the Army prepared to move thousands of families to land in the West designated as Indian Territory. Many of those who fell ill simply gave up—they preferred to die near their beloved mountains rather than leave them. Not until late October 1838 did the long journey westward begin.

John Burnett, one of the cavalrymen charged with removing the Cherokee, recalled the day they started the long march westward:

> *In the chill of a drizzling rain on an October morning I saw them loaded like cattle or sheep into 645 wagons and started toward the West. One can never forget the sadness*

Cherokee people of the early 1800s typically wore a mixture of modern and traditional clothing.

> *and solemnity of that morning ... many of the children rose to their feet and waved their little hands good-bye to their mountain homes, knowing they were leaving them forever. Many of these helpless people did not have blankets and many of them had been driven from home barefooted.*

On that fateful day, Cherokee men, women, and children began their long walk to their new home in the West. They walked through towns, where people would come out to watch them as though they were in some kind of parade. Their supplies soon ran out, and the wagons that carried their belongings could not hold up under the difficult conditions, including roads that were choked with mud and, later, covered in ice and snow.

A Cherokee man remembered many years later:

> *Long time we travel on way to new land. People feel bad when they leave old nation. Womens cry and made sad wails. Children cry and many men cry, and all look sad like when friends die, but they say nothing and just put heads down and keep on go towards west. Many days pass and people die very much.*

They trekked through the mountains, trudging through snow-covered passes and struggling to stay warm and fight off starvation and sickness. At sunrise, the soldiers would count the dead. There was no time for proper burials. Shallow graves chipped into the hard earth would have to do.

A traveler heading north to Maine later gave a New York newspaper an account of what he saw:

> *A great many ride on horseback and multitudes go on foot—even aged females, apparently nearly ready to drop into the grave, were traveling with heavy burdens attached to the back—on the sometimes frozen ground, and sometimes muddy streets, with no covering for the feet except what nature had given them.*

> *We learned from inhabitants on the road where they [the Native Americans] passed, that they buried 14 or 15 at every stopping place, and they make a journey of 10 miles [16 kilometers] per day only on average.*

As winter howled down through the Mississippi Valley, the survivors reached the ice-choked Mississippi River. There they waited until it was safe to cross. Many Cherokee died waiting. With the ground frozen solid, the dead were buried under piles of stones.

After walking more than 800 miles (1,280 km)—through parts of Tennessee, Kentucky, Illinois, Missouri, and Arkansas—the sad procession finally arrived in what today is eastern Oklahoma, near

A Haunting Silence

In his book *Democracy in America,* writer Alexis de Tocqueville described the haunting vision of what was left of the once great Cherokee Nation being forced to cross the river. "They possessed neither tents nor wagons, but only their arms and some provisions," he wrote in the 1830s. "I saw them embark to pass the mighty river. Never will that solemn spectacle fade from my remembrance. No cry, no sob, was heard among the assembled crowd; all were silent."

The mountains of North Carolina and Tennessee had been Cherokee land for centuries when the first European settlers arrived.

the Arkansas River. To the southwest were the relocated Creek and Seminole tribes. Beyond them were the relocated Chickasaw and Choctaw tribes. All were tribes native to the Southeast that had been forced to move.

By the time the Cherokees' journey ended, soldier John Burnett was filled with disgust:

> *The long painful journey to the West ended March 26th, 1839, with 4,000 silent graves reaching from the foothills of the Smoky Mountains to what is known as Indian Territory in the West. And covetousness on the part of the white race was the cause of all that the Cherokee had to suffer.*

The Cherokees were one of five groups of Native Americans required to leave their ancestral lands in the Southeastern United States with the passage of the Indian Removal Act. Hardship, sadness, and suffering accompanied the Choctaw, Chickasaw, Creek, and Seminole people in their treks to the West as well. But the 15,000-plus Cherokee people forced to move during the winter of 1838–1839 suffered especially appalling losses. Those who survived called this ordeal *Nunna daul Isunyi*, or the Trail Where They Cried. Today we know it as the Trail of Tears.

Poor planning by the government, disease, a lack of provisions, and harsh weather created a disaster along the Trail of Tears. Approximately one-third

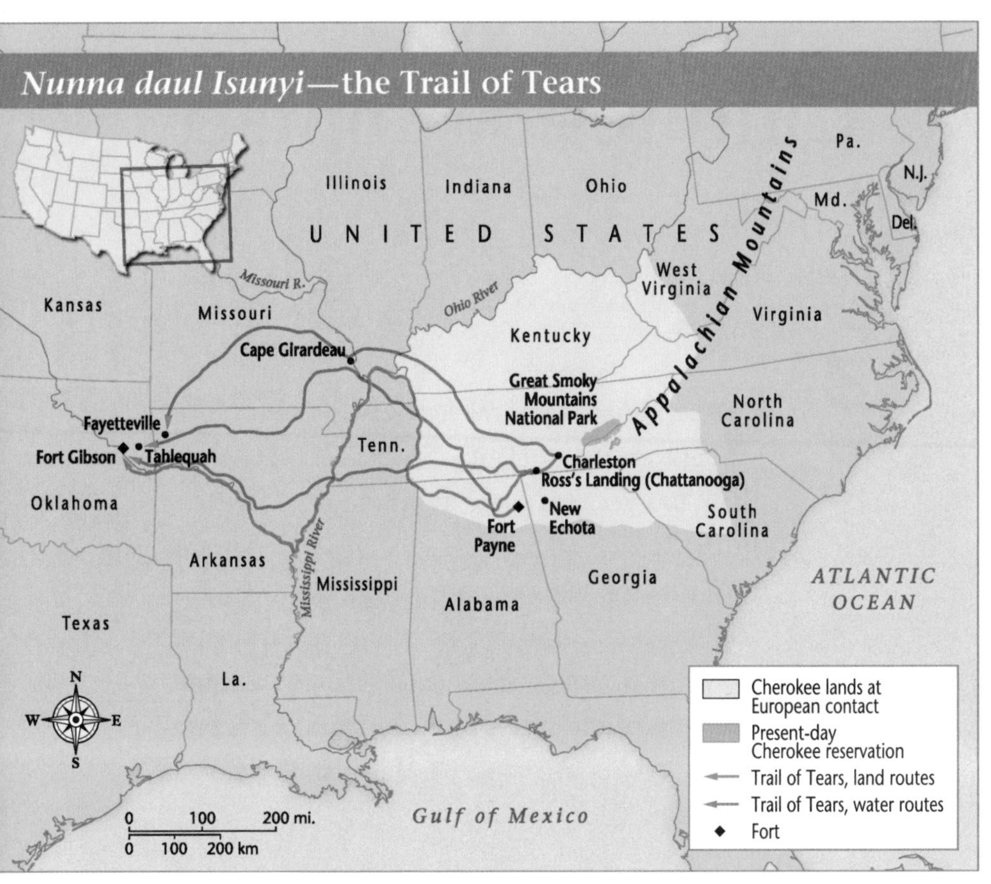

of those who started the journey did not live to see their new home. The Trail of Tears was the sad culmination of events triggered by the Indian Removal Act of 1830. However, the story begins long before that fateful year.

Most Cherokee people removed from their homelands walked on what became known as the Trail of Tears.

Cultures in Contact

Chapter
2

The Indian Removal Act was the result of a process that took place over a period of more than 200 years. It came at a time when settlers in the United States were pushing west toward the Mississippi River. During this time, the rights and property of the Native Americans living along the frontier were in grave jeopardy. But the violation of the rights of Native Americans had begun even earlier—when the first Europeans arrived in North America.

The first contacts between the five tribes and European settlers came during the 1500s and 1600s, when the Spanish, French, and British began arriving in the Southeast from the Atlantic Ocean, Gulf of Mexico, and Mississippi River. While Native Americans living along the coasts of New England and the South, and near the

Great Lakes and the Mississippi Delta fell victim to slave traders and European diseases, the Cherokee, Chickasaw, Choctaw, Creek, and Seminole people had only occasional contact with the Europeans. Sometimes they exchanged gifts and ideas with the newcomers, and sometimes they exchanged blows.

The Creek tribe lived near the Gulf of Mexico.

The tribes most affected by the Indian Removal Act were the Cherokee, Chickasaw, Choctaw, Creek, and Seminole. Together, they occupied millions of acres of fertile land stretching from Mississippi to South Carolina and from Florida to Tennessee. These tribes were practically unknown to Europeans when they began colonizing this part of the New World. Because their land was largely undisturbed in these early years of contact, the five tribes did not sense the outside world closing in on them. However, as the American frontier pushed ever westward, members of these five tribes came into greater contact with European settlers.

The Spanish began to make regular contact in the 1600s from the south, through Florida. The French came later in the century from the west. The English began to make inroads into the area from the east in the early 1700s.

The native people of this region were enthusiastic traders, and over time they formed friendships and even alliances with these foreign groups. For

AMBUSH!

In 1540, Spanish explorer Hernando de Soto was ambushed in present-day northern Alabama by a group of Chickasaw. His party was nearly wiped out. The blood-curdling cries of the Chickasaw and other Native American warriors became famous in the region and are believed to be the origin of the "rebel yell" used later by the Confederates during the American Civil War.

Trade between Europeans and Native Americans had existed since first contact in the 1500s.

example, in 1729, the Natchez people of Louisiana went to war against the French. But the French and the Choctaw were allies, and together they defeated the Natchez.

Each European country wanted to colonize North America and control its resources. Each country lavished the Native Americans with new technologies and materials to secure their friendship. The leaders of the five tribes eventually came to understand that European traders, soldiers, and adventurers were in fierce competition with one another. They tried to use this competition to their advantage.

In making agreements or treaties, the chiefs of the five tribes expected to be paid special tribute in the form of gifts. When the five tribes were later pressured to cede land to white settlers—often against the best interests of the native people—

the chiefs agreed in part because they were paid a separate fee. This led to mistrust of chiefs among their people. In turn, it weakened the resolve of Native Americans to fight for their rights.

As contact with the native people in the region increased, the Europeans increasingly began to marry Native American women. Although the children of these marriages typically lived as natives, many did not. It was not uncommon for a European trader to marry a Native American woman, settle down on a plot of land, start a business, and raise a family. The five tribes—particularly the Cherokee—were open to the idea of bringing white men into their extended families. It helped them to understand their new neighbors and, they assumed, strengthen the bonds between Native Americans and European settlers.

Adopting European Ways

Although it was the goal of all people in the Southeast to survive and thrive, the Native Americans and European settlers approached this challenge in different ways. The settlers sought to build permanent structures on pieces of land they owned, which was the European system. The native people, however, believed the land belonged to everyone in the tribe, and they moved from one place to another depending on the season and the availability of food. Hoping to coexist with their new neighbors, many native people of the Southeast began to adopt the ways of the settlers—from the concept of land ownership to styles of dress to adopting Christianity as a religion.

Thanks to intermarriage, there was a great exchange of customs and cultures during the 1700s. Scottish traders in particular married into Creek and Cherokee families. These families lived European lifestyles but considered themselves to be Creek or Cherokee. Their success in business and farming intrigued other tribe members. In the early 1800s, many full-blooded Native Americans in the Southeast began to adopt the customs of those born to couples who had intermarried. This led to the Cherokee, Chickasaw, Choctaw, Creek, and Seminole becoming known as the Five Civilized Tribes.

The Five Civilized Tribes had much in common, but they were also distinct from one another in a number of ways. The Cherokee Nation occupied a vast area. Today it would include the mountains and foothills of Tennessee, Virginia, Georgia, Alabama, North Carolina, and South Carolina.

The Cherokee spoke a language different from that of the four other so-called civilized tribes. These tribes spoke variations of a Muskogean tongue, which had originated in the southern part of the continent. The Cherokee language, however, was Iroquoian, originating in the northern part of the continent. In the early 1800s, a scholar named Sequoyah assigned symbols to the 85 syllables in the Cherokee language, making it the first Native American language to have a written form.

Cherokee Alphabet.					
Ꭰ a	Ꭱ e	Ꭲ i	Ꭳ o	Ꭴ u	Ꭵ v
Ꭶ ga Ꭷ ka	Ꭸ ge	Ꭹ gi	Ꭺ go	Ꭻ gu	Ꭼ gv
Ꭽ ha	Ꭾ he	Ꭿ hi	Ꮀ ho	Ꮁ hu	Ꮂ hv
Ꮃ la	Ꮄ le	Ꮅ li	Ꮆ lo	Ꮇ lu	Ꮈ lv
Ꮉ ma	Ꮊ me	Ꮋ mi	Ꮌ mo	Ꮍ mu	
Ꮎ na Ꮏ hna Ꮐ nah	Ꮑ ne	Ꮒ ni	Ꮓ no	Ꮔ nu	Ꮕ nv
Ꮖ qua	Ꮗ que	Ꮘ qui	Ꮙ quo	Ꮚ quu	Ꮛ quv
Ꮜ sa Ꮝ s	Ꮞ se	Ꮟ si	Ꮠ so	Ꮡ su	Ꮢ sv
Ꮣ da Ꮤ ta	Ꮥ de Ꮦ te	Ꮧ di Ꮨ ti	Ꮩ do	Ꮪ du	Ꮫ dv
Ꮬ dla Ꮭ tla	Ꮮ tle	Ꮯ tli	Ꮰ tlo	Ꮱ tlu	Ꮲ tlv
Ꮳ tsa	Ꮴ tse	Ꮵ tsi	Ꮶ tso	Ꮷ tsu	Ꮸ tsv
Ꮹ wa	Ꮺ we	Ꮻ wi	Ꮼ wo	Ꮽ wu	Ꮾ wv
Ꮿ ya	Ᏸ ye	Ᏹ yi	Ᏺ yo	Ᏻ yu	Ᏼ yv

Sequoyah used letters he had seen in English writing to create the 85 symbols of written Cherokee.

Descendants of the mixed European and Native American couples who had married in the 1700s gained great influence in Cherokee tribal matters, for they had an intimate understanding of both white and native cultures. In time, they formed an elite class among the Native Americans. Years later—by the 1820s—many of them ran vast plantations and owned dozens of slaves.

Cherokee villages were typically permanent farming settlements. They were often built on or near rivers, with 50 or so windowless log cabins. The center of social and religious life in Cherokee villages was a large meeting house with a sacred

Slave Ownership

Slavery had been a part of the picture in the New World since the first European settlements were established. For the native people of the Southeast who adopted the culture of their white neighbors, this was one more way of showing how they fit in. At a time when there were few machines to do the back-breaking work of agriculture and construction, many families and businesses depended on enslaved people. Most were African in origin.

fire. The people raised crops, hunted and fished, and were highly skilled with both the bow and arrow and the blowgun.

During the 1700s, when colonists began encroaching on Cherokee lands, the Cherokee had been convinced it would be in their interest to fight on the side of the British during the American Revolution. The Cherokee had been an important part of the British deerskin trade for many years and did not want to side against their business partners. When the colonists won their independence, the Cherokee were punished. They were forced to give up much of their land in Georgia and the Carolinas.

The Creek tribe occupied lands in parts of Tennessee, Georgia, Alabama, and Florida. Like the Cherokee, they had lived in this region for many centuries. The Creek built their villages along rivers, with mud-thatch houses arranged around a town square, where religious celebrations were held. The most important of these events was the Green Corn Ceremony, which celebrated the last ripening of the season.

Warfare played an important role in Creek culture. Creek warriors were skilled with all kinds of weapons and had a number of time-tested offensive and defensive strategies. The Creek often formed military alliances with other tribes, and even with European countries. When European powers began to grapple over the region, they courted the Creek as allies. Like the Cherokee, the Creek sided with the British in the American Revolutionary War. As a result, the new government of the United States would come to view the Creek as a people sympathetic to its enemies.

Among the traditional enemies of the Creek were their neighbors to the west, the Choctaw. The Choctaw mainly lived in present-day Mississippi, with some groups in Alabama and Louisiana. They were the region's most skilled farmers, and they

The French and Indian War

The French and Indian War began in 1754. Great Britain, its American colonists, and a handful of Native American tribes loyal to the British fought together against the French and their Native American allies. At stake was control of North America. Regardless of whether the French or the British won, it seemed to the native people that they would end up losing. Many Native American tribes were forced to choose sides. But many Southern tribes were spared this decision, since no actual fighting took place in the Southeast. After the British won the war, life for the Five Civilized Tribes returned to normal.

also maintained herds of cattle. The Choctaw befriended the French in the 1700s and fought alongside them in their battles with other Native American tribes.

One of the tribes in conflict with the French was the neighboring Chickasaw tribe. The Chickasaw spent many centuries as a seminomadic people in the northern sections of Alabama and Mississippi. They absorbed members of other tribes during this time and settled into a permanent agricultural society in the 1500s. The Chickasaw farmed the rich soil in the flood plains of Mississippi, as well as sections of Tennessee. Chickasaw warriors were skilled raiders.

The Seminole people shared a common heritage with the Creek. They lived in Georgia until pressure from white settlers and other tribes pushed them south. They moved to Florida in the early 1700s.

The British made alliances with Native American tribes during the American Revolutionary War as well as during the earlier French and Indian War.

The Seminole were farmers, hunters, and gatherers. They had an intimate understanding of the land on which they lived, which ranged from fertile farmland to impenetrable swamps. This was important when food was scarce, because they knew where to find edible plants in harsh environments. It also was important when they went to war. The Seminole moved easily across terrain in which entire armies would become lost. They defeated much greater forces because of this advantage. These skills also made the Seminole a

The Five Civilized Tribes occupied much of the land in the Southeast before settlers arrived.

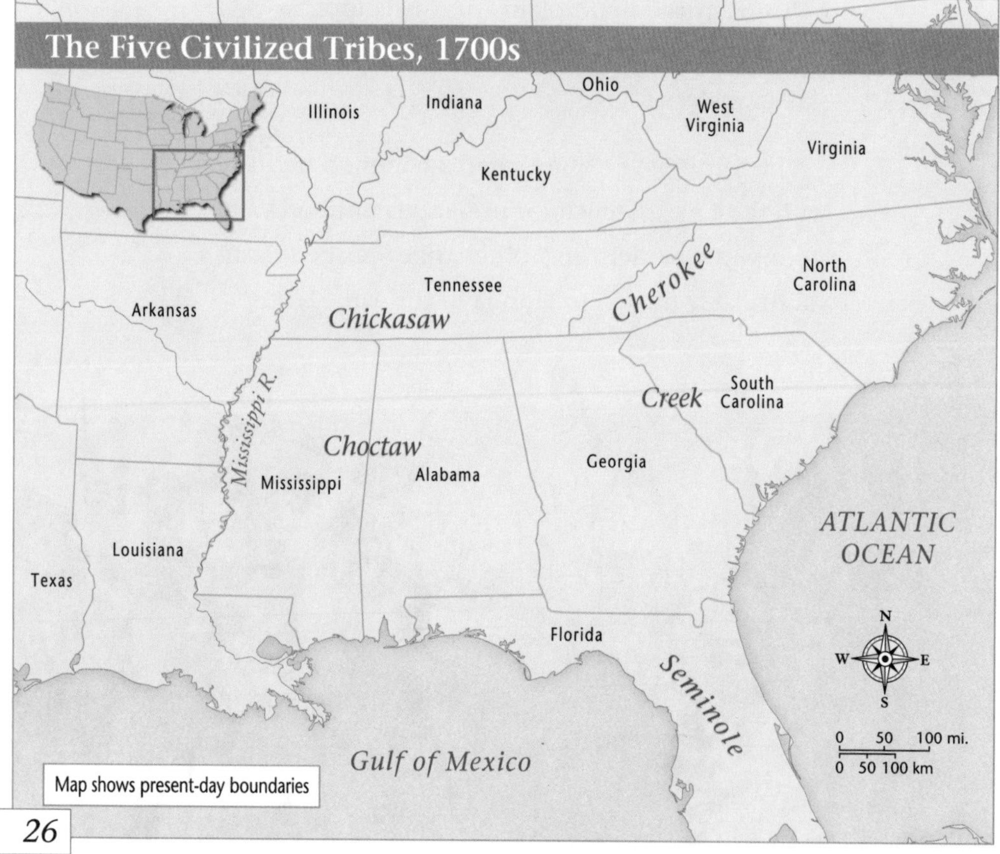

haven for runaway slaves. Once a slave was taken into a Seminole village, there was little chance his master would attempt to retrieve him.

During the 1700s, the most important thing the five tribes of the Southeast shared was their place on the map. To the east, the British had colonized much of the Atlantic Coast and were beginning to push into the interior of North America. To the west, the French, moving down from their stronghold in Canada, had established themselves along the Mississippi River. To the south, the Spanish occupied Florida and much of the Gulf Coast all the way to Mexico. And to the north, rival tribes had made powerful alliances that included the British and French, countries that were hoping to expand their territory. The Cherokee, Creek, Chickasaw, Choctaw, and Seminole suddenly found themselves being squeezed from all directions.

Because their lands were in the interior of the Southeast region, away from coastal areas, they had survived the diseases that had wiped out many other Native American populations. Nor had the tribes experienced floods of settlers into the region. Yet few doubted that these catastrophes would come. The French and Indian War, fought from 1754 to 1763 between the French and British (and their respective Native American allies), illustrated that the European powers were willing to fight and die for power in the New World.

A New Nation

Chapter 3

The French and Indian War was fought primarily in the north, but during the American Revolution, fighting was much closer to home for the five tribes. In many cases, the Native Americans sided with the British against the colonists. At many points along the frontier, they took up arms and fought against each other. After the colonists won their independence from Great Britain, the fate of the Cherokee, Creek, Chickasaw, Choctaw, and Seminole tribes would be determined by the new United States of America.

The first order of business for the new nation was to create a political structure that could protect and govern the territory it had won from the British. George Washington was elected president of the new country. President Washington had fought both beside and against Native Americans for more than 30 years. He understood that they could be good friends or dangerous enemies.

Washington accepted the assertion in the U.S. Constitution that Native American tribes were sovereign nations. He instructed Henry Knox, secretary of war, to make treaties with them, giving Native Americans the right to make and enforce their own laws within their own borders. Those borders, in turn, were to be respected by American settlers. Native American lands were like little islands within the United States, and it was not always easy to see where U.S. territory ended and Native American lands began.

George Washington served as president from 1789 to 1797.

As settlers journeyed south and west in search of opportunity, many simply stopped when they reached the first piece of good-looking land that wasn't owned by another settler. They cleared forests and built farms without knowing exactly where they were or whether anyone had a claim to the property. Often they built homes on Native American soil. This angered the owners, who felt they had been cheated by the U.S. government.

President Washington knew that making peace with the native people living on the American frontier was a matter of national security. If settlers continued to live as squatters on Native American land, he believed, it would lead to violent conflict. This would require the intervention of troops, which the U.S. government could not afford. It also might encourage the Native Americans to make alliances with foreign powers—such as Great Britain and Spain—as they had done before.

Though their territory was protected through treaties, the Native Americans of the Southeast still found themselves fighting to keep control of their land. Time and again squatters built cabins and cleared fields on tribal land. Many tribes took matters into their own hands. There were Native American raids and white reprisals throughout the region. The U.S. Army, occupied by warfare with the tribes of the Ohio Valley, could not always respond to these conflicts. At the same time, local militia leaders were told they could only fight defensive battles and could not enforce laws.

Meanwhile, the leaders of the new country looked on the five tribes with increasing greed, fear, and suspicion. They lived on the kind of fertile land that would soon be needed to feed and clothe a growing country. They populated the country's southern border, which was still vulnerable to invasion from Spain, France, and England. The five tribes had made alliances with these world powers in the past, so what would keep them from doing so again?

Although the idea of "removing" these native people to the West was not being discussed in the late 1780s, the forces that would lead to this decision were already present. Cultures in contact were about to become cultures in collision.

As more territories became states, some order was restored along the frontier. This was because the states established state militias. They were more powerful and organized than the ones that had existed when these lands were mere territories. Many conflicts were settled before they became crises, and an attempt was made by these militias to enforce the laws that applied to Native Americans and settlers alike. In many cases, squatters were driven off tribal lands,

Making States

William Blount was appointed by President Washington to govern the vast territory south of the Ohio River. Blount saw statehood as a solution to the conflicts between Native Americans and settlers, since a state militia would have greater authority to deal with the tribes. Georgia and Kentucky had become states in 1788 and 1792, respectively, and had formed their own state militias. Blount pushed for Tennessee to become a state, and in 1796 it did.

and their houses were burned. When tribal leaders felt they had been wronged, they were encouraged to use the state courts. And when settlers had claims against Native Americans, they were also handled through the states' legal systems.

One of the unstated goals of the U.S. government at this time was to discourage the traditional movement of Native Americans across the countryside. This would weaken tribal claims to land that was not permanently occupied. During the 1790s and early 1800s, the U.S. government urged the native people of the Southeast to change their way of life. They were given modern agricultural tools so that they would become less dependent on hunting and more reliant on farming and herding. This was called the Civilization Plan. The native people were also compensated with trade goods for lands that had been taken illegally by whites. This plan made the Native Americans more dependent on purchasing what they wanted, instead of using only what they needed, as they had done in the past.

The trading and selling of commercial goods to tribe members led to many abuses. Through Washington's presidency and through those of John Adams and Thomas Jefferson, stores along the frontier were told to extend credit to the Native Americans. When natives were unable to pay for the goods they purchased on credit, storeowners used the courts to recover what was owed. Since the Native Americans had no money, they were forced to give up the only thing they did have: land. This turned out to be a good way for the United States to obtain the territory belonging to tribes without violating their sovereignty. Native Americans lost thousands of acres in this way.

Also around this time, the United States bought from France the vast region of land west of the Mississippi in the Louisiana Purchase. This region was home to more than 150,000 Native Americans. Most had lived in this part of North America for many centuries. Thousands, however, had been pushed into a large area just to the west of the Mississippi by settlers to the north. When the United States bought this land from France as part of the Louisiana Purchase, some Americans thought that it would make a fine place to relocate other Native American groups such as the Cherokee, Chickasaw, Choctaw, Creek, and Seminole.

The Louisiana Purchase

The thought of France owning much of the land to the west of the recently formed United States worried President Jefferson. He began pressuring the French to sell this land. He threatened to make an alliance with the British, and he threatened to support a slave uprising on the island of Haiti that would drive the French from the Caribbean. When France needed money to fund the cost of fighting the Haitians and other wars, Napoleon decided to sell France's vast territory to the United States in what would come to be called the Louisiana Purchase. This land included more than Louisiana. It stretched north to Canada and west to the Rocky Mountains, and its acquisition doubled the size of the country.

One of these people was Andrew Jackson, who at that time was head of the Tennessee militia. He and his soldiers spent much of their time trying to ensure that the native people and settlers respected one another's rights. He soon came to the conclusion that this was a losing battle. Sooner or later, Jackson believed, the Native Americans would be driven from their lands by an unstoppable wave of settlers and would cease to exist as a people.

Jackson and other influential whites in the Southeast began to support the idea that Native Americans should be required to exchange their land in the Southeast for land west of the Mississippi. Jackson often claimed that he had no wish to see a race of people driven from their

Andrew Jackson believed that Native Americans would one day be overrun by settlers.

ancestral lands, but he believed this was a better option than annihilation.

In 1812, tensions between the United States and Great Britain were reignited, and the United States declared war. The War of 1812 officially ran from 1812 until 1815. Among the many issues that led to President James Madison's declaration of war was the suspicion that the British were encouraging the tribes along the southern frontier to attack American citizens. One of these tribes was the Creek, who had attacked a homestead in an area where Jackson had invested in land.

Jackson's anger toward the Creek exploded after an 1813 Creek rebellion at Fort Mims on the Alabama River, during which more than 250 people were killed. Jackson and an army of 2,500 men were ordered south to stop the Creek rebellion. It was the beginning of a journey that would ultimately take him to the White House.

State of Mind

In the early 1800s, most people in the United States thought of themselves as belonging to a state. If you lived in Virginia, you were a Virginian first and an American second. When Andrew Jackson looked at the United States, however, he saw a country. To him, the Creek rebellion was an attack on the United States and was no different than the British attacks on the country during the War of 1812.

The roots of the Creek rebellion at Fort Mims dated back to the fall of 1811, when the great Shawnee chief Tecumseh gave an impassioned speech at the grand council of the Creek Nation. He reminded the people how the whites had taken their land, destroyed their traditions, and trampled the bones of their ancestors. Tecumseh stated that whites should be destroyed before they destroyed Native Americans. He urged Creek warriors to fight the whites and drive them back into the ocean from which they had come.

However, a chief named Big Warrior and other influential Creek leaders had long believed that their people's best chance for survival was to learn to live alongside the whites. Big Warrior refused to go to war. He was opposed by a group of Creek who felt as Tecumseh did. This group's leaders claimed they could change the course of bullets, make the ground tremble, and call down lightning strikes upon their enemies. These mystical powers attracted thousands of young warriors who painted their war clubs red and were known as the Red Sticks. The Red Sticks began attacking frontier families, but they did not only attack whites. They also attacked Creek people who did not agree with them. This split the Creek Nation in two.

Jackson's Native American Son

After one of the first battles of the Creek War, an infant boy was found alive, still clutched in the arms of his dead mother. He was the last surviving member of his family. The child, named Lyncoya, was brought to Andrew Jackson. An orphan himself, Jackson decided to give Lyncoya a home, and he raised the boy as his son. Lyncoya died of tuberculosis in his late teens and was laid to rest at Jackson's Tennessee estate, known as the Hermitage.

The Creek massacre of settlers at Fort Mims triggered events that would propel Andrew Jackson to the presidency.

The conflict exploded into full warfare after the attack at Fort Mims. The Red Sticks had not only attacked a U.S. town, but they had killed many women and children and mutilated the bodies afterward. Americans were outraged—and terrified. President James Madison, fearing that other tribes might join the Red Sticks, began to see the situation as Jackson did: The rebellious Creeks had to be defeated.

Although this conflict was called the Creek War, Jackson was aided in his campaign against the Red Sticks by many friendly Creek warriors. Big Warrior contributed more than 100 soldiers to Jackson's army. Chief Pathkiller, the head of the Cherokee Nation, sent more than 500 warriors to help defeat the rebellious Creek. Neither Big Warrior nor Chief Pathkiller wanted to see the conflict grow, and both believed that their tribes would earn favor with Jackson and the U.S. government.

In March 1814, Jackson attacked the Creek at a heavily wooded peninsula in the Tallapoosa River called Horseshoe Bend. Jackson's troops overwhelmed the Creek and destroyed their forces in a bloody battle. Approximately 1,000 Red Stick warriors perished, while only 50 or so attackers lost their lives.

The Creek War ended in April 1814, when Red Stick leader Red Eagle surrendered to Jackson. The Creek chiefs friendly to Jackson were then summoned to sign a treaty. Expecting to be rewarded for their loyalty, they were shocked to find that they were being punished instead. Jackson demanded more than 20 million acres (8 million

Andrew Jackson rode into battle against the Creek.

hectares)—most of present-day Alabama and a fifth of Georgia—as payment from all Creek people for taking up arms against the United States.

For the Americans, the Creek War ended just in time. The British—still fighting the War of 1812—were planning to land on the Gulf Coast, and they would have joined forces with the Red Sticks. Jackson went south and took control of Pensacola, Florida, a port town in Spanish territory that was run by a British trading company and was therefore friendly to the British. Jackson's capture of Pensacola forced the British to attempt a much more difficult landing in the bayous of Louisiana. Jackson then raced to Louisiana to meet the British there. He defeated the invaders in the Battle of New Orleans and was hailed as the country's greatest hero.

After the war ended in 1815, Jackson became head of the country's southern army. He turned his attention to Florida, which was still a Spanish possession. The Seminole were conducting raids along the southern frontier. Jackson, again suspecting British involvement in the attacks, made war on the Seminole in 1817. Many important Seminole chiefs were killed, and the Seminole people were pushed deeper south. The First Seminole War led to the United States acquiring Florida from Spain in 1819. Jackson was named governor of the territory, and soon he began thinking about the presidency of the United States.

Land Exchange

Chapter 4

A flurry of treaties began after the War of 1812 whereby tribes in the Southeast exchanged land with the United States. In treaties signed in 1816 and 1818, the Chickasaw gave up millions of acres in Kentucky, Tennessee, Mississippi, and Alabama. Mississippi was granted statehood in 1817 and Alabama in 1819. In 1821, the Creek agreed to sell much of their land to the United States in the Treaty of Indian Springs. They also agreed to relocate to land in the West—in what is now Oklahoma—by 1826.

Some of the groups that agreed to move found that they received less land and less money than they were promised. Others were dismayed to find that white settlers were again squatting on their new land. During this time, the leadership of the five tribes began to change.

Agreements in Georgia and other states eventually forced the removal of Native Americans in the 1830s.

ACTS

OF THE

STATE OF GEORGIA

AN ACT

To ratify and confirm certain articles of agreement and cession entered into on the 24th day of April 1802, between the Commissioners of the State of Georgia on the one part, and the Commissioners of the United States on the other part.

WHEREAS the Commiffioners of the State of Georgia, to wit: James Jackfon, Abraham Baldwin, and John Milledge, duly authorized and appointed by, and on the part and behalf of the faid State of Georgia; and the Commiffioners of the United States, James Madifon, Albert Gallatin, and Levi Lincoln, duly authorized and appointed by, and on the part and behalf of the faid United States, to make an amicable fettlement of limits, between the two Sovereignties, after a due examination of their refpective powers, did, on the 24th day of April laft, enter into a deed of articles, and mutual ceffion, in the words following, to wit:

ARTICLES of agreement and ceffion, entered into on the twenty-fourth day of April, one thoufand eight hundred and two, between the Commiffioners appointed on the part of the United States, by virtue of an act entitled, "An act for an amicable fettlement of limits

Bicultural leaders who had a better understanding of the American legal and political systems were replacing full-blooded Native American chiefs. These leaders desperately wanted to remain in the Southeast and feared that their tribes would one day be required to leave their farms and homes for the wilderness of what is now Oklahoma. They urged their people to continue adopting aspects of white culture, believing that this would make it more difficult to force them out.

In 1824, Andrew Jackson ran for president and defeated John Quincy Adams and two others in the popular vote, but he did not gain the clear majority needed for a victory. The House of Representatives convened and chose Adams as president. Many Americans were outraged by this result. This caused political alliances in Washington, D.C., to shift dramatically, leading to the formation of the Democratic and Republican parties we know today.

Republicans and Democrats

After the splintered results of the election of 1824, American politicians recognized the need for strong, well-organized political parties. Martin Van Buren formed a group that later became known as the Democratic Party to support Andrew Jackson's bid for the presidency in 1828. Supporters of John Quincy Adams and Henry Clay, who were more relaxed in matters such as Native American affairs, joined to form an opposing party known as the Whigs.

John Quincy Adams was thought to be more open-minded than his political opponent, Andrew Jackson, when it came to the rights of Native Americans.

One of the first orders of business for President Adams was to deal with the Creek people still living in Georgia. Some Creek chiefs complained that they had not agreed to the Treaty of Indian Springs, and after an investigation, this was found to be true. James Barbour, the U.S. secretary of war, argued that making treaties with Native American tribes as if they were sovereign nations was foolish. Barbour believed—as did Jackson and many others—that because these people lived within the boundaries of the United States, they should do what the federal government said. People who favored removal thought that George Washington had made a mistake in supporting the sovereign status of Native American tribes and that it was their duty to correct it.

President Adams, on the other hand, believed the wishes of the country's founding fathers should be respected. He not only recognized the legality of treaties but declared the Treaty of Indian Springs void because it had not been properly ratified by the Creek Nation. When Georgia Governor George M. Troup threatened to protect his state's rights by having soldiers force the Creek out, Adams threatened to use any means necessary to stop him.

This controversy had to be settled before it ripped the young nation apart. The Senate appointed Missouri Senator Thomas Hart Benton to lead an investigation into the dispute. The feeling in government—and the mood in much of the United States—was that the Native American nations of the Southeast had to move for their own good and the good of the country. If they stayed, they would be scattered or destroyed as so many northern tribes had been when waves of settlers arrived on their lands.

Furthermore, the fertile land in Georgia, perfect for growing cotton, was vital to the growth of the country. Fueling this shift in policy was the fact that many Americans started to believe the white race was superior and that Native Americans were childlike in the way they clung to old traditions and their ancestral lands.

In the end, Benton's committee found in favor of Georgia. The decision was a critical blow to the rights of Native Americans everywhere. It meant that the land exchanges were entirely legal. The next step would be forced removal. And it would start soon.

By standing up to Georgia—and losing—Adams lost his support in the South and now would be unable to win a second term as president. That left the presidency open for Andrew Jackson, who was utterly convinced that Indian removal was the only option the government should consider.

Missouri Senator Thomas Hart Benton headed a committee that dealt a severe blow to the rights of Native Americans in the Southeast.

Prior to the election of 1828, Jackson was asked to consult on treaty negotiations with the Chickasaw and Choctaw nations. Based on his experience with their leaders, he knew that they would resist giving up pieces of their land, as the Creek and Cherokee had done. It was more prudent, Jackson said, to negotiate an exchange for all of their land—taking the government yet another step closer to an Indian removal policy.

Andrew Jackson believed the five tribes of the Southeast would thrive in their new lands west of the Mississippi.

Jackson made suggestions to the government negotiators. He advised them not to worry about the amount of money and land promised—the government would find a way to come up with whatever was necessary. He also warned them that the Chickasaw and Choctaw leaders might protest because they were unfamiliar with the territory being offered. Jackson said it was worth delaying the negotiations so that representatives of the tribes could be escorted to see the land for themselves. Most of all, Jackson told the negotiators, do not lie. Be forceful and be blunt if necessary, but do not be deceitful.

On Jackson's advice, the Chickasaw and Choctaw were offered an equal amount of land west of the Mississippi River, along with a promise they would never be asked to move again. They were also told that they might form a mighty nation with their relocated neighbors, and that once their children became educated, they might join the Union as a new state.

Despite Jackson's counsel, the treaty negotiators failed. This proved to Jackson and his supporters that the time for talk had ended. After defeating John Quincy Adams in the 1828 election, he declared that a president's duty was to obey the will of the people. As President Jackson saw it, the people's will was to remove the Native Americans and relocate them in the West.

A Swift Removal

Chapter 5

In his inauguration speech, Andrew Jackson promised Native Americans that his administration would give their rights "humane and considerate attention." Jackson's words softened his intent. He planned to involve Congress in passing laws for Indian removal. Jackson appointed John H. Eaton as secretary of war and John M. Branch as attorney general. Both men supported removal. Jackson also replaced many of the Indian agents who had served as liaisons between tribal leaders and the government with pro-removal Indian agents.

For years, Jackson had developed his argument that the five tribes would be safe from whites in the vast territory that lay to the west of the Mississippi River. There, they would not be subject to the same laws as the rest of the country, and the U.S. government would exert minimal control over them. But Native Americans did not see things this way.

In 1827, anticipating Jackson's election, the Cherokee Nation wrote a new constitution modeled on the U.S. Constitution. In it, the Cherokee declared themselves a sovereign nation. This infuriated Georgians. State leaders had been angry for more than 25 years about a promise to cease any Native American claims within Georgia's borders that the Jefferson administration made—and then failed to keep. And now the Cherokee seemed more determined than ever to stay.

In 1829, Andrew Jackson was sworn in as the seventh president of the United States.

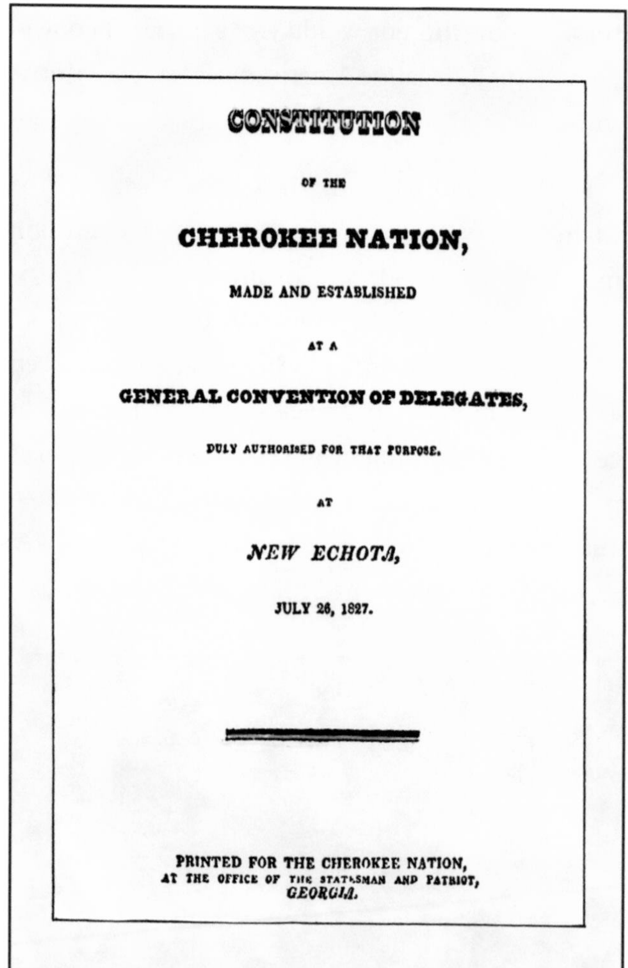

CONSTITUTION

OF THE

CHEROKEE NATION,

MADE AND ESTABLISHED

AT A

GENERAL CONVENTION OF DELEGATES,

DULY AUTHORISED FOR THAT PURPOSE.

AT

NEW ECHOTA,

JULY 26, 1827.

PRINTED FOR THE CHEROKEE NATION,
AT THE OFFICE OF THE STATESMAN AND PATRIOT,
GEORGIA.

The Cherokee constitution used language similar to that of the U.S. Constitution.

In retaliation for the Cherokee constitution, the Georgia legislature passed a law on December 20, 1828, stating that all Native Americans living in the state would fall under state laws after six months. The state assemblies in Mississippi and Alabama planned to do the same. Passage of the Georgia law fell between Jackson's election and his inauguration.

Jackson was a man of action, and here was an opportunity to send a message that he would continue to be decisive as chief executive. He saw a chance to start the presidency by acting on three of his strongest beliefs: national security, unifying the United States, and protection of the native people. Jackson's thinking was that by forcing Native Americans to move west, he would be able to secure the country's southern frontier, keep Georgia, Mississippi, and Alabama from defying the federal government, and ensure the survival of an entire race of people.

In 1829, Jackson sent two generals to meet with Cherokee and Creek leaders. The generals were instructed to tell the native leaders that Jackson agreed with Georgia's declaration and that he could no longer guarantee their safety. If they voluntarily moved west, however, their safety would be assured. The Cherokee and Creek, however, refused to give up what remained of their ancestral lands. Furthermore, they said they would advise other tribes to do the same.

Jackson felt that he had exhausted every option. He also believed that the time to act might be slipping away. Gold had been discovered in the mountain wilderness of northern Georgia, and by 1828, prospectors had begun flooding into the state. It was only a matter of time before there would be conflict and bloodshed. Meanwhile, several church groups had taken up the cause of the Cherokee, Chickasaw, Choctaw, Creek, and Seminole. Jackson was concerned they might argue against his "moral" reasons for relocating the five tribes.

Jackson ordered troops to chase squatters off Indian land. He also asked Thomas L. McKenney, a highly respected Indian agent who shared Jackson's views, to convince missionaries that their actions were hurting the tribes, not helping them. Finally, Jackson made it clear to state leaders that if they took action on their own, it would cause a rift with the North, making the passage of a U.S. government policy of Indian removal almost impossible.

On December 7, 1829, Congress listened as a clerk read Jackson's official plea to develop a policy of Indian removal. The document described the worsening situation in the Southern states and compared the plight of the native people there to that of the Mohegan, Naragansett, and Delaware nations, which had been wiped out in the North. These tribes had ceased to exist when their people died, assimilated, or joined other tribes. Jackson wrote that "humanity and national honor demand that every effort should be made to avert so great a calamity." He acknowledged that the government had once ensured the sovereignty of the country's Native Americans but said this was an error that could be changed. The reality was that measures had to be taken to protect the rights of states while ensuring the survival of what he called a "much-injured race."

Jackson's solution called for setting aside a vast tract of land that was not part of any state or territory. There, he wrote, relocated tribes would have a place where they could once again find the freedom and self-government they enjoyed before the arrival of the white man. Jackson added that the only time the United States would venture into this territory would be to preserve peace on the frontier. This fair exchange of land, Jackson added, would show the "humanity and justice" of the government.

Jackson Takes Action

In the early months of 1830, debate over a removal bill raged in the government. The issue found the two political parties split and also created a rift between representatives from the North and South. Andrew Jackson sat in on many of the meetings and tried to sway opinions, which his political opponents deeply resented. They claimed his actions were unconstitutional. Today the president is not allowed to sit in on law-making sessions.

Although forced removal was not part of this plan, Jackson made it clear that any person or tribe that elected to stay would become subject to state and federal laws. He could not guarantee any tribal land claims against actions by the states, nor could he prevent the inevitable loss of culture that would come if the tribes chose to stay. The removal policy would involve treaties, as in the past, only this time if they refused to deal with the government and did not agree to the treaties, they would be at the mercy of the people who had been trying to take their land for decades.

Jackson expected to be roundly hailed for his visionary idea. He was surprised when petitions began flooding his office. This plan broke every promise ever made to the Native Americans, his critics claimed. Worse, it dumped thousands of helpless people into an unknown wilderness. The people of the five tribes were astonished by the removal policy. To them, it sounded like a "leave or else" ultimatum. And basically, it was.

Those who stood against Indian removal claimed that the white race had already taken too much from the Native Americans. "We call them brothers, but steal their land," pointed out Theodore Freylinghuysen, a U.S. senator from New Jersey. It had to stop, he said. Those in favor of a removal bill said their opponents were hypocrites. Northerners had been wiping out Native Americans for two centuries, claimed Georgia Senator John Forsyth. It was unfair for them to oppose the same process in the South.

New Jersey Senator Theodore Freylinghuysen opposed Jackson's removal plan.

The bill's supporters countered by arguing that as the country grew, it would have to grapple more and more with the nation's rights versus the rights of states. Adding Native American rights to these discussions would create total havoc.

The debate lasted into the spring. Members of Jackson's Democratic Party had the majority to pass a removal bill, but some Democrats were afraid of voting for it because they would lose the votes of important religious groups, such as the Quakers. These groups feared that the Western territory designated for relocation was little more than a desert and that removal would amount to a death sentence for women, children, and the elderly.

Congressman Joseph Hemphill, a Pennsylvania Democrat, proposed a bill that would delay any new law until a commission was sent to the Western territory to determine whether it was fit for human habitation. This sounded like a good plan to the politicians, who welcomed the chance to delay the decision. But the Hemphill proposal outraged Jackson. To his mind, by the time a journey was made and a report completed, more than a year would go by, and the chances of a removal bill's passing might be ruined. Jackson wanted to accomplish many things as president, but if his Indian removal plans were delayed or defeated, he feared his presidency would be a disaster, and he would accomplish nothing.

The vote in the House of Representatives on Hemphill's proposal ended in a tie. Fortunately for the president, it was defeated by the tie-breaking vote cast by his ally, Speaker of the House Andrew Stevenson. When a removal bill was later presented to the House, it passed by a vote of 102 to 97. After some minor changes, the Senate also approved the bill, and Jackson signed the Indian Removal Act into law on May 28, 1830.

In part, the Indian Removal Act stated:

> *That it shall ... be lawful for the President of the United States to cause so much of any territory belonging to the United States, west of the river Mississippi ... to be divided into a suitable number of districts, for the reception of such tribes or nations of Indians as may choose to exchange the lands where they now reside, and remove there; and to cause each of said districts to be so described by natural or artificial marks, as to be easily distinguished from every other.*

Those who supported the Indian Removal Act claimed it would preserve native cultures in danger of being overrun by white settlers. Those opposed to it said it was an unjust land grab. The Indian Removal Act authorized the president to exchange land west of the Mississippi River for land held by tribes east of the Mississippi. It guaranteed the tribes perpetual ownership of their new land and monetary compensation for buildings they left behind. The government was responsible for the cost of moving people west and for a year's worth of supplies after they arrived. A total of $500,000 was set aside to cover the costs.

Jackson was impatient. He was unwilling to experience any delays in the removal process. Taking a cue from their president, Americans went to extraordinary lengths to force the Native Americans from their lands, often ignoring the basic justice upon which the new country prided itself. In the end, the rush to relocate the five tribes of the Southeast would contribute heavily to the great loss of human life. Removal may have looked like a simple matter on paper, but the reality of making the policy work would prove almost impossible.

Targets for Removal

Although the Indian Removal Act applied to other Native American tribes, it was specifically aimed at pushing the five tribes out of the Southeast. Jackson felt that the Native Americans would not stay in the region anyway. He thought that for them, the thought of living among white men, in a white culture, and under white laws, would be too terrible to consider. Sooner or later, they would realize that their only option was to resettle in the West.

Chapter 6

A Matter for the Courts

One of the first signs that removal would not go smoothly had come earlier that year, in May 1830, in the form of a treaty proposal from Greenwood LeFlore, chief of the Choctaw in Mississippi. He had agreed to exchange his people's land—but not unless the government agreed to the then-astronomical sum of $50 million. If the other tribes demanded this much, the government would go bankrupt. The U.S. government declined the Choctaw treaty offer.

Remembering the government negotiators' recent failures with the other tribes in the region, President Jackson decided to talk to Southeastern tribal leaders himself. Instead of inviting them to Washington, D.C., he returned to his home in Tennessee and called the chiefs together for a conference. To his surprise, the Choctaw declined to meet with him. The Creek and Cherokee declined Jackson's invitation as well. Instead they hired William Wirt, a former U.S. attorney general, to take their case to the U.S. Supreme Court.

Jackson did meet with the Chickasaw, but they were not interested in talking about a land exchange. As expected, Mississippi had passed a law similar to Georgia's, which placed Native Americans there under state control. This violated government treaties, the Chickasaw leaders told Jackson, and it was his duty as president to uphold and protect those treaties. Jackson told a group of 21 chiefs there was nothing he could do. He predicted that whites would soon overwhelm them and that they would disappear and be forgotten. The dejected Chickasaw eventually agreed to move on the terms the president dictated in August 1830.

William Wirt served as attorney general from 1817 to 1829, the longest tenure in this position in American history.

A land exchange treaty was drawn up and signed. The Chickasaw would receive $15,000 a year for 10 years. There was just one problem: When tribal members inspected their new territory, they found it to be very different from what had been described. The Chickasaw waited for a new deal. It never came.

In October 1832, the Chickasaw accepted Jackson's original offer and moved to present-day western Oklahoma. Each family was given a new parcel of land. The size depended on how many slaves a family owned. The Indian Removal Act affected many African-Americans who traveled west, not as members of the relocated tribes, but as their property.

The Choctaw also suffered under Mississippi's jurisdiction. They finally agreed to meet with two of Jackson's most skilled and trusted negotiators, Army General John Coffee and Secretary of War John Eaton. A land exchange treaty seemed close until Tushka Mastubbee, an old chief who had attended many negotiations with the whites, suddenly accused the two men of lying. There would be no treaty, he informed them.

The Choctaws were deeply divided. Following Mastubbee's accusation, many of the chiefs left the discussions. But the two Indian agents persuaded the remaining Choctaws, including the three leading chiefs—LeFlore, Nitakechi, and Mushulatubbe—to sign the Treaty of Dancing

Rabbit Creek on September 27, 1830. Each of these chiefs, as well as several other Choctaw, received personal sections of land in Mississippi as a form of bribery to ease their resistance to removal. These Native Americans either stayed in Mississippi, as did LeFlore, or they sold their sections for profit.

Later that year, as agreed in the Treaty of Dancing Rabbit Creek, thousands of Choctaw were escorted by government troops to present-day Oklahoma in the first of numerous mass relocations under the Indian Removal Act. The operation was a disaster. When harsh winter weather closed in on the long line of travelers, the people began to freeze and starve. Many died along the way.

Part of the problem was that the U.S. government was intent on running the removal process as a

John Guthrie's painting Solemn Tears *depicts the harsh reality of winter removal that many Native Americans faced.*

military exercise. Assigned to each operation was a superintendent whose job was to count the number of people to be removed, estimate what they would need to survive the journey, and then figure out the amount of supplies to be left at depots along the route. Next, an Army officer took over. He would use the estimates of the superintendent to buy and distribute the supplies. He was also responsible for the safety of the people being relocated. At almost every step of this process, there was a chance for government officials to steal money or supplies or to inflict cruelty on the travelers.

In March 1832, the Creek dropped their suit against the government. They signed the Treaty of 1832, agreeing to move. Over the next few years, the entire Creek Nation relocated to present-day central Oklahoma, but it was not a peaceful process. In many areas of the Southeast, squatters and land speculators competed to see who could take possession of Creek property first after a family had left. Sometimes the first ones on the scene found that the family was still packing its belongings. Not wanting to lose their prize, they would throw the Creek family out.

This led to violent confrontations, and by May 1836, the Creek had had enough. A group of warriors formed under Chief Jim Henry, who led them in a clash against the Georgia state militia near the Chatahoochee River. The Army was sent in to subdue the Creek, with orders to remove them by force. Several bloody battles followed,

INDIAN TERRITORY

In 1834, the U.S. government created Indian Territory as part of the Indian Removal Act. It originally covered most of present-day Oklahoma, as well as smaller sections of Kansas and Nebraska. The southern part of this territory was reserved for the Cherokee, Chickasaw, Choctaw, Creek, and Seminole. In 1907, Indian Territory became the 46th state and was renamed Oklahoma, from the Choctaw words for people, *okla,* and red, *humma.*

and it took nearly 10,000 Army troops to defeat them. Later in 1836 and 1837, approximately 20,000 Creek were led away under military guard, with many making the westward trek in chains. Once again, hundreds of lives were lost because of poor planning and corruption.

Like the Creek, the Seminole also consented to removal in 1832, as part of the Treaty of Payne's Landing. Perhaps learning from the mistakes of the Chickasaw, they reserved the right to approve their new land before signing a treaty. A delegation was sent to inspect the land, and the members did not like what they saw. But it did not matter. The delegation was given the choice of signing the treaty or being abandoned by its government escorts in the wilderness. They signed, but upon returning home, they said the treaty was no good because their signatures had been forced.

Meanwhile, the government was becoming angry with the Seminole people, who did not own slaves themselves but who were sheltering a growing number of escaped slaves. These slaves believed that being free and "removed" was more appealing than continuing to toil for white masters. They hoped to travel west with the Seminole.

By 1834, two years had passed since the signing of the first removal treaty, yet not a single Seminole had left Florida. General Duncan Clinch, who was in charge of Florida's federal troops, gathered the tribe's important chiefs and so offended them with his arrogance that there was suddenly talk of war. Clinch had no regard for Native American rights and showed no respect for the tribal leaders he had invited. He addressed them as if they were misbehaving children and refused to recognize their importance or authority. The meeting was a disaster. John Eaton, who was now governor of the Florida territory, confirmed to President Jackson that the Seminole were ready and willing to fight until they got a better deal.

Eaton also warned the federal government about Osceola, an emerging Seminole leader. Osceola was young and dynamic, and he told his followers that they should die before accepting removal. He was captured in the spring of 1835 but was released soon after when he signed a statement accepting the validity of the removal agreement. The Army believed it had broken his spirit, but it was just a clever trick. Osceola declared war not only on the United States, but also on any Seminole who agreed to move west. He enforced this threat when his warriors attacked a group, led by Chief Charlie Emathla, that had sold their belongings and agreed to move across the Mississippi River. Osceola killed Emathla, flung his money on the ground, and left his body to rot in a swamp.

In December 1835, the Second Seminole War began when Osceola captured an Army wagon train. The war lasted for seven years and cost the U.S. tens of millions of dollars. Osceola was captured and died in 1838, but the war dragged on until 1842. Approximately 4,000 Seminole were then removed by ship to Indian Territory, while several hundred fled into the Everglades in Florida. The Seminole were the last of the five tribes to be removed. By the time they were defeated, the U.S. government had also forced the Cherokee from their lands. The Cherokee battles were still to come, and they would be waged in the courtroom.

As the relocated tribes began moving across the Mississippi, the native people already living there saw their world turned upside down. The Osage tribes had signed a treaty with the United States in 1825 that guaranteed them territory that included

Seminole Chief Osceola led the fight against the removal of the Seminole people.

present-day Kansas. This was part of a series of treaties that had cleared Illinois, Wisconsin, and Michigan of its remaining tribes, including the Chippewa, Winnebago, and Sioux. Now the Osage found members of the relocated Southeastern tribes on their land in the south, and members of the Sac and Fox people, who had been removed from western Illinois, on their land in the north. These hardships were compounded by the fact that the annual payments they had been guaranteed in their removal treaties were late.

The Numbers

During the 1830s, more than 30 Native American tribes exchanged their eastern territory for land west of the Mississippi River as part of the Indian Removal Act. In addition to taking total control of the Southeast, the United States gained valuable land in Illinois, Indiana, Kentucky, Louisiana, Michigan, Ohio, and Wisconsin. In all, more than 60,000 Native Americans were moved west across the Mississippi River during this period.

The Sac and Fox were angered by the situation, too. They decided that they had not received what was promised, and they moved back into Illinois in the spring of 1832. The settlers and state militia were unable to prevent them from resettling, so the Army was called in. They were able to drive the Sac and Fox north into Wisconsin, where the tribes made a desperate last stand under Chief Black Hawk. The Native Americans were defeated, and the proud old chief was captured and paraded around the country to show Americans that the government was in complete control of the frontier.

The U.S. government then turned its attention toward resolving its differences with the Cherokee. The government would have to deal with a very different type of leader. His name was John Ross, and he had once fought side by side with Andrew Jackson at Horseshoe Bend against the Creek. He was only one-eighth Cherokee, but was now regarded as the nation's principal chief.

Ross lived in a large home and ran a very profitable plantation with many slaves. He was also the man who controlled the annual payments given to the Cherokee for the land they had ceded to the government in the past. He was a very crafty leader who moved as easily in the white world as he did in the Cherokee world. Ross promised his people that if they stood together, they would win, and they believed him.

The Cherokee Nation had become very different from other Native American tribes in ways that made many Americans think long and hard about the fairness of the Indian Removal Act. The Cherokee had their own written language, their own constitution, their own newspaper, the *Cherokee Phoenix*, and their own schools. Many Cherokee worshipped in Christian churches. Their homes and style of dress were similar to those of whites who lived along the frontier, and in many cases, they were much better educated. In the course of two generations, Cherokee leaders had determined that it was better to live alongside settlers than to fight against them.

Before deciding to take their case to the Supreme Court, the Cherokee had tried to defend their rights in many ways. They possessed a keen understanding of the legal system and believed that they could win a legal battle to remain on their lands. A delegation was sent to Washington, D.C., to ask that the federal government intervene against the state of Georgia, whose laws they believed were unjust. They appealed to President Jackson, whom they considered to be a man of laws and a man of his word. Jackson said their problem was with Georgia and he refused to help them.

When it became clear that they would receive no aid in their plight, the Cherokee gave William Wirt permission to take their case to the Supreme Court. The Creek had dropped their case by this time, accepting their fate and moving west. The

Taking It to the People

Cherokee leaders also appealed to the American public. They issued a notice that was distributed throughout the country, asking the American people for their support. It appeared in newspapers, was circulated in handbills and on posters, and was read aloud in many churches. Referring to themselves as civilized and Christian people, the Cherokee asked why—after 40 years of peaceful coexistence—they had to move merely because the state of Georgia wanted their land. Many Americans were shocked that their government would trample the rights of the Cherokee. Most, however, were unswayed. They believed, as their president did, that removal of the Cherokee would ultimately save the tribe from destruction.

Cherokee vowed to stand and fight, believing that a willingness to work through the legal system would win them public favor. In *Cherokee Nation v. Georgia,* the Cherokee people asked for an injunction that would protect them from the state of Georgia and would allow them to keep living there. Wirt argued that the treaties signed by the Cherokee and the United States recognized the tribe as an independent and sovereign nation.

The Supreme Court's decision in *Cherokee Nation v. Georgia* came on March 18, 1831. John Marshall, the chief justice, paid particular attention to arguments surrounding the legal status of the Cherokee people. Marshall denied the Cherokee the right to call themselves a sovereign nation. But he also decided that the Cherokee did not have to abide by state laws, either. Marshall called the Cherokee a "domestic dependent nation," which meant that they were part of the United States but not part of a state. The federal government and its courts were to play the role of guardian, protecting the rights of the Cherokee, who technically were not citizens. The Cherokee celebrated this complicated decision. They believed that they had won and that Georgia had no right to take their land and property.

One year later, Marshall seemed to uphold this idea when the court ruled in *Worcester v. Georgia*. In this case, the state had made it illegal for whites to enter Cherokee land. That way, the state could arrest white missionaries who were helping the Cherokee organize themselves. Eleven missionaries were arrested and nine were pardoned after agreeing to stop their work. The remaining two, Samuel A. Worcester and Dr. Elizur Butler, were sentenced to hard labor when they refused to stop helping the Cherokee. The Supreme Court heard the missionaries' case and overturned the Georgia court's decision, thereby freeing the two men. Marshall said that the state had no right to pass laws that dealt with what the Cherokee did on Cherokee land.

The decisions were seen as setbacks by the U.S. government, but they did nothing to stop the government from seeing its removal policy through. Squatters continued settling Cherokee land, and neither the state nor the federal government did anything about it. When the Cherokee tried to force squatters out, violence often followed. Although Jackson did not encourage the actions of squatters, he had to feel that they were proving his point. As Jackson had predicted, the longer the Cherokee resisted removal, the worse the situation became.

In 1832 and 1833, a Treaty Party was formed by several Cherokee leaders who decided to ignore the wishes of John Ross and agreed to listen to the removal scheme the government was willing to offer. This group included many influential individuals, including the speaker of the Cherokee National Council, Major Ridge, his son, John, and Elias Boudinot, the former editor of the *Cherokee Phoenix*. John Ridge traveled to Washington, D.C., and asked President Jackson if he planned to force Georgia to uphold the Supreme Court decisions. Jackson answered that he did not and convinced Ridge that the only way his people could survive was to move west. He, his father, and Boudinot were later murdered for agreeing with Jackson. But first he brought a strong message back to his people: We are out of options—it is time to make a treaty and move.

Fearing that his nation would soon be divided, Chief John Ross went to Washington, D.C., to see whether he could find some way to persuade Jackson to let the Cherokee stay in Georgia. Jackson did not trust Ross, whom he considered part of a bicultural upper class among the Cherokee who were mostly interested in protecting their wealth. The truth was that Ross was much like Jackson—both were hard-edged fighters who believed in the power and the rights of their people.

Major Ridge's Cherokee name was Kah-nung-da-tla-geh.

The two leaders met in February 1834, and Jackson quickly made it clear that he would do whatever it took to move the Cherokee to the West. Ross tried to bargain with Jackson, which angered the president. Then, fearing he might leave Washington, D.C., with no solution, Ross agreed that his people would consider whatever offer the Senate voted on. Jackson agreed, and the Senate approved a sum of $5 million for all of the Cherokee land. This was far less than Ross had hoped for. He rejected the offer and left Washington, D.C.

Jackson instructed his chief negotiator, John Schermerhorn, to make a deal with Ridge's group. In March 1835, an agreement was reached for a payment of more than $4 million in exchange for 8 million acres (3.2 million hectares) of land—a million dollars less than the offer Ross had rejected. Fearing a violent uprising among their own people

Cherokee Chief John Ross passionately resisted the Indian Removal Act.

when the treaty was announced, another group of Cherokee leaders traveled to Washington, D.C., to plead with Jackson for another solution. The president was pleasant and respectful, but he reminded them what happened to the Creek when they took up arms.

The Treaty of New Echota was presented to the Cherokee National Council in December 1835. Schermerhorn told tribal leaders that anyone who failed to show up for the vote would be counted as a "yes" vote. Still, more than 90 percent of the Cherokee chiefs refused to attend out of protest. Instead, 12,000 Cherokee sent a petition to Washington, D.C., denouncing the treaty, which was fraudulent according to both Cherokee law and the Indian Removal Act itself. Jackson dismissed the petition as the work of Ross and his wealthy friends. The treaty was sent to the U.S. Senate, passed by one vote, and signed into law by Jackson on May 23, 1836. It stated that the Cherokee were required to leave their land within two years.

Ross spent that time pleading with his people to continue their fight against removal. A few thousand gave up hope and left for the West, but most stayed, believing Ross would find a way to save their land. Jackson left office after the 1836 presidential election and was replaced by Martin Van Buren. As a senator, Van Buren had supported removal, and now he meant to enforce the law. When the two-year grace period expired, the new president unleashed the Army on the remaining Cherokee.

Leaving the Land

Chapter 7

In May 1838, men armed with muskets and bayonets stormed through Cherokee towns and settlements, rounding up families and marching them toward specially built stockades. They were designed to be temporary holding areas, but for many Cherokee this would not be the case.

Throughout the Cherokee removal, basic human decency was routinely ignored. There were many stories of families being interrupted as they sat down to dinner and forced from their homes. They were given little or no time to round up belongings. Protest was sometimes met with a gun butt to the head. One soldier, who also witnessed the carnage of the U.S. Civil War 25 years later, said the Cherokee removal was the cruelest thing he had ever seen.

The Cherokee people began their long march to Indian Territory in 1838.

Looting the Land

Behind the removal troops was another army—of looters. As soon as a Cherokee family was driven from its home, the property was stripped of anything of value and its livestock led away. This was equally true for tiny farmhouses and large estates. Men with shovels dug up family graveyards, hoping to find valuable trinkets in the coffins. Many Cherokee homes were burned down in full view of the families who lived there.

That spring, more than 17,000 people were forced from their homes. By June 1838, nearly every Cherokee in Georgia was either in a stockade or on his or her way west. There were distressing signs from the start. The first groups to leave the stockades did so in June, during the worst drought in more than a century. Moving slowly in the extreme heat and parched by thirst, more than 3,000 Cherokee found themselves in a nightmarish situation.

The original plan had them traveling by water for much of the journey, but river levels were too low for navigation. On land, there was not enough water to keep the group moving at a good pace, and when a supply depot was finally reached, the food was often spoiled or stolen and the water gone. Many of those who survived to reach Indian Territory were sick or dying. In one group, three to five people died each day. A decision was made to halt further removal until conditions improved. This meant that between 13,000 and 15,000 people would have to remain in the temporary camps.

Life in the stockades was grim. Food and shelter were poor, and with so many people crowded into unsanitary conditions, hundreds of people fell ill each day. Their terrible conditions were made worse by a feeling of sadness over having to leave their homes and land. Many Cherokee died in the stockades. More than 3,000 Cherokee may have perished before they had a chance to start the 800-mile (1,280-km) journey to their new land in Indian Territory in present-day Oklahoma.

During the summer, the Cherokee chiefs again tried to assert their tribe's status as an independent nation. Their arguments were ignored, although Chief Ross was appointed superintendent of the removal, and he was able to persuade the government to increase the amount of food and clothing that would be available on the march westward. Unfortunately, the drought did not break until September, which meant that the move west did not start again until late October 1838.

The Cherokee were divided into 12 groups of roughly 1,000 individuals for the journey. Although riverboats were available when conditions permitted, most would make the entire trip on foot. Horses and wagons carried soldiers and supplies. There was not enough money to move thousands of people by wagon train. The last group to leave their homeland included Chief Ross, who carried with him the records and laws of the Cherokee Nation. From the mountains of North Carolina, they moved northwest through Tennessee and Kentucky and then through southern Illinois. Weather conditions were bad from the start. Autumn rains turned the dirt roads into muddy quagmires. Thirsty children drank from puddles, only to become violently sick. So went the infamous journey that came to be known as the Trail of Tears.

The first of the groups reached the Mississippi River in November. Already a harsh winter had set in. The river crossing was delayed for several days by ice floes. Up to this point, many of the women, children, and elderly had died from disease and exhaustion. Now, poorly clothed and cut off from their supplies, many more began to fall ill.

The groups that followed found conditions even worse. A relentlessly bad winter gripped the Mississippi Valley, and thousands were trapped between the ice-choked Ohio and Mississippi rivers. Their delayed departure now doomed them. They found themselves trapped, with no means of gaining new supplies and only crude tents for shelter. Each day, more and more people died. The ground was too frozen to dig proper graves, so the dead were buried under stones or simply covered in snow.

After dragging themselves through Missouri and Arkansas, the first group finally reached Fort Gibson on the Arkansas River in January. Ross' group, which now included the weak and ill from other groups, was still in Kentucky and in danger of being completely wiped out. As soon as weather

permitted, they were loaded onto a riverboat. They did not reach Fort Gibson until March. Ross' wife was among the many who died on the way.

When they reached Fort Gibson, the Cherokee were officially in Indian Territory.

The number of deaths on the Trail of Tears differs by account, but most historians believe that more than a quarter of the nearly 20,000 Cherokee rounded up in the spring of 1838 were dead by March 1839.

Once they had arrived in Indian Territory, the surviving Cherokee immediately began organizing themselves. Within a year, they had formed a constitutional government, which consisted of an elected chief, a senate, and a house of representatives. Their capital was located in Tahlequah, in northeastern Oklahoma. The Cherokee started a public school system in 1841 and within a decade had established two colleges. Still, life for most tribe members was a daily struggle.

Living in the West

Chapter 8

Few of the Native American tribes removed to the West thrived in their new homes. The terrain and the climate were dramatically different from that of their former homelands, and in many cases, the amount of property they received yielded only a fraction of what they had been able to grow on their land in the Southeast. They had lost everything except for one another, and that is where they turned to find the strength to survive as a people.

In 1898, Congress passed the Curtis Act, which helped to clear the way for the Bureau of Indian Affairs. This law called for the elimination of the courts and governments of the five tribes. It also gave the U.S. government greater control over the lands it had exchanged with the tribes during their removal in the 1830s. Later, in 1906, Congress gave the president power to remove any of the chiefs in Indian Territory and gave the U.S. government the authority to sell buildings that were owned by Indian governments. Much of what made a nation a nation—self-government, rule of law, and national borders—was now gone.

In 1907, the Cherokee government disbanded when Indian Territory became Oklahoma and was admitted to the Union as the 46th state.

Some Cherokee people today live on land that was reacquired by the Cherokee in North Carolina in the 20th century.

Today more than 250,000 people trace their heritage to the Cherokee Nation, making them the largest group of Native Americans in the country.

Like the Cherokee, the Creek had formed a constitutional government in Indian Territory. It was run by a tribal organization made up of elected leaders. They, too, dissolved their nation when Oklahoma was preparing for statehood, but a century later many Creek still live in traditional towns, maintain cultural traditions such as the Green Corn Ceremony, and speak the Creek language.

The Chickasaw also formed a representative government, but it, too, was dissolved before Oklahoma achieved statehood. In 1983, the Chickasaw Nation ratified a new constitution and again has a representative government. About 39,000 Chickasaw people live in the United States, mostly in south-central Oklahoma.

Since removal, the Chickasaw have lived with and beside their former Choctaw neighbors. The Choctaw were able to maintain many of their cultural traditions, and today there are more than 80,000 Choctaw living in the United States. About half still live in Oklahoma.

Of the five Southeastern nations removed to Oklahoma, the Seminole were and still are the smallest in number. They are better known for their continued presence in Florida, where recently they have been successful in the tourism and gambling industries. After the Second Seminole War, a few hundred Seminole escaped into the Everglades. A third Seminole War was fought in the 1850s between U.S. government forces and about 100 warriors. After that, the Seminole seemed to simply disappear. More than a century passed before the Seminole would again play a role in the culture of the state.

After the Indian Removal Act forced their relocation to Indian Territory, most Native Americans had an uncertain status. They were not U.S. citizens, nor were they foreigners. Over the next 50 years, a series of laws granted citizenship to certain Native Americans under certain conditions, but as the 19th century drew to a close, there were still countless thousands of native people who belonged to no country at all. Even as the territories in which Native Americans lived became states, they still had no status as citizens. For

Those Who Stayed Behind

Despite the government's determination to remove all Native Americans from the Southeast, many never left the area. Some who remained behind were those who profited from the Indian Removal Act at the expense of other Native Americans. They were given land in the Southeast when they signed treaties requiring their Native American tribes to leave the area. Others remained but had no rights as U.S. citizens.

example, in 1907, when Indian Territory became the state of Oklahoma, many of its residents had no official citizenship. Finally, in 1924, every Native American residing in the United States was granted citizenship.

Young tribe members are instrumental in maintaining their people's cultural identity.

Many of the tribes pushed out of their homelands by the Indian Removal Act have regained the rights to some of their native land, which has been set aside by the U.S. government for the exclusive use

of tribal members. Some have used federal laws to open highly profitable businesses, including gambling casinos and tobacco companies.

A series of court rulings that Native American lands are not subject to certain state laws has created business opportunities and employment for thousands of Native Americans.

The Indian Removal Act of 1830 marked a dark chapter in American history and created a scar that has never fully healed. The law went against the founding notion of the United States that all people are created equal. If, as its supporters claimed, the law did indeed save entire cultures from extinction, it did so through brutal enforcement and preventable deaths.

The consequences of the Indian Removal Act were profound. Debates over its fairness helped to define politics for decades to come. The role of the president was changed in two important ways: The president's personal influence in the law-making process was weakened, and the president's ability to guide national policy in the name of national defense was strengthened. This is still the case today.

If there is anything positive to be said about the Indian Removal Act, it is that it serves as a lesson about the terrible things one race can do to another when its members consider themselves superior. And as many times as we are reminded of this, it is a lesson that we have yet to fully learn.

Timeline

1540

Hernando De Soto fights with Chickasaw warriors while exploring what is now Alabama.

1729

The Choctaw form an alliance with the French against the Natchez people of Louisiana.

1783

The colonists win independence from England and take Cherokee land in the Carolinas.

October 1800

France is granted land west of the Mississippi River by Spain.

May 1803

The United States buys French land as part of the Louisiana Purchase.

June 18, 1812

The War of 1812, between the United States and England, begins.

October 1813

Andrew Jackson's troops are ordered south from Tennessee to subdue a Creek rebellion.

March 1814

Jackson's forces defeat the Creek at the Battle of Horseshoe Bend.

1819

The United States takes control of Florida from Spain.

1821

Sequoyah assigns 85 symbols to the syllables in the Cherokee language, creating the first written form of a Native American language.

November 1828

Andrew Jackson is elected president.

December 1828

Georgia passes a law giving it jurisdiction over Indian lands; Mississippi and Alabama soon follow.

1829

President Jackson pushes congressmen and senators to create a law authorizing exchange of territory west of the Mississippi River for Native American lands in the East.

May 28, 1830

The Indian Removal Act is signed into law.

1831

The Choctaw start moving west, beginning the removal process; many die en route during the winter of 1831–32; the Supreme Court decides *Cherokee Nation v. Georgia*.

1832

The Chickasaw agree to relocate; the Supreme Court decides *Worcester v. Georgia*; state jurisdiction over Indian lands is found unconstitutional.

June 1834

The government officially creates Indian Territory, now part of Oklahoma.

1836

The Treaty of New Echota is ratified, giving the Cherokee two years to leave their land; Martin Van Buren is elected president.

May 1836

The Creek resist removal, touching off a war that lasts seven years.

1837

The Creek are forcibly removed after violence breaks out.

May 23, 1838

The roundup of Cherokee begins.

June 1838

The first groups relocated west are thwarted by severe drought; the removal process is halted.

July 1838

Hundreds of Cherokee begin to die in overcrowded stockades.

October 1838

The removal process resumes.

November 1838

Ice blocks the path of the first groups to reach the Mississippi River.

December 1838

The harsh winter traps 5,000 Cherokee east of the Mississippi.

January 1839

The first groups reach Fort Gibson in Indian Territory.

Timeline

March 1839

The final group reaches Indian Territory; the death toll of the Cherokee removal is estimated at more than 4,000.

1842

The Seminole are defeated in Florida and forcibly removed to the West.

1898

The Curtis Act is passed.

1907

Indian Territory is renamed Oklahoma and becomes the 46th state.

1924

All Native Americans are granted American citizenship.

On the Web

For more information on this topic, use FactHound.

1 Go to *www.facthound.com*

2 Type in this book ID: 0756524520

3 Click on the *Fetch It* button. FactHound will find the best Web sites for you.

Historic Sites

Trail of Tears State Park
429 Moccasin Springs
Jackson, MO 63755
573/334-1711

Park and memorial dedicated to the Cherokee Indians who lost their lives because of forced relocation.

Fort Gibson Historic Site
907 N. Garrison
Fort Gibson, OK 74434
918/478-4089

Site includes a reconstructed 1824 log fort and outbuildings, plus original structures from the time of Indian removal.

Look For More Books in This Series

Brown v. Board of Education:
The Case for Integration

The Chinese Revolution:
The Triumph of Communism

The Democratic Party:
America's Oldest Party

The Japanese American Internment:
Civil Liberties Denied

The Progressive Party:
The Success of a Failed Party

The Republican Party:
The Story of the Grand Old Party

The Scopes Trial:
The Battle Over Teaching Evolution

A complete list of **Snapshots in History** titles is available on our Web site: *www.compasspointbooks.com*

Glossary

annihilated
reduced to nothing

appalling
causing shock or horror

assimilated
found a way to fit in to a new culture or ethnic group

bayonet
a blade attached to the end of a rifle and used as a weapon in close combat

bicultural
belonging to two cultures or races

carnage
great and usually bloody killing of a large number of people

cede
give up property as part of a treaty or pact

convened
gathered together

culmination
the highest or final point reached

designated
chosen for a particular purpose

elite
a class of people who believe themselves to be above others in society

encroaching
taking by small steps the property of another

haven
a safe place

hypocrites
people who act differently than their stated beliefs

ice floes
large pieces broken loose from the frozen surface of moving water

Indian agent
a person who acted as the U.S. government's representative in negotiating with Native Americans

infamous
known for a negative act or occurrence

injunction
decision by a court ordering a party to refrain from a specific act

inroads
paths for progress

intervention
involvement in a problem or dispute

jeopardy
danger of harm or death

jurisdiction
legal power to interpret and administer the law in a specific area

land speculators
people who invest money in land believing it will rise in value

lavished
gave a large amount to

liaisons
people who establish contact and understanding between two groups

militias
citizens who have been organized to fight as a group but who are not professional soldiers

Mississippi Delta
the region where the Mississippi River fans out and enters the Gulf of Mexico

mutilated
harmed by taking off or destroying parts

negotiators
people who handle a matter through discussion and compromise, rather than by force

perpetual
meant to last forever

quagmires
soft, wet surfaces that give way under a minimal amount of weight

ratified
formally approved

reprisals
acts of force committed in response to a perceived wrong

retaliation
an attack in response to a similar attack

seminomadic
a way of life that includes both permanent villages and movement during the seasons

sovereign
having an independent government

status
a person's position in relation to others

squatters
people who occupy unused property that belongs to others

ultimatum
final proposition, demand, or condition

unconstitutional
a law that goes against something set forth in the Constitution, the document that set up the government of the United States

vulnerable
open to attack or danger

Source Notes

Chapter 1

Page 10, line 27: John Ehle. *Trail of Tears: The Rise and Fall of the Cherokee Nation.* New York: Doubleday, 1988, pp. 393–394.

Page 12, line 2: Ibid., p. 358.

Page 12, line 17: Ibid., p. 357.

Page 13, sidebar: Alexis de Tocqueville. *Democracy in America*, Vol. I. New York: Random House, 1945, p. 353.

Page 14, line 8: Ibid., pp. 393–394.

Chapter 5

Page 48, line 3: Robert V. Remini. *Andrew Jackson and His Indian Wars.* New York: Penguin Books, 2001, p. 226.

Page 52, line 19: Ibid., p. 232.

Page 52, line 26: Ibid.

Page 53, line 10: Ibid.

Page 54, line 8: Ibid, p. 233.

Page 56, line 11: U.S. Government. *The Indian Removal Act of 1830*. 25 Sept. 2006. www.civics-online.org/library/formatted/texts/indian_act.html

Chapter 6

Page 69, line 18: Chief Justice John Marshall. "Cherokee Nation v. Georgia." *The Oxford Guide to United States Supreme Court Decisions*. Ed. Kermit L. Hall. New York: Oxford University Press, 1999, p.51.

Select Bibliography

Ehle, John. *Trail of Tears: The Rise and Fall of the Cherokee Nation.* New York: Doubleday, 1988.

Foreman, Grant. *Indian Removal.* Norman: University of Oklahoma Press, 1972.

Green, Michael D. and Thelda Perdue, ed. *The Cherokee Removal: A Brief History with Documents*. Boston: St. Martin's Press, 1995.

Remini, Robert V. *Andrew Jackson and His Indian Wars*. New York: Penguin Books, 2001.

Remini, Robert V. *The Legacy of Andrew Jackson: Essays on Democracy, Indian Removal, and Slavery*. Baton Rouge: Louisiana State University Press, 1988.

Rogers, William Warren, Robert David Ward, Leah Rawls Atkins, and Wayne Flynt. *Alabama: The History of a Deep South State*. Tuscaloosa: University of Alabama Press, 1994.

Further Reading

Bruchac, Joseph. *The Journal of Jesse Smoke*. New York: Scholastic Inc., 2001

Burgan, Michael. *The Trail of Tears.* Minneapolis: Compass Point Books, 2001.

Morgan, Ted. *Wilderness at Dawn: The Settling of the North American Continent*. New York: Simon & Schuster, 1993.

Rozema, Vicki, ed. *Voices from the Trail of Tears*. Winston-Salem: John F. Blair, 2003.

Index

About the Author

Author Mark Stewart is a graduate of Duke University with a degree in history. He has written more than 100 nonfiction books for the educational market. He lives with his wife and two daughters in Sandy Hook, New Jersey.

Image Credits

The Bridgeman Art Library, **back cover** (middle and right), pp. **9**, **22** and **86**, **37** and **86**, **38**, **41**, **46**, **65**, **72**, **75** and **87** (Peter Newark American Pictures); Corbis pp. **13** (David Muench), **43** (Corcoran Gallery of Art), **59** (Stapleton Collection), **2** and **81** (Raymond Gehman), **84** (Lindsay Hebberd), **11**, **6** and **19**, **5**, **79** and **87**; Getty, **cover,** pp. **17**, **29**, **34**, **45**, **54** (Hulton Archive); John Guthrie p. **61**; Library of Congress pp. **49, 71**; North Wide Picture Archives, **back cover** (left), pp. **25**, **50**.